MW01593834

THE
FRATERNITY

BY

CHRIS CJ JONES

This book is a work of fiction. Places, events, and situations in this story are purely fictional. Any resemblance to actual persons, living or dead is coincidental.

© 2003 by Chris CJ Jones. All rights reserved.

No part of this book may be reproduced, stored in a retrieval system, or transmitted by any means, electronic, mechanical, photocopying, recording, or otherwise, without written permission from the author.

ISBN: 1-4107-1640-6 (e-book)
ISBN: 1-4107-1638-4 (Paperback)
ISBN: 1-4107-1639-2 (Dust Jacket)

This book is printed on acid free paper.

1stBooks – rev. 02/27/03

To Dave, Michael, and Vick,

for the fun of college friendships

ONE

"Billy! It's J.D.! How ya' doin'!?" Jimmy Donovan yelled his normal greeting into his car phone.

"Hi, Jimmy. What's up?" replied Billy, even though he knew what Jimmy normally called about on a Monday morning, as Jimmy usually did his research over the weekend.

"I've got a few more clients for us." Jimmy snickered at his choice of words to describe unsuspecting people he discovered during the past two days. "Three in Mountain View, one in Los Altos, and another two here in Palo Alto. Let me give you their names and numbers."

"Hang on a minute, Jimmy," interrupted Billy. "Let me find a pen and paper."

"That will probably take quite a while in that messy truck of yours you call an office," Jimmy chided. "You'd think you'd have a pen and paper ready when opportunity comes knockin'. And Lord knows when Jimmy Donovan calls, opportunity is beatin' down your door."

Jimmy smiled and waited a few seconds for Billy. Jimmy was always amazed Billy could find anything in the cab of his F250 Ford pickup truck. Jimmy loved teasing Billy every time he got the chance, and the lack of cleanliness in Billy's truck and other parts of his life were Jimmy's prime targets on many occasions.

"Billy! Maybe you can find a pen in your shirt pocket!" Jimmy laughed. "And a piece of paper is probably under your spittoon. Why don't you give up that nasty habit, anyway? Don't you know smokeless ain't harmless?"

"Okay, Jimmy," came Billy's voice back over his cell phone. He disregarded the teasing as he knew if he tried to retaliate it would just get worse. "Give me those names."

"There are three in Mountain View. First one is a lady by the name of Johnson. Second one is a couple named Hunter. The third

1

one is Martinez. You'll probably need to be a little more careful with the last one as I got a feeling the mister has more on the ball regarding roofing than most folks I find for us. I remember seeing a lot of power tools in the garage, but nothing like a table saw or drill press. It also looked like there were a lot of unfinished projects going on in the garage, so I don't think he's one to check your work very closely, but you ought to proceed with a little more caution."

"Did he have a ladder, Jimmy?" Billy asked. He knew one way to determine if someone could easily check his work was to find out if they owned a ladder long enough to provide access to their own roof.

"Give me some credit, Billy. Of course I checked. Isn't that the first thing you taught me when we started this? And yes, Mr. Martinez has one of those segmented ladders you can extend to a full sixteen feet. That's why I'm telling you to be more careful with him. None of the others had anything more than an eight-foot wooden painting ladder. And the two in Palo Alto didn't have a ladder anywhere I looked. Reckon how those folks get by without even a small ladder, Billy? You reckon they call some handyman for every light bulb which burns out in a room with a vaulted ceiling? You gotta believe if they pay someone with a ladder to come in and do any work in their home, we can shake some dollars from them for some roof work when they want to sell their home." Jimmy smiled and let out another hearty laugh. This felt like taking candy from a baby to him.

Jimmy and Billy continued their conversation as Jimmy gave Billy all of the names, addresses, and phone numbers of the new contacts. As they finished Jimmy delivered his closing line. "Billy, the ball is in your court. Don't miss it."

"Thanks, Jimmy. Talk to you later." Billy pushed the end button on his cell phone. He pondered for a few moments before he started his calls to the new clients, or potential ones, knowing it was necessary to close the deal with each of them. It seemed to him he was the one taking most of the risk, but he and Jimmy always equally shared the profits of their little scheme. It was Jimmy's idea in the first place, and Jimmy did the initial work to identify and contact their targets, so maybe it was fair.

Billy also genuinely liked Jimmy. He always liked Jimmy. He enjoyed Jimmy's zest for life from the moment they first met more

2

than twenty-five years ago. Although Billy usually couldn't remember his first meeting with most people, he never forgot his first chance encounter with Jimmy.

Billy thought back to their first meeting. What an impression Jimmy made. The two of them were freshmen in college at Memphis State University, and the fall semester was just starting. Jimmy was on his way to a fraternity rush party, and he was hurrying down the dormitory hallway trying to get his arms into his sport coat while also trying to stick a whiskey flask into his back pocket. Billy was locking the door to his dorm room as he exited, simply minding his own business. But then Jimmy bumped into Billy and things changed.

Billy's mind wandered further as he reminisced about his first impression of his freshman dorm room. It was small. It was lifeless. It needed painting. It was too dark. It was old. He remembered he thought it was like a dungeon, although he'd never seen a real dungeon. He remembered he couldn't believe he was planning on spending at least the next school year of his life in that room. Being caught in an animal trap in the woods couldn't be any worse.

In a hurry in the hallway of the dormitory, and without even knowing Billy, Jimmy asked Billy if he wanted to go along to the party. Billy was not too sophisticated, and never had a desire to join a fraternity, but he went along with Jimmy due to his contagious personality. Jimmy was genuinely nice to everyone, including total strangers, talking about everything from fishing to sports cars to politics. Jimmy seemed so outgoing and fun, always full of stories which made everyone laugh.

Billy remembered how Jimmy was able to sneak the bottle of whiskey into the party at one of the fraternities courting him. The act was clearly against the rules, and Billy was amused at how Jimmy always felt more fulfilled when he disregarded rules, policies, and laws.

Prior to meeting Jimmy, Billy adhered to all of the rules. It was how he was raised. Prior to going to college in Memphis, Billy lived all of his life just outside Tupelo, Mississippi. He and his younger sister were both born in Tupelo, and his father farmed some land north and east of the city. His mother never worked outside of the home as she was dedicated to raising her children. When he and his mother talked about dreams during his high school years, it was clear she suppressed many of hers in lieu of being an obedient wife and a providing and loving mother. His impression of his mother was she didn't want him to live the same sheltered life she lived, and the evidence was in the constant encouragement she provided. Even though he never stepped foot in the state of Tennessee until his orientation the summer before his freshman year, his mother practically pushed him until he couldn't refuse to go to college there.

When Billy attended his freshman orientation, he could tell most people's impression of him was he was a country boy who wasn't too smart and would never make it through college. It wasn't that he wasn't smart, as his grades were quite good. It was just he was fairly quiet and reserved, talked slowly when he did speak, and wore mostly blue jeans and t-shirts. He owned a suit and a sport coat his grandmother purchased for him one Christmas, as she thought every young man old enough to work on the farm should have something nice to wear to church on Sundays.

Billy wasn't uncomfortable going to new places and meeting new people, it was just he didn't seem to need as much of it as Jimmy. Jimmy was tremendously impatient waiting on Billy to change clothes into something more suitable for going to a fraternity party. Jimmy was so excited he was going to be meeting so many new people, as the only fear Jimmy seemed to have was of being alone. Once Billy changed his clothes and was ready, he practically needed a leash to hold Jimmy back from running to the party.

Jimmy and Billy attended several parties the first night, and they continued to attend more parties on subsequent nights. At first, Billy went along with Jimmy just to experience more of the college life his mother so strongly encouraged him not to miss. After a few nights of attending so many parties and meeting so many interesting people, Billy was warming to the idea of actually joining a fraternity.

It was clear all of the fraternities liked Jimmy and wanted very badly for Jimmy to pledge theirs. Although not as vibrant as Jimmy, Billy made a good impression at enough of the houses, so he thought he too would be wanted. He also knew being a friend of Jimmy's would help. It turned out he was right, as Jimmy and Billy both pledged Sigma Chi.

Billy remembered the excitement in his mother's voice when he broke the news to her about his pledging a fraternity. She was so happy. His father on the other hand was neutral on the idea, but he wasn't one to stand in the way of his wife's desires for her children. Billy's mother always felt having a larger group of boys Billy could study with, share experiences with, and rely on like a family were good things. She certainly didn't anticipate any negative effects.

Both being enrolled in the college of business, Billy stuck with the standard curriculum, while Jimmy always took a lot of seemingly unrelated classes. Jimmy liked real estate, so he enrolled in any class remotely connected to the subject. Also, any class attended by sorority girls was of huge interest to Jimmy, as he always had an eye for the sexiest coeds on campus.

Their friendship grew during their college years, and all of their social activity centered around their membership in the fraternity. Each year members would graduate, a few would give up on college and quit, new pledges would arrive, new members would get initiated, and life would go on. Billy thoroughly enjoyed his first three years in college, and he knew most of it was due to his association with the fraternity and his friendship with Jimmy and others.

It was Billy's senior year he didn't enjoy. Early in the fall semester his mother became sick with something resembling the flu, but the doctors never could figure out quite what it was. The doctor bills mounted as treatments continued, but nothing seemed to help. The farm always did well financially, and it was still doing alright. However, his father informed him during the Thanksgiving holiday the doctor bills would become too much of a hardship if they continued at their present rate for several more months.

Billy remembers the somewhat somber mood during the Christmas break of his senior year, as there was no excitement at home due to his mother's condition. He was also disappointed he skipped a trip to Europe with many of his fraternity brothers. His mother wanted him to go on the trip, but he felt compelled to be with her while she was feeling badly.

The spring semester was in session for more than a month when Billy's mother showed signs of improving. As a result, he planned on spending his last spring break with many of his fraternity brothers in Cancun. The excitement around the fraternity house overpowered everyone, and very little studying got done amidst all of the planning and conversational dreaming of how much fun everyone would have in the sun, on the beach, and chasing women.

It was the Wednesday evening nine days before the scheduled departure of the trip when Billy received the horrible news. His sister called him and could barely get out all of the words between her tears. His parents were killed in a car accident coming home from the church. A drunk driver, traveling at a high rate of speed in the south bound lane, apparently crossed over the median of the road, and struck his parents' vehicle in the north bound lane. He always hated the way a newspaper was forced to state the details of what happened. Why couldn't they simply state the drunk ran into his parents? Both his mother and his father died within minutes of the accident.

The accident caused Billy to not only miss the long-awaited spring break trip to Mexico, it also forced him to drop out of classes completely. He was fifteen hours short of finishing his business degree, and at the time he planned to take care of his parents' estate and enroll again in the fall semester to complete his degree requirements.

As Billy worked during the spring and summer with the lawyers, accountants, bankers, and others to close the estate, he realized it was going to take more of his time than he first thought necessary. It was becoming clear to him he wouldn't be able to attend classes in the fall to finish his degree. Although it bothered him, the thing perturbing him more was he would have to sell the farm. He couldn't figure out how to make the finances of the farm work by leasing the land, mostly due to the immediate need for money to pay the doctor bills which accumulated during his mother's long illness. Insurance was not something his father trusted, and now he certainly appreciated it more. He also knew he didn't want to spend the rest of his life farming the land like his father.

By the time Billy resolved everything, including selling the farm, it was October and too late to enroll in the fall semester. If he wanted to finish his degree, he would have to wait until the spring semester. Thinking depressingly about how those in his freshman orientation group who predicted he wouldn't finish college would be right after all, he almost wanted to finish just to show them. The reality was money was tight, and he lost much of his enthusiasm for college during the past several months. So remembering the encouragement of his mother to do new things and not to worry about what others think or say about it, he decided to pick up and move to California.

Billy previously visited both northern and southern California with some of his fraternity brothers during college breaks and holidays, and he always liked the climate of northern California, certainly compared to what he was used to in Tupelo and Memphis. His fascination with the west coast and particularly California was like a magnet. He liked the mountains and the ocean. He liked the wineries and the vineyards. He liked the many Asian restaurants, although he missed the good barbeque he knew could only be made in the South, for reasons unknown to him. He liked the diversity of the people living there. He even liked the golfing, even though he was a lousy golfer, as he still had never broken ninety-five. Putting was his downfall, he and everyone who played with him always concluded.

Billy thought it somewhat fateful he stumbled onto some job opportunities in the California Bay Area while doing some tax research during the depressing time in Tupelo when he was working on his parents' estate. He was in contact with two of his Sigma Chi brothers who were seniors when he was a freshman. Their fathers were involved with estate planning in California, and it was his hope they could provide assistance with his situation in Mississippi. Although they weren't much help due to the differences in the state laws, they did send him a few issues of the San Jose Mercury News which contained some good background articles. It was late one night when he decided by chance to look at the jobs advertised in the classified section when he encountered a few listings striking his fancy.

The one catching Billy's attention the most was from an industrial construction company located in San Jose. The employment advertisement specifically stated a college degree was preferred but not required, although a junior college degree or at least two years in a major college was required. The job was also not a labor job, but rather a purchasing job. He was intrigued by it, and when he contacted them he felt somewhat lucky he was looking for a job at a time in the year when other college students were still focusing on their fall classes instead of searching for a full-time job.

The company would not agree to pay Billy to relocate to San Jose from Mississippi, but he decided to take the job anyway. He felt the same uncertain excitement going to San Jose as when he first enrolled at Memphis State University. The drastic change was welcomed and provided motivation. Adapting to all of the newness and learning so much as a result of his employment kept his mind on the present, which helped to suppress his unanswered questions regarding the abrupt end to his parents' life.

Billy recognized his involvement in the fraternity during college helped him develop his people skills, which he was thankful for then, but even more so now as those talents were absolutely necessary in his purchasing agent role. Over the years, he felt normalcy returning to his life, as the routine of work provided emotional stability for him.

Financial stability was a completely different issue. Billy didn't realize during his visits to California while in college how high the cost of living in San Jose was. So much of his paycheck went simply to paying the rent. He was able to save some money from time to time when business improved and he worked more overtime, but he usually was quick to spend those extra dollars in short trips to meet with his old college fraternity brothers. The dilemma between saving money and seeing his old friends was still unsolved.

Billy remembered when he thought he first solved his financial difficulties. It was about the time he turned thirty. One of the suppliers with whom he worked for five years or so and knew quite well provided him with the tip. He was hesitant at first, but he took the chance anyway, and things worked well.

During a routine visit the supplier told Billy their parent company was going to purchase two other companies in the near future. Urge was too soft of a term to describe how the supplier pushed him to invest. He never invested in the stock market due to the uncertainty of it all and his own ignorance of how it worked, but in this case he decided to take a chance. What a winner it turned out to be. In just three years, his small sum of ten thousand dollars grew to one hundred thousand. It was a ten-bagger! The dream of every individual investor was captured by none other than Billy Wicks on his very first try. With more investments like this, he would become a millionaire before he was forty. Unstoppable was the new feeling dominating his thoughts.

With his newfound fortune Billy decided to start his own roofing company. The idea came to him over time as the managers of his company were always complaining about the roofing part of their construction jobs. He felt like he knew what would be required for a roofing company to satisfy the customer since he was on the customer side for so long, and he also knew profits for the roofing jobs were good. The other part of his realization was after working for his initial employer for more than ten years, the company's owner was the only one profiting significantly from the business. Now more knowledgeable, financially stable, and more daring, starting his own business was the natural next step.

Valley Roofing was the name Billy settled on, and he sure hoped all other decisions of the business didn't require as much time and energy. That's why he contracted an outside group to develop the company's logo for a fixed amount. Some of his employees liked the logo, and some did not, but he would retell the story quite often of how little money he spent on the logo versus how much time he spent on the name. The story always ended with a challenge to the complainers to develop a better one, while not doing it in a day-dreaming fashion when they should otherwise be working.

Billy quickly came to appreciate why the owner at his previous company was the one who made most of the money. After working at his business for the first six months, he realized he was doing more work than he ever did before. The stress and strain of having the leadership and responsibility was tiring yet fulfilling. Particularly satisfying was the success which came during the first four years for Valley Roofing. He often times wondered why he didn't start his own business earlier, but he was quick to remember he was without the financial capability before his first successful investment.

Unfortunately, Billy's subsequent investments didn't yield anything close to a ten-bagger. As a matter of fact, most of them were big losers. How he ever got involved in trading futures and options he couldn't fathom, but it was addictive. When he was unable to buy low and sell high on normal stocks, his broker suggested trying mutual funds. The first few did about average, but then he invested in some international funds which were bad investments to say the least. The jargon of the market fascinated him, as terms like covered calls and naked puts seemed to be like a different language, yet he truly loved the chase. And with Valley Roofing turning a nice profit quarter after quarter and year after year, he could afford to play the market.

It was Billy's business becoming sluggish coinciding with his worst investments to date which were financially crippling. His broker warned him about buying stocks on margin, but it was a wonderful means for leveraging a small amount of money, when it worked. He also was warned about selling short, and he now knew the potential loss from a short sale was infinite while the potential loss from going long was only the invested amount. Although not richer, he felt smarter, and he was confident his roofing company could return to the profitability of the first few years. In the meantime, Jimmy Donovan concocted a wonderful scheme to help put more dollars in Billy's pocket.

A blaring car horn jarred Billy's attention, causing him to look back at the names and phone numbers Jimmy gave him. He dialed the first one and hoped he would get a live person instead of their recording. No such luck as the answering machine played a standard greeting. When it got to the beep, he offered his services. "Hi, Mrs. Johnson. This is Billy Wicks of Valley Roofing calling to follow up on the inquiry Jimmy Donovan of Donovan Realty made over the weekend. Mr. Donovan said you were in need of a roof inspection at the request of a client of his. He also said he informed you he would put someone in contact with you who could handle it. Well, I'm the one who can help you with the roof inspection and any repairs which may be needed, although I'm hoping nothing major is required, as I'm sure you are, too. I hope Mr. Donovan or your real estate agent have already informed you a positive roof inspection is mandatory for a residential real estate deal to close in California, so it is inevitable the roof be inspected." Billy concluded his message by leaving his cell phone number and his office number, and by wishing Mrs. Johnson luck in selling her home. He always found it helped his chances if he did two things to someone hoping to sell their home. The first was to provide them with encouragement, and he always did this by saying he hoped there were no major repairs. The second was to inform them of the law. Those two items seemed to always be part of the winning formula.

Billy continued with the remaining five clients—talking with two, leaving two messages similar to the first one, and not being able to reach the other. By the end of the day, he talked with four of the six, and all four agreed for him to inspect their roof so Jimmy's potential buyers would be comfortable with possibly making an offer knowing their roof was in sound condition. Further, he informed them he would complete the inspection tomorrow and his report would be in the mail to them by Wednesday. They were all now comfortable they would have his report by the end of the week, and if repairs were required, he would contact them again to schedule the work.

When Billy returned to his office he took care of the billing for the roofing jobs he completed last week based upon contacts made the week before. This was one of the beauties of this scheme. The entire length of time was usually less than two weeks.

Jimmy scoped out new listings in the multiple listing service. He looked for properties listed by those realty agencies not normally asking the sellers to get a roof inspection done prior to listing their property. Jimmy made an appointment with the seller to preview the property, and then he visited the house, where he checked for signs indicating what capability the seller possessed to check Billy's work. If the seller was home, Jimmy simply asked them a lot of questions about their house, their employment, and many other normal and unsuspecting questions. Most sellers liked the attention since they were completely focused on helping a real estate agent sell their home. This was all part of Jimmy's research to identify new clients. He then contacted the sellers, usually the very next day, telling them he had a potential buyer, but also stating the buyer was insisting on a roof inspection prior to making an offer. He offered to have a licensed roofing company contact them to make it easier and more efficient. Jimmy then passed the contact information to Billy as he did this morning. Once a seller agreed to have the inspection, Billy inspected the property and sent the report to the seller. Billy was prompt to follow the report with a call to schedule what were normally minor repairs. On occasion, major repairs were required, and Billy welcomed those, too, as they also helped his business. In both cases, minor repairs were exaggerated or were simply not needed, yet they were always billed as completed work.

On one of the particular bills Billy prepared this afternoon, there were the three fairly standard items he often used. The first was the sealing of burn spots where holes in the thin part of the shakes exposed the underlayments to destructive ultra violet rays. The second was the sealing of crack-over-crack shake areas which also exposed the underlayments. The third was the sealing of exposed nails at flashings and in the field. How could someone consumed by the sale of their home possibly understand this roofing language, Billy mused. The total repair bill was $740, and Billy knew only one of the three items was completed, normally costing $120. So a $620 profit from this one customer would provide Billy and Jimmy each with an extra $310.

Billy knew he certainly needed the money. His business was mediocre the past few months, and his recent stock investments were once again negative. If he could only find another ten-bagger, things would be fine. Maybe it was a good thing half of the profits from this scheme went to Jimmy, as at least he wasn't losing it in the stock market like Billy.

TWO

When Jimmy Donovan hung up the phone after his conversation with his long-time friend Billy Wicks, he immediately began wondering the wisdom of including the Martinez house in his latest list of contacts for Billy. They never before encountered a problem, and Jimmy knew his initial research was a prominent reason for the success. He eliminated many people he met and talked with under the guise of previewing their home for the possible sale to a hot client. A much longer list of homeowners were rejected from his review of the listing information, as over the years he developed a checklist of items which were definite show-stoppers. The list became so lengthy he actually wrote it down, and the first item included was to look for a new roof. Even though he knew Billy inspected each roof before preparing the quote for repairs, and Billy would not suggest any repair work for a new roof, Jimmy always tried to spare Billy the time which would otherwise be wasted.

There were three such clients the past weekend Jimmy eliminated. Two not only bought and sold multiple homes in California, they were planning on remaining in the local area, so Jimmy knew it best to avoid them. The third was a man who replaced his roof with his own hard work just three years ago. Jimmy was glad Mr. Baumgartner was home during his preview just two days ago, as the listing sheet did not specifically advertise a new roof, and the new roof wasn't obvious from the street due to two large overgrown plum trees obscuring the front of the house. Only Jimmy's seemingly unobtrusive conversation allowed him to uncover this feature which actually helps sell a home. He could only shake his head at the negligent realtor who listed the property without highlighting the attribute.

There was another item which did catch Jimmy's attention last Saturday in Mr. Baumgartner's study. A complete set of leather-

13

bound books for coin collections was located on a shelf above the roll top desk. To allow himself more time to let his eyes wander around the room, he asked about the wood used to make the desk. While not listening carefully to the answer, he paid careful attention to the fact there were books for buffalo nickels and mercury dimes in addition to the current Jefferson nickels and Roosevelt dimes. He only hoped he would find the more valuable coins in the collection when he was able to complete a private review at a future time. When Mr. Baumgartner commented he was being transferred to the east coast, his wife also worked, and their children were grown, Jimmy couldn't believe it was going to be so easy.

Jimmy contemplated once more if he should call Billy back and advise him to skip the Martinez house, but the thought didn't last long as he continued his drive to the Baumgartner residence. He opted to drive his Cadillac Seville this sunny and beautiful June morning, as he was in his Audi TT on Saturday, and using two different cars to visit the same property on different days always seemed like the safe thing to do in such a covert operation. He couldn't smile big enough as he thought of his own genius.

The thought really holding Jimmy's attention was the trust homeowners implicitly gave to all realtors. Did homeowners really understand every realtor had total access to their homes via the house key contained in the lockbox hanging on the front door? Sure the computer system would know which realtors accessed the box, but he could easily dodge any accusation by simply stating he showed the house to a prospective buyer, and there were certainly a lot of prospective buyers viewing properties at the start of summer. The other half of the deal absolutely astounding him was since most prospective buyers liked looking at a home without the homeowner being present, most homeowners would gladly arrange to be away from their home if requested. It was an amazing inconvenience to the homeowner to leave their home vacant for a few hours providing a total stranger accompanied by a local realtor complete and uninterrupted access. It was even easier in the case of Mr. Baumgartner and his wife since they both were away from home at work on this Monday.

As Jimmy turned into the neighborhood, he took note of how many people were out walking their dog, with a friend, or just by themselves. He counted very few adults as it was almost ten o'clock, and he figured most did their walking earlier. Since school was out for the summer break, there were many children riding skateboards and motorized scooters, but nothing which concerned him. He did wonder if bicycles were becoming extinct, as he always saw so few kids on bicycles. He knew his two girls hadn't ridden theirs for years.

Jimmy first parked two blocks from his destination. He used his cell phone and dialed the Baumgartner's phone number hoping for no answer. After four rings the answering machine picked up. At the tone, he left a brief message thanking Mr. Baumgartner for his time and hospitality last Saturday. He learned not to simply hang up since he was previously caught off-guard when caller identification first became available. At the time he didn't know caller ID was sophisticated enough to capture the caller's phone number even if the caller hung up prior to the answering machine starting. He remembered scrambling to think of a good reason for his call when a homeowner unexpectedly returned his call. He was so stunned at the time he was barely able to calmly tell the caller he dialed the wrong number from a long list of phone numbers. He apologized for the intrusion, but he was thankful he learned a lesson without paying a penalty. What a rush it was though, and he truly enjoyed the times his heart beat uncontrollably with excitement. It was his life's spice, just like the spice cajun cooking provided to food he thoroughly enjoyed.

Jimmy next parked on the side of the street across from the Baumgartner's home. He grabbed his folder from the passenger seat and reached in the console storage compartment for a small black pouch he specifically remembered to bring from home earlier. Inside the pouch were several coins he was hoping could be swapped for others.

Jimmy walked quickly to the door, inserted his access computer into the front of the lock box, and typed in his code. Out fell the key to the door, and he let himself in. He proceeded directly to the study and took a moment to review the exact position and condition of each of the coin collection books. The books looked to be in the same position as before, as they were in order of currency denomination, and there was only a little dust on the binding of each. He was glad as it was harder to cover his tracks if a significant amount of dust was on the books.

Jimmy went first to the mercury dimes. He begrudgingly learned about coins from his grandpa long ago. He didn't care much for it at the time, but now he was glad he developed enough appreciation for it to allow him to exploit it for his own financial gain. He knew one valuable coin would be the 1916D mercury dime, if indeed it was included in the collection. Only 264,000 mercury dimes were minted in Denver in 1916, and the cost for one of those at any basic coin shop was now several hundred dollars, even approaching a cool one thousand, depending upon the coin's condition of course. As he opened the book, he was ecstatic! The 1916D mercury dime was present! He quickly extracted the coin from its holding spot and replaced it with a 1916S mercury dime. Since over ten million mercury dimes were minted in San Francisco in 1916, the exchange was profitable yet not detectable at just a glance since someone would have to look very closely at back of the coins to distinguish the D from the S.

Jimmy next opened the book containing Lincoln pennies. He was hoping to find a 1909-S V.D.B. Once again he hit pay dirt! Only 484,000 of these were minted in San Francisco before the initials of the designer Victor D. Brenner were removed, and he used a 1909-S from his black pouch as a replacement. The 1909-S was itself valuable since less than two million were minted, but the swap would net him several hundred dollars.

Jimmy was certain anyone having both the 1916D mercury dime and the 1909-S V.D.B. Lincoln penny would also own the rare buffalo nickels and Washington quarters. He was not disappointed as the 1913S type I, 1913S type II, 1913D type I, and 1913D type II buffalo nickels were in their respective locations. He swapped all four for ones of the appropriate type from the Philadelphia mint from the same year. He still couldn't believe there was a total of six different buffalo nickels minted in 1913. Why there were both raised ground and recessed ground versions was beyond him today, but he was glad someone decided to do it long ago.

Jimmy was hoping to get another exchange for Washington quarters. With the Denver and San Francisco mints generating fewer than 500,000 Washington quarters in 1932, he wanted to capture each of those for a couple of the more than five million minted in

Philadelphia in the same year. As expected, the coins were indeed there, and he promptly switched the last of the coins.

He replaced the books on the shelf in their original order, reminded of how easy it was when someone kept their things clean, neat, and organized. The danger of course was anyone so meticulous might also be someone who checked their collections regularly. Jimmy was fairly certain though the home sale and employment relocation would occupy Mr. Baumgartner more than his coin collection.

Jimmy left the study and headed for the kitchen where he could use the table for one last item. He pulled a small case from his shirt pocket. The case was no bigger than a business card and about a quarter of an inch think. As he opened the case, the smell of the clay entered his nose. He took the house key, placed it in the clay, and closed the cover. He waited for a few minutes before opening the case again. The key was extracted from the clay with a magnet from his key chain. The result was a perfect outline of the house key, and he could turn it into a fully functional key for his own use at any future date. As he headed for the door, he almost caught himself whistling, as it was more than a year since he last accomplished a clean sweep of coins.

Jimmy exited the house and smirked as he locked the dead bolt of the door. If only people knew how little this helped, he thought. He replaced the house key in the lock box and walked across the street to his car. He glanced at his watch to see it was about half past ten, and he debated whether he should make his next stop before or after lunch. Expecting traffic to be light, he decided he could make it to another stop well before lunch to complete more of his day's work. Once settled in he started his car's engine and let down the windows to enjoy the beautiful weather.

The drive to his next stop took about forty-five minutes, but it was a pleasant ride as traffic was not heavy. It was a typical northern California June day, with the temperature around eighty, the sky a crystal clear shade of blue, and almost no humidity. Jimmy simply loved the weather and being outside. He was so thankful he and Susan escaped the oppressing heat of the Memphis summers, but living in the South until his graduation from college allowed him to appreciate the temperate climate much more than he knew his

17

daughters could. They spent their entire lives in Palo Alto, and the perfect weather was not the only thing he and Susan made available to their offspring. The girls' mother made sure to provide everything for them at any expense. Now fifteen and thirteen years of age, they were both turning out to be very beautiful teenagers. It was a compliment to their mother, but they still seemed unable to appreciate everything given to them. Maybe someday they would understand money didn't grow on trees, but he knew they wouldn't learn it from their mother. On the contrary, the girls were learning parents were wells of money. He sighed at the thought of the rude awakening awaiting any boys who dated or married his daughters, as he was sure no teenage boy could yet imagine how much money women in general, and the three in his life in particular, could spend.

Jimmy easily navigated the many turns required on the way to his next stop. He was very adept at finding his way to most places, and this was a neighborhood he visited more often than probably any other he could remember. As he parked a few blocks away from his destination, he saw it was not yet half past eleven, and he proceeded to make a phone call. He dialed the number using his cell phone, fully anticipating no one would be home to answer. The answering machine clicked on after just the second ring, indicating to him a message or messages by other callers were not yet retrieved. This was consistent with his research from the past weekend. After the beep, he left his message. "Hi, Mr. and Mrs. Windermere. It's Jimmy Donovan of Donovan Realty. I know your home sale went pending about four or five weeks ago, but I was wondering if there was any problem with the close of escrow, as I have a client who is particularly interested in living in your neighborhood, and there are not many houses in the area which fit the exact needs of my client as well as yours does. If everything is fine, then good luck to you with your upcoming move. If not, then please call me at my office." He left his phone number, thanked the nice couple, and pushed the end button.

Jimmy knew he wouldn't receive a call back from the Windermeres, as a neighbor two doors down was amazingly open with information during a conversation just two days ago. Jimmy made the call as a precautionary measure simply to confirm the Windermeres were indeed not at home. The neighbor just listed his house, and Jimmy made a visit to preview the home and do his usual research. Early in the conversation Jimmy commented about how quickly he thought the property would sell, as evidenced by the home just two doors down staying on the market for less than a week before two offers were made. The man commented he was well aware of the quick sale, and he was hoping for the same. By the end of the conversation Jimmy learned the Windermeres just left town the previous evening, they would not return until late Wednesday evening, the packers were coming on Thursday to prepare for their move to Chicago, all the papers for the sale of the home would be signed Friday afternoon, the movers would load everything on Saturday, and the change of occupancy would occur at midnight on Saturday. How could a neighbor not only know so much, but so freely communicate this to a realtor he just met? Phenomenal was the only word Jimmy could find coming close to describing it. He guessed the neighbor must have felt talking about it would allow his home to sell more quickly. It was just another example of how homeowners wanting to sell their property acted in uncharacteristic or inappropriate ways.

Jimmy drove the few blocks to the Windermere's home, careful to approach the house from the direction opposite of the informed neighbor. He parked on the street behind another car which helped hide his car from the neighbor's view. He first grabbed his folder, and then he reached into the glove compartment and grabbed a house key he made five weeks ago after a previous visit to the Windermere residence. He walked quickly to the front door and was happy the key worked without any problems. There were times when his duplicating process didn't work, as some locks were more difficult than others, but it hadn't happened for several months now.

Jimmy stopped just inside the front door to take account of the condition of the house. Many things were moved from his recollection of a month ago. It was obvious some things were already packed and other items were ready for the upcoming packing. All of the pictures were removed from their hooks and were now on the floor leaning against the wall. The CD racks by the stereo were now empty, but two packed boxes sat unlabeled and unsealed on the floor near the racks. He opened the flaps on top of one of the boxes and saw the CDs were stacked inside in a somewhat orderly fashion. As

19

he walked toward the stairway to the downstairs, he peeked into the kitchen and saw a few boxes were packed and a few others were laying on the floor in their flattened configuration. He saw through the bay window the wind chimes hanging from the arbor on the back porch were still there, but quiet due to the calm of the late morning.

Jimmy became more anxious as he descended the stairs. Nothing to this point was of tremendous interest to him. He was simply forming his own opinion of how organized or unorganized the Windermeres were at this stage. What awaited him in the downstairs family room was his real agenda.

In his initial visit to the Windermere house, they were not home, and Jimmy was surprised at all of the different things they collected. Their music collection was most likely their largest, as it looked like they had as many as a thousand CDs. Since those cost them probably fifteen dollars on the average, the investment was not great. Their artwork was quite extensive, too, and it included mostly limited edition prints. He didn't know the artists, but the pictures were attractive, with many bright flowers included in the different landscapes. In several of the rooms, Wedgwood dishes of varying colors were displayed. He knew those were expensive, but he wasn't connected with a secondary market which allowed him to profit from a sale of those items. Mr. Windermere also had a large collection of books, ranging all the way from leather bound classics to romance paperbacks his wife or possibly his daughters read. Surely Mr. Windermere wasn't the one reading those, too, Jimmy hoped.

The prize in the downstairs family room was the Department 56 collection of Christmas village houses. There were close to two hundred different houses, and there were also all of the accessories, including people, cars, trees, roadway, and cotton filling acting as the snow. Jimmy hoped the collection would be mostly packed, as most collectors of these houses keep the original boxes and do their own packing prior to the relocation of their entire household goods. Much to his delight the houses were no longer on the shelves beneath the track lighting, but in what looked at first glance to be eight large cardboard moving boxes. He opened the flaps of the boxes and searched for anything resembling an inventory. When he couldn't find any such listing, he walked into another downstairs room where a desk was present. He went through every drawer looking for anything representing a full account of their collection. When he didn't find one, he decided the Windermeres could make their move with a few houses missing.

Once back in the family room Jimmy quickly hunted through the large boxes. He was knowledgeable of the fact the limited edition houses or the ones retired for many years were the most valuable. Some of the houses could easily command in excess of a thousand dollars, and he did business with a dealer in southern California on many occasions for buying and selling these collectibles, mostly for selling.

In the first box Jimmy found the Dickens' Village Mill from 1985. The Chesterton Manor house from 1987 was in the third box. The sixth and seventh boxes produced two more limited edition houses, the Green Gate Cottage from 1989 and the Norman Church from 1986. Those four alone could net Jimmy about six grand! In the last box were the original seven shops of the Dickens' Village series from when it was first released in 1984. The set was now worth over ten thousand dollars, but he felt those seven possessions would be missed on the other end of the Windermere's move. Plus he only had two hands for carrying these, so he opted to take only the four.

Jimmy headed up the stairs and hurriedly made his way to the front door. His heart was beating ferociously as he realized he didn't bring a plastic bag from a grocery or department store. Peering out the front window and not seeing any cars or anyone walking, he exited the house and swiftly got into his car and drove away. Seeing the clock on his car dash indicate it was past noon, he headed toward his office for some lunch.

THREE

Donovan Realty leased some office space in downtown Palo Alto on a side street just off University Avenue. Jimmy liked the many delis and restaurants within walking distance, and the atmosphere of this town coupled with the wonderful June weather made him happy he chose to live here. It was a long shot at best when he first proposed marriage to Susan, but it was an even longer shot when he further proposed they move to northern California.

Both Jimmy and Susan were raised in Tennessee—Jimmy in Germantown, just ten miles outside of Memphis, and Susan in Jackson, less than one hundred miles or two hours to the north and east from Memphis. Susan was not one to stray too far away from her family or her home, and the thought of moving to the west coast was the same as moving to the other side of the world in her mind. While in college at Memphis State, she would often times drive home on a weeknight, have dinner with her folks, and return to campus the next morning. Having to get on an airplane to visit her folks was not something she welcomed, but his persistence won out.

Jimmy first met Susan during their sophomore year at Memphis State at a party between his fraternity, Sigma Chi, and her sorority, Delta Gamma. He was awed by her beauty, and she was intrigued by his personality, charming smile, and style. They only dated a few times during the school year, as she was hesitant to go somewhere strange with a boy she hardly knew. She did permit him to escort her to the home football games, but nothing more. She lost track of the number of times he asked her to go to a blues festival, an art show, or some other special activity somewhere in downtown Memphis, and she always pleasantly declined his offers. She was flattered by his interest to the point it almost embarrassed her.

During the summer between her sophomore and junior years, a high school friend of hers was killed in a motorcycle accident, and

Susan changed. She began to appreciate a lot of simple things so much more. When she returned for her junior year, she had feelings of confidence and urgency, allowing her to throw caution to the wind and gladly accept Jimmy's invitations for dates. As time passed she recognized she was not only enjoying the events they attended, she was also thoroughly enjoying his company. She began to regret not venturing out with him the previous year.

At the start of their senior year, Jimmy proposed to her. Susan didn't accept immediately, as she was still somewhat frightened. She drove home to her mother that evening for one of their many mother-daughter chats, and she returned to Memphis the next day with an acceptance. The proposal to move to California came a week later, and it was a much bigger pill to swallow. Her mother did not encourage her one way or the other, but the excitement of trying something new finally overcame the fear of the unknown.

Jimmy on the other hand wanted to move to California since the summer after his freshman year at Memphis State. He worked in Las Vegas at a casino that summer, and it was a chance conversation with a wealthy business man from San Francisco which convinced him.

Late one night after finishing his shift at the casino, he shared the bar at a diner with a gentleman he guessed was forty-five to fifty years old. The man seemed out of place in the messy diner due to all of the expensive jewelry he was wearing, and Jimmy guessed he just lost a large sum at the tables and was recuperating at this somewhat deserted spot. The jewelry was Jimmy's first clue the man had some financial success, and to satisfy his curiosity, he engaged in a conversation with the man. He remembered talking with the man for more than two hours, and the thing he learned was this man thought real estate in the San Francisco Bay Area was going to boom over the next few decades. This man already made a fortune in commercial real estate in downtown San Francisco, but he told Jimmy he fully expected it to continue for many years to come, as the peninsula from San Francisco to San Jose was prime for commercial and residential development. Jimmy also learned the man won big at the craps table, and he just liked the quietness and good food of this particular diner.

With Jimmy's zest for real estate and this new tip from someone who was already successful in the same field, he began his mission to finish college and move to California to chase his real estate dreams.

When he returned to Memphis State after the summer in Las Vegas, the first thing he did was subscribe to the San Jose Mercury News and the San Francisco Chronicle. He wanted to learn as much as possible about the local economy, and this seemed like the best way to accomplish it.

After the joyful junior year when he spent so much time with Susan, it became apparent to him his love and lust for her was possibly a barrier to his dream. He wanted to marry her, and he wanted to move to California, but he knew she was a southern girl through and through, which meant she dreaded the thought of living more than a day's drive from her parents. Only his previous persistence and subsequent success at convincing her to date him in a steady fashion provided the motivation for him to suggest such an inconceivable thing. When she agreed to the move, his feet didn't touch the ground for an entire week. He was uncontrollably happy he was going to marry this amazingly beautiful woman and sell real estate in California.

Things did not work out well though, as Susan and Jimmy fought constantly, mostly regarding money. Susan's father spoiled her to no end, and her spending habits could not be curbed. It was never enough to simply buy a table, a chair, a bed, kitchen items, or a dress. She shopped for everything at the most expensive stores. She always equated price with value, and Jimmy could not dissuade her. Fortunately, they waited until they were thirty before the first of their two children was born, so their financial situation was more stable when the expense of a child was encountered.

When Jimmy and Susan married and subsequently moved to Palo Alto, he was an agent in the local office of a national real estate company. She decided not to work outside of the home even though she had a degree in Elementary Education from Memphis State. Instead she did volunteer work, which on occasion would provide a new client to him.

During the first five years in California, Jimmy was having moderate success selling residential real estate. He built up enough contacts and joined a smaller, local realty office. The new office allowed him to keep a larger percentage of the commission paid to the brokers, so he made more money by selling the same value of property.

The big move in his career came when he decided to start his own realty office. His two girls were five and three years old, and he just turned thirty-six himself. With Susan certainly capable of taking care of the children, Jimmy decided to spend his energy building his own business, in hopes he could garner a substantially larger portion of the financial pie. His efforts paid huge dividends, but there were times he still thought he couldn't make it faster than she and the girls were capable of spending it. If there was a hall of fame for shoppers, surely she would make it on the first ballot. His girls would then be second generation inductees.

Jimmy didn't care much for shopping, unless hunting down a delicious deli and ordering their signature sandwich counted. On this lovely June day he opted for a hot roast beef and cheddar on a toasted french roll, accompanied by a brown gravy sauce for dipping. It was one of his favorite sandwiches, and he felt his actions of the morning were deserving of such a treat. He ordered the sandwich to go and returned with it to his office just around the corner.

Jimmy walked in the front door of his office building and greeted his assistant. The rest of the office was vacant as all of the agents working for him were out either having lunch, showing property, or doing whatever it was they did on Mondays at this time. Mondays were always slow days for showing property, as realtors worked with clients mostly on weekends and holidays, so many of his agents used this day to catch up on paperwork or take the day off. His assistant handed him a few messages from people who phoned earlier in the morning, and a quick glance indicated no one of import called.

Jimmy proceeded to his office in the front corner of the building. The walls were decorated with maps of the Bay Area, and he constantly studied them on every occasion when he ate lunch in his office. He was insistent on having the latest maps, and he remembered firing a previous assistant who was unable to keep the maps current.

After finishing his sandwich, Jimmy proceeded to the back of the office building to a locked storage room with no windows. He was the only one with a key, and he used this room for many different purposes. Once inside the room, he turned on the light, closed the door, and headed to a corner containing a desk. He opened a desk drawer and extracted a key duplicating kit. Using this kit and the clay imprint he made earlier, he duplicated the key within minutes. He labeled the duplicate key and walked to a wall totally covered with cabinet doors. He opened one of the doors and placed the new key next to hundreds of other keys for that particular neighborhood. He knew all of the keys wouldn't provide access to their original homes anymore, as most new homeowners changed the locks shortly after they occupied a new dwelling, but he also knew many homeowners didn't go to the trouble of buying and installing new locks. He duplicated close to four thousand keys over the last ten years, and he expected about one thousand of them still were useful today.

On another wall of this storage room were several books on collectibles. Jimmy grabbed this year's volume of the Department 56 houses and flipped to the section on the Dickens' Village series. He checked the pricing of the four houses still in his car. Out of curiosity he checked the previous year's pricing to see the annual increase. It was over ten percent on the two oldest, and roughly seven or eight percent on the others. He made a note on a scrap of paper and stuck it in his shirt pocket. On another shelf were books on coins, but he passed over those as he knew he could get more current pricing from an internet site using the computer in his office. He exited the storage room and locked the door as he headed to his office.

Back in his office Jimmy turned on his computer and waited impatiently for the operating system to boot. After a few minutes he was reviewing the latest prices for the coins he now possessed. He also checked the prices for the coins he used as replacements so he could calculate the real profit he would realize. It was a tidy sum indeed and kept him in good spirits. A profitable day, a wonderful deli sandwich, and the beautiful California weather were a combination always providing ecstasy.

Jimmy picked up the handset of the phone on his desk and hit a speed dial button. The gentleman who answered was the dealer in southern California with whom Jimmy bought and sold Christmas houses on many previous occasions. It was several months though since their last transaction, but he didn't expect any problems. It was arranged for him to mail the houses at his earliest convenience, and upon receiving the houses, the dealer would mail a check to Jimmy's office. The agreed upon price was what he noted just a few minutes ago minus a small commission for the dealer.

Jimmy grabbed a department store bag from the corner of his office on his way out. He informed his assistant he would be out of the office for the remainder of the day and to call him on his car phone if she needed him. He wished her a good day and headed back to his car. He was glad she was the one required to stay inside and answer the phone while he could enjoy more of this gorgeous day.

Jimmy's first stop was at a local shipping shop. He placed the four Christmas houses in the department store bag, and after walking through the entryway he permitted the older lady behind the counter to box the houses for shipment to southern California. He didn't remember previously seeing her working here, but she seemed capable of handling this fairly simple task. He paid her for the wrapping and shipping and then headed to his next stop.

Within forty minutes Jimmy arrived at the coin shop. It took only a few minutes to agree on a price acceptable to both him and the coin dealer, and Jimmy was given cash from a wad of bills in the dealer's pocket big enough to choke a horse. Maybe he was in the wrong business, Jimmy thought, as no one he knew carried such a large amount of spending money in a pocket of their pants. Jimmy speculated the wad of money might be the dealer's entire life's savings, so he decided he would stick with real estate and all the extra business it provided him.

Jimmy called back to his office to check for any new messages. He also instructed his assistant to check on the status of several closings taking place over the next few weeks. He finally reminded her to be sure to check any new listings from the last two weeks in Alameda county, as he hadn't previewed any homes in the East Bay for more than a month, and he wanted to keep his finger on the pulse of the activity in that part of the Bay Area. After completing the call he saw it was almost four o'clock, so he decided to head home to check on a few other things from his office there.

It was less than an hour-long drive to his home, so he was able to beat the upcoming rush hour traffic. It was one thing he didn't like about their locale, but Jimmy knew his business would only get better with more and more people flocking to the area. As he approached the turn onto his street, he passed two trucks from a local flower and garden business heading in the opposite direction. He hoped Susan hadn't already started her summer spending frenzy. Surely she wouldn't ruin this wonderful day.

Once his house was within his sight, his good feeling began to evaporate. There were new flowers throughout the yard. As he pulled into the driveway he saw some exotic-looking flowers he didn't recognize. After parking in the garage he walked to the yard to take a quick inventory of the damage. He saw a large number of impatients of all different colors under two of the trees. There were other plants he didn't know the names of. Susan probably didn't even know their names either. He was sure these were probably annuals as well, meaning the same expense would be encountered again next year, and the next year, until forever probably. Why didn't she plant some perennials like agapanthuses or day lilies he wondered. And why didn't she buy all of these at Walmart or Home Depot and plant them herself instead of paying the higher cost at the local garden shop in addition to the labor charge for having them do the planting? It was exasperating to him how her mind worked regarding money.

Jimmy decided to let it go for today since he knew Susan would be so happy the yard looked pretty again. The flowers were quite colorful, and he didn't want to crush her spirit, so he figured he could worry about this some other day. As he entered the house through the garage door, he bumped into several shopping bags. He noticed a few from Macy's and a few from Nordstrom in the pile. He could hear the excitement of the conversation in the kitchen between Susan and his girls, so he knew the bill for the flowers was minute compared to the bill for the day's purchases at the mall. His anger was about to get the best of him, so he walked to his office instead of first going to the kitchen to greet his family.

A few minutes after entering his office, Susan came in to greet him with a big kiss. She was clearly excited, but he could only think of the cost. "How much did you spend for the flowers, Susan?" Jimmy started in a calm tone.

"Not nearly what the new summer clothes for me and the girls cost," she replied.

"So how much did the female bonding experience set us back?"

"Only five thousand or so, but we got most of it on sale, and we did buy you something."

"Only five thousand!" Jimmy hollered. He couldn't believe it. How could three women spend so much money? "What did you buy?! A new outfit for every day of the summer!"

"Well, the girls needed to have new clothes for the summer. You know how a girl dresses is so important for her self-esteem. Plus we need to have new clothes for our vacation next month."

"Why do you need to have new clothes on a vacation? No one who will see you will know the difference. New clothes or old clothes. They'll be the same in other people's eyes."

"Jimmy, you know how you feel makes the difference. You just can't feel new if your clothes are old, and people can tell the way you feel."

Jimmy couldn't understand or believe this logic. Did she really believe what she was saying? She was a beautiful woman, and their girls got all of their good looks from her, but he would gladly trade some of her beauty for some financial intelligence. He surrendered. "Let me finish some work I need to do. Someone's got to pay all of the bills around here."

"Okay. But the girls want to give your gift to you before dinner, and we want to go out and eat tonight since we're all a little tired from our shopping today. So please finish up by six as we have a reservation at seven."

Jimmy was mystified. They were tired from spending money, so he had to take them out to eat! He couldn't see how he was ever going to win when it was three against one.

FOUR

It was June 20th, the sixth anniversary of his divorce, and Mickey Ross planned to spend it the same way as the previous five. As a matter of fact, Mickey wished he spent the divorce day six years ago playing golf instead of signing the papers. He knew his ex-wife deliberately scheduled the paper signing at noon to totally disrupt his day. She knew a noon appointment would prohibit him from golfing in the morning and the reality of the settlement would depress his afternoon to the point he would only get as far as the bar at the golf course instead of the first tee.

And how right she was. Mickey made it to the course by 1:45pm and started his third beer at 2:05pm. Sometime around nine or ten that evening the bartender called a cab for him. Mickey stumbled into his hotel room, fell onto the bed, and stayed there until nine o'clock the next morning when he was awakened by the cleaning lady and immediately realized he was experiencing one of his worst hangovers. It took two days for his head to clear, and he resolved every anniversary of his divorce would be spent playing golf and enjoying an outstanding meal. He wasn't about to give up drinking, but he figured he could get by with far less than he consumed on his divorce day.

So far Mickey made good on his resolution from six years ago. On this day he left his Monterey town home prior to dawn, watched the sun rise from the front seat of his jaguar, and then ate breakfast at one of his favorite spots on Ocean Avenue in Carmel. The three-egg omelet with chorizo sausage accompanied by hash browns, sourdough toast, cranberry juice, and black coffee was an excellent start to what he hoped was a great day of golf and food. He referred to this day as the Sixth Annual Mickey Ross Golfing and Dining Extravaganza, and as was the case for the previous five, he kept all his scorecards and dining receipts in a scrapbook as if it were some kind of official event. The dining location varied from year to year, but the golfing venue was always the Pebble Beach Golf Links, and he presently did not intend to change this part of his annual celebration.

Mickey loved this golf course. It was clear to him the decision long ago to build the houses on the hills and place the golf course along the ocean was the right one, and he was glad those who wanted to do the opposite lost their battle. Hopefully they ultimately agreed the correct decision was made. How could they not since it turned out perfectly, he wondered.

It was a typical start to an early summer day on the Monterey peninsula. The temperature was in the fifties, which required him to don a sweater. The clouds were pushing back from the coastline, maybe a little earlier than normal, hinting by mid afternoon the temperature would be in the eighties. The waves crashed softly into the rocks along the bank, and the wind rustled slowly through the trees. Various birds were flying in all directions, and Carmel residents and tourists were walking along the Carmel bay. Mickey knew the ones with dogs were the residents and those without were probably the tourists, and it made him think back to when he and his ex-wife walked their dog along the same beach many times years ago.

Mickey met his ex-wife at his first job after finishing his engineering degree. They couldn't be more different. Mickey was born and raised in Vicksburg, Mississippi, while she was a California girl whose family resided in Santa Cruz for most of her childhood. She attended college in California at Cal Poly in San Luis Obispo, while Memphis State University in the middle of the South was his alma mater. He was a true sportsman—being a fan of all sports, playing golf regularly, and participating in other outdoor activities like hiking, skiing, and hunting. She on the other hand despised any activity demanding physical exertion. He enjoyed dining at fine restaurants, while her preference was for cooking something simple at home. He couldn't remember liking anything she cooked, and it was the source of many arguments. Why they ever got married in the first place, let alone having it last more than ten years and producing a daughter and a son, was beyond his and anyone's imagination or comprehension.

They did have something in common, and if it could've been avoided, his life would have been and would still be easier and less complicated. They both possessed engineering degrees and their first jobs were with a small engineering firm in Monterey. It must have been bad luck when they started employment on the same day, and even though they worked in different departments, they were part of the same orientation group. Both were in an unfamiliar setting and situation, and loneliness was a common foe they battled, so they dated a few times during the first couple of years.

The relationship was not really headed anywhere, but they enjoyed each other's friendship since it helped the loneliness subside. The company was going through a difficult period on a few projects, and fate landed them on the same task force. It was during this intense nine-month period the common goal of working together for the good of the company provided the basis for a stronger attraction. They both recognized they were two of the smarter workers assigned to the team, and they agreed almost universally on all aspects of the work, including the data needed, the experiments to conduct to gather the data, the interpretation of the data, and the proposed solution to the problems. It was close to the time when the task force was about to disband when they looked deeply into each other's eyes during an evening work session and felt being smart was enough commonality to provide a solid foundation for a successful marriage.

Their marriage coincided with the company performing better. Pay raises came more often and were more generous. Additional vacation time was also granted to all employees. While good for most others, this only created tension between Mickey and his wife. They never could agree on how to spend the extra money or the extra time off. Mickey always wanted to go to some exotic golfing resort where they could hike or snorkel or take part in some other invigorating activity, while her desire was to simply stay home and read a mystery novel or go to a local attraction. The result was Mickey would often times take a golfing trip and leave her to do whatever she wanted. At least while they were physically separated they didn't fight.

Another seven-month task force near their third wedding anniversary helped things improve for a short while. It was during this discreet moment of happiness they recommitted themselves to each other and their marriage. Thinking producing a child would help them remain closer, their son was born nine months later. At the time of his birth, however, things returned to the dominant, unpleasant state.

Shortly after Mickey celebrated his thirtieth birthday he did some soul-searching and determined his chosen profession was not providing him with the fulfillment he needed. Although his son was now less than two years old, he convinced his wife he should enroll in law school at Santa Clara. He would continue to work in Monterey, but he would use his vacation time and go to a reduced-hour schedule, part of the company's continuing education program. She agreed to continue working so they could make ends meet. Their celebration of the expected future resulted in the birth of their daughter nine months later.

Mickey did not conceive how hard and time-consuming the decision turned out to be. Even with a reduced work schedule in Monterey, the commute time to and from law school coupled with the class and study time was almost too much for him. He knew he was not being a good father or husband, but he desperately wanted to accomplish this career change. He also knew his wife was contemplating divorce, but for some reason the topic was never discussed. He could only figure she was enjoying however little time she spent with their children more than any time with him.

After four long years of working on his law degree, Mickey finally finished. He was so happy, and his wife seemed genuinely proud of him. Mickey immediately quit his job with the engineering company and embarked on his new career. He started a law firm named Ross and Associates, even though there was only a single paralegal assistant. Although working long hours trying to get his new business venture on solid ground, he no longer endured the long commute which plagued him during law school, so he was much more content.

Mickey's new career was difficult. Not having any clients and not having the mentoring normally provided to a new lawyer by a senior lawyer in a larger firm, many days there was little or no work. Without significant work, he contributed almost nothing to their financial well-being. Still intent on making good on his career change, he began to pursue clients with personal injury claims.

Two and a half years after starting his firm, and after working with several clients ending in a handful of small settlements and others still in litigation, Mickey finally won a case netting his client millions of dollars. His fee was several hundreds of thousands of dollars, and he felt vindicated. Shortly thereafter his wife was pregnant with their third child.

Seven months later the pregnancy ended in an induced abortion. Difficulties arose during the fifth month, and she took a leave of absence from her job. By the seventh month the doctor recommended the abortion as the only way to ensure Mickey's wife would remain safe. Depression overcame her, and she refused to return to work. She constantly blamed Mickey for the lifestyle she was forced to live to support him and take care of the children while he was attending law school and starting his own business. Within a year of the lost child she was asking for a divorce.

Mickey fought the idea at first, thinking the uncompleted pregnancy was dominating their lives and after enough time things would return to normal. Then he remembered normalcy wasn't much fun, and he finally realized their marriage was a mistake from the beginning. Mickey chose to represent himself in the settlement, while his wife hired an experienced lawyer. It was clearly a mistake on his part as the woman judge gave everything to his wife.

Mickey thought the alimony payments were excessive, but the judge ruled he must provide compensation for her not working, ruling the difficulty and failure of this last pregnancy was the cause. Also included in the judge's ruling was the financial and emotional support provided by his wife while Mickey was in law school and while he was getting his law business started from nothing would solely benefit him unless he was forced to pay more to her each month. The child support seemed unreasonably large, although Mickey didn't mind the basic idea of paying it since they were after all his kids. The amount was the part he just didn't agree on. She received the house, while he of course kept paying for it, forcing Mickey to make do with a hotel room he could now not afford until he was able to find a one-bedroom apartment. Her having custody of the kids was the one item Mickey didn't mind relinquishing.

That was six years ago, though, and Mickey was a much happier man now. The one-bedroom apartment lasted a little more than a year, and he was content with his two-bedroom town home with a wonderful view of the Monterey bay from the deck. The decision to study law and consequently start his own firm provided the fulfillment which was missing in his previous career. His love for golf was rejuvenated since he dedicated more time over the years to improving his game. Even though he was enthusiastic prior to every round of golf about playing the elusive perfect round, he was particularly cheerful today since it was the golfing and dining extravaganza he invented.

The tee time wasn't until 10:30am, yet Mickey arrived well before nine. He paid his green fees of $350 and stopped for a few moments to browse through the sweaters, shirts, and hats for sale, all bearing some form of the Pebble Beach lone Cypress tree logo. Mickey made many purchases here on previous visits, but he overcame the temptation on this occasion. What did he need with yet another golfing shirt from Pebble Beach when the closet in the secondary bedroom of his town home was full of golfing attire from courses throughout the country? He knew he owned so many hats from different golfing venues he was sure he couldn't wear all of them during the course of a year, even if he was to wear a different hat every time he played.

Earlier this morning Mickey opted for a navy pair of slacks, a predominantly white shirt, and a yellow sweater. The sweater covered the logo on his golf shirt from a course he played during a golfing trip the previous summer. Matching his white golf shoes was a white cap he purchased at St. Andrews during his most recent trip to Scotland four weeks ago. He was hoping the hat would be good luck on this day as he began to play much better near the end of his Scotland trip, and his good play continued since his return to the Monterey peninsula.

Since Mickey arrived before his playing companions, he headed to the driving range alone. Surprisingly the range was almost devoid of other golfers. Mickey knew it was expensive to play golf here, but more golfers participating in their dream vacation in some form or fashion were usually present on a Wednesday near the end of June. All the better, he thought, as having the course less populated made a round of golf here more comfortable.

Mickey's first few swings with a six iron showed promise, as his balance was good and his grip felt right. He knew many days he left his game on the range, while on a few rare occasions he was somehow transformed into a perfect swinging machine between a poor warmup and the first tee. He expected every golfer experienced similar outings, so he continued to experiment with a few other clubs in his bag. All he tried seemed satisfactory, so his confidence remained high.

Mickey then heard his name being shouted as two other golfers approached in a golf cart. A quick look revealed two others of his foursome arrived. They smiled broadly indicating they too were as excited as Mickey at the day's golfing agenda. The three barely exchanged the normal handshakes before the verbal jabs started.

"How long have you been out here practicing, Mickey? You better be getting an early start if you're going to take my money today," was how one started.

The next added, "Do you want to just pay me now and save the embarrassment at the end of the round, Mick?" They both laughed at their early-morning wit.

"Boys, I must warn you," Mickey started his reply. "I don't think you brought enough money with you to pay me what you will owe me when we finish. But on the bright side, I'm willing to accept IOUs from each of you, payable within thirty days of course."

"Of course!" the two said in unison. All three laughed as silently each hoped today would be their day.

After pounding balls with various clubs for another fifteen minutes, Mickey decided to head to the putting green. If his putter was hot he knew he could pocket a few thousand dollars by the end of the round. Waiting for Mickey when he arrived at the practice green was the fourth member of his group. "Good morning, Mick. How are ya?" was the reserved greeting he received.

"Not bad. Not bad," Mickey responded as they shook hands. "It's a beautiful day, it's a work day for normal folks, and I'm going to play golf on my favorite golf course. How 'bout you?"

"I'm doin' fine. How's your golf game been treatin' ya?"

"Pretty good. I started playing much better in Scotland. It's been a good summer so far, and I'm hoping it continues on some of the other trips I planned for later this year."

"Where all are ya' goin' this year?"

"Well, I leave for Chicago tomorrow morning to play at Cog Hill with some buddies of mine living near there," Mickey offered. "I have four other trips planned, but two of them are short ones here on the west coast."

"Just a normal year for ya' then."

Mickey didn't respond as he wanted to get a feel for the speed of the green. They both continued putting silently as another foursome sharing the green with them was called to the first tee. After a few more moments, the silence was broken. "Let me ask ya, Mick, how do you afford all of these trips? Is your law business really that profitable?"

"Business has been quite good," Mickey answered. "And the neat thing is once you get enough clients to make you think you're really going to start making some dough, the referrals come pouring in. I'm getting close to thinking I need to hire an additional lawyer to handle all of the wills and other fairly simple work. Plus, taking money from golfers like you every so often is a nice supplemental income." Mickey laughed at his last comment. He knew he usually struggled to compete with the three he invited to play with him on this occasion, but he was feeling confident about his game and wanted to give it a good test on this special occasion.

Once the group gathered together at the practice green prior to their tee time, the wagers for the day were made. One standard bet was the player with the day's best score would have his green fees paid by the other three. They agreed to play a revolving game of partners where each player would team with one of the other three for six holes of match play. Each player of the winning team for the six-hole match would pocket $100 from a loser. A game of skins worth $50 per skin was standard fare and was also included. Beyond those bets Mickey knew there would be other side bets and presses added as the round progressed. As a result, he knew playing well later in the round usually counted for more dollars in your pocket than playing well early in the round.

Mickey's game was superb for the first four holes. He carded three pars and a birdie, with the birdie on the third hole being good for three skins since the first two holes were tied. Every shot was hit where he was aiming, and he felt good about his putting stroke. His team was also ahead by two holes with two holes left in the first six, so they accepted the day's first press. Bad luck on the sixth hole when his putt lipped the cup kept his team from winning the press, but they made good on the original bet.

It was the change of partners on the seventh tee which seemed to be the turning point of the round for Mickey. His new partner encouraged him to aim at the flag on his tee shot on the short seventh as opposed to playing to a safer part of the green. Knowing better but being confident at the time, Mickey's shot was blown by the wind into a greenside bunker. When they arrived at the green, a buried lie awaited him. The result was a double bogey five, and the one ill-advised play gnawed at him for several holes. He and his new partner lost the original bet and two presses during the middle six holes, while Mickey also did not capture any more skins for himself. He was now looking forward to the last six holes with his final partner.

The highlight of the remaining part of the round was a birdie on the fifteenth hole. A good tee shot followed by an approach stopping a mere four inches from the cup provided a tap-in birdie and a skin. Unfortunately, there were no carry-overs from the previous hole, so it only counted as one skin, bringing his total to a respectable four skins.

The team bet was halved on the final six holes, so Mickey won one bet and lost three others in the revolving team game. His four skins netted him $600 from the other three competitors, but the fourteen skins captured by them cost him $700. His total score of four-over-par 76 was only third best in the group, so he also paid his third of the green fees of the day's winner. The disappointing part of the round to him was not necessarily the double bogey on seven, but the way it came about and its lingering effect. He was discouraged he played stupidly based on someone else's advice, and then he bogeyed three of the next four holes while steaming over the bad choice. Those five strokes were the difference between finishing first and finishing third, and his bogey on number nine cost him five skins since all the others bogeyed the ninth when there were four carry-overs.

Once resigned to the bar, the not so insignificant task of figuring out who owed whom how much began. There was the normal bickering over what bets were made and for how much, along with who pressed and when. In addition there was the replaying of different shots with the standard would've, could've, and should've. When all the figuring for the bets was completed, Mickey's damage was just under $500. He lost much more on many occasions, but he knew just a couple of breaks could have him walking away with $500 or more instead of the reverse.

After a few beers with his group, the pain of the round began to subside. He began to contemplate his choices for the dining part of his celebration, and the joy of playing golf on one of the game's greatest courses helped his spirits return to where they were at the start of the day, despite the monetary setback of the golfing portion.

"I hear you're off to play at Cog Hill tomorrow, Mick," was a comment from one of his friends.

"Yeah. I leave first thing tomorrow morning. I'm heading up to San Jose tonight for a relaxing dinner before I go. Wish me luck so I can make up the losses from today in addition to all the expenses."

Everyone said their goodbyes as they departed and went their separate ways. It was always a little depressing for Mickey to drive away from Pebble Beach after the completion of his round. On this occasion though he felt good since he expected his golf game was ready for the test awaiting him at Cog Hill.

The drive to San Jose was uneventful, as Mickey drove this route so many times before while working on his law degree. He listened to music from some old CDs from his college days, including the Eagles, Lynyrd Skynyrd, ZZ Top, and the Allman Brothers. This music soothed his soul so much more than rap or most of the music of today. His reservation was at the Fairmont, and when he pulled between the columns supporting the roof to let the valet park his car, he noticed it was half past six.

Mickey enjoyed both large and small hotels, as what was particularly attractive to him was expensive flooring, tall ceilings in the reception area and bar, detailed trim, and fine art hanging on the walls. The Fairmont was small but well-situated in downtown, providing access to several nice restaurants. Since it also included all of the features Mickey liked, it was one of his favorite hotels.

After checking into his room, he showered and dressed for dinner. On the drive from Monterey, he decided to eat at the restaurant located in the hotel. He also decided his attire should be simple, so he wore a pair of khaki pants and a medium blue shirt proudly displaying the Greek letters of his college fraternity.

Mickey ordered a cocktail while he studied the menu and wine list. He wondered what would be appropriate for the Sixth Annual Mickey Ross Golfing and Dining Extravaganza, and he first chose the filet mignon covered with fried onion strings, which was advertised to be one of the house specialties. To accompany the food he opted for a bottle of Silver Oak cabernet sauvignon. He finished the meal with a cigar and a cognac, and he was satisfied the meal was exactly what he envisioned six years ago when he decided to celebrate his divorce in this fashion. The tab was well over $300, mostly due to the wine, but he thought it was a reasonable amount for such a special occasion.

Before going back to his room, Mickey decided to take a walk through part of downtown San Jose. The night was pleasant as he enjoyed the view of the buildings and the sound of planes on their approach to the airport. Content with the results of the day, he returned to his room hoping his ex-wife and kids were eating takeout pizza for dinner.

As Mickey stuck the hotel key in the slot on the door, he looked down and noticed a drop of wine on his shirt just below the two Greek letters, Sigma Chi. Disappointed he didn't have any stain remover with him, once inside the room he removed his shirt and stuck it under the faucet in the bathroom. Satisfied the shirt would not be permanently stained, he grabbed his cell phone to check his messages.

He was dumbfounded there were nineteen messages in all. He told his paralegal assistant not to bother him with any work until Monday when he returned, unless of course it was an emergency. Someone must have confused his cell phone number with his fax number and automatically redialed numerous times when the document did not get transmitted. It happened before, but never enough times in one day to account for this many messages.

Not really in the mood for going through the messages, Mickey reluctantly dialed the number of his voice mail. The first four were from his assistant and dealt with some details of his Chicago trip, including a change in the tee time for Friday's round and the phone number of one of his friends he was meeting there which he previously couldn't find. There were indeed three messages containing those annoying beeps associated with a fax machine. Two other messages were from golfing friends of his in Boston and New York, asking Mickey if he wanted to participate in a special golf outing they were planning for this September. The next three were also from a fax machine, and Mickey wondered what document could be so important for someone to send it a total of six times now. There were two more messages from other golfing friends regarding trips which Mickey had already purchased his airline tickets and made hotel reservations. Why everyone considered their calls so urgent was presently escaping him as he kept adding notes to the growing list.

As he listened to the next message, a chill came over his body. It was Jimmy Donovan, and Mickey certainly wasn't expecting to hear from Jimmy today. "Hi, Mick. It's J.D. I hope you are enjoying your annual golfing and eating experience, or whatever you call it." Jimmy's message started innocently enough, but then it took a turn for the worse. "We have a problem with one of our special closings next week, and I'm not sure it can wait until you get back into town next Monday. We should be able to work it out over the phone between now and your return, so how about giving me a call tomorrow night when you get settled in Chicago, and we can go through the details? Have a good flight, and I'll talk to you then. I hope you played well today at Pebble." Jimmy didn't provide any more details, but Mickey knew something was seriously wrong from the tone of his voice. After listening to the message a second time, he debated about returning Jimmy's call tonight, but decided to let it wait until tomorrow as Jimmy suggested.

Nothing of particular import was revealed in the remaining messages, so Mickey turned off his phone and began a night of uncomfortable sleep. Every time he awakened he found himself thinking about Jimmy's message. What could be wrong with the upcoming closures, he pondered. He didn't think anything out of the ordinary was included in any of those.

When Mickey saw it was 3:30am, he concluded he wasn't going to get any more useful sleep. He leaned over and turned on the light next to the bed and then turned on the television. ESPN's SportsCenter detailing the previous day's sporting events was on. Baseball dominated the telecast, but it was only slightly interesting to Mickey. After thirty minutes he switched over to CNN Headline News. Not finding it very stimulating, he turned the set off. Knowing Jimmy was probably still sleeping at this early hour, Mickey decided to get dressed and head to the airport. He figured the least he could do was get a good start on one of the novels he packed for the trip.

FIVE

Mickey's flight to Chicago was as smooth as he could remember. The comfort of the ride combined with a fairly boring book allowed him to nod off from time to time during the five-hour trip. Upon arriving he wasn't feeling particularly refreshed or extremely tired as he walked through the terminal, just sluggish from his poor night's sleep and the long ride. He hoped a better night's sleep tonight would help his body recover. He definitely didn't want to struggle through three days of golf with this lethargic feeling. Mickey made his way to the baggage area to claim his suitcase and golf bag. He was delighted the airline delivered his belongings without incident, as there was nothing worse in his mind than playing golf with some rented or borrowed clubs.

Mickey hurried outside to where the shuttle bus was located for the short ride to the Hilton hotel located at O'Hare airport. He was eager to get checked in and return Jimmy's call from the previous day. He noticed it was a warm day in Chicago, and certainly a lot more humid than what he left behind in California. Why his friends enjoyed this kind of weather in the summer and the bitter cold of the winters versus the climate he was accustomed to in Monterey was beyond him.

Mickey found his way to the elevator after completing his registration. The worker at the front desk was very pleasant, but he figured it was easy when accepting someone's credit card for a room with a rate of over $200 per night, not counting the ridiculous local taxes always imposed on travelers. He asked her for a recommendation for a nice Italian restaurant, and she strongly encouraged him to dine at a place located fifteen miles away. Mickey didn't plan on picking up his rental car until morning, but he figured it could easily be changed, and he really craved a huge plate of pasta accompanied by a nice Chianti. He also figured getting out and about

43

a little bit would be better for him than staying around the hotel for the remainder of the day. But before doing anything about eating, he was going to check back with Jimmy.

When the elevator doors opened on the sixth floor, Mickey exited and quickly found his room. The door unlocked on his second try with the key, and he opened the drapes upon entering. He could see several planes in the distance, all in a line preparing to land.

Mickey sat in one of the available chairs and turned on his cell phone. The ensuing beep indicated he had some new voice mails, so he pushed the buttons necessary to access them. Fortunately, there were only four messages, which seemed to him to be more normal than yesterday's outrageously long list. The first one was almost an exact duplicate of one from his assistant yesterday, confirming Friday's tee time was indeed changed to shortly after noon. Mickey realized then he didn't do anything with the page of notes he made from yesterday's calls, so he searched for those in his small bag while he punched a key to skip to the next message.

The second message was also from his assistant, and it was a reminder the office would be vacant on Friday as the assistant was taking a personal day they agreed to a few weeks ago. Mickey did forget, so he was thankful for the reminder, and he figured the answering service could take messages from anyone who happened to call.

The third message was from one of Mickey's friends he was golfing with on this trip. The friend was confirming the change in the tee time while also inviting Mickey to join them for lunch at the course around eleven. Mickey didn't need to reply, but they hoped he could make it. The caller also hoped the flight was fine, and he left his number just in case something came up Mickey needed to call about. The message concluded with a comment about how he was looking forward to taking some of Mickey's hard-earned money during the next three days, and of course a hearty laugh.

Jimmy's familiar voice came through loud and clear once the fourth message began to play, and his tone was definitely more upbeat than the previous day. The urgency from yesterday subsided due to the closing now being delayed for a few weeks for other reasons unrelated to Mickey. There were still some things they needed to take care of, but it could wait until Mickey's return on Monday. Jimmy didn't want to bother Mickey with the details, and he also didn't want him worrying too much about business while on his golfing trip, so Jimmy only wished him luck instead of leaving a more detailed message.

After listening to the message a second time, Mickey breathed a sigh of relief, but he was uncomfortable something unexpected developed in the first place. He debated whether or not to call Jimmy, but he decided to just leave it until his return next week. He could call him on Sunday evening to arrange a meeting on Monday afternoon. His flight would return him to San Jose, which was convenient for meeting with Jimmy in either San Jose or Palo Alto. As he looked out the window, he saw the line of planes preparing to land still present.

Instead of taking the hotel's shuttle van back to the airport to the rental car agency, Mickey decided to walk, thinking the exercise would do him some good. He always found it much tougher to get physically adjusted to a two-hour time change or more when traveling from west to east versus going the opposite direction. It was one reason he planned a golfing trip to Hawaii each year. The trips to the east coast were much harder, and every time he went to Europe it seemed to take him until the end of the trip to get adjusted, only to then be required to make a significant adjustment on the return. He knew it was one cause for his poor play in Scotland during the first part of his most recent trip there, but a minor adjustment in his stance seemed to be the more important factor.

As Mickey walked he could hear and feel the bustle of people on the move, as there was a constant stream of cars in addition to the sounds of planes taking off and landing. The rental car agency was quite busy with business travelers, as most were carrying briefcases and no children were in sight. It was typical of a Thursday or any other weekday evening he thought.

Once Mickey successfully garnered a full-size car and a map of the area, he ventured into the traffic, which was moderately heavy compared to his last trip to Chicago. With only a few checks of the map sitting in the front seat, he negotiated his way to the restaurant. It looked reasonable enough from the outside, and he was not disappointed once he entered. He noticed a large number of waiters and other staff moving about quickly in their efforts to service the huge dinner crowd. Mickey checked at the hostess stand and was told it would take about twenty or twenty-five minutes to be seated, but he could enjoy a drink in the bar while he waited if he liked. He liked the suggestion very much, so he found his way and promptly ordered a martini.

As he stood and sipped his cocktail, Mickey began to wonder again about what could possibly have happened prompting the two phone calls from Jimmy. There was such a sense of urgency in the first message, yet Jimmy made it sound like no big deal during the second. Mickey wondered if he shouldn't just call Jimmy tonight once he returned to the hotel to satisfy his curiosity.

Mickey decided on the veal for dinner, and he couldn't be more satisfied with his choice. The sauce had a taste he found hard to place exactly, and the side order of spaghetti was large enough to feed him and his two children. This was just what he had in mind when he asked for a recommendation from the hotel staff. Choosing against any dessert after being tempted by his waiter's strong urging for the cheesecake, Mickey paid the bill and debated once again about whether or not to call Jimmy later.

Finding his way from the restaurant back to the hotel took only thirty-five minutes, and it wasn't enough time for him to find a suitable radio station. Mickey wondered if maybe the person who checked him in and recommended such a wonderful restaurant might still be working and could also suggest a station he might like. As he walked past the registration desk, he took a look but didn't see her, so he continued on his way. Instead of the elevator he decided to walk up the five flights of stairs to provide a last bit of exercise for the day. He hoped his body would feel good enough tomorrow to play a solid round of golf and start this trip on a winning note.

Continuing to contemplate whether or not he should call Jimmy, Mickey decided to sit and read more of the novel he started earlier in the day. After reading a few more chapters, Mickey put the book down and reached for his phone. After dialing the area code, he stopped and decided to let it go. Jimmy said it could wait, and Mickey trusted his advice, so Mickey vowed to try and put it out of his mind until the end of the weekend. He turned on the television in hopes of finding an old movie to put him to sleep. Settling on something short of his original hope, he turned the volume down low and was asleep within minutes.

The phone rang with a wakeup call at seven as Mickey requested. The TV was still on, but now an infomercial advertising yet another home fitness apparatus was being aired. He wondered how many fools actually purchased those things, and he guessed there were enough to keep paying for the ads. After showering he realized he was still full from the previous night's meal, so he figured he should skip breakfast and meet his friends for lunch at eleven as they suggested. In the meantime, he decided to make his way to the golf course and spend some time on the driving range and practice green.

Mickey walked out of the hotel shortly after eight. He could tell it was going to be another hot and humid day in the Chicago area, as it already felt hotter at this early hour than it was in the middle of the afternoon just yesterday. Blue shorts and a white shirt were his choice for the day, hoping he could stay somewhat cool in the Midwestern summer heat. He was careful to pack extra golf gloves as he knew he would sweat much more here than what he was used to.

The thirty-mile drive to Cog Hill in the town of Lemont took almost an hour as Mickey was slowed somewhat by the morning commute, and he wondered if the Friday morning version was lighter or heavier than the other days. Once at the course he walked into the golf shop to register and see what shirts and hats were for sale. He found a visor with the course logo which also matched his shorts, and he figured it would work better than the hat he packed, so he bought it and headed to the practice range.

His body was indeed a little stiff at first, probably due to the inactivity during yesterday's flight, but once he loosened up Mickey felt good. His swing had a good rhythm, and he was striking the ball solidly. At the practice green his putting stroke also felt encouraging, so Mickey was beginning to get more excited about the upcoming round. Once he saw it was almost eleven, he made the short walk to the restaurant and confidently entered.

His three friends were already talking and laughing loudly. When they saw him they all shouted to him and welcomed him with warm smiles and handshakes. There was talk of the three of them coming to visit Mickey some time the following summer so they could play on his turf as they called it. As the lunch was finishing the more serious business of agreeing to the betting for the upcoming three days started. They decided to rotate partners on a daily basis so everyone would team with each of the others by the end of the weekend. There were bets for individual scores each day and for the total score for the three days. Skins were set at $100, and there were numerous other side bets. Mickey knew additional bets would be made on subsequent days, and his anticipation was building since he knew his game was improved significantly since the last time he played with this particular group.

Cog Hill has four different courses, and the first day's play was on the famous course #4, nicknamed Dubsdread. With the PGA tour's Western Open being played starting the following Thursday on this course, Mickey knew the course would be set up to be its most difficult. They would play the following two days on two of the other courses, and the scoring was definitely expected to get easier as the weekend progressed.

Mickey's good ball striking from the morning's practice continued through the first nine holes of the round. He won three holes worth five skins from the carry-overs, and his team was ahead on multiple bets. Mickey played even par for the front nine, and it provided him with a two-shot advantage over his closest competitor. The back nine was going smoothly with only a few hiccups. As the group approached the eighteenth hole, it was clear he would be a big winner if he could avoid a disaster.

Mickey's drive was in the fairway, but he hooked his approach into the pond guarding the front left of the green. A bogey resulted, causing him to either tie or lose several of the presses which were made late in the round. His total of three-over seventy-five was the day's best round by three shots, and he still was the biggest winner for the day, pocketing a little over a thousand dollars. He knew his winnings could've been substantially more if only he had stayed out of the pond on the last hole.

Family commitments prohibited Mickey's friends from entertaining him for dinner, but he didn't mind since his wallet was much thicker from money which began the day in their pockets. He assured them he would be fine on his own, and he would most likely enjoy a wonderful steak at a fancy restaurant. He knew Morton's was not far from the airport and his hotel, and he hoped either a reservation wasn't necessary or he could make one during the drive.

As Mickey left the golf course, he turned on his phone to dial information. He was greeted by a beep indicating there were new messages, and it reminded him of the messages he received the previous two nights from Jimmy. He disregarded them for the time being and dialed information, and upon receiving the phone number for the restaurant, he jotted it down on a corner of the map. When he called about a reservation he was told he could indeed be seated, and they would be glad to have him dining with them this evening. He confirmed the address and directions and then hung up.

Feeling good about the prospect of a wonderful steak, Mickey decided to check his messages while he continued his drive. There was nothing from Jimmy, and nothing of particular importance was contained in the other messages waiting for him, so he continued on his drive still feeling the high of having played a fulfilling round of golf on a very difficult course. Having won some serious cash was the icing on the cake.

The dinner was a real treat for Mickey. Ordering the prime rib medium rare, he declined a cabernet and opted for a blend from a California winery he visited on several occasions. The prime rib was cooked to perfection, and the creamed horseradish provided just the right amount of spice. A piece of cobbler topped with ice cream capped the incredible meal. He gladly paid the check and left a healthy tip from the day's winnings. A feeling of contentment dominated him for the remainder of the evening as he anticipated the rest of this trip.

The second day of golfing was quite different from the first. Mickey didn't feel comfortable on the driving range, and he couldn't quite figure out why. He expected the first day to be the toughest due to the long flight and the time adjustment, but after only a few holes into this second round he realized he was mistaken. He struggled to hit his driver into the fairway, and he had difficulty with the speed of the greens. He knew the old saying was "drive for show and putt for dough," but he couldn't do either today.

The result was a fat eighty on a much easier course than the one he carded a seventy-five on just yesterday. Two of his friends played much better on this second day, while the other one continued to fight with erratic iron play. Unfortunately, this last friend was Mickey's partner for the day, and the two of them lost every team bet. Mickey managed to win two holes for three skins, so he wasn't the day's biggest loser, but he lost almost as much as he won the day before, and now he was behind in the big bet for the lowest total score for the three days.

Mickey left the course dejected, mainly due to the fact he wasn't able to fix his swing during the round, although he certainly tried a lot of minor adjustments from shot to shot. He hoped the third day would be better, and he also knew his partner for the last day was the best of the three other golfers. Knowing an outstanding day of golf could come close to paying for his trip's expenses, he decided to have a light dinner and get some rest so he could spend some time on the driving range prior to the last round. He found his way to a restaurant where he dined on a previous occasion, and the sauce topping the halibut lifted his spirits. A little bit of reading and some plane-watching from his hotel window were the only activities for the rest of the night.

Feeling refreshed when he awakened for this final day of golf on this trip didn't help. The day turned out to be the worst of the three for Mickey. He worked out a few kinks during his practice session, and most of his tee shots were better than what he managed on the second day. The problem was he hit three very wayward shots which were either out of bounds or couldn't be found, accounting for six penalty strokes in total. His iron play was better than average, but his putting didn't provide adequate help as he was unable to see some of the subtle breaks on many occasions. The result was an eighty-two, his worst round since one of his early rounds on his recent trip to Scotland. To make matters worse, his partner for the day played below his standard, too. Their team lost numerous bets, and Mickey finished the day with only a single skin. His losses totaled just over two thousand dollars when everything was settled. What a disaster, he thought, particularly after having started so well. With the golfing completed he looked forward to getting back to California and meeting with Jimmy.

SIX

Mickey's flight from Chicago to San Jose departed shortly after eight o'clock on Monday morning and touched down on schedule about fifteen minutes before eleven. He didn't enjoy the flight due to his disappointment with his poor play during the past two days. He was also discouraged with the ending of the novel he finished reading somewhere over the state of Nevada.

He tried to call Jimmy on Sunday evening from his hotel room, but Mickey was only able to leave a voice mail message. He missed Jimmy's return call since he turned his cell phone off and went to sleep. Jimmy left a message for him which he retrieved prior to boarding his flight. Jimmy said lunch sounded like a great idea and he'd meet him at the airport. There was no trace of worry in Jimmy's voice, so Mickey decided not to worry about last week's business concern during the flight. He knew worrying wouldn't help the situation anyway since he didn't have the details.

As Mickey walked into the gate area, he couldn't help but begin to smile as he saw his good friend bearing the contagious smile he knew since their first meeting in college long ago. "Mick! How ya' doin'? How was the trip?" greeted an exuberant Jimmy.

"Hey, Jimmy. How are you? You certainly gave me a scare last week."

"Tell me about your golfing outing first, and we can cover all that once we get in the car. How did you handle the famous Dubsdread course at Cog Hill? I know you were really excited about playing there, and your game has been better since your trip to Scotland."

"Well," Mickey started as he thought back to the excitement he owned less than a week ago. "The day we played Dubsdread was the first day. It was a wonderful day, from the start on the practice tee to the mighty steak I ate in the evening. If only every golfing day could be so enjoyable. The fun ended there though, as the other two days were horrible. It's a good thing summertime is the height of the house-buying season, as this trip set me back a few thousand or so."

"Is that all?" Jimmy mused. He knew Mickey was notorious for not only spending extravagantly on these trips for hotels, green fees, and dining, but he also wagered heavily and didn't win as much as he lost. Seeing Mickey was not amused by his comment, Jimmy reassured him. "Don't worry, Mick. We'll get it back. We always do."

The two silently continued their walk to the baggage area to claim Mickey's belongings. Mickey was anxious to get the full story, but he knew it should wait until they were alone in Jimmy's car. The airport was fairly busy for a Monday morning, as several families with animated children were waiting at many gates and in the line at the counter for baggage checkin. It reminded Mickey of some of the vacations he and his wife took with their children years ago, although they almost always drove somewhere instead of flying.

As they walked Jimmy was reminded of his upcoming vacation, and he shivered at the thought of how much money it would cost him. Rays from the sun filtered through the many windows they passed, indicating another cloudless day was upon them.

Mickey's bags were delivered along with those of his flying companions, and Jimmy hoisted the golf bag onto his shoulder for the walk to the car. "You're pretty good with the bag, Jimmy," Mickey commented. "Why don't you become a caddy when you retire? You could caddy for me."

"That's not my idea of retirement, Mick."

"Well, as my caddy, you'd be my best friend, along with some bartender and a chef of course." Mickey began laughing at his joke.

"Yeah, right," Jimmy replied as he joined in the laughter.

Jimmy was driving his Cadillac today so there would be plenty of room for Mickey's bags. "I thought we would drive to Pleasanton for lunch," Jimmy said as he closed the lid to the trunk. "I want to check out a few properties, and the drive is about forty minutes or so at this time of day, which will give us time to chat."

"Sounds good, Jimmy. I can't say I've ever eaten anywhere in Pleasanton. Come to think of it, I'm not sure I've ever been there other than just passing through on the freeway. I'm sure you know a good deli."

"Actually, there's an Italian restaurant downtown I hear has wonderful fish and pasta dishes. I thought we could give it a try."

Once he exited the parking garage and paid the fee, Jimmy smiled as he began to tell Mickey the story from the previous week. "Mick. You know we've been at this game of ours for several years now. I don't know about you, but I still get a real rush from this whole business. From all aspects of it. From the big-dollar ones to the small-dollar ones. But I have never experienced a rush quite like last week, and we're probably not going to profit anything on this. And even though we may not make anything, it still made my heart pound."

"Which deal was it."

"It's the Rogers' house. He's the sales guy living in Mountain View. He's relocating to the east coast to work as a sales manager for the tech company his sales firm here in the Bay Area represents."

"Yeah, I know it," replies Mickey. "It's supposed to close this week. I remember the buyer is a couple named Smith. What happened with it."

"Well, our problem is it turns out Mrs. Smith works at the same tech company Mr. Rogers is joining, which of course Mr. Rogers has worked with for several years in his role as a sales representative."

"How did that happen? I thought we checked it carefully."

"Well we didn't, or we got bad information. You know Mr. and Mrs. Rogers are my clients, so I knew their situation. Mrs. Rogers doesn't work, so no problems from her. Mr. Rogers' employment is with Bay Tech Sales, which is only about a dozen people, and the major company they represent is this big semiconductor company he is joining as a full-time employee, to be a sales manager in Boston.

"When the offer comes in from the Smiths, we check out both of them. The problem is we paid a little more attention to Mr. Smith than to Mrs. Smith, plus we got bad data on her. Mr. Smith is not a problem as he works at a different company in a totally unrelated field. When we checked out Mrs. Smith, she also worked at some other company, or so it seemed. But, it turns out she recently changed jobs. When we checked her, she'd already made the change, but somehow we got the wrong answer. My expectation is she'd been at her previous company for so long she just said the old company name instead of the new company name. Probably just some ditzy blond

53

who can't remember where to go to work each day anyway, let alone do her job."

Jimmy paused for a moment with an exasperated look on his face as he pondered once again how this came about. Mickey's mind was working while he was taking all of this in. He knew they always avoided working a special deal when the buyer and seller were well acquainted with each other, which didn't happen very often for them or in any other sale of residential property in an area with as many millions as were in the Bay Area.

Mickey interjected, "But the company is quite large, Mrs. Smith just joined, Mr. Rogers is going to the east coast, and most people don't compare notes on financial deals anyway. So what's the problem?"

"Oh, there's more. Just listen for a while." Jimmy had the excitement back in his voice as he continued the story. "So Mrs. Smith is recently employed by the company Mr. Rogers is also joining after having sold their products for years anyway while with the rep firm. The company has a party for all of its employees and their significant others. Some kind of annual or quarterly event where they rent out a movie theater and eat pizza and drink beer or whatever. You get the idea. The event was last Tuesday.

"Well, Mrs. Smith is in a marketing role, which of course interfaces directly with the company's sales force. She doesn't know which territory she'll be covering since she has only been there one or two months. She's been on a training program and hasn't yet landed in her permanent assignment. However, her training mentor takes it upon himself to introduce her and her husband to as many sales people as he can while everyone is eating before the movie starts. And of course, one couple she and her husband meet is the new sales manager and his wife, soon to be located in Boston, Mr. and Mrs. Rogers."

"Amazing," Mickey offers. He almost wanted to ask what movie was showing, knowing Jimmy would pride himself on knowing that detail, too, but he resisted. Imagining the size of the company and the party, he stated, "But they probably got introduced to maybe a hundred people that night. And as I said before, most people don't compare notes on financial deals. Why do we think this is different?"

"Hang on. It gets better. So Mrs. Smith and her husband get introduced to all of these people, including Mr. and Mrs. Rogers. As you said, they do get introduced to so many people they can't keep all of them straight, or most of them anyway. They hadn't met Mr. Rogers before, but when they were introduced to Mrs. Rogers, they recognized each other. It turns out the three of them attended some charity event for cheetahs, leopards, pumas, and all other kinds of cats just the previous weekend. They didn't make a connection at the cheetah thing because Mr. Rogers was not with his wife, and they only met briefly. They didn't talk about jobs or houses, only briefly about the cats. So at the company party, it's like some massive reunion between the two women when they realize they met briefly just a few days prior.

"So with this cheetah thing in common, they get to talking more. The Rogers mention they are moving to Boston along with some details of their move, including they'll be renting for a while until they can find a home they like. The Smiths then mention they are buying their first home, some place in Mountain View. One thing leads to another, and they find out the Smiths are buying the Rogers' house."

"Unbelievable. Just unbelievable," said Mickey as he shook his head from side to side in disbelief. "So how did you uncover all of this?" was Mickey's first question. He followed with, "And what is our exposure? And what do we need to do to correct it?" His anxiety was growing.

"Well, on Wednesday morning I get a call from the realtor working for the Smiths. She wants a copy of the preliminary closing statement delivered to her on Friday for her review. Nothing out of the ordinary. I knew I could get it from your assistant while you were away.

"But later in the day I get a call from Mrs. Rogers. She just wants to let me know about this amazing thing she learned within the last twenty-four hours. She gives me the whole story about the company party and the cheetah charity event. She goes on and on about how wonderful it is that someone who just started working at her husband's company is buying their house, and they all love animals. Her enthusiasm was quite remarkable. She was truly excited.

"Then she somewhat teases me by saying I should reduce my commission on the house sale since friends of theirs are buying the property. I think she was serious but trying to be nonchalant just to see what I would do. She even went so far as to suggest I call the other agent and advocate the same thing from her. I of course almost fall out of my chair at the suggestion since I know it's our intention of not only sticking them with a lot of our normal extra fees, but cheating them by a large amount on the taxes, too.

"That's when I decided we should talk and put this deal on the up-and-up. I didn't really want to bother you while you were enjoying your golf at Pebble and the nice dinner I know you planned afterward, but I knew we needed to talk. So I called your cell phone sometime Wednesday evening. When you didn't have it on, I left my voice mail saying something came up. Little did you know it was this whole mess."

Mickey interrupted, "But then your message on Thursday said everything was fine, or it could wait until I got back. What happened to change everything?"

"Oh, this is beautiful. Just listen. I'm sitting there in my office worrying what to do. I'm looking at one of the maps in my office and the phone rings. It's the Smith's realtor again. At first I think she is going to kindly remind me again she wants the preliminary settlement statement, but instead she says for me not to bother, as things are going to be delayed due to a problem with the financing. Turns out Mr. and Mrs. Smith were struggling with getting the down payment. He was expecting a bonus at work, and it got delayed, was smaller than he anticipated, or just got canceled. Without the bonus they were about six grand short of what they needed. So they decided to borrow the money from their credit cards by getting a cash advance. The mortgage company found out and balked. The expectation now is we'll get closed in a few weeks once the Smiths collect a few more paychecks or the remainder of the bonus. In the meantime we can clean up the paperwork and go on about our lives."

Jimmy exited from the highway and made his way through the downtown of Pleasanton where he found a parking spot just off the main street. The two walked quietly the two blocks to the restaurant and enjoyed the shade provided by the buildings on this sunny day. The temperature was about eighty-five on its way to ninety, and the walk was quite comfortable, particularly since they both knew they may have just narrowly escaped.

Jimmy and Mickey enjoyed their lunches as Jimmy chose the fish of the day while Mickey opted for the pasta special which was lobster and linguini covered in a spicy cream sauce. Jimmy commented several times how much he liked fish grilled over a mesquite fire more than broiled, and the delicious meal helped keep the conversation light and away from their business. They both knew the ride after lunch would provide additional opportunity for them to discuss their work.

Jimmy picked up the tab for lunch knowing Mickey was still feeling the sting of spending and losing so much money on the recent golf trip. Jimmy lost count long ago of how many times he consoled Mickey in this fashion, but he knew Mickey was an invaluable partner in completing the schemes.

Jimmy was proud he did most of the initial thinking and conniving, but he recognized Mickey was the one who handled a large part of the execution. In addition to being a lawyer, Mickey set up his own title company and was an escrow agent for handling the closings of real estate transactions in the state of California. Jimmy was the first to convince Mickey to expand his law firm into that capacity, which seemed like a reasonable thing to Mickey. The thing really exciting Mickey was Jimmy's suggestion to try and hide the income from his ex-wife and her lawyers through a simple maze of multiple companies.

Once Mickey completed his first closing as an escrow agent through his own title company, it didn't take Jimmy long to think of other means for the two of them to profit from the situation of a realtor working with an escrow agent who was a trusted fraternity brother. The first few schemes were simple experiments to see what was possible with different clients and others involved in a residential real estate transaction.

In one case a neighborhood utility origination fee, payable to a company Mickey created and owned, was added to the buyer's closing statement. Jimmy was the buyer's realtor, and a simple, five-second explanation amongst the signing of more than thirty documents was sufficient. The seller and seller's realtor were completely unaware since their closing statement was different from the buyer's and contained no mention of this concocted neighborhood fee.

In a second case a parks and recreation fee was paid by the buyer. This one was payable to another company created by Mickey, and the company's name made the buyer feel like it was a normal charge to some part of the city government. A third deal included a fee payable to an arts association, and Jimmy remembered the buyer didn't even blink when all of the papers were reviewed and signed.

The next set of schemes Jimmy and Mickey used were merely extensions of the first set, but were utilized when Jimmy was the realtor for both the buyer and the seller. In these cases, having both parties pay for notary fees, attorney fees, the appraisal, the survey, or even overnight shipping fees were successfully completed.

Once comfortable with the basic process of cheating the buyer, the seller, or both—whichever party or parties Jimmy represented—and hiding it from the other party by generating different closing statements, Jimmy enlisted the help of Billy, beyond the trickery of roof-related items. The idea came to Jimmy one day while eating a pastrami on rye in his office and gazing at his maps. Jimmy was exacerbated with a home inspector with whom he experienced previous difficulties. Jimmy's frustration was he thought a home inspection was not a difficult thing, should be done at the time scheduled, and should be completed in an hour. Further, he thought the report should be submitted within one day of the actual inspection, and this particular home inspector was under-performing in all these areas. Jimmy knew things would be more efficient if the home inspectors were just a little more computer literate.

The idea which hit Jimmy was to ask Billy to do the home inspections. Billy was certainly capable enough, and having another trusted fraternity brother involved in an additional part of his real estate transactions gave Jimmy extra opportunities to extract money from unsuspecting homeowners for his, Billy's, and Mickey's gain.

The basic scheme used was for Billy to identify in his report to the seller one or two things which didn't work properly when in reality those things were working fine. In most cases the work was scheduled in a short period of time between the exit of the seller and the entry of the buyer. The company completing the work was one of Mickey's creations, and while no actual work was performed, payment for services was included in the closing and was billed accordingly. In a few cases Billy would return in a different company van bearing a generic home repair name to seemingly complete the stated repair work prior to the closing. The name was yet another company crafted by Mickey.

The most lucrative yet most dangerous maneuver Jimmy and Mickey attempted was a relatively new one, as they successfully executed it in only three previous closings, all within the past five months. It was an honest mistake on Mickey's part almost one year ago which opened their eyes to the possibility, and Jimmy wasted no time in following the new avenue with some on-line research in his office to further develop the strategy. It was fairly simple in its final form, but the two debated the implementation for several months before striking.

The error Mickey made the previous July was prorating the taxes incorrectly on the closing statement. The seller previously paid their property taxes through the end of the year, and was due the appropriate refund as part of the closing. This amount would show as a credit to the seller, in effect adding money to the selling price. The buyer was required to pay the same amount being refunded to the seller. Mickey's miscalculation was he simply got confused about the number of months remaining in the year, as he figured the taxes as if it was September instead of July. This was indeed rare for Mickey since he was usually well aware of the calendar due to his constant planning and scheduling of his golf outings.

The error was identified prior to closing when the realtor representing the seller reviewed the statement. Fortunately for Mickey the statements for the seller and the buyer matched on the tax calculation, so an apology for an incorrect calculation quickly followed by a corrected version allowed the closing to proceed without further problems or inquiries.

The very next day Jimmy spent his afternoon in his office searching how taxes are prorated in other states and counties. He also kept in mind the amount of prepaid taxes to be refunded to the seller through a payment by the buyer was something which could be negotiated just like any other item related to a real estate transaction. Instead of implementing an extravagant scheme, Jimmy and Mickey decided to simply show a smaller credit to the seller on their statement than the buyer was paying according to their statement. When Jimmy represented the seller, the buyer's statement was legitimate while the seller was the one cheated. When he represented the buyer, things were reversed so the buyer was deceived.

When developing this scheme Jimmy and Mickey acknowledged more dollars could be made for transactions completed earlier in the year as opposed to later. That was because more of the full year's tax liability was the starting point. Their agreement in light of this was to avoid this deception during the last four months of a year, so the planned attempt of cheating the Rogers on their taxes was going to be one of the last until after the new year.

"Why are you checking out properties here in Pleasanton, Jimmy?" questioned Mickey as the two opened their respective car doors following their short walk from the restaurant.

"Well the real estate business has changed during the last year," Jimmy started. "Used to be we only worried about a relatively small area since different areas utilized different means for the agents to access a property. In the case of a national real estate firm, an agent from one office in a town in the Bay Area would refer a client to an agent in another office in the other town if the client was uncertain of where exactly they wanted to buy a home. As an example, someone relocating to work in San Jose might explore living up the peninsula somewhere between San Jose and San Francisco, while also looking at houses south toward Gilroy or even Monterey, while even considering here in Pleasanton. In the past, they would work with three or more different agents, although it may still be with the same company, like Coldwell Banker or some other similar company.

"Now an agent such as yours truly can represent a client in all of those areas. The two things making it possible are the common access boxes and the internet. It is absolutely amazing how much information can be found in the confines of a small office equipped with a computer and a phone line, in the real estate business or any other."

"But isn't it almost impossible to adequately cover the entire Bay Area as opposed to what you used to cover?"

"Depends on the person and the client, Mick. In just the past two weeks, an agent from Concord, one from Walnut Creek, and one from Dublin all showed a property in Palo Alto I have the listing on. I also know of an agent in Burlingame who routinely shows clients houses here in the East Bay, mainly Pleasanton. I thought I'd drive by a few of the places here just to see what first impressions I get."

"But do any of these remote agents ever find a house for their client?"

"I've heard of it happening, but it is rare. As you can imagine, it is quite inefficient having to drive between some locations in this part of the world. Plus, no agent can really know the details of different neighborhoods in an area where they only have limited exposure. I just thought it wise to keep my eyes open for new opportunities, just like you are always on the lookout for new golf courses to play."

Mickey laughed at Jimmy's last comment. He momentarily forgot about his lost weekend in Chicago, but he was always cheered up by just being in Jimmy's company. Mickey felt fortunate to have a friend he'd known and trusted for so many years. "Thanks for the lunch, Jimmy," Mickey said as Jimmy navigated through a neighborhood.

"You're welcome, Mick."

SEVEN

"And now, the starting lineup for your San Francisco Giants!" Jimmy heard the female announcer's voice over the public address system as he hurried to find his way to the skybox for the evening's baseball game. He still wasn't used to the idea of a female doing the job which used to be universally and was still predominantly performed by men. He resigned to himself it would be this way in San Francisco forever, or certainly for a long time to come, since the Giants were the first major league team to employ a woman in this capacity, and the first woman was replaced with the present one at the beginning of this season.

Even though the female announcer's voice was somewhat foreign to him, the sounds and smells were familiar. He heard the recognizable buzz of the large number of fans already gathered. He could also smell hot dogs, nachos, and other food. Even though the game was yet to start, the concrete below his feet was littered with cups, food wrappers, and spills of beer.

As he walked along the corridor at Pacific Bell Park among several other fans, Jimmy counted the suite numbers he passed while checking each to the one on his ticket. He felt the cold wind, a staple of Candlestick Park and still present throughout most of this new ball park. Even though the team management and stadium planners promised things would be different at the new location, he was skeptical. He knew this was still San Francisco, and it gets cold in the evenings even during the middle of summer. Tonight was the first day of August, and if there wasn't a baseball game being played, he would not know it was summer.

As he neared the number of the suite matching his ticket, Jimmy noticed the door was propped open. He didn't hear any voices which surprised him, as he expected to be one of the later arrivals since the first pitch was only the singing of the national anthem away. As he entered he saw only one well-dressed man, who was leaning over to gain access to the refrigerator under the counter.

"Charlie!" he greeted the man with a shout. "How ya' doin'?"

Charlie Bates was so startled by the sudden sound he bumped his head on the underside of the edge of the counter covering the small refrigerator. As he turned to see his invader, a huge smile came across his face.

"J.D.! How are you?" Charlie responded. "Thanks for coming. Let me get you a beer. You still prefer a Budweiser, or have you come to like something with an international flavor?"

"A Bud will be fine, Charlie. I learned to drink the simple domestic beers while growing up in the South, and I've never strayed. I'll leave all of those fancy imports for you."

"Oh, you don't know what your missing, Jimmy. You know what the Germans say about Budweiser."

"Yeah, yeah, Charlie," Jimmy interrupted. "I know. I know. Please spare me the criticism."

"Here you go," said Charlie as he handed Jimmy his beer. "Hey, have you eaten, or should we order a few hot dogs?"

"That would be good. I haven't eaten since lunch, and this body will need some food to go with the beer."

"Okay. Let me call the suite service now. They sometimes are a little slow right at the start of the game so I'd better get the order in. There are some peanuts in the cabinet on the end which will have to suffice in the meantime." Charlie pointed behind Jimmy as he grabbed the phone on the wall and dialed the food and beverage service number.

Jimmy found the peanuts and made his way to the front row of seats. The window between them and the remainder of the crowd and the playing field was partially open, and a small breeze was blowing through the suite from the open door in the back through this window in the front. The breeze didn't feel nearly as cold as the wind during his walk from outside the ballpark, but he knew it would get colder as the night wore on. He was glad they could simply shut the back door to stop the breeze, and if it got significantly colder, the front window could also be closed.

The public address announcer was introducing a male trio, assembled on the field behind home plate and ready to perform the anthem, so Jimmy put his beer on the table between two of the seats and stood ready to place his hand over his heart. He could hear Charlie in the back finishing with their order, and he was reminded once again of the good manners Charlie displayed in dealing with people. Jimmy knew those served him well in his banker profession.

Similar to Jimmy's passion for real estate, Charlie was always interested in the banking industry. Charlie's version was he started his banking career at the age of twelve when he convinced the owner of a local bank in his hometown of Little Rock, Arkansas to let him wash the windows of the bank for free. Charlie would take extra care not only to make sure the job was perfect, but to use the extra time while cleaning to gaze at all the activity taking place inside and outside the bank. He was just fascinated at all the money being handed back and forth between the patrons and the tellers.

The owner of the bank took a strong liking to young Charlie, and instead of paying him a salary, different tours of all parts of the bank were his reward. Charlie particularly enjoyed the times he was escorted to the safety deposit boxes and the vault. He knew this contributed to his outgrowing of board games with play money by the age of fourteen.

As Charlie progressed through high school the bank owner allowed him to do more than provide custodial service. By the middle of his sophomore year he did all of the courier work available after school. That summer he worked full-time doing all jobs not requiring him to handle money. The best part was now he was getting paid for the work he was doing.

When Charlie graduated from high school in Little Rock, his biggest decision was not his major, but the college to attend. He knew banking and finance was the path for him, and he settled on Memphis State University since it was only a short drive from Little Rock. The choice easily allowed him to help at the bank during his breaks between school terms and work full-time in the summer.

The one activity Charlie allowed himself besides his focus on his college classes and his work at the bank was his fraternity. The bank owner strongly encouraged Charlie to join a fraternity so he would have the opportunity to meet people other than just the patrons of the bank in Little Rock. The owner knew Charlie would enjoy the camaraderie of being in a fraternity, while he also knew studying and working needed to be complemented with a sufficient amount of rowdiness and outright fun.

Charlie pledged Sigma Chi and never regretted it. He wasn't as active as many of his fraternity brothers, certainly not like the crazy Jimmy Donovan who was one year his senior, but his genuine kindness made him one of the most well-liked members. Charlie was also a favorite of all of the mothers of his fraternity brothers since his manners were far superior to any of their boys' behavior.

The summer preceding his senior year at Memphis State was a difficult one for Charlie as he contemplated his future. It was his dream for many years to work permanently for the bank in Little Rock so one day he could be the owner, but the bank owner threatened to fire him if Charlie didn't consider his contrary advice. Charlie listened on several occasions to the owner's argument, saying he could more easily achieve greater things in his banking career by starting in a large bank in a big metropolitan area. The compelling part of the argument was it would be fine if he wanted to run a small bank in a southern town later in his career, but Charlie would be better prepared by working for a long time in a large bank in a variety of roles.

Charlie's parents also agreed with the banker regarding their son's career. His dad was predominantly in favor of Charlie taking his first job far from home to give him a chance to see more of the country. With so much pressure to not disappoint those he trusted most, he decided prior to his senior year of college to search for banking jobs in New York, Chicago, and San Francisco.

Charlie would probably have taken a job in New York as opposed to San Francisco if it wasn't so cold and windy during his interview trip in early December. Not being accustomed to such cold weather pushed him to the more pleasant climate of California. He knew New York was the financial capital of the country and the world, but he just couldn't bear the thought of enduring the winter's cold every year there.

His choice of San Francisco worked well. As he was promised by the bank owner in Little Rock, there was more opportunity for him to perform and learn in a large bank. Charlie's abilities and dedication allowed him to move quickly through ever-increasing positions of responsibility and income. After slightly more than fifteen years with the bank, he was promoted to vice president. Having worked in that capacity for over five years, he now felt he was in position to become the president when the current one retired in two or three years.

"So can the Giants finally win a game tonight?" Charlie asked as he took a seat in a chair on the other side of the small table from Jimmy. "What have they lost now; four or five in a row?"

"Four in a row, and six of their last seven," Jimmy replied. "The last game they won was in San Diego when the guy pitching tonight pitched a four-hit shutout. Other than that win, they either haven't pitched well, haven't hit well, haven't played good defense, or just haven't been very lucky on this recent stretch. But being back at home now after nine games on the road should be a big boost for them."

"They've won almost every time I've been here to watch them this year."

"Yeah. They presently have the best record at home of any team in the National League, and only two teams in the American League have better home records. I'm convinced a good team on the west coast can be a great team at home due to the time difference."

"Why is that?" Charlie hesitantly asked, not knowing what Jimmy's latest sports hypothesis might be.

"My theory is with games starting at seven o'clock or seven thirty in the evening, the bodies of the players on the visiting team from the east coast or the Midwest think it is nine or ten just when the game is starting. By the seventh inning stretch, it's close to or past midnight, and they're ready for bed. In a tight game, the west coast team can make the one extra play which wins the game."

"Hmmm," Charlie contemplated what he just heard as he watched Jimmy take another swig of his beer. "But J.D., I've found I have much more trouble with my body clock when I travel to the east coast than others who travel from the east coast to meet with me here in the Pacific time zone. How do you explain that?"

"Well, the difference is your business day is typically from eight in the morning until five in the evening. There's time required before eight to get up, get ready, eat something, and drive to work. And of course there is time required after five to drive home, take care of some things at home, eat, and so on. However, there are usually a few extra hours in your day at the end of the day as opposed to the beginning. Do you agree with everything so far."

"Sounds about right, but I'm not sure where you're going with all of this and how it relates to baseball on the west coast."

"Well when you travel to the east coast for business, you have to shift your work day by three hours, and those three hours must be earlier than your normal day, not later." Jimmy emphasized the word earlier, so he paused for a moment to let it sink in. Seeing Charlie not totally confused, he decided to continue. "So we previously agreed, in your normal time zone, your extra time is at the end of the day. But when going to the east coast you have to shift your clock forward where you don't have any extra time. That creates the problem for your body when you travel to the east coast for your business."

Jimmy was watching Charlie absorb all of this. Jimmy could tell he was becoming somewhat fascinated since Charlie was the one who did so much more traveling than Jimmy, yet Jimmy was the one who contemplated this part of life's idiosyncrasies.

"Now for your counterparts on the east coast coming to the west coast, it's just the opposite," Jimmy continued. "They are required to shift their work day three hours later, but it's easily done since the end of the day is where the extra time is. So they simply get up around their normal time, which is real early here on the west coast, do some extra work or whatever with the extra time which is now at the start of their day, do their business, and then don't have any extra time at the end of their day." Jimmy smiled broadly as he finished this explanation.

Charlie smiled as well and waited for it to fade before asking his next question. "That sounds interesting, but it only explains why I have more trouble on business trips to the east coast than my colleagues on the east coast have when they come here. How does that relate to your theory of the west coast baseball teams having such a huge advantage at home?"

"Well for baseball, the work day is skewed toward the end of the day, except for the Cubs who play most of their home games during the day. Similar to your work day being skewed toward the beginning so your extra time is at the end, a baseball player's work day provides him with extra time at the beginning. Therefore, a baseball player from the west coast can adjust to games on the east coast more easily than the reverse." Jimmy smiled broadly again and added, "Don't you agree?"

"You're incredible, J.D. When do you find the time to ponder these kinds of things?" Charlie replied as they were interrupted by the banging of a cart into the back door of the suite.

The two turned to see a young lady trying to push a food and beverage cart through the partially open door. She was unsuccessful as the door opening was not as wide as needed, and she obviously misjudged it. Her hat displayed the vendor's company name, but it was slanted significantly on her head and needed to be adjusted. Her hair was exposed and a little unkept, although it was probably neatly tucked under her hat when she started her shift. "Sorry," she stated when she saw she gained their attention. "Here's your food order," she continued as Charlie hustled from his seat to lend her a hand.

"Here, let me help you, ma'am," Charlie offered. His smile and soft tone eased her, allowing her to also display a pretty smile.

"Thanks for your help, sir."

"My pleasure. Is it a busy night?"

"Very much." She unloaded the order for them as Charlie helped arrange the food on the counter.

"Any particular reason why?" Charlie continued the conversation.

"It's always busy on the first day of a series, particularly at the start of a new homestand. And for some reason we always have less people working. I guess some people just can't remember when it's time to come back to work. Either that or the scheduling isn't done right. I don't know. I just know it's real busy tonight.

"I think that's everything. You can check it here against the order." She handed the ticket in Charlie's direction for his approval.

"I'm sure you've got it right. Please charge it to the account. And here's a tip for you," Charlie said as he reached into his pocket and handed her five dollars.

"Thank you, sir." Her eyes widened as she looked at the money he placed in her hand. "Enjoy the game," she seemed to shout as she wheeled the cart around and easily managed to exit without bumping into the door.

"You're amazing, Charlie," Jimmy commented as he walked toward Charlie. "You really made her day."

"Thanks. That was easy though. A smile, a kind word, a little assistance, and a few dollars aren't much, and that's all it took for her. I wish it was so easy with everyone. Grab a bun and let's eat these hot dogs while they're warm."

The two prepared their dogs to their liking, grabbed two more beers, and returned to their seats to focus on the game. "Are others from your bank joining us tonight, or do we have the suite all to ourselves?" Jimmy questioned.

"It's just the two of us. A few of the others who normally would've been interested are busy with the upcoming banking seminar we present every August. There's always a handful of games where the bank doesn't get good use of this for one reason or another."

"Seems like somewhat of a waste," Jimmy wondered out loud.

"We figure it is better to waste a few days as opposed to the alternative of not being able to accommodate some of our employees and clients on certain occasions. With over eighty home games each year outside of the possibility of the playoffs, using this more than seventy times is a much better return than we get from any of our other promotions."

"Well you can count me in for those handful of games if you're looking for someone to fill a seat," Jimmy offered. "This is really nice. The view is good. You get replays on the TV. The food service is nice. And best of all, it is warmer in here than anywhere else in this ballpark. Thanks for inviting me."

"You're welcome, J.D. I thought it would be advantageous for us to get together and catch up on some things. You know once I got married eight years ago we haven't talked as often as we did prior to then." Charlie paused to take a sip of his beer as he contemplated how to lead the conversation to the business of the evening which was part of his agenda. "And of course the last five years have been busier for me at work, too. I never knew how many extra activities a bank vice-president is required to attend for the sole purpose of making sure the bank is represented. It's a necessary function and just takes someone's time."

"How's your wife, Charlie?" Jimmy politely asked as he continued to eat his hot dog which was covered with so much mustard, ketchup, onions, and relish he could barely keep it from spilling in his lap.

"She's doing real well, thanks. She truly gets pleasure from living here in California, mainly because she was born and raised here in the Bay Area and can't imagine living anywhere else. She does travel with me when she can, and she and I thoroughly enjoy those trips. It's becoming more difficult for her to break away from her volunteer work."

"Does she still do her volunteer work for children?"

"Yes. You know we can't have children due to her accident shortly after she and I first met, so she's always compensated by working for so many children's organizations."

"Are you still trying to convince her to consider adoption?"

Charlie let out a deep breath before he answered. "I haven't pushed her on it for many years. It was always such a difficult discussion for her, so one day I just decided to save her the pain. Me, too, for that matter. I trust if she's ever ready to discuss it she'll approach me. She knows I'd be willing to adopt as many children as she would ever want, so I just leave it alone."

Jimmy paused as he realized his long-time friend was reminded of the pain of not being able bear children with his chosen mate. Although Charlie could hide his feelings from many people, Jimmy could see the hurt. It also reminded Jimmy of how fortunate he was to have two beautiful daughters who were becoming more like their lovely mother every day.

"How's your family doing, J.D.?" Charlie broke the silence. "I haven't seen Susan in over a year, and it's probably been almost two since I've seen your daughters. Are they still as pretty as I remember them being?"

"They're doing great, Charlie. It's amazing how they translate spending money on them into love for them." Jimmy scoffed at his own remark as he remembered how much money he spent for clothes for those three while on their vacation the previous month. He remembered how utterly amazed he was when Susan and the girls bought enough clothes before the trip for two vacations and still managed to buy more clothes during the trip. He was a little disgusted the memory was not erased, but Charlie's warm presence was comforting. "And yes, the girls are amazingly pretty, just like you and I remember their mother from her pictures at about the same age."

The crack of the bat brought their attention back to the game. They both looked up in time to see the baseball fly over the left field wall and into the seats for a home run. With two men on base, the hit accounted for three runs, pushing the lead for the Mets to four runs.

"Darn it!" hollered Jimmy as he watched the runners circle the bases. "Four runs behind already."

"It's okay, J.D. It's only the top of the fourth inning. There's plenty of innings left for the Giants to catch up."

"I don't know. The offense hasn't scored more than four runs in a game for a week. This lead may be more than they can overcome, particularly if the pitcher doesn't shut them down for the rest of the game." Jimmy was clearly disgusted with the events of the game. "Shoot! I can't believe he just gave up a homer to that guy!"

Charlie waited to let Jimmy's vocal outbursts pass, then offered, "Let me get you another beer. I need to stop in the men's room first though. Just give me a few minutes."

When Charlie returned to the suite, the Giants were batting with runners on first and third and no outs. Jimmy's spirits were improved as he was now standing, hoping for another hit. Charlie grabbed another beer from the refrigerator and walked to the front to root as well. As he handed the can to Jimmy, the batter hit a routine double-play grounder to the shortstop, scoring the runner from third but killing the rally.

"Shoot! Another poor at bat! Man! I can't believe they pay him two million a year! The Giants would be better off giving him away! Don't even bother trading him. Just give him away! A great chance to get back in the game, and he hits into a double play. He's useless!" Jimmy finally stopped as Charlie was almost laughing at his intensity for the game. Jimmy had to smile as well as he looked at Charlie.

"I thought you had this whole east coast-west coast, time difference theory worked out," Charlie said wryly.

Jimmy just shrugged his shoulders. "I thought I did, too. Although what I expected was for the pitcher to have another good outing tonight. He pitched a shutout last week, and he pitched well both times before the shutout. He's traditionally been a better late season pitcher, so I figured all of that coupled with being back at home would be enough for them to win. At least it's what I was betting on."

"How much did you bet, J.D.?" Charlie asked, as he knew Jimmy always bet on games he attended.

"A few thousand."

"A few thousand?!" Charlie was surprised at the amount. He knew Jimmy was a gambler, but he didn't realize the stakes were so high. "That's a pretty steep bet, J.D."

"It's okay. I'll win it back next week or the week after."

"Actually, J.D., that's something I wanted to talk about with you tonight. You always said you had some ideas for how we could both profit if I was just willing to do a few things. Well, my finances are not going as well as I'd like, so I thought we should chat."

EIGHT

"Wow, Charlie," Jimmy replied as he soaked up what Charlie said. "I didn't realize you were in such financial difficulty. I thought you were in pretty good shape with your banking job and your standard investments. I never knew you were involved in the wine business."

Charlie just finished giving Jimmy the details of his financial problems stemming from his investments in different wineries in the Napa and Sonoma valleys. Having invested in five wineries, only one was proving profitable. While a second was breakeven, the other three were small disasters growing toward large ones, each with a different set of problems.

The first of Charlie's losers was an old winery with aging equipment. The inefficiency resulting from the equipment cost the winery more than was gained from the price increases of the past few years. The higher prices were not well received by their base of restaurant customers and distributors, thus causing a drop in sales. Instead of selling out of one vintage before the next was released, inventory was building during the last two years. New equipment would help with the production costs, but the investors were being asked to ante up more money for the capital purchases. Even with a better cost structure, it wasn't clear the previously lost customers could be won back.

The second winery with problems experienced severe damage to two of its three vineyards, lowering the production significantly. One of the vineyards was completely replanted one year ago, but it still was not producing any grapes. The hope was for some yield the next year, but it would be lower than previous levels for several years while it matured. The other vineyard was not yet replanted as the decision was to wait and see the outcome of the first. Having land not generating anything was worse than not owning the land, but selling it under the present circumstances was unlikely. The vineyard not experiencing any damage was the smallest of the three, rendering the production equipment underutilized. There were efforts to rent the equipment to other wineries, but so far there were no takers since the other winemakers were leery of a competitor with two damaged vineyards.

The problem with the third failing winery was somewhat of an enigma. It seemed to be a management issue, but Charlie and the other investors hadn't determined the root cause of the problem.

"But aren't you doing well with your stock options at your bank?" Jimmy asked as he wondered what Charlie's complete financial standing was.

"That's been good," he answered. "That's how I raised the money to invest in the wineries. Unfortunately, I decided to diversify into the wine business while I should've kept my money where it was. While I've squandered away a lot of money, the bank's stock has doubled."

"But don't you have stock options vesting every year? You should be continuing to make more money from those, and with the bank's stock going up, you should've been able to make up for your losses."

"You're right. I do have stock options vesting all of the time. Every month actually. That does provide more income, but my investment problems don't stop with just those wineries." Charlie paused for a moment before he continued. He wanted to talk with Jimmy about ways to make money, and he knew it was required to discuss his financial problems as a preliminary. What he didn't realize was how hard it was going to be to recap his failures, even to a trusted friend.

"So what else did you do to squander your money, Charlie?" Jimmy prompted him to continue. "Did you lose it in the market trading stocks or commodities?"

"Not in standard investments, I didn't. I invested in mutual funds, some bonds, and some individual companies. And those did all right. My blue chip stocks and other large-cap companies grew steadily over the years, with some winners and losers. But the last year those I still own are almost all down, so it hasn't been too pretty to watch.

"The unfortunate thing I did a few years ago was to take my gains from those fairly safe investments in the market and invest in some high-tech startups. At first it was a wonderful thing. My first three were all going up seemingly without any bounds. The gains were phenomenal. It was intoxicating. It was the most fun I think I've ever had. Even though the wineries were doing poorly, I didn't worry too much since I'd found a way to make more money than I could ever imagine losing in any wine business.

"Then I got greedy. And then the dot.com euphoria fell as quickly as it rose. It was horrible. I lost so much money so quickly I couldn't keep up with the losses. I must've invested in ten or twelve more startups after those first three, and only one of those is still in business today."

"Wow. I'm sorry, Charlie." Jimmy couldn't help but feel for his friend. The thought of asking him how the first three startups were now doing came to mind, but Jimmy let it pass. He knew it didn't matter.

"Thanks for your understanding, J.D. So let me ask you, why have you always asked me about working with you to make some extra money? Isn't your real estate business going well?"

"The real estate business is fine." Jimmy smiled as he prepared the remainder of his answer. "My biggest problem is the spending habits of the three ladies in my life. At least you lost money trying to promote business. I feel like I just sit and watch as they throw it away."

The two watched the final few innings of the game without much more discussion about their finances, as each was wondering silently what their next move should be. The Giants continued to fall further behind as the game progressed, and many from the previously excited crowd made an early and quiet exit.

When the Giants rallied for two runs in the bottom of the ninth, only about half of the original crowd was present to see it. Those remaining barely cheered since they were tightly bundled in their coats and hats in an effort to stay warm. It seemed every run relinquished by the Giants caused the temperature to drop one or two degrees while the wind steadily gained momentum, thus making for a cold and unsatisfying night at the ballpark. Even the dedicated fans contemplated leaving early, but stayed out of loyalty. The final score was 9-4, and Jimmy wondered when he should bet again on the Giants winning.

"Why don't we go get a cup of coffee on our way back to Palo Alto and talk some more, J.D.?" Charlie offered as they watched the disappointed fans shuffle toward the exits.

Jimmy was a little tired but not ready to let weariness get in the way of what seemed like a golden opportunity to arrange a working relationship with a banker and trusted fraternity brother. "That sounds fine. Do you have somewhere in mind?"

The two agreed on a place in San Mateo which was on their way home to Palo Alto from San Francisco, and they made their way down the exit ramp to the street beside the ballpark. The streets were filled with cars even though many fans left early. The hustle and bustle of the big city was present as people and cars competed for space, but the honking of car horns normally accompanying a Giants' victory was absent. "Which way did you park, J.D.?" asked Charlie.

"I'm up this way several blocks," Jimmy said as he held his coat tight with his left arm and pointed with his right arm. "Right into the teeth of the wind. Man, what a cold walk this is going to be."

"I'm in this direction," Charlie commented as he, too, held his coat with one hand and pointed with his other. "I think I'm walking into the wind as well. How can it be the wind is in your face no matter which direction you walk?" Charlie mused as they readied to depart for their respective cars.

"That's just the beauty of San Francisco. It's our payment for all of those wonderful summer days without the high humidity we endured in Memphis."

"Well let's go before it gets any colder. I'll meet you there as soon as I can."

"Sure thing. See you there," Jimmy yelled over his shoulder as he already was walking quickly toward his car.

Charlie turned and walked toward his car in the cold. The wind was blowing the fog in from the ocean as it does on most every summer night in San Francisco. As he walked amongst the other baseball fans, Charlie began reflecting on his financial situation. He couldn't believe how he got himself into so much debt from his prior position of having some wealth and seemingly being on his way to complete financial security. He knew it was partially due to his impatience and partially due to his greediness, but it was also due to his perception of people in his profession. His view was bankers invested in a variety of things, many with significant risk, but they somehow were immune to the pitfalls affecting other amateur investors. He now realized his earlier misconceptions, but it didn't change the facts. He was broke and had huge debts to pay.

Arriving at his car, he inserted his key into the ignition of his Lexus and began to think about his wife. She trusted him completely with the finances. She wrote checks from their main account, but she certainly didn't balance the checkbook as she didn't even bother to calculate the balance regularly. She knew their account was protected against any accidental overdrafts, and her husband was a vice president at the bank for heaven sakes. Certainly there weren't any financial difficulties, so why bother to expend energy keeping up with any of it. It wasn't that she couldn't, she merely chose not to.

Charlie hadn't told her any of the details, and he had no intention of doing so. It was difficult to discuss it with Jimmy, and he couldn't bear the thought of his wife's reaction. Although he was in favor of adopting children, he knew their financial situation would be exposed if she suddenly changed her mind and was ready to start the proceedings. He wasn't sure what excuse he would use if that happened. He hoped he could somehow find a way to work out of his debt quickly enough to keep everything hidden in case she abruptly changed her mind, but he wasn't sure it was possible. He knew Jimmy had some ideas about ways to make money, and he expected they might push legal boundaries, but he was ready to listen.

As Charlie was parking his car he looked for Jimmy's Cadillac but didn't see it. However, when he walked through the front door, he saw Jimmy already seated and talking with one of the waitresses. The place was quiet as he noticed a couple to the left and a group of three men far to his right. Making his way to the table he uttered, "I thought I made it first when I didn't see your Cadillac parked anywhere."

"Coffee, sir?" the lady asked as she interrupted.

"Yes, please. Black will be fine. Thanks." Charlie sat without taking off his coat.

"Want anything to go with that?"

"No, thanks. Coffee will be plenty."

"The danishes here are really good," she begged.

"I'm sure they are, but I'll pass. Thank you for offering though."

"Two coffees coming right up," she said as she turned and walked toward the group of three men.

"Oh yeah, I'm in my Audi TT tonight," Jimmy picked up the conversation from where Charlie stopped. "You know me. I'm never satisfied with a car for too long, so I trade one in every year or two it seems."

"An Audi TT," Charlie repeated. He was amazed Jimmy always seemed to be driving a new sports car from the last time he saw him. "That's nice. How long have you had it?"

"About six months."

"So how does it handle?" Charlie asked.

"Superb. Awesome. It's breathtaking. It's beyond what I imagined."

"How does it compare to the others you've tried?"

"It's the best so far. I might just keep this one for longer than normal. That would at least help keep me from having to buy Susan a new car the next time she thinks she needs one," Jimmy added. He watched the waitress finish with the men and make her way to where she could grab two clean cups and a pot of coffee. He knew he and Charlie could get down to business after their coffee was delivered.

Once the cups were filled and the waitress departed again, Jimmy broke the silence. "So what's really on your mind, Charlie?"

"It's simple, J.D. As I told you earlier, I'm in a significant amount of debt. For several years you've always told me you thought we could work together to make some money on the side. Now I'm ready to discuss what we can do."

"Okay," Jimmy started as he adjusted his position in his seat, readying himself for his monologue. "You may not realize it, but in my line of work I have tremendous access to a substantial amount of information about people. Most people buying or selling a home recognize they give me some data, but none of them really knows what I can find out about them with the access provided, particularly regarding the seller.

"When a seller lists their property with me or any other agent for that matter, they put their trust in me or their agent. That part they understand. What they don't realize is the trust they put in all other real estate agents in the area. Once a house is listed and a lock box is installed, every real estate agent within fifty miles or so has access to the home. If people really understood it, they might change their mind or at least do some things differently, but their overbearing thought is to get their home sold and get on with their life, wherever they're going.

"So I have access to every home listed in the entire Bay Area. I can come and go almost as I please, provided I take a little care." Jimmy paused for a sip of his coffee as he watched Charlie's reaction. The mug was warm on the outside, and it felt good against his cold hands.

He decided Charlie was ready to hear more so he continued. "If I want, I usually can find every financial account a person has, including the name of the institution and the account numbers. I can determine which branch they normally do their banking. On some occasions I can even determine the username and password they use for on-line banking.

"And here's the real beauty. They don't have a clue some small real estate agent with an office in Palo Alto has all of this information. They only know I was one of many different agents who showed their house to a potential buyer who chose not to make an offer on their property. And if the truth were known, ninety-nine percent of them probably don't even remember that much."

"So what do you do with all this information, J.D.?" Charlie politely asked.

"Nothing, so far," Jimmy replied. "But, I'd like it to change."

"What do you want from me?"

"Well the first thing I need is some basic information to better understand what is possible, what is not, how some things are done, what the chances are of getting caught, and what the consequences might be. Beyond that I may need some outright help executing some things." Jimmy looked at Charlie and thought he was not yet fazed, so he asked, "Still interested?"

Without hesitation Charlie answered, "Yes. I'd like to keep listening."

"Good," Jimmy said as he resumed. "Here's one of my thoughts. What is to keep me or someone else from going into a branch of a bank with the account number and other personal information about someone who has an account with the bank, filling out a withdrawal slip, and withdrawing a few thousand dollars from someone's account?"

Charlie's eyes widened as he heard the blatant tone in Jimmy's voice. "Well, a couple of things come to mind. First, our tellers would require some form of identification, with a picture of course. And it would most likely have to be a driver's license, as other forms of identification, although valid, raise red flags, particularly with large withdrawals using a generic withdrawal slip."

"Okay," Jimmy interrupted. "What if the person withdrawing the money has a seemingly valid California driver's license with appropriate name and address matching the name and address of the account holder? I can even match the driver's license number to the account holder's real driver's license number. And what if the withdrawal slip being used is not the generic one anyone can get in the lobby of a bank, but one from the back of the book of checks from their very account?"

"It would certainly help," Charlie said as he was amazed at Jimmy's comfort with this while also being more than slightly impressed with Jimmy's insight into some of the details. "But what are you going to do when the account doesn't balance at the end of the month?"

"I'm not worried about that part. By then, the game's over. And believe it or not, when a family is moving, they may not even notice the money is gone. There are so many other items consuming them, I expect they'll figure they just forgot about something."

"I'd be surprised if someone doesn't miss a few thousand dollars. Plus to make it worth the risk, it seems like you would need to withdraw ten thousand or more, which would make it much more obvious."

"Well tell me this, Charlie, what would someone do if they found a discrepancy when balancing their account and thus suspected someone else withdrew several thousand dollars from their account?"

"They would call the bank and ask about it."

"And what would the bank do?"

"We'd check the records and see if there was any possibility of fraud."

"But would you expect fraud initially, or would your gut say they just couldn't keep up with their own banking?"

"It would depend, J.D.," Charlie started as he thought about what his bank did in the past but not certain of the policies of all other banks. "It would depend upon the customer, the branch, and the bank of course. I would expect every bank would look through the daily activity of deposits, checks clearing, and withdrawals, and they would easily identify a withdrawal matching the amount of the unbalanced account. If it was a single withdrawal at a single branch, the branch would then do some auditing of the day's business for the particular teller who handled the transaction."

"Okay. So they find the withdrawal, the branch, and the teller. What next?"

"Depending upon the amount of time having elapsed, most banks would search through their videotapes from their in-bank cameras. I think every bank utilizing video security keeps their tapes for anywhere from three months to a year. In our case, we would go back and view the tapes from the day of the withdrawal to see if we can identify the person who made the withdrawal. Since the withdrawal is stamped with the time and date, it would be pretty easy to find the correct spot in the tapes."

"So a little bit of disguise on the part of the person making the withdrawal would be necessary."

"Yes, it would help. Believe it or not, J.D., the success rate of identifying people in this fashion is about eighty percent, so you'd be fighting the odds."

"So what happens in that eighty percent?"

"We get the account holder to complete an affidavit allowing us to prosecute the criminal. Our insurance provides an immediate refund to the account which we later recover."

"And what about the other twenty percent?"

"Our insurance covers that, too, but only because we allow our policies and procedures to be reviewed on a regular basis."

Charlie watched intently as his friend absorbed all of this. He could tell Jimmy was not deterred, but excited at the possibilities and the challenge.

Finally, Jimmy said, "Okay. So with a little bit of planning and execution, it can be done."

Charlie was amazed at Jimmy's confidence. "It's possible, J.D."

As Charlie looked at his friend, he could tell without a doubt Jimmy decided he would try the scheme they just discussed. He also expected Jimmy would be successful. He wondered about two things. The first was what Jimmy would ask him to do. The second was how he personally would profit.

"So what's in this for me, J.D.? From what we've discussed, you don't need my help."

"You're right. I don't need your help in the execution, but I do want your help advising and planning. I want you to take me to your bank and show me exactly how everything works regarding the security. I then want you to inform me of what you know regarding all of the other banks in the area. Which ones are similar. Which ones are more sophisticated. Which ones are less. That kind of information. For being an advisor acting in such a capacity, I'll give you a cut of what is earned."

Still being preoccupied with the internal moral conflict he was presently having regarding all of this and not wanting to sound greedy yet, Charlie chose not to ask how much of a percentage he would receive or how much Jimmy intended to steal in this fashion. He figured it could wait until another time to be discussed. He needed to give all of this some more thought.

The waitress came with a pot of coffee in her hand to refill their cups. "Gentlemen, can I get you anything else besides coffee? I'm sure you'll enjoy the danishes if you'd just try one."

"That would be fine," Jimmy responded. "We're going to be a little while longer, so a few danishes will be perfect."

"Any particular flavor?" she asked happily.

"Your choice."

When the waitress returned with two danishes, she placed one in front of Jimmy with a cheese filling in the center. Charlie received one with a fruit filling. Both men took a bite and were presently surprised with the taste.

"This danish is quite good," commented Charlie.

"It certainly is," agreed Jimmy.

"So what are some of your other thoughts, J.D.?"

"Well here's another idea. Let's talk about cashier's checks for a while." Jimmy continued to explain his second idea as Charlie was staggered at the creativity and imagination he was witnessing. Clearly Jimmy thought long and hard about this idea, too, and Jimmy's reaction to new obstacles Charlie proposed astonished him. Jimmy was obviously not intimidated or discouraged.

As Jimmy proposed several more ideas, Charlie's attitude was transformed. In addition to providing likely obstacles, Charlie recommended possible courses of action. Jimmy had several schemes in mind associated with on-line banking, but Charlie cautioned him substantially due to the electronic trail which most often can be easily followed.

When the two noticed it was almost two o'clock in the morning, they agreed to continue their discussion the following week. They made an appointment to meet at the bank the following Tuesday in the late afternoon for Charlie to review his bank's security with Jimmy. In the meantime Charlie would conduct some specific discussions regarding security with some of the employees who recently joined his bank from other banks. It was a common topic of discussion in different meetings, so he didn't expect it would raise any suspicion.

On his drive home from the café in San Mateo Jimmy spent more time thinking and researching an idea he was developing for quite some time. He was always adept at using computers, and he did a significant amount of his banking electronically. He had accounts with three different banks. The initial motivation for banking at two different institutions was to separate his home finances from his business finances. The third bank stemmed from his desire to hide some of his money from his wife to allow him to bet on sporting events without her knowing.

One thing initially annoying him was the difference between the information provided by the three banks and how it was presented. One bank he particularly liked allowed him to sort his transactions in almost any fashion imaginable. The other two were not nearly as capable, and one was particularly difficult to track due to the limited number of characters in some of the displayed fields. Often times names were truncated or changed in such a cryptic fashion he was unable to decipher the transaction other than from his own knowledge of what happened for a particular amount or on a specific date.

His attitude about the differences and difficulties changed when a wonderful idea popped into his head during a quiet lunch in his office. He still remembered it was while he was enjoying a Philly cheese steak sandwich with mushrooms, onions, hickory sauce, and extra cheese. While he stared at one of the maps on his wall, the name of a street almost matching the name of one of his banks caught his attention. For some unknown reason he then realized he might be able to prosper from the complexities associated with electronic banking. If he was having trouble on occasion deciphering a particular transaction, surely there were others who were having as much or considerably more difficulty.

Since then Mickey and he did several experiments. One experiment started by having Mickey set up a company and open a banking account for the company. Jimmy then began a monthly electronic transfer from one of his accounts to the company's account, similar to the way monthly bills are paid. After reviewing the transaction for two months to determine how it was logged, Mickey set up a second company with the name exactly matching the name on the logged transaction, which was similar but different from the first name. Jimmy and Mickey then used the home computer of Mickey's assistant to access Jimmy's account via his username and password. They discontinued the first monthly payment and initiated a second monthly payment, payable to the second company. To their mutual surprise and excitement, the logged transaction looked identical, even though the money was paid to the second company instead of the first.

Over the last several months Jimmy and Mickey repeated this experiment numerous times with different company names. It didn't always work, but the logged transactions were always very similar. In a slight variation of the experiment, Mickey one time changed the name of the first company without setting up a second company and without having Jimmy change the monthly transfer. Mickey did this without Jimmy's knowledge to see what would happen and if Jimmy would notice it in his detailed review. Jimmy was flabbergasted yet ecstatic when he didn't notice the switch and Mickey pointed it out to him. That was when the two began to figure how they could exploit this interesting discovery.

Being in the real estate business, Jimmy's grand scheme was to change someone's automatic bank draft for their home mortgage payment to be paid to a company Mickey could set up. That would allow money to come directly to them without the homeowner even noticing it. The problem with the idea was the homeowner would soon be alerted by the mortgage company when the first payment or two was missed.

After continuing to ponder how he could make this work, Jimmy thought of letting the homeowner be notified and allowing the bank holding the mortgage to proceed to a possible foreclosure. The key piece in his scheme was having the banker working as part of his team, and Charlie was his candidate to fill the slot.

As Jimmy neared his home in Palo Alto, he felt the excitement inside of him growing. He was shocked about Charlie's financial situation, but he knew it provided him a much better chance of convincing Charlie to work with him.

NINE

Jimmy parked his Cadillac in the parking lot of the bank shortly after four o'clock on Tuesday afternoon for his meeting with Charlie. Jimmy could not remember the last time he was in this branch of the bank. He didn't physically go to the bank for much of his banking due to his substantial use of electronic banking, and when he did he used the branch located closer to his office. Also, this was the bank he used for his personal accounts as his business and gambling accounts were at other financial institutions. However, since his meeting with Charlie last week Jimmy made special efforts to walk into as many of the branches of his different banks as possible. He wanted to get a feel for the amount of traffic, the location of security cameras, the number of people who used generic withdrawal and deposit slips versus those using ones from their checkbook, and numerous other details he thought were valuable to know.

Jimmy took a moment to gaze at the outside of the two-story building, and he knew Charlie's office was on the second floor, but the exact location escaped him. The outside walls were a tan-colored stucco like most other buildings and homes in northern California. Several similarly sized palm trees were planted in the walkway, helping to make sure the patrons recognized they were in sunny California.

Three ATM machines were on one of the outside walls of the bank. Jimmy did a quick count of eight people in three different lines, not counting the two men and one woman presently using the machines. The woman looked particularly frustrated as she held in her left arm a child of about two or three years of age. Jimmy wondered why she didn't put him down so she could use both hands to complete her transaction.

Upon entering the bank Jimmy noticed a line of seventeen people waiting for one of the two tellers on duty to help them. A few couples were included in the line, and two mothers were accompanied by their children, but this was still the longest line he witnessed during the entire past week of his information gathering.

Jimmy stopped and looked at the other activities present. To his left was a woman in her late forties or early fifties assisting a young couple. He expected they were completing the paperwork to open a new account based on the sign hanging from the ceiling above the desk. A man was seated behind a second desk, and he was staring at the information on a computer screen. A few other desks were vacant with only fake potted flowers beside them.

Behind those desks were offices with full-length glass windows and wooden doors with placards denoting the name of the person occupying the office. Two of the offices were dark with closed doors. Two others were without people but with the doors open and the interior lights on. A woman busily typing on her keyboard was seated in one. Her door was open, allowing Jimmy to notice the four pictures on the wall. Taking a moment to determine the theme, he quickly concluded the images depicted the four seasons of the year. Knowing California did not experience the four seasons as other parts of the country, he decided she probably was raised in a small town in the Midwest and found her way to California like he and many others. In another of the offices a small conference with three participants was in progress. The man behind the desk listened intently as a younger man waved his arms in his efforts to make his point. The third man was between the ages of his two colleagues, and he seemed disinterested.

Jimmy looked back at the line of people waiting for service and did another quick count. No one joined the end since he entered, and sixteen were still in line. Seeing from the clock on the wall about four minutes passed, he calculated the last person might be required to wait in excess of twenty or even thirty minutes in the line if things continued at this pace. He thought Tuesday afternoons would be less busy than other afternoons, so he made a mental note to ask Charlie what was normal.

Jimmy walked slowly past the line of people toward the stairway he knew was near the back entrance. He noticed only one man in the line who filled in numbers on a generic withdrawal slip while all the others were waiting patiently having already completed their preparation.

There clearly was no dress code for coming into a bank to do business. On one end of the spectrum was a male barely old enough to drive. He was wearing blue jean shorts and a t-shirt. The shorts hung to a few inches below his knees, quite different than the style Jimmy remembered from his late teenage years. The boy wore no hat so his bleached blond hair was on full display. A pair of sandals with their better days far in the past completed the ensemble.

Two patrons were at the other end of the spectrum. One was a middle-aged man in a dark business suit with a white shirt, a conservative tie, and dark dress shoes with shoelaces as opposed to the slip-on variety many now enjoyed. The other was a lady in her late twenties wearing a blue skirt and matching jacket. Her brunette hair was nicely curled, and when she turned to glance at Jimmy he saw the outfit matched her eyes. He also saw the sparkle of a diamond earring as she quickly turned away after noticing him looking at her.

Only one man of those in line wore a hat. He was in blue jeans, tennis shoes, and a golf shirt with a collar. On the left of the front of the shirt was a small logo from a resort Jimmy didn't recognize. As Jimmy continued his walk to the stairs, he pondered which of those clients attracted the most attention of a security person. He knew his attention would normally be drawn to the most attractive female, but he expected he could be trained otherwise, as he noticed many different things during the past week.

Upon finding his way to the top of the stairs, Jimmy felt a slight sense of familiarity and thought he now knew where Charlie's office was. He read the names displayed on the doors he passed as he walked, while also saying hello to one man going in the opposite direction in quite a hurry. As he approached another man exiting an office, the man asked if he needed any help. Jimmy stated he was on his way to see Charlie Bates and was hoping he was heading in the correct direction. The man pointed further down the row of offices and watched from behind as Jimmy made his way.

"J.D.! Come in. Come in." Charlie greeted him with a large smile and a hearty handshake. "Good to see you. Please, have a seat," Charlie said as he motioned with one hand to a table surrounded by four leather chairs while closing the door with his other hand. "Can I get you something to drink?"

"No thanks, Charlie," Jimmy answered as he took a seat.

"So how are you doin', today?" Charlie continued with his politeness as he sat across the small table from Jimmy.

"I should be asking you." Jimmy let out a short laugh and then his face became serious. "Look, Charlie. You've known me for a long, long time. You know I have a zest for life, and you also know I don't like playing by the rules. I never have. I was always pushing the limits and going beyond them. You saw it when we first met in college. You said it yourself so many times. You used to refer to me as 'that crazy Jimmy Donovan' during college. I enjoyed your friendship then, and I've enjoyed it as we've grown older, too. We've each done our own things since college, and now here we are. You're in a tough financial spot, and I want to have more money, too. I'm convinced we can work together in a variety of ways to benefit both of us. We simply have to agree we'll work together, plan carefully, execute flawlessly, and stick together while making things better for both of us. So, given that as a starting point, what are your thoughts since we last talked?"

Charlie paused for a few moments. He looked hard into Jimmy's face, and he saw the conviction and certainty. Having waffled with his feelings for the last several days, he didn't decide until earlier in the afternoon what he would do. He knew he could dedicate himself to his work for several years and slowly raise himself out of his current debts. He expected it would be required to tell his wife all about his investment failures and thus live with her disappointment in him. He wasn't sure who else would find out, but he feared the circle would grow.

On the other hand was this proposition from his fraternity brother. He knew Jimmy was selfish yet caring, so he expected Jimmy was in it for his own benefit while also truly wanting to help a friend.

The event swinging his decision was his reading of an email earlier in the afternoon. One of his partners in one of his winery deals outlined a new plan. The spending required for new equipment was only part of the cost proposed, as a new tasting room and picnic area at the winery coupled with new advertising and distribution programs were also included. While he agreed with most of the change in strategy, the suggested price was far beyond what Charlie imagined.

It was the last comment in the email which solidified his decision. After outlining all of the strategy and costs, with predictions of future revenues and profits, his partner stated, "Let's not turn a large fortune into a small one like so many before us. Let's stay the course, fight the odds, and win this one."

Charlie's reaction to the closing sentences was one of awakening. He realized they lost significantly with their earlier investments, and something needed to change for the outcome to be altered. However, change could come in many forms.

"Let's go for it, J.D," Charlie firmly stated as he looked squarely into Jimmy's eyes.

A broad smile came across Jimmy's face. When Charlie began to smile, too, Jimmy said, "So let's talk about bank security. What do you have for me?"

Charlie got up from his chair and walked around his desk to access some papers in one of the drawers. He pulled out a folder and began to open it as he seated himself again, this time next to Jimmy. "I've gathered four different things for us to review first. After we go through all of this, we'll take a walk around the bank so you can see what it looks like in real life. Then we can meet again back here to discuss what I know about other banks in the area. There are several good targets, but we should start with a few I think are excellent ones."

Charlie proceeded to spend the next seventy-five minutes reviewing the information he gathered and organized during the past week while he contemplated what to tell his friend. It was a few minutes before six o'clock when the two started their tour. Since the bank closed at six there were a few last customers being helped. Jimmy didn't recognize any of them from the line of people he studied earlier, and he hoped they were all helped before their patience expired. He couldn't imagine they would wait this long anyway without threatening to withdraw all of their money with hopes of getting better service at a competitor.

After a detailed tour including many polite comments by Charlie to several of the employees, the two returned to Charlie's office. Charlie reached into his desk for another piece of paper containing some notes. Jimmy quickly learned Charlie made a tabular comparison of most of the banks in the area. The number of branches for each of the banks was one of the first pieces of data of particular interest to them. Another important detail was the number of fraudulent claims and the outcomes of those expressed as a percentage. This data was not available for all banks, and Charlie explained those were only guesses based upon interviews he recently conducted with the employees hired from those who worked at the other banks within the last year.

The two further discussed strategy and timing among other details. Jimmy's earlier question about the normalcy of Tuesday afternoons was answered, and it was agreed the best time to get helped quickly while having enough traffic to not be noticed was around twenty minutes past eleven o'clock in the morning. The noon rush would not be started, so the line for service should be relatively short. However, the business of the lunch hour would be quick to follow so activity would be increasing. Also, many regular weekly meetings are scheduled in the morning and would still be in progress.

As the two completed their review, Charlie asked, "So how much can I expect to profit from this J.D.?"

"You'll get one-third of the total. I'll be getting one-third as well, and the other one-third will take care of some other details of the operation."

"What other details?"

"Charlie, you're better off if you don't know. You just have to trust I won't cheat you. I promise you I will only get as much as you from this. Is it a fair deal?"

Realizing not knowing the details of the day, bank, branch, or anything else was probably a good thing, Charlie replied, "Yes."

"Let me get to work then, Charlie," Jimmy said excitedly as he pushed himself to his feet. "Thanks for all the information. I'll be in touch."

"I'll have to let you out since the bank is now closed, J.D." Charlie also stood and opened his office door for his friend as Jimmy led the way to the stairway. The man Jimmy spoke with briefly on his way to Charlie's office was still working in his office. Jimmy saw him seated behind his desk, and the man looked up and waived as the two walked by. Jimmy was tempted to ask about his position and why he was there so late, but decided to let it pass.

Charlie unlocked the door to the bank and held it for Jimmy. The two quickly said good night, and Jimmy headed for his car. He didn't take the time to absorb all of his surroundings as he was excited and in a hurry for his next appointment.

Jimmy started his car and began to drive to his office. It was only a five-minute drive, but it allowed enough time for a phone call. Jimmy confirmed he would be expecting his guest to arrive at half past eight. When Jimmy arrived at his office, he quickly seated himself in front of his computer to review his notes about people and their banks.

Jimmy previously completed his research on five candidates, while several others were in progress. For those five he had names, physical descriptions including pictures, addresses, phone numbers, social security numbers, drivers license numbers, account numbers, historical balances, spouse names, names of children, maiden names of mothers, and other information possibly of value. He gathered this information for some of the candidates through a relatively quick but detailed search of homeowners' desks. For most people he additionally searched through files on their home computer. He was amazed so few utilized the password features available for files associated with different computer applications, mainly word processing programs. On two occasions a single file named 'PersonalInformation.doc' was quickly found from a file search, and the file contained everything imaginable in it. He figured either the man or the woman of the home, whoever managed the finances, generated the file for use by the other or by their children in case of an emergency. Thinking they were protected was exactly the opposite of what in reality was the case.

He compared the banking institutions for these five to the top two targets Charlie determined. He found two matches for the first one and a lone match for the second. He reviewed the home addresses and business addresses against a list of addresses for all of the branches of the two banks to determine the best fit. He wanted to pick branches far enough away from where they normally did their banking but not too far away. He was familiar with the addresses so he didn't utilize the maps surrounding him. Finding what he thought

92

were good choices, he highlighted the appropriate ones and printed a single page for each of the three candidates.

His guest arrived promptly at half past eight, and Jimmy greeted him at the front door of his real estate office. "Who's car is that?" Jimmy greeted him. "It's better than what you normally drive."

The man approached Jimmy, and the two shook hands. "It's just a car I borrowed from someone at work. They were glad to trade for a few days," was the reply. The two walked to his private office in silence as the main lights were off and all was quiet since his staff left for the day several hours ago.

Jimmy took the first of three printed pages and wrote Wednesday at the top. All of the details were reviewed, and then Jimmy conducted a quick test to see if the details were committed to memory. Determining most of it was from this initial review, Jimmy was satisfied. He folded the page, handed it to his guest, and directed him to review it a few more times later to make certain everything was known before tomorrow morning.

Jimmy placed a blank sheet in front of his guest and handed him a black ink pen. "Sign Liston's name on this sheet," Jimmy directed. "And try to make it look something like this," he added as he placed a small sheet of paper beside the first one. The second sheet contained Jimmy's version of Liston's signature which was copied from a check Jimmy found while at Liston's house gathering all of the other information.

"That looks good. Write it a few more times. You may want to practice more later tonight and tomorrow morning as well."

Leaving the signatures on his desk, the two then walked to the back of the office to the locked storage room. The guest took a seat in a barber's chair while Jimmy found the color of dye most closely matching Mr. Liston's hair color, who was Wednesday's target. "This shade will work fine," Jimmy said.

He proceeded to dye his friend's hair. When finished he handed him a mirror and asked how he liked it. "It will do for now, but when can I get back to my normal color?"

"The way I've organized the next three days, we'll be back to your natural color on Thursday night since Friday's person is pretty much the same color as you. Now stand over here so I can get a picture of you."

Jimmy cleaned his hands in the sink of his all-purpose storage room and took a picture of the changed man using a digital camera. "Just stay put for a minute while I download this to my computer. Review the information I gave you, and we'll test you again when I return. I'll be back in a flash."

Jimmy walked back to the front of the building to his office. He transferred the image to the computer and double clicked an icon allowing him to size the photo properly. He then transferred the small picture to another computer application permitting him to add text and other graphics. The name of the state of California was boldly displayed in all upper case blue letters across the top. Below that was Mr. Liston's driver's license number in green. Mr. Liston's name, address, and physical details were listed to the right of the picture. His date of birth along with an expiration date for the license were in red in the correct places. The seal of the state of California was contained in the background, along with two DMV logos in the top two corners and other detailed printing in appropriate spots. Jimmy lastly scanned one of the signatures he previously obtained and added it to his creation. Taking one last look at the finished artwork, he smiled and clicked on the print icon.

He heard the printer make some noise behind him, and he reached into his desk for a pair of scissors. He grabbed the hardcopy and cut along his dotted lines. Placing the remains in his trash can he headed back to the storage room.

"How are you doing with the profile information?" Jimmy greeted him as he entered.

"Real good, Jimmy. I think I've got it all. Ask me anything."

"Great." Jimmy walked to another counter to use a lamination machine for completing the driver's license. "What's your social security number, Mr. Liston?"

"3. 0. 3. 8. 4. 2. 5. 9. 6."

"That's not a social security number from California. Where'd you grow up?" Jimmy asked as he was almost finished with the license.

"Indiana."

"There. Here's your official California driver's license, Mr. Liston, from Indiana originally. Thanks for stopping by the DMV tonight." Jimmy laughed at his mockery of a DMV employee and handed the small card to his friend.

"Wow. That's pretty good. This looks like a real California driver's license."

"Here. Use this. This is one of Liston's," Jimmy said as he grabbed a hat from a shelf on the wall. The hat was one he retrieved from Mr. Liston's closet, which he hadn't yet determined if he would return or just keep as a souvenir. "And here. Use this withdrawal slip. It's one from Liston's checkbook."

Jimmy cleaned his hands once again while the two went through tomorrow's plan one more time. Jimmy decided ten thousand dollars would be an appropriate starting amount since Liston had more than seventy thousand in one of his accounts, more than fifty in a second one, and slightly less than ten in a third. The middle account was chosen somewhat randomly, although Jimmy knew the small account was used on an everyday basis for normal purchases and bills while the other two were less active. Avoiding the largest account seemed like a better way to possibly conceal their withdrawal during a cursory review of the monthly statement.

As he escorted his guest to the front door, Jimmy once again noticed the car his guest borrowed as instructed. He smiled as he was certain this scheme would work. He then returned to his computer to do some additional work for Thursday's and Friday's activity. After making a few phone calls, he called Susan but found she must already be in bed with the phone turned off.

Noticing it was almost eleven in the evening, he realized he hadn't eaten since lunch. He wasn't one to forget meals very often, but today's excitement and the anticipation of the next few days temporarily put dinner out of his mind. He told Susan he would be working late and would fend for himself, but this wasn't what he had in mind. Now feeling hungry he wondered what would be appropriate. He decided to try to get a few slices of pizza from a place a few blocks from his office. He figured the walk would be fun.

The next morning was a typical August day. The sky was a cloudless blue, the temperature was a moderate eighty-three degrees, and a slight breeze of about ten miles an hour was blowing. It was quite hazy since the last rain was in early April. The highways and main roads were full of cars moving faster than the speed limit, as the morning commute finished well over an hour ago. At fifteen minutes past eleven o'clock, the borrowed car pulled into a parking spot at the Milpitas branch of Mr. Liston's bank.

The imposter opened the car door, put the borrowed hat on his head, and walked casually to the front door. Upon entering he was glad when he noticed only three people in the line with three tellers helping others. He made his way to the end of the line and stood calmly with his head slightly lowered and eyes fixed on the floor a few feet in front of him.

Within less than a minute he moved up two spots in the line as two of the tellers quickly finished with their clients. The third teller was having some difficulty completing the transaction, and the man was beginning to talk in a louder voice than normal. He hoped things didn't escalate to the point of requiring additional bank personnel to assist the flustered teller and disgusted man.

A few more people joined the line behind him. One was a mother with two children, a boy and his older sister. He kept his head lowered and hoped the kids were well-behaved. After another minute the capable teller on the end finished another transaction and waved for the lady in the front of the line to come forward. He was next, and he felt his heart start to beat a little faster than normal.

He transferred the withdrawal slip from his right hand to his left, and he noticed he was beginning to sweat. The teller experiencing difficulties was asking the man in front of her to please not shout as it would only take a few more minutes to resolve the problem. Suppressing the desire to look around to see how much attention they garnered, he continued to stare at the floor near his feet.

"Sir, can I help you?" he heard someone say. "Sir. Sir. I can help you right here."

He looked up and saw the teller at the end waving her hand at him so she could assist him. He almost stumbled on his first step as the little boy was playing with the rope and made a sudden twist toward him. "Oh. Excuse me," he said as he avoided the child and made his way to the teller. He knew his steps were a little awkward, but he hoped she wouldn't notice.

"How can I help you?" she said with a smile.

He looked up and saw she was a brunette with her hair tied in a bun. She had big brown eyes and bright red lipstick.

"Hi. I'd like to make a withdrawal," he said as he handed the withdrawal slip to her.

"I'll have to see some ID, and you'll need to sign this slip here."

With his right hand he grabbed the pen which was dangling over the counter. Simultaneously, he reached with his left hand into his back pocket for his wallet. Trying to do both of these at the same time caused him to drop his wallet to the floor. When he quickly leaned over to pick it up, he hit his head on the corner of the counter. "Ow!" he exclaimed as he reached to rub his head where he bumped it. The hat was now on the floor, too.

He felt his heart racing mightily, but he let out a big breath as he grabbed his wallet and hat. "Just a little clumsy today," he muttered as he became upright again and put his wallet on the counter. He placed the hat back on his head as he noticed the teller typing on the number pad of her keyboard. When she hit the enter key, she looked intently at her screen.

"Here's my ID, ma'am," he said handing her his fake driver's license. He once again grabbed the dangling pen and began to sign his name on the slip. His hands were damp, and he was having difficulty keeping the pen from sliding.

He finished with the signature and pushed the slip slightly toward her. She wrote his license number on the withdrawal slip and initialed it. "How would you like your cash, Mr. Liston?" she asked.

"Uh," he stuttered. "Hundreds will be fine."

"I'll have to do a little work for this much cash. Please wait for just a minute," she said as she walked behind the teller stations.

He took in another deep breath and let it out slowly as he tried to wait patiently. The man previously having problems was gathering his wallet, cash, and other items as he loudly stated he was tired of being treated so poorly. He now had the attention of everyone in the line, including the young boy who stopped his game and was holding his mother's hand.

After a few moments which seemed like several minutes, his teller approached him with a smile on her face. "Here you are, Mr. Liston. One, two, three, four, five, six, seven, eight, nine, one thousand," she said as she counted the money in front of him. "One, two, three, four, five, six, seven, eight, nine, two thousand," she went on as he watched. She continued all the way to ten thousand and then offered, "Have a great day."

"Thanks, ma'am," he said as he grabbed the money, folded it neatly, and stuffed it in his front pocket along with the fake license. He turned and walked as smoothly as he could muster toward the door. Once outside he quickly continued to the borrowed car. He let himself in and started the engine. He checked behind him, and seeing no one coming he backed up. He stopped to put the car in a forward gear and navigated his exit from the parking lot.

After driving a few minutes he turned into the parking lot of a gas station. He put the transmission in park and reached for his cell phone. He punched a few buttons to retrieve the number and hit send. The call was answered on the first ring.

"Jimmy Donovan," he heard from the other end.

"Hi, Jimmy. It's Billy. I got the money." Billy Wicks let out a huge sigh of relief. He wasn't sure he could pull it off, but with enough coaching from his friend Jimmy, he was convinced to try. Now it seemed like the first one was successfully completed.

"That's great, Billy!" Jimmy yelled into his phone. "Good job! I'll see you tonight around eight. You'll like tonight's hair color."

TEN

"Jimmy! Jimmy! Wake up, Jimmy!" Susan Donovan exclaimed from the bathroom.

Jimmy rolled over and peeked at the clock. It was a few minutes after seven o'clock in the morning, and he wanted to sleep longer after having been up late the previous night. With despair he watched UNLV's football team lose a home game to Northwestern, 37-28, in a special Friday night college football game. His bet was on UNLV since they played so well in their season opener on the road at Arkansas just one week ago. Arkansas won by only four points, 14-10, and he lost his bet on Arkansas since they did not cover the point spread. He still couldn't believe UNLV played so well at Arkansas. Having underestimated UNLV in their opener, he hoped to benefit this week since they were back at home, but his strategy failed.

Watching the special broadcast put him behind his normal Friday evening fall schedule of completing his analysis of the final point spreads for Saturday's college football games and calling his bookmaker with his bets. This week he finished the call at almost two o'clock in the morning, and now his wife was yelling at him to get up before seven.

"Jimmy! I know you're awake!" she yelled. How could she tell he was awake when she couldn't see him from her position in front of the mirror he wondered. "You have to get up and take the girls to the school for their trip! They have to be there in less than an hour! So get up and get in the shower!"

Now he was mystified. He knew the girls' trip was today, but he didn't remember having the responsibility of driving them to the school. Did he really agree to this? He tried to remember but was too tired from poring over all the numbers late last night. Things will certainly be easier when his oldest gets her license to drive next year he thought at first. But then he quickly came to his senses and sat up in bed as he realized the scariness of the thought.

Shaking his head as he got out of the bed and walked toward the bathroom, he couldn't imagine the difficulty awaiting him with his girls when one and then both of them were driving. Of course they would require their own cars, and his resistance would be futile since their mother would be in full support of them.

"I thought you agreed to take the girls this morning," Jimmy commented to his wife as he passed her in the bathroom on his way to the shower. "I was hoping to sleep a little longer."

"If you remember from early last night, I informed you I have my fundraiser meeting this morning."

It was now coming back to Jimmy. He totally forgot their discussion during dinner after having consumed himself with the scores, stats, point spreads, and other pertinent college football details. "Oh yeah," he acknowledged she was correct. "Now I remember."

"Thank you," she replied with satisfaction.

Jimmy pulled the shower door closed and felt the warm water on his body. While washing his hair he thought about his girls and their trip. Then he remembered his surprise plans for the day. "Hey, Susan. When will you be home from your meeting?"

He waited a few moments for a reply. Not hearing one he decided she was no longer in the bathroom, so he yelled. "Susan! Hey! Susan!"

"You don't have to shout, Jimmy," Susan said as she walked back into the bathroom. "I'm right here."

"Well I asked you a question just a moment ago, and you didn't answer. So then I hollered for you, and you're right here. Why is that?"

"I don't know, Jimmy. And I don't care. Maybe if you got out of bed on time your timing wouldn't be all messed up. What is it?" She stopped and put her hands on her hips as she waited for him to tell her what was so important.

"What time will you be home from your meeting?"

"Around ten or so," she bluntly stated. "Why?" Her hands remained on her hips.

"Well," he said slowly. "With the girls gone for the day, I thought we would spend the day together."

"Well," she began as she mocked how he started his last comment. "What did you have in mind?"

"Well," he returned the mocking favor as he started, "I thought we would grab a couple of deli sandwiches and have a picnic around eleven-thirty."

"Sounds like fun," she said in a somewhat skeptical tone. "And where are we going to eat this picnic lunch?"

"I thought we would eat it outside of Stanford stadium before going inside for the football game this afternoon."

Jimmy could tell this caught her totally off guard, so he silently continued with his shower. "What a great idea, Jimmy. I'd love to go." Susan was truly excited. She was now disappointed in her earlier tone as she loved the few times each year Jimmy would take the girls and her to a college football game at Stanford, San Jose State, or Berkeley, and this time it would just be the two of them.

"And to top it off, I thought we could enjoy a nice dinner in downtown Palo Alto at your favorite Italian place." Jimmy turned off the shower and opened the door to grab his towel.

"Wow," she said as she stuck her head passed the door and kissed his wet face right on the lips. "I can hardly wait. I'll be sure to hustle home from my meeting. Please hurry so the girls aren't late. Bye!" Susan turned and hurriedly walked away from her husband and out of the bathroom. She had a teenage bounce to her steps. Jimmy smiled as he knew he pleasantly surprised her once again.

After dropping the girls off at their school, Jimmy returned home to review his bets for the day's games. He was excited with the new season, as last weekend proved quite profitable. He was off to a good start and hoping to gain momentum with this weekend's schedule.

Before reviewing this week's bets, Jimmy took a few moments to gaze at the prior week's results. He reached into a folder in his desk and pulled out a single page summarizing his activity. There were always five main categories for how he thought about the games. The first grouping included teams ranked in the top ten nationally. The second contained the remaining teams ranked in the top 25, but not in the PAC-10 or SEC conferences, as these were the conferences he followed most. The third and fourth categories contained games with the PAC-10 and SEC conference teams not in the first group. The fifth group included any special matchup, such as one played on a day of the week other than Saturday or a game played between a PAC-10 team and an SEC team.

Looking at last week's first group of games, Jimmy smiled as he saw he won seven of his eight wagers. The one he lost was Oregon's close win at home against Wisconsin, 31-28. He picked Oregon, but they were unable to cover the point spread. So even though Oregon won, he lost his bet. Two of the games did not have a betting line since the odds makers determined each was such a mismatch they couldn't determine a fair point spread. This happened quite often for teams ranked in the top ten, particularly early in the season when some of the teams played what many reporters claimed were warm-up games, insinuating it was nothing more than a scrimmage or glorified practice.

His second group contained only three games, and Jimmy didn't bet on any of these. One of the three was Clemson hosting Central Florida. Although priding himself on knowing something about most teams, those were two teams he didn't follow. Another contest in this category was Colorado hosting Colorado State. State was the ranked team, but Colorado was at home, so Jimmy hesitated to bet even though he was leaning toward the home team. His gut was right as Colorado whipped their in-state rival 41-14, but unfortunately he couldn't claim a victory since he didn't bet on it.

For the PAC-10 games he won one bet and lost one. The winning one was USC's win over San Jose State. He knew San Jose State was not as good as a year ago from comments made by two local newspaper reporters who were known for having accurate information. The losing one was Cal's 44-17 drubbing at home at the hands of Illinois. Illinois must be really good because Cal couldn't possibly be so bad when playing at home he thought.

For the SEC games Jimmy won two and lost three. LSU and South Carolina were his winners, while Vanderbilt, Kentucky, and Arkansas were the losers. Vanderbilt hosted Middle Tennessee State and lost. Vandy did not pick their warm-up game opponent very well this year Jimmy decided. Kentucky also lost at home, but to a respectable Louisville team. The surprising part was the score of 36-10. Quite a pounding to an in-state team Kentucky should be able to beat, particularly at home. The Arkansas contest was the stinger, as they won over UNLV by four points but did not cover the spread.

The special category had the final three games, and he had two losers and a winner. The first was an interesting matchup between UCLA and Alabama, played in Tuscaloosa. UCLA was ranked #15, and Alabama was #25. Jimmy really liked these kinds of games, especially early in the season, since it was difficult to determine who would win. Jimmy's expectation was for Alabama to play well at home with UCLA being somewhat weary from the long flight. So much for logical thinking as UCLA won 20-17. The second was a special Sunday game in Fresno with Fresno State hosting Oregon State, who was ranked #12. Fresno dominated and won 44-24, which Jimmy missed along with most others. The last game was a special Labor Day game, with his alma mater playing at Mississippi State, who was ranked #19. Jimmy found it difficult to bet against Memphis, but he knew the Bulldogs were a good team and played well at home. Although close through the first half, Memphis couldn't keep up in the second half, losing 30-10. Their loss was his gain since it capped off an excellent weekend on his tally sheet.

Eighteen total bets. Eleven winners and seven losers. With each bet being two thousand he netted eight thousand, minus only one percent for his bookmaker since he was a valued client. If he only managed half of that amount for each of the next ten weeks or so he would pocket around fifty grand for the season.

Placing last week's sheet back in the folder, Jimmy grabbed today's summary page. He was already one bet behind due to the outcome of the Northwestern/UNLV game from last night, but he could easily overcome the small setback. Looking at his first group he saw all of the top ten teams were playing, although five did not have a betting line. Florida, ranked number one, was hosting Louisiana Monroe. Having grown up in nearby Tennessee he didn't remember any college in Monroe, Louisiana having a football team. No wonder there's no betting line he thought. Don't even bother to play the game, he decided. It would be more entertaining to just let the tailgaters have multiple games of flag football between their burgers and beers, right on the field instead of in some parking lot.

Number five Florida State was hosting UAB. Since when did UAB have a football team he wondered. Another top ten game with no betting line. The same folks in charge of some of these schedules must be the ones running the Bowl Championship Series, which still didn't make any sense to Jimmy.

There were three interesting matchups involving top ten teams. Fourth-ranked Nebraska was hosting #17 Notre Dame, tenth-ranked Michigan was traveling to #15 Washington, and seventh-ranked Tennessee was playing at Little Rock against Arkansas. Charlie's advice was to bet on Arkansas based upon comments from contacts Charlie maintained back in Little Rock, and Jimmy trusted his friend on this one. Plus, Jimmy found it difficult to root for Tennessee as the fans in Knoxville thought they were superior to him and anyone else from the western part of the state.

The second group of games was almost a waste. Wofford, whoever they are, was playing at Clemson. Tempted to get on-line to find where Wofford was located, he resisted and continued his review. Fresno State was playing at Wisconsin. Wisconsin played well on the road last Saturday in their three-point loss at number seven Oregon. Fresno was coming off a big home win, but they played on Sunday and spent all day yesterday flying to Wisconsin. Surely Wisconsin would win today.

In the PAC-10 group were seven games. USC was hosting a good Kansas State team, and Jimmy expected the Wildcats could withstand the early-season trip to the west coast. Oregon State and UCLA were scheduled for road trips for the second straight week. Jimmy's bet was for Oregon State to play better and win, while he was passing on UCLA as they should be down after last week's big win at Alabama. Arizona and Arizona State both were hosting teams today, and Jimmy bet on Arizona to cover against Idaho but was not willing to gamble on Arizona State covering against San Diego State. Surely Cal would be better this week in another home contest against BYU, who was certainly not as good as Illinois.

The SEC category indicated conference play was beginning, as three conference games were slated in addition to the Tennessee/Arkansas one in his first group. Vandy was hosting Alabama, and the Crimson Tide should handle them as easily as Middle Tennessee State did was Jimmy's thinking. Ole Miss was at Auburn, and even though he hated all of Ole Miss' sports teams, he particularly despised their football team. Their cheerleaders were pretty, as were the sorority girls, but it didn't make up for his hatred of their athletics. Still, he tried to put it all behind him and judge the game objectively. Since the quarterback for Ole Miss was once again named Manning, Jimmy's bet was on the Rebels. The other SEC conference game was South Carolina and Georgia. Both teams were ranked, and he opted for Georgia since they were the home team.

One more matchup was on his sheet, and it was Stanford hosting Boston College. He put this in the special category along with Friday night's game. This was his way of giving it the extra consideration it deserved since he was attending the game, and he hated losing bets while he watched helplessly except for his cheering. Stanford was favored, and he expected them to cover the spread. He was so certain of this he doubled his betting amount to four thousand.

Jimmy counted fifteen bets for Saturday's games. Having lost the Friday night game, but having doubled his amount for the Stanford game, he would win thirty grand if all fifteen games fell in his favor today. Just a ten and five mark for the day with Stanford on the good side would be worth ten thousand for the weekend. His excitement for the day and the season were at an all time high as he returned the betting sheet to his desk.

As he stretched his arms above his head he heard the sound of his wife's car returning from her appointment. Knowing Susan would need to change clothes, he found his way to the kitchen to pack a few things in their picnic hamper for lunch.

He opened the basket and saw the plates, glasses, and cutlery precisely packed in their respective places. A blue and white checked tablecloth and matching napkins were laying loosely in the bottom. He opened the refrigerator and grabbed the bottle of Susan's favorite Chardonnay from the bottom shelf. It was one he placed there late last night before going to bed so it would be chilled for today. Remembering one picnic when he forgot to pack a corkscrew, he promptly opened a drawer containing several. He snatched one and set it in the basket along with the wine, while making a mental note to leave the corkscrew permanently in the hamper for future picnics.

Jimmy reached into the refrigerator once again in hopes of finding some bottled water. He didn't mind drinking from a public fountain, but he knew Susan felt it was unclean and would want some water in addition to the wine. Four bottles of water were neatly stacked along the right side, and he added three of those to the basket.

Knowing Susan would want to clean up as best as she could after the picnic and before the game, he searched for some handi-wipes he expected were hidden somewhere. After unsuccessfully looking in several cabinets and drawers, he walked out of the kitchen to the base of the stairs and yelled to his wife, "Susan, honey! Do we have any of those handi-wipes somewhere in the kitchen?"

Waiting for a response but not receiving one after a few moments, he climbed the stairs in pursuit of her. Once reaching the top he remembered they would need a blanket, so he walked into their guest bedroom to locate an appropriate one. While opting for the one bearing Stanford's colors and logo as opposed to one of a rival's shade, he remembered where he last saw the handi-wipes. As he walked back to the stairs Susan emerged from their bedroom wearing a flowered summer dress and sandals. He stopped and stared as he was reminded of how beautiful she still was after all of these years.

"You certainly look lovely," he commented.

"Thank you. I wanted to feel like I was in college again. This was such a great idea, Jimmy."

The two descended the stairs and walked into the kitchen. Noticing the picnic hamper she took a peek inside. "Oh! Aren't you a sweetheart? You packed my favorite wine along with some water," she said as she turned and embraced him. They kissed several times as Jimmy thought about how much he loved Susan when she was happy and loving him. Susan once again felt the fun of being married to Jimmy.

After buying the sandwiches and other necessary items, Jimmy expertly navigated through traffic of both cars and people to a parking location where he knew the attendant. Slipping a twenty dollar bill to the man allowed him entry to the private lot normally reserved for special boosters. Once parked the two grabbed their picnic items and made a short walk to an area where several tall trees provided ample shade for those wanting to avoid the sun. Even though the temperature was in the mid-seventies on another cloudless day, the decision was to utilize the shade now since the remainder of the afternoon would be in the bright sunshine.

As they ate the sandwiches and sipped the wine, there was little talk as they mostly watched others making their way toward the stadium. Susan wondered aloud if any of the college girls she saw were unknowingly walking with their future husbands as she did long ago. Jimmy simply smiled and didn't reply as he enjoyed the perfect day.

The opening kickoff was underway as they found their way to their assigned seats. Jimmy particularly noticed the excitement of the crowd, which looked to be about forty thousand or so. Although Boston College played last week and won against West Virginia, it was Stanford's season opener, so part of the excitement was due to the newness of the season.

Having attended more baseball games than football games in the past several months, Jimmy immediately felt the difference between the two sports. More attention was placed on each play in football versus each pitch in baseball. He also recognized the difference between the spirit displayed at a college event versus a professional one. The cheerleaders in college actually cheered, while those for pro games mostly danced and waved to the crowd. He determined yet again this was one of the many reasons he preferred the college game. That was his rationale for limiting his betting activity mostly to the college games. Occasionally he would bet on the Sunday games during the season, but he made up for it during the playoffs.

Boston College struck first for a 7-0 lead, putting an early strain on Jimmy's nerves, but Stanford answered with two touchdowns to go ahead 14-7. Late in the second quarter an interception by Stanford was returned inside the Boston College ten. The result was another touchdown, putting Stanford ahead 21-7 at the half.

Jimmy was ecstatic. He completely forgot about losing his bet on last night's game since he doubled his bet for the game he was watching and Stanford's present lead easily covered the spread. Tempted to call his bookie and check on how his bets on the other games were doing, he resisted and remained with his wife for the halftime show. Susan expected him to go somewhere during the half as was his habit, so she was pleasantly surprised he chose to stay.

Boston College scored early in the third quarter and followed with another score later in the quarter to close the gap to 21-16. Jimmy's nervousness returned as he hoped for a Stanford rally. On the very next drive with the ball on their own 31-yard line, Stanford threw a short pass to their wide receiver. The receiver made the catch, broke a tackle, and scored on a touchdown as the crowd roared its approval. It was 28-16 with only one quarter remaining.

In the middle of the fourth period, Stanford scored on another pass play. This one was for fourteen yards, making the score 35-16. Jimmy could now breathe easier as the game was in hand.

The final score was 38-22 for Stanford. As the gun sounded Susan turned to her husband and hugged him tightly. She thoroughly enjoyed the game and was glad he thought to do this while their girls were away for the day.

As Jimmy steered his car through the maze of traffic to exit the game and head home, he thought about his other bets of the day. Noticing on the clock it was almost a quarter of five, he turned on the radio and tuned it to KCBS for the sports update at forty-five minutes past the hour.

Jimmy heard the short musical introduction to the sports segment which was followed by a summary of the major league baseball games played during the afternoon. Additionally, a few night games on the east coast were in the early innings, and Jimmy wondered why precious radio time was being wasted on those unimportant updates. After a brief commercial the announcer finally started to give the day's college football scores.

Florida won their game easily, as did Miami and Oklahoma. Nebraska won over Notre Dame, and Jimmy remembered his bet was on Notre Dame. Florida State won, and so did Texas. Jimmy couldn't remember if he bet on either of those games, and now the scores were coming a little faster than he could comprehend since he was busy with the fairly heavy traffic, too. He wished his betting sheet was available for reference.

"Jimmy! Watch out!" Susan screamed.

He quickly turned the steering wheel to the left while also stomping on the brake in his efforts to avoid another driver who was changing lanes. Out of the corner of his eye he saw the car in the lane to his left narrowly steer clear of him. Sensing the car behind getting close, he looked in his rearview mirror and saw he was almost hit, but the driver stopped in time.

"Man. That was close. Why doesn't that idiot pay more attention?" Jimmy breathed a sigh of relief. Then he stepped on the gas pedal and continued.

"South Carolina and Georgia are scoreless early, and rounding out the top twenty-five, it was Fresno State beating #23 Wisconsin, thirty-two to twenty. And there's your sports update." Jimmy heard the music indicating the conclusion of the sports segment and realized he missed most of the scores. It also registered with him his bet in the last game was on Wisconsin. Now another loss to go with the one on the Nebraska game. He hoped the scores of the games he missed were favorable as his excitement from the Stanford win was rapidly being extinguished.

Jimmy turned into the driveway and stopped the car. He grabbed the picnic basket and blanket from the back seat as Susan walked to the mailbox to retrieve the day's delivery. He unlocked the front door and waited for his wife to walk up the drive. He enjoyed watching her and hoped other men noticed her and were jealous.

When she arrived at the door she stopped and kissed him. "I had a wonderful time at the game today. Thank you for taking me. I love you, Jimmy." They kissed again and then walked inside.

"I want to check a few things before we go to dinner," Jimmy said as he made his way to the kitchen with the remains of the picnic.

"Okay. What time is our reservation?" Susan turned toward the stairs. "I'd like to fill the tub and enjoy a nice bath before we go."

"Seven. It will only take us fifteen or twenty minutes including parking, so we have over an hour. Take your time and enjoy your bath. I'll be in my office if you need me."

Jimmy sat the basket on the table and hurriedly made his way to his computer to check on his bets. As the college football scoreboard page loaded on his screen, he reached into his desk and retrieved his summary sheet. First he marked the Stanford game as a two-star win since it was twice his normal bet. Two winners against the loser from Friday night's game in the special category.

Turning his attention to the top ten category, Jimmy wrote a minus sign indicating a losing bet next to the Nebraska game against Notre Dame. He saw from his notes he did not bet on either of the Florida State or Texas games. There was no betting line on Florida State, and he chose to skip Texas since he wasn't expecting them to play well for a second straight week. He wondered if Texas was going to continue to play at the same level in subsequent games. The next game was seventh-ranked Tennessee at Arkansas, the one Charlie handicapped for him. Tennessee's defense dominated as the final was 13-3. Another lost bet. Eighth-ranked Oregon covered the spread at home against Utah, so a check indicating a winning bet was added to the sheet. It was offset by Washington's five-point win against Michigan. One winning bet and three losers in the top ten category. Too many games without betting lines he thought as he shook his head in disgust.

In the second category he only bet on the Fresno State game at Wisconsin. He knew it was a loser since he remembered hearing the score at the end of the sports update on the radio. This was now another category with an overall losing score for him.

The third category included the PAC-10 games. USC lost to Kansas State, who was ranked #11, but only by four points. Jimmy double checked the spread and realized he lost this bet even though his team won the game. Oregon State, ranked twelfth, beat New Mexico State in another close game. The winning margin was just five, which meant Oregon State won but did not cover, and Jimmy lost another bet. UCLA won easily, but they were on the road at Kansas so he did not bet on the Bruins. Cal got pounded for the second straight week, and another minus was added to the sheet. Washington State won easily on the road, and Jimmy realized he passed over another potential winner. Arizona State handled San Diego state easily, but Jimmy bet on Arizona instead. The Arizona game was a night game in Tucson, so the game was still to be played. No wins and three losses in this category with one game left.

Greatly subdued, he turned his attention to his last category, the SEC. Surely he could still pick the games from teams he followed all his life. The LSU game was still in the first half since it was a night game in Baton Rouge two time zones to the east. LSU was winning as he expected and hoped. South Carolina and Georgia were also still in the first half in a real tight game. He hoped Georgia's crowd could help the Bulldogs pull out the victory. Alabama only beat Vanderbilt by three points. Vanderbilt lost to Middle Tennessee State the previous week by nine points, and now they held 'Bama to twelve points and only lost by three. Another bet lost against the spread.

Kentucky won their game after their horrible showing a week ago against Louisville. How could they play so well this week after being so bad just seven days ago Jimmy wondered. The last game on the sheet was Ole Miss at Auburn, which Auburn won. Jimmy was now zero wins and three losses in this group with the two night games still being played.

What a disaster Jimmy thought. He resisted the urge to pound on the desk at his misfortune. How can Fresno State be playing so well while he is betting against them? How can Oregon State be playing so poorly while he is betting for them? Wisconsin cost him twice as they played well on the road in the first week and now badly at home in the second week. UNLV is the same. Cal must be horrible. Last week was 44-17 and this week was 44-16, with both games at home. He lost both weeks on Arkansas, and they played at home both times, too. Charlie will have to start getting better information if this keeps up he thought.

Jimmy closed his eyes and mentally counted how he stood for the week. Two up and one down in the special category. One up and three down in the top ten for a total of three and four. One loss in the other ranked category for a three and five total. Three losses in the PAC-10 with one game left, bringing the total to three and eight. Three more losses in the SEC with two games left. A grand total of three and eleven with three games to go. The best he could do was six and eleven, which would put him below even for the year. The worst was three and fourteen, which would be a real catastrophe.

"Jimmy! Are you showering before dinner?" Jimmy heard his wife coming down the stairs. He opened his eyes and swiftly stuck the betting summary sheet in his desk. "Are you going to take a shower before we go? It's almost six-thirty," Susan said as she walked into the room.

"Yeah. I was just checking on the scores we missed when that idiot almost caused us to have a wreck on the way home." Rising from his chair he kissed his wife on the cheek and headed for the stairs.

While in the shower Jimmy closed his eyes and thought about his horrible fortune from the day's football. His worst picks were in the PAC-10 and SEC conferences, and many of those were games where the winning team simply didn't cover the point spread. He clearly needed to do more homework on the spread. Next week he would pay more attention and make up for this week's bad performance.

Then he thought about all of his other money-making schemes. He smiled as the thoughts of his next maneuvers with Billy, Mickey, and Charlie passed through his head.

ELEVEN

Jimmy Donovan was sitting in his office eating a pastrami on rye with a side of potato salad. He stared at the maps in front of him without paying attention to any details. It was Wednesday, and he was still steaming over the betting results from last Saturday. Only one of the three night games went his way, bringing his final betting total to four wins and thirteen losses. Thankfully he doubled his bet on the Stanford game, or his monetary setback would have been twenty thousand instead of the eighteen he did lose.

On Monday he printed the point spreads for the upcoming weekend's games along with the new rankings for the week, but it was still buried deep in his office desk as he only gave it a cursory review before disgustedly stuffing it away. He debated instead of buying a dartboard and re-labeling it with the names of different teams. Anything random could do better than he did last week. Finished with his sandwich he wiped his mouth and took another drink from his cup of water. As he threw the wrapper in his trash he took a deep breath and turned toward his computer.

Two offers were received for his listed properties on Sunday. The offers were lower than the asking prices by about eight percent in one case and by over ten percent in the other. The date of occupancy was a sticking point in both situations, too. After a few counter offers went back and forth on Monday and Tuesday, he hoped each would result in a sales contract sometime today, but he wasn't completely confident it would happen. His strategy was to compromise more on the occupancy and less on the price, thus providing him with the maximum commission at the inconvenience of the sellers to move earlier than desired. On occasion he would recommend accepting a lower price, but he knew most buyers were emotionally attached at this stage and would pay more than their first offer.

As Jimmy thought more about how to reach a deal in these two cases, a new idea suddenly popped into his head. He found the phone number of the agents representing the buyers and dialed the first. His proposal was to offer additional assistance to complete items normally performed by them. He would do this for no additional commission, but in return the other agent would lower their commission by one-half of one percent. It amounted to three thousand dollars on a selling price of six hundred thousand dollars, which should be enough for the seller to accept the price contained in the latest counter offer. The agent requested something in writing, and Jimmy was more than happy to oblige.

Jimmy phoned the second agent with the same basic offer. This agent was not as receptive until Jimmy also agreed to reduce his commission, but his reduction was only one-quarter of one percent. Jimmy knew he would gain more than the quarter point by having control over some of the details, particularly the home and roof inspections, so he quickly agreed and moved forward.

Jimmy completed the drafts of the documents the other agents requested and handed them to his assistant for faxing as he walked out of his office with other papers in manila folders tucked under his arm. He intended to meet with each of his counterparts later in the afternoon to close the deals, but he first wanted to meet with both of his clients to gather more information.

Jimmy sat in his car and phoned his two clients. In both cases the wife was home and the husband was at work. He expected and wanted this, as he usually was able to coerce the women into providing him with a little more data. Each lady was a little suspect about meeting with him alone, but he convinced them nothing would be decided until they were able to talk with their husbands later in the evening while also reassuring them the paperwork requiring immediate review was generally more easily analyzed by the wife.

After completing the calls Jimmy started his car and rolled down the windows to enjoy the drive in his Audi TT. It was another cloudless day with the temperature close to eighty. A slight breeze ruffled the leaves of the trees, and he noticed some of the leaves were already beginning to turn shades of yellow and brown.

His first appointment was in Mountain View, and he quickly made his way down a less-traveled route to avoid traffic on other roads.

When he arrived at the McVey residence, Mrs. McVey was standing at her opened door waiting to welcome him. He grabbed one of the folders and smiled as he walked to the door.

"Hello there, Mrs. McVey," Jimmy greeted her. "Lovely day, isn't it?"

"Yes it is, Mr. Donovan," she replied.

"Please, Mrs. McVey, call me Jimmy," he said with a grin. Jimmy knew she was older than him by more than twelve years, and he just wasn't used to older women calling him Mr. Donovan.

"Okay, Jimmy. Please come in. We can sit at the kitchen table and chat."

As they walked through the front door and made their way to the kitchen, he thought about an earlier conversation with her. She told him she wanted to move back to the Midwest, and after years of discussions and outright pleading, she convinced her husband to get transferred back to the Midwest where they lived until fifteen years ago when they first moved to California. Why she wanted to move back was beyond him, but he'd seen it many times over the years.

"Your house sure is beautiful," Jimmy stated as they walked through the living room. "I know it's been an inconvenience keeping it so clean and showing it so often, but I feel we are getting near the end." The house was an older home, having been built twenty-seven years ago, but it seemed well maintained. The furniture was attractive, and the colors of the drapes accentuated the fabric covering the chairs and sofas. Jimmy knew this house showed well, but he also knew many shoppers for homes preferred much newer homes, independent of the condition.

Once seated at the table in the kitchen, Jimmy first placed a copy of the document he prepared earlier in front of Mrs. McVey. "This is a proposal I faxed to the agent representing the buyer around lunch. She and I discussed it over the phone prior to my drafting it, so she is in total agreement with it. She wanted it in writing to protect her client, as she should."

Jimmy explained he was offering a slight difference in the way activities normally get completed from the time of the sales contract to the actual closing. He would do some extra work, for free he emphasized, while the agent representing the buyer would take a slightly less commission. He knew it wasn't much, but it indicated

115

how much both realtors were willing to go the extra mile to help the buyer and seller come to terms. He also advised her to reconsider the occupancy date, as it was the item with the most leverage after the selling price.

Mrs. McVey was receptive to his presentation, and she boldly said she would try to convince her husband when he returned home from work. Jimmy pledged to meet with the other realtor later in the afternoon to help persuade them to offer a higher price for the concession on the occupancy date. He was hopeful it could get completely resolved by the next day at the latest.

The other item Jimmy wanted to review with Mrs. McVey was the disclosure document Mr. McVey and he completed and signed at the time of the listing. Everything was stated to be in normal working order other than a few minor details, and Jimmy wanted to make sure it was accurate. He confided in his client one additional sticking item of this deal was a concern on the part of the buyer regarding the age of the home.

He asked Mrs. McVey to think about anything in the house which didn't work completely correctly, however minor the problem or intermittent the operation. Seeing how hard he was trying to help her, while wanting desperately to sell the house, she proceeded to provide a list Jimmy could only hope for in his wildest dreams.

The oven temperature didn't regulate like she thought it should, as one of her loaves of homemade bread burned last week. The dishwasher didn't dry the dishes the way she remembered it drying them several years ago. Two of the eyes on the cook top didn't get as hot as quickly as before. Every so often the toilets would not stop running when flushed, and the handle had to be jiggled. The downstairs was colder last winter than in earlier years, and she suspected the heater didn't work as well as it used to. The exhaust fan in the kitchen ran a little slower on the high setting than she remembered, although she recognized it was just a feeling. The disposal made a funny sound at times, particularly when she put slices of tomatoes in it. When her husband walked around upstairs while she was downstairs, she could hear the floor creak slightly. On the days she showered immediately after her husband, the water wasn't as hot as she remembered it from before. She expected the water heater needed replacing. It also took longer for hot water to begin running out of the sink in the kitchen, further supporting her position. A few light switches in the house would stick a little from time to time, and she blamed the wiring although admitting she had no further justification. The timer for the automatic water sprinkler system seemed to work properly, yet the yard appeared to not get watered as much as was needed during their first extended vacation this past June. The garage door would not go all the way down every once in a while, and as a result it was left open one Friday evening while they were dining in San Francisco. Fortunately nothing appeared to be stolen when they returned.

Jimmy didn't make any notes while he listened to Mrs. McVey. He simply nodded and shrugged as he listened in amazement. When she finished, he couldn't muster the nerve to ask her if there was anything else. He assured her everything would be fine and told her not to worry about those items. He encouraged her to speak with her husband as he expected to be calling them around seven or eight that evening with the feedback he would have from his anticipated meeting with the buyer's realtor.

After being let out by Mrs. McVey, Jimmy returned to his car and quickly started the engine. After driving three blocks he pulled over to the side of the road. He snatched a blank piece of paper from a separate folder, grabbed a pen from his pocket, and wrote a detailed list of all of the items his client just stated may not be working in excellent condition. When he finished writing what he remembered, the page was full. A smile came to his face as he returned the car to a driving gear and headed to the Addison residence in Cupertino, once again amazed at how open and unassuming some wives were.

His meeting with Mrs. Addison was gratifyingly similar to the one with Mrs. McVey. She too was older than Jimmy, and she also was more desperate than her husband to sell their house. Jimmy easily won her over with his charm, and she agreed whole heartedly he was working in their best interests. She liked his proposed strategy of not giving up too much on the price while compromising on the occupancy date, as she mentioned saying the same thing to her husband the last few days. She was happy and knew her husband would be ecstatic with the concessions suggested by the realtors representing both sides.

Similar to the McVey house, the Addison home was twenty-three years old and well maintained. When asked about the working condition of all of the things in the house, her list was not as lengthy as Mrs. McVey's, but just as entertaining. It wasn't enough for Mrs. Addison to simply state the items. She made extravagant hand motions or mimicked the sounds to enhance her explanation. She even offered to give him a personal demonstration for a few things. Mrs. Addison was fixated on some of the screens being stuck in the windows, which prohibited them from cleaning every window prior to listing the home, as she mentioned this on three separate occasions. They no longer used the tub in the master bedroom since an occasional leak around the base of the water spout caused some water to accumulate and sometimes drip down the side of the tub and onto the floor. Her husband caulked it several weeks ago, but he instructed her not to use the tub. He was never much of a handyman, and she was certain he probably didn't fix it right anyway, so she avoided using it. She was tired of bathing in the guest bathroom, but it allowed her to get her way with her husband on other issues. All of the exhaust fans in the bathrooms made a funny noise when first turned on, but after achieving their normal speed they sounded fine. Jimmy wondered how women paid attention to these items, yet he heard them many times, including earlier when Mrs. McVey described her disposal.

Jimmy's departure from the Addison house found him in high spirits, as his plan from only hours ago was materializing quite well. If he could just get the other realtors to agree with the terms and convince their clients likewise, he could begin the next phase.

His afternoon was considerably hectic. After the meetings with Mrs. McVey and Mrs. Addison, he met with the realtors representing the two buyers. Both of those meetings lasted nearly an hour as multiple phone calls between the realtors and their clients were made in both cases. In each case the only remaining item to be settled was the date of occupancy, and Jimmy vowed to resolve the final issue by noon of the next day.

The phone call to the Addisons was relatively simple, as Mrs. Addison easily convinced her husband when he returned home from work. The agreement was for Jimmy to bring the paperwork by their house early the next morning for them to sign. Mr. Addison was quite gracious as he said he could work from home during the morning and drive to the office after lunch, and Jimmy expected Mr. Addison would use the morning hours to make arrangements with the moving company and take care of other personal business.

The phone call to the McVeys was quite the opposite, but Jimmy was used to dealing with emotional clients. In a way he preferred emotional people since he knew they didn't always think as quickly and clearly as they otherwise would, which provided him with more opportunity.

Jimmy was hanging up the phone after a long and unpleasant discussion with Mr. McVey. After listening an uncountable number of times to the same reason why they couldn't grant occupancy on the date the buyer was requesting, Jimmy's patience and persistence won out. Mr. McVey cursed him on three occasions during the call, but Jimmy did not retaliate. He simply stated how everyone, including the buyer and both realtors, was compromising in some form or fashion, and a deal would be agreed upon if Mr. McVey could find a way to move ten days earlier than he preferred. Finally Mr. McVey relented and told Jimmy to bring the paperwork by the house immediately before he changed his mind.

Jimmy looked at the clock in the corner of his computer screen and saw it was 8:17pm. He hurried to his car and figured he could phone his wife while he drove back to Mountain View.

Jimmy dialed his home number as he drove. He was disappointed he would be missing another dinner with his wife and girls, and he knew Susan would be upset he didn't called earlier. He listened as the phone rang four times, and finally the answering machine picked up. He shook his head in disgust as he knew Susan chose to disregard his call in her anger over him not calling sooner. As he awaited the beep he tried to calm himself so he could use his most polite tone.

"Hi, honey. It's me. I'm sorry I didn't make it for dinner. I've been busy all afternoon working to get those two deals closed I told you about the last few days. I thought I was going to be finished around seven and home by seven thirty, but I just listened to Mr. McVey go on and on for over an hour. Fortunately, I was able to convince him, but he demanded I bring the paperwork to him this evening for him to sign. So I'm on my way to Mountain View, and when I finish there I'll be home. I expect I'll be there by nine thirty or ten at the latest. I would appreciate it if you would leave me a plate of food I can heat up in the microwave. Thanks. I love you. Please tell the girls I'm sorry I missed dinner with them."

After meeting with the McVeys and getting all of the paperwork signed, Jimmy hurried home. It was ten minutes before ten as he pulled in the driveway, and only the light above the stove was on in the kitchen. The girls and their mother were somewhere upstairs, and he knew this signaled they didn't appreciate him missing another dinner without calling at a reasonable time. He felt they didn't appreciate how hard he worked or how he adjusted his plans to match the demands and schedules of his clients. Certainly they didn't translate efforts like his from today into money they spent everyday. He shook his head as he thought about how quickly Susan's feelings shifted. Just last Saturday she was so appreciative of him and loving toward him, and now she wouldn't even answer the phone when he called, greet him when he arrived home, or sit with him while he ate his dinner.

The next morning after acquiring the Addisons' signatures on the contract, Jimmy returned to his office. He was happy he was able to convince both clients to move earlier than they originally wanted, as they would be more occupied with moving than with the other items he was handling. He picked up his phone and dialed the number. The call was answered on the second ring.

"Billy! It's J.D.! How ya' doin'?" he yelled his normal greeting into the phone.

"Hi, Jimmy. What's up?" Billy replied as usual.

"Listen. I've got two clients needing home inspections. In both cases, the closing date is roughly three weeks away. Both homes are older, and I've got an inside list of things which may not be working quite right. I want you to complete the inspections a week from tomorrow, on Friday, and we'll deliver the reports to the clients the following Monday. There won't be adequate time before the closing to complete all of the work you'll suggest in your report, but I'll handle it. Things really needing to get fixed we'll get done, but the other stuff will just turn into money for us. I also think we'll be able to include some ventilation and roof items in these two cases. I'd like to meet with you next Thursday afternoon prior to the inspection to review these lists and finalize some specific plans. Can you make it at four o'clock next Thursday, and can you handle the inspections next Friday?"

"Sure, Jimmy. I'll juggle anything I need to. I'll also bring your portion of the money for the last few weeks of roof work. Will that be okay? Sorry I didn't bring it to you sooner."

"That'll be fine, Billy. See you next Thursday at four here at my office."

Jimmy pushed the hook switch to end the call with one hand as he kept the receiver in his other. He really liked Billy. The man was simple and genuine, and he could trust him to return to him as little as five dollars if it was owed. He was really happy Billy was the one who dyed his hair and made the withdrawals, as he knew he wouldn't be able to dye his own hair and hide it from Susan. Jimmy was also glad Billy was able to share in the profits, as he knew he was still hurting from his stock market investments while he was working hard on his roofing business but only turning a slim profit.

Jimmy lifted his hand and dialed Mickey's number next. His assistant answered the phone and transferred the call. After hearing several tones and clicks from Mickey's phone system, Jimmy was greeted by the familiar voice.

"Mick. It's J.D. Welcome back from your latest golfing trip. How was it?"

"Thanks. It was fun. I played fairly well, and the weather was nice."

"Tell me again where you were."

"I was in Oregon, at a course called Pumpkin Ridge. They played the U.S. Amateur there a handful of years ago, and I made my first trip there the next year. This was my second trip, and I'm thinking of going back more often, maybe every other year."

"So did you win or lose?" Jimmy asked as he was anxious to know how Mickey fared.

"Pretty close to even this trip. Clearly my best outing of the year. One of the guys I played with had three great days, and he was the big winner. I beat the other two guys, which made up for what I lost to the other one."

"Congratulations on not losing then. Any good restaurants?"

"Absolutely. There was this one place. They had a wonderful blackened catfish. It was as spicy as anything you'd find in the South.

And to top it off was a delicious dessert served in a tall glass. There was chocolate cake at the bottom, then a layer of chocolate fudge, then some chocolate mousse, and about half of a chocolate bar sticking out the top just in case you didn't get enough chocolate." Mickey took a breath as he thought back to the dish. "Wow! It was phenomenal."

"I'm sure it cost a pretty penny, too."

"Of course. As it should." They both laughed as the foreplay of the conversation came to an end. "So what's up?" Mickey asked.

"I've got contracts on two houses for real quick closings, in about three weeks. I represent the sellers, but the buyers' agents have both agreed to let me handle some things they normally take care of. As a result, you'll get to do the paperwork while Billy will perform the inspections."

"How'd you swing this from the seller's side?"

"All part of my charm my friend. I offered to go the extra mile if the other realtors would take a little smaller commission, all in our efforts to assist our clients in their efforts to close the gap on the price each had in mind."

"Wow," Mickey said in amazement. "That's pretty good. How come the closing dates are so soon?"

"That's the best part," Jimmy replied as he laughed. "The occupancy date was another sticking point in both of the negotiations. I convinced my clients to agree to give ownership sooner if the buyers would give more on the price. So my commission won't get reduced, and my sellers' heads will be spinning in their efforts to get all of their personal stuff in order."

"You're a genius, Jimmy. So what do I need to do first."

"I'll fax you a copy of the contracts when we get done. Do all of the normal title search and other stuff like always. But I want to meet with you and Billy next Thursday to discuss the inspections. You'll be even more amazed when you see what I gathered from the two wives."

"Okay, Jimmy. You've peaked my curiosity, but I'll let it wait until next Thursday, as I've got plenty of other things to keep me busy after having been away from here. What time next Thursday?"

"Four o'clock. We can have dinner afterward if you like. I think Susan and the girls have something planned, so I won't be missing another meal with them on account of business."

"I'll see you next Thursday. I'll let you know if I have any questions in the mean time after I get those contracts from you."

"See you then, Mick."

Jimmy once again hung up the phone by placing his finger on the hook switch while continuing to hold the receiver in his other hand. He lifted his finger and listened for the dial tone. When he heard it he dialed Charlie's direct line at the bank.

"This is Charlie. How can I help you?"

"Charlie. It's J.D. How ya' doin'?"

"Hi, J.D. I'm fine, thanks. What's up?"

"I'd like to meet with you early next week if you can make it. I've got a few new ideas I want to discuss."

"Let me check my calendar, J.D. Do you want to do it near the end of the work day, or would you prefer something at noon?" Charlie asked as he looked through his schedule.

"The end of the work day is better. Any day but Thursday works for me."

"How about Monday? We could go to a pub and have a few beers during the Monday night football game if you like."

"That sounds good. How about if we meet there around six thirty? Where do you suggest?"

The two finalized their meeting for the following Monday and said their goodbyes. As Charlie hung up the phone, he wondered what Jimmy had in mind now.

TWELVE

Jimmy Donovan noticed Charlie's Lexus as he hunted a parking space. There was an empty spot one aisle over, but the cars in the two adjacent locations were both parked slightly over their respective lines. Jimmy knew he couldn't fit his Cadillac in the tight spot and wished for a moment he was in his Audi. Then he saw a vehicle vacating a space much closer to the door, so he hurriedly steered his car in that direction. He easily parked as a handicap parking space was vacant next to him. Leaving several folders of paperwork on the front passenger seat, he got out and walked the short distance to the door of the pub.

Jimmy last visited this establishment a few months ago, but he was familiar with the seating arrangement and easily found Charlie sitting alone in a booth big enough for four people. A pitcher of beer, flanked by two mugs, proudly sat in the center of the wooden tabletop. The mug nearest Charlie was full minus either one big gulp or two smaller drinks, and Jimmy guessed it was the former. The other mug was empty but noticeably cold having clearly been out of the freezer no more than a few minutes.

"How ya' doin', Charlie," Jimmy greeted his friend in a much softer tone than he used when talking on his cell phone.

"Fine, J.D. Thanks," was the reply as Jimmy took a seat opposite Charlie.

"So what are we drinking?" Jimmy asked as he reached for the pitcher of beer displaying a light color, hoping it was Budweiser or at least some other domestic brew.

"It's your favorite," Charlie answered knowing it was an import masquerading as a domestic beer. He watched Jimmy pour a full glass and return the pitcher to the middle of the table. "I know what you like, and as a beneficiary of your brains and efforts, I figured the least I could do was buy you a pitcher of your favorite beer." Charlie raised his mug in a toasting fashion and took a drink. Jimmy, too, raised his glass toward his friend and proceeded to take a long drink.

Before Jimmy could comment about the beer, Charlie asked, "So what's on your mind, J.D.?"

"I wanted to talk more about electronic mortgage payments, or automatic payments, however you refer to them," Jimmy started.

"Before we get into that, there's something I need to know first." Charlie was bold with his interruption of Jimmy, but he couldn't concentrate on a new issue until his mind was cleared. The seriousness of his statement was stunning.

"What is it, Charlie?" Jimmy inquired being surprised Charlie asked him what was on his mind only to cut him short so abruptly.

"We had a call from a patron of our bank this afternoon complaining about their account balance not matching their statement. They claimed there was a withdrawal listed which they didn't make. We checked into it and found all of their withdrawals during August were in the branch where my office is, which is the bank branch where they normally do their banking. They claim the withdrawal for six thousand dollars on August 30th was one they didn't make. We haven't looked into it completely yet, since we only received the call late this afternoon, but I have to ask you. Is this one you, or we for that matter, are responsible for? I know I agreed I didn't want to know the details, and I still think it's better that way, but I thought you were going to avoid my bank in this scheme."

"Charlie. It wasn't me. I told you I would avoid your bank on the fraudulent withdrawals, and I have." Seeing Charlie was not totally convinced, he reiterated his statement. "You have to trust me. It wasn't me. You told me yourself this stuff happens all the time. And the withdrawals are always made at a different branch from where the account holder normally does their banking, to make sure one of the tellers or other employees doesn't recognize the person. Sounds to me like you need to beef up the security in your own bank, Charlie." Jimmy lifted his glass and took another drink.

"I believe you, J.D. I just needed to ask to be certain. I'm sure we'll find the person responsible from our video security." Charlie was satisfied with Jimmy's explanation, so he took the last swig of his beer. As he sat his empty mug down, he added, "It's just difficult being involved on one side as well as also being on the other side."

Jimmy finished his first glass and poured himself a second one. He also refilled Charlie's beer as he allowed some time for Charlie to get satisfied before he proceeded to his agenda. "I told you this would make your heart race, Charlie. That's why I love it so much. It's as emotionally demanding as it is intellectually challenging. You have to trust your instincts, and you have to trust the right people. That's why I chose you. I trust you, just as I have from the day you uttered the oath required to join Sigma Chi."

Jimmy raised his glass between the two of them. "Here's to Sigma Chi and all it stands for," Jimmy stated proudly. Charlie raised his glass until it touched Jimmy's, and they both took a long drink.

"So let's get back to mortgage payments, Charlie," Jimmy stated.

"Okay," Charlie replied as he nodded his head and adjusted his position in his seat. "What do you want to know?"

"Let's say someone has their mortgage paid each month by a bank draft. What is to keep someone who knows their account number and electronic username and password from logging in to the bank website, stopping the payment to its intended destination, and having it go instead to some other account? Why would it be any different than the person who actually owns the account making the change?"

"Well for starters, bank drafts can't be changed electronically, at least not in our bank, and I'm pretty sure it is universally true, but I could be wrong. There may be some banks who do it a little differently. But assuming the bank is like mine, you have to fill out some paperwork at the bank, and sign it, to initiate, terminate, or change a bank draft.

"Now electronic bill paying is different. Those transactions are handled in the fashion you describe. Someone can pay their mortgage either way, and we have customers who choose one versus the other for whatever reasons, but most do their mortgage using bank drafts if they want it done automatically. So, you'd have to find someone who has it set up as an electronic bill pay as opposed to a bank draft."

"Hmmm," Jimmy twisted his mouth as he digested this information. He grabbed his mug and took another drink to stimulate his thinking. "So what you're telling me is I can change bill paying directions electronically, but I have to change bank drafts in person at the bank."

"That's correct."

"And further, most mortgages done automatically use bank drafts, not bill paying."

"Yes."

Jimmy took another drink as he let this sink in. Charlie also took a drink from his glass.

"You realize, J.D., to redirect a payment to another account, the other account has to exist, which provides a trail. Plus, don't forget the mortgage company's account won't get credited with the payment, which will get flagged along with all of the other missed payments for the month. When a payment is late by more than the allowed time period, usually fifteen days, the mortgage company notifies the person or party responsible."

"Yeah, I realize what you're saying. But I've done some experiments with electronic transfers and I'm convinced there's a way to do what I'm suggesting. Let me ask you this. When the notice is sent by the mortgage company the first month a payment is missed, is it always done by mail, or is a phone call sometimes made."

"Almost always by mail, certainly in the environment of this area. Now if you were asking me about how my bank in Little Rock did it, we usually just told the person the next time we saw them in the bank. Typically, they simply forgot to send us the payment. They were generally so embarrassed by it they didn't forget again, or at least not for a long time." Charlie laughed as he thought back to some of the times he remembered this happening during his high school and college years long ago. He was constantly amazed at how much things changed since then.

Jimmy continued to listen carefully while thinking about how to make his idea work. He filled his glass again and offered the remaining contents of the pitcher to Charlie. Charlie nodded, and the pitcher was emptied. One of the diminutive waiters of Mexican descent noticed and walked toward them as the two watched him approach.

"Another pitcher of Heineken, gentlemen," the young man said.

Jimmy's head turned quickly to his friend. Charlie simply shrugged his shoulders. "I thought you said this was Budweiser, you ol' dog," Jimmy said in an accusatory tone.

"I never said it was Bud. What I said was it was your favorite. Here's to your new favorite beer, J.D.," Charlie laughed as he raised his glass for a toast.

"Real funny," Jimmy replied as he raised his glass and began to laugh as well. "Yeah, bring us another pitcher. But be sure to charge it to this guy."

"Coming right up," the waiter said with a grin as he grabbed the glass pitcher and walked toward the bar to fetch another.

The two continued to discuss how mortgage payments could be sent to the wrong or right account, depending upon the perspective. Charlie's suggestion was to create only one account for receipt of the payments in an effort to limit the exposure. He further advocated using someone else's identity for the account, including their real address, as opposed to setting up a new company with a post office box address or using a false address. He knew a bank would check the address of the account holder while setting up the account and easily identify a mismatch. He also expected the best implementation was to redirect multiple mortgage payments to this one new account on the first day of a given month, and then close out the account before the payment becomes late.

Jimmy agreed with the merits of this plan, but he wanted to get more than a single month's payment for his efforts. His point was no one would know their payment went to the wrong account if two things were done. First, their statement needed to show a payment of the correct amount to an account with a name closely matching the name they were used to. Second, they didn't receive the notice from the mortgage company stating a payment was late.

Jimmy's proposal was to take care of the first item if Charlie would take care of the second. Charlie now realized Jimmy wanted him to effectively steal from his own bank. Astounded at how persistent and ruthless Jimmy was, while remembering his large debt and not wanting his wife to discover it, Charlie agreed he would insure notices of late mortgage payments would not get mailed for three accounts for the first two missed payments. Jimmy agreed to the limitations knowing he would have nine missed payments to divide between everyone who would play a part.

After the two left the bar and were driving home, Charlie was amazed at what he just agreed to do. He wondered if part of his willingness was a result of all of the beer he consumed. He was already beginning to regret what he did. Jimmy was happy as he drove home. He continued to think of how to make this work for bank drafts, but he wasn't sure Billy could handle performing the job of completing the necessary paperwork.

Billy arrived at Jimmy's office building a few minutes before four o'clock on Thursday afternoon. Jimmy greeted him at the door and quickly led him to his office. "Have a seat, Billy," he said as he motioned with one hand to a couple of chairs in front of his desk located under a map of Santa Clara county. He closed the door and proceeded to take his normal seat behind his desk.

"So what's up, Jimmy?" Billy asked anxiously.

"I wanted to review my thoughts with you regarding the home inspections scheduled for tomorrow. We have a unique opportunity to make a nifty sum if we do this right, as this is the first time I've had Mick doing the closing when I did not represent the buyer. By the way, I asked Mick to drive up from Monterey to meet with us, as I thought it would be best for the three of us to make sure we're in sync on this. He should be here any minute. He must have run into some traffic somewhere. Anyway, let's cover some of the details and he can catch up when he gets here.

"Now, even though what we'll be doing won't be much different from anything we've done before, I think we just need to be a little more careful to make sure we don't have any problems. As you know the first one is the McVey house in Mountain View. The second one is the Addison house in Cupertino. Both homes are older homes, and when I completed the disclosure for each, I did it with the two husbands. In both cases only one or two minor items were listed as not working completely correctly. I suspected they weren't being totally honest with me, but their houses are maintained well, so they don't show their age like some houses do.

"Now last week when I was working to get the buyers and sellers to agree on the terms of the deals, I met with the two wives. And as I expected, their views were quite different from their husbands. Based upon my past experiences, I don't think they would have provided me with as many details as they did if their spouses were present, but it doesn't matter much since I got what I usually only dream for.

Billy continued to listen carefully without interrupting as Jimmy kept going.

"Here is a list of what Mrs. McVey told me was suspect in terms of everything in the house working properly." Jimmy handed Billy a typed list which was more organized than the quick notes he made after his conversation with Mrs. McVey. "Quite a laundry list for a home inspector to have prior to the inspection, wouldn't you say?"

Billy was amazed as he looked at the list. Oven temperature, dishwasher drying, two eyes on the cook top, toilets running, heater, kitchen exhaust fan, disposal, floor creaking, water temperature in shower and sink, light switches in garage and by back door, water sprinkler timer, and garage door were all included.

"And here's a similar list from Mrs. Addison," Jimmy continued as he handed him a second list.

"Hey. There's Mick," Jimmy said as he jumped from his chair and hurried to greet his expected visitor.

"Mick. How ya' doin'?" Jimmy said as he smiled broadly and extended his hand.

"Fine, Jimmy. Sorry I'm late. There was an accident on north 101 down near Morgan Hill. So even though I was going opposite the commute direction, our side was slower than the other one for about three miles. Reminded me of some of those days when I was attending law school and made the drive regularly."

"At least you don't fight it every day like we do. Come on in. I was just getting started with Billy."

Jimmy led Mickey into his office. Billy stood and offered his hand as he said, "Hi, Mickey."

"Hi, Billy. How are you?" Mickey replied.

"Doin' fine."

"How's the roofing business?"

"Okay, but a little slow. I've been working on a deal with a production builder who's going to start developing about two hundred acres near East Ridge Mall in the foothills. Right now he tells me I'm his number one choice for doing the bulk of the roofs for him. He wants to give one person seventy percent of the business while giving two others fifteen percent each. His thinking is to give one a bigger portion to control his costs, while giving some of the pie to two others as a backup. It's going to take another month or so for him to decide, but it would be a huge boost to my business."

"What's going to be the deciding factor?" Jimmy interrupted.

"I think he'll pick the one he expects can get the job done right and on time. I've heard of a few cases where this builder got held up significantly because the roofer didn't do his job, so I think he's worried more about that part of it than anything else. Price will also be a concern, but I think he'll be willing to pay a little more to avoid any problems."

"Well good luck, Billy," Mickey offered. "I hope you get it."

"Yeah, me too," Jimmy chimed in as he made a mental note of this new information which could change Billy's financial standing.

Then Jimmy turned his attention back to the matter at hand. "Mick, Billy and I were just going over some of the details of the home inspections he will be completing tomorrow for the two closings the first week of October. In each case the wife verbally listed several items which the husband failed to disclose to me when we completed the form prior to the listing. I don't want to cause the husbands any problems for maybe not being completely honest, but I will use it as a threat if I run into any problems with them.

"My plan is for Billy's inspection reports to the sellers to indicate every one of these items requires repair. But I want the buyers to get reports stating everything is fine. Since the closings are so soon, we won't have time to fix everything. I'll suggest to the sellers we go ahead with the closings by withholding some funds for fixing all of these things, and I'll take care of coordinating everything since they were so nice in agreeing to move earlier than they would have preferred. I won't have to do any convincing of the buyers and their agents since their reports will say everything is fine. I also won't have to spend any effort coordinating any repairs, only getting false invoices generated.

"Now on these lists, Billy, I want you make two additional notes. For the Addison home you should be able to take the bathroom exhaust fan item and turn it into some ventilation and minor roof repair work.

"For the McVey house I want you to suggest a completely new roof. The house is twenty-seven years old, and the roof is eighteen years old. The McVeys have been in the house fifteen years. The former owner put a new one on before the first one was worn out, for who knows why."

"The house may need a new roof in five or seven years anyway, Jimmy," Billy stated matter of factly.

"I'll let the new owners deal with it when the time comes. Mr. McVey was as rude as any client I've dealt with in the past few years, and I think he deserves to pay for a new roof."

The three continued to discuss the details of the timing and paperwork necessary to complete this grand scheme. It was half past six when everyone was satisfied with the plan and understood the specifics of their role. It would all start tomorrow, shortly after lunch, when Billy planned to pull into the Addison driveway.

After Billy left, Jimmy and Mickey decided to have dinner in Santa Clara at a quiet Italian restaurant. Arriving shortly after seven, the parking lot was sparsely populated as the full evening crowd was yet to arrive. Once seated the business discussion was postponed as they studied the menu and wine list. Having a craving for some spicy pasta, Mickey chose the penne pasta and sausage covered with a cream sauce. Jimmy opted for the veal marsala with garlic mashed potatoes and mixed vegetables. After much debate the two finally agreed on a Sonoma County zinfandel.

"Billy seemed really excited about the possibility of landing the roofing job in the new development," Mickey started as he reached for a bread stick. "How's his business doin', Jimmy."

"It's okay, but he really needs something like that to give it a good boost."

"He must or he wouldn't be willing to generate all of these false items in his inspection reports. Do you think there's any chance he may not want to keep working with us if his business improves?"

"No," Jimmy stated firmly. "He's never been one to save his money, and he's got a lot of debts from his stock market activities. Trust me, Mick, Billy's tremendously thankful for the opportunities provided him for making some extra money. He's helped me on a few other things, so he'll keep helping us on the home and roof inspections.

"I hope you're right."

"I am, Mick. I'm a lot closer to Billy than you are since he lives so much closer than you do. He's just a very loyal person to those

132

who are nice to him. But let's talk about the banking business for a while."

"What's there to talk about."

"You know all of those experiments we've done with bank transfers. Well I've finally got Charlie Bates to agree to work with us."

"You're kidding," Mickey said with astonishment. As he looked at his friend's face he could see the familiar Jimmy Donovan smile indicating he wasn't kidding, just satisfied with being able to do the unexpected. Jimmy noticed the waitress walking toward them with a tray containing their main dishes, so he continued to let what he said sink in.

"This really looks good," Jimmy commented to the waitress as steam rose from the plate placed in front of him. She placed the bowl of pasta before Mickey as he continued to stare at Jimmy.

"Please enjoy," she said as she picked up the bottle and poured more wine into each of the two glasses. "And please let me know if there is anything else I can get for you."

"Thank you," Jimmy said as he watched her walk away.

Before picking up his fork, Mickey leaned forward and said, "I can't believe it, Jimmy. I never thought you'd be able to convince Charlie to join us. What motivation does he have? He's got to be making plenty of money with his vice president position at the bank. Shucks, in salary alone he's got to be in six figures. And I'm sure he's got a boatload of stock options. He and his wife don't have kids, so he doesn't have some of those expenses like I do." Mickey stopped abruptly and just looked at Jimmy. He saw an expression of contentment from having conquered something believed to be unconquerable. He shook his head for a few moments and then grabbed his fork and took his first bite.

The two ate and drank with a vigor fueled by thoughts of how they would profit having a trusted fraternity brother who was a banker helping them. "This pasta is delicious, Jimmy."

"I'm glad it is. My veal is outstanding. It's amazing how tender they get it. Susan tried to cook veal on one or two occasions, and I thought I was eating my front tire. Now whenever she suggests we eat out, I pay a little less attention to the price since I know what the alternative might be."

"So what has Charlie agreed to do?"

"Well," Jimmy started as he put his fork down. "First he's provided advice and helped develop a plan which only requires you and me to execute. And then second he's agreed to keep some missed mortgage payment notices from being mailed for a few months."

"And what do we have to pay him for the advice portion?" Mickey asked with a tone hinting his disapproval.

"I've agreed to split everything evenly. We'll all get one-third."

"That's not fair, Jimmy," Mickey said loud enough for several others in the restaurant to hear. Leaning forward and lowering his voice he added, "He gets the same as you and me when all he does is provide a little advice." Mickey couldn't believe what he was hearing.

"Now Mick. Take it easy." Jimmy tried to calm his friend so others in the restaurant wouldn't notice. "His advice is valuable. Without his input we would've done something stupid. So my view is his advice is worth every penny. Plus, he'll feel indebted to us, which will help in the times when we need his outright assistance."

Jimmy's look was worth more than his words. Mickey could see Jimmy truly felt this was the best way to proceed. "Okay, Jimmy. Whatever you think. I trust you know what you're doing."

Jimmy raised his glass and said, "Here's to the Sigma Chi banking business." Mickey smiled as he raised his glass and lightly touched it to Jimmy's. After finishing what remained in his glass, Jimmy asked, "Do you want another bottle of wine or an after-dinner drink?"

"No. I've got the long drive to Monterey in front of me, and I've got more work to catch up on tomorrow. I'm still buried from my last golfing trip, and these two closings are coming up real soon. Have Billy fax me copies of his reports over the weekend so I'll have them first thing Monday morning."

THIRTEEN

The official arrival of fall came on Friday, September 21st, and it was announced with another summer-like day with temperatures in the lower eighties, a cloudless sky, low humidity, and only a slight breeze. Days like this reminded Billy Wicks how fortunate he was to have a job allowing him to be outside for a portion of the day. Although he enjoyed his previous job as a purchasing agent and was thankful for the learning it provided along with the many construction contacts, he despised having to watch beautiful days through a window.

Days like this also reminded Billy of how much he loved the fall of the year growing up. The summer in Mississippi was so hot and humid, and he now often wondered how he worked outside on his dad's farm as a teenage boy in the heat. Certainly he was much tougher in his youth than he was now in his mid-forties, but he still couldn't imagine spending eight or ten hours working outside when the temperature was close to the century mark and the humidity was above ninety percent. The winter in Mississippi was a constant transition from relatively warm days with temperatures in the fifties and sometimes sixties to cold spells with temperatures barely making it above freezing. The winter in Mississippi was certainly better than other places farther north, but he still preferred the California winter. The spring and fall seasons of the year in Mississippi both had moderate temperatures, yet the pollen from the trees in the spring, mainly from the many tall pines adjacent to his family's land, were a constant bother to Billy and others who suffered from different allergies.

Billy arrived at the Addison residence at ten minutes after one o'clock. He called earlier in the morning to confirm the appointment, and Mrs. Addison said she was expecting him shortly after lunch. When she further stated her husband was required to attend some meetings at work and would not be available other than by telephone, Billy phoned Jimmy, and the decision was to let Billy handle this without Jimmy's presence to avoid any suspicion on Mr. or Mrs. Addison's behalf. The agent representing the buyer was going to try to attend for at least a portion of the time, but he wasn't sure he would be able, given other conflicts in his schedule. This calmed Billy since he felt he could adequately handle any questions or concerns Mrs. Addison might have.

Billy grabbed a clipboard from the passenger side of the bench seat in his pickup truck. The floor resembled a trashcan, as fast food bags and soda cups, old portfolio reports, and empty tobacco pouches lay on top of the pile. He shook his head at his untidiness and could hear in his mind the comments both Jimmy and his mother would be making. Jimmy would call it a mess at first, and then continue with more profound descriptions in his teasing fashion. His mother would say it was the worst looking pig sty she'd ever seen, and unlike many mothers who used similar references, his could actually be considered somewhat of an expert, having lived on a farm all her life.

Billy knocked on the door to announce his arrival. When he previously completed the roof inspection prior to the listing of the house, neither Mrs. Addison nor her husband were home, and Billy was thankful now. Mrs. Addison greeted him warmly as she was clearly happy to see someone responsible for anything related to the sale of their home and their move to another part of the country.

Billy indicated he would start on the outside and knock again when he was ready to check the inside. He did however want her to open the garage door to provide him access. He told her not to be alarmed if she heard his footsteps or other noises on the roof, as there were things he needed to check even though a satisfactory roof inspection was already performed. He also indicated he would be operating the garage door.

Being left alone to perform his inspection of the exterior, Billy first checked the topography, making sure downspouts were present and drainage seemed sufficient. The landscaping was colorful from the many flowers located along the borders of the sidewalk, driveway, and walkway. The trees were tall, and he guessed they were planted around the time the house was built. The lawn was freshly mowed, and he knew the Addisons heeded Jimmy's advice to have it cut each week on Friday morning during the duration of the listing. From the green appearance of the grass, he expected the automatic sprinkler system worked properly, but he planned to check it manually when he was in the garage. The fence along the two sides and back of the property looked new from a recent painting. Billy could tell a few boards were replaced prior to the painting, providing further evidence of the Addisons' efforts to show their older home in the best light possible.

Billy continued his scrutiny of the exterior by checking the condition of the moldings, trims, eaves, and overhangs. Except for a wall of stone surrounding the garage and some wood facing which covered the remainder of the front of the house, the exterior was mostly a tan colored stucco. Many of the houses in this neighborhood were similar, and Billy wondered if he should expand or change his business from roofing to stucco exteriors. Realizing he knew far less about this part of the building, he let the idea pass quickly.

He retrieved an extendable ladder from the top of his truck to show the appearance of checking the roof, even though he checked this roof personally a few months ago without finding any problems. He still wasn't sure how they were going to successfully translate the bathroom exhaust problem Jimmy learned about from Mrs. Addison into ventilation and minor roofing repair work, but Jimmy assured him not to worry.

Billy spent little time on the roof as he only wanted Mrs. Addison to hear him doing a thorough job, and he hoped her hearing was adequate. Once down from the roof, he checked the lower level windows and noticed some of the screens were indeed stuck. The pattern seemed to be the ones receiving the bulk of the sun were problems while those in the shade were fine. Not wanting to waste his time climbing up and down his ladder too many times, he concluded the second level screens would follow the same pattern.

After returning his ladder Billy walked inside the garage. He pushed a button thinking it would lower the door, but nothing happened. He pushed it a second time, but there was still no activity. Two more quick depressions were still not successful. Then he was startled when the door behind him opened.

Realizing she scared him momentarily, Mrs. Addison said in a soft tone, "Did I frighten you, Mr. Riggs?"

"Excuse me," he replied not recognizing the false name he gave her previously to hide his identity. He could feel his legs shaking at the knees. "Oh! Yes. As a matter of fact you did," he said now realizing she was addressing him.

"Well I heard you ring the doorbell the first time, but I couldn't make it to this door until you rang it two or three more times."

"Oh! I'm sorry, Mrs. Addison," Billy said as he comprehended his error. "I thought this button operated the garage door." He felt himself take a breath, but it seemed unnatural.

"Oh no. This one is the doorbell. I don't know why they put one here, as no one ever comes to this door and rings the doorbell. But it's here nonetheless. The garage door button is the big one here," she said as she pointed on the other side of the door.

"Thank you, Mrs. Addison. Thanks for your help.," Billy said sheepishly. "I need to check a few more items here in the garage and then I'll be ready for the inside. I'll just ring the doorbell here when I'm ready, since I now know what each one of these buttons does."

"I'll leave you alone then. Please let me know if you need anything. I'll just be inside." Mrs. Addison smiled at him and then turned and walked away. Billy felt stupid for not being able to tell the difference between the buttons, and he could feel his anxiety level was much higher than when he first arrived. Based upon what Jimmy told him about Mr. McVey, he only hoped the rest of the day passed quickly and without incident.

Getting back to his business at hand, Billy punched the garage door button and watched the door slowly lower itself to the ground. Another touch raised it. As it was lowering a second time, he quickly walked to the laser beam eye and tripped it to make sure the door stopped its descent. After a few more experiments he was satisfied the door was working properly.

Billy walked to another wall inside the garage to a small box. He unlatched the door and saw the many controls associated with the automatic sprinkler system. This one was different from most of the ones he was familiar with, but he operated a similar one just a week or so ago. He flipped a switch from the auto setting to the manual setting and then turned all six of the other switches to their on position. He heard water start to run and walked to the yard to see if the sprinkler heads were spraying in an acceptable fashion. Not seeing any problems, he opened the door of his truck and retrieved a screwdriver.

Billy returned to the garage and turned the sprinkler system off, also moving the main switch back to the automatic setting. He walked to another wall where the circuit panel was located. He opened it and saw all of the switches properly labeled. He undid a few screws to provide a view of the wiring. Everything looked fine, as none of the insulation on any of the wires was worn, so he screwed the cover back on.

Billy checked the water heater located in the corner of the garage. There was only a single strap, and the current California law required double strapping to keep it from falling in case of an earthquake. He knew this was a commonly required repair for older homes, so he made certain to bring two strapping kits with him. Confident he could make this simple repair in about ten minutes, he made a note to offer to Mrs. Addison to fix it himself if she wanted.

Billy made one more trip to his truck for a small can of lubricant and a rag before gaining access to the interior. He walked to the front door and gave it several raps with his knuckles. The door was oak with a light finish, like many other homes on this street. There was no window, only a peephole for viewing from the inside.

As Billy waited for the door to be answered, he put his ear to the door to listen for some movement from within. Not hearing anything, he continued to wait. After a few more moments he reached to knock again. As he swung his clenched fist forward, his target moved as the door was being opened. Not expecting this he partially lost his balance, which startled Mrs. Addison.

"Mr. Riggs!" she exclaimed. "You scared me." She put her hand to her chest in an effort to quiet her heart. "I thought it was you when I came to open the door, but I certainly didn't expect to see a fist come swinging in my direction. I thought you were going to ring the doorbell in the garage."

Feeling awkward Billy tried to explain. "Well, I went to my truck to get a few things for the inside, so I was closer to the front door and I just came here instead. You see, I always find squeaky doors, and I use this to fix it. I'm careful to wipe up any excess with this rag," he said as he showed her the can and dirty cloth he was holding in addition to his clipboard. "Most homeowners appreciate the extra effort even though it's the new owner who benefits, but I'm not sure the new owners even appreciate it's been done."

"That's awfully nice of you Mr. Riggs. I sure hope someone like you is looking out for us when we purchase our new home."

"I hope so, too. Here, let me check this one." Billy grabbed the handle and moved the door slowly from completely open to almost shut as he looked away and leaned his head to position his ear for better listening. After slowly returning the door to its fully open position and not hearing a sound, he repeated the closing and opening at a faster speed. "This one is fine," he announced as he turned his attention to the second door which was anchored at the top and bottom since it was not normally used.

Releasing the door to allow it to open, Billy once again moved the door slowly on the first cycle and quickly on a second cycle. A squeak was heard, so he placed the clipboard on the floor and removed the cap from his can. A few quick sprays to the hinges at the top and the bottom satisfied him, so he repeated the opening and closing. The squeak was gone, and he wiped the door and its frame in the vicinity of the hinges to clean them of the lubricant.

"That was nifty," Mrs. Addison stated. "You probably could handle a lot of things my husband has attempted over the years. I wish I'd known you all of these years. You'll have to leave me a business card so I can give your name to all of my friends whose husbands are as handy as mine."

"Thank you for the compliment, but it's nothing really. I'm certain your husband could do this as easily as me."

"Oh, you'd be surprised. I'll let you finish your inspection. If you need me I'll be in the kitchen preparing a dessert." Hesitating to return to her kitchen, she inquired, "Do you like cherry cobbler, Mr. Riggs?"

"Very much so, especially if it's warm."

"And with a big scoop of ice cream, I'm sure," she interrupted him.

"Oh, yes ma'am," he replied.

Hearing a drawl to his words, she asked, "Do I detect a bit of a southern accent, Mr. Riggs?"

"Yes, ma'am. I was born and raised in Mississippi, but I've lived here for more than twenty years now. I guess some things you never lose."

"I guess so," she agreed. "Well, I wish I could give you some of this cobbler, but it most likely won't be done until after you're gone, and I'm making it to take to a home for battered women. They probably wouldn't appreciate it too much if I took it with a few servings missing."

"I guess not," Billy replied as he began to have a craving for the dessert she described.

"Well, as I said, I'll be in the kitchen if you need me."

Billy checked the walls, the floor, the baseboards, the windows, and the ceiling. He detected no cracks, and he could tell the walls were recently painted. The hardwood floor was a little worn in the normal traffic areas, but not nearly as bad as many others he inspected which were this old. He expected the house was carpeted originally, and at some point the Addisons must have changed it.

Seeing the steps to the upstairs, Billy decided to check the second level first and leave the kitchen and other downstairs rooms for last. He checked the two secondary bedrooms and bonus room, finding nothing wrong. When he turned on the exhaust fan in the guest bath, he did hear a strange noise as it first started, but the sound did not persist once it reached its full speed. This was an item Jimmy mentioned to him, and Billy expected he may not have even noticed it if he wasn't paying particular attention. There was plenty of water pressure even with the shower on, the sink on, and the toilet being flushed. Hot water was available after a short wait, so Billy made the appropriate notes on his form.

The master suite was fine except for a similar noise with the fan in the bathroom. After turning on the faucets in both sinks and the shower, and also flushing the toilet, he twisted the handle to begin to fill the tub. Jimmy's list indicated there may be a small leak around the base of the water spout, but it was working fine now. Leaving the tub running, Billy turned the shower and sink faucets off. Looking back at the tub he now noticed a few beads of water forming where an amateur caulking job was previously performed. He pulled slightly at a loose piece of caulk and a long strand easily lifted from the surface. Now more water was leaking, and he knew no amount of caulking

141

could solve the problem. This was a needed repair requiring a plumber's services.

Returning down the stairs he checked the dining room, fourth bedroom, family room, and laundry room. Finding no problems he entered the kitchen and saw Mrs. Addison working a crossword puzzle at the table. He could smell the cherry cobbler baking in the oven, reminding him again of the insufficiency of his lunch.

"Just a few more things to check here in the kitchen, and I'll be done," he said to her.

"Let me ask you something, Mr. Riggs. Have you ever heard the term or phrase 'Yella Fella', similar to 'yellow fellow', only with the letter A at the end of each word instead of the letters O-W?"

"Yeah. That's what we called someone in the South who was afraid, or chicken as we called it. We called them yellow. Why?"

"Well this puzzle sure has some funny things in it. One of the answers was jelly belly, another was chick flick, and based on the letters in the other direction, I think this one is yella fella. There's one here I think is piggle wiggle, but I can't get the E's at the end to work."

"Is the clue something like a southern grocery?" Billy asked.

"Yes. Southern market. It's forty-three across."

"It's probably Piggly Wiggly then, with Y's at the end. That's the name of a grocery in the South, maybe only in Mississippi."

"That's it!" she exclaimed. "Now this other answer makes more sense. My, you are more useful than my husband for a lot of things," she said as she quickly erased the incorrect letters.

"I don't know, Mrs. Addison. I'm sure he's pretty good with a lot things," he said to reassure her as he walked near the sink. "I'll need to run part of a cycle on your dishwasher. Are the dishes in here clean or dirty?"

"They're dirty. Do you want me to put in some soap?"

"No. I'm only going to run it for a minute to make sure the water gets hot and it drains properly." Billy latched the dishwasher door and touched the start button. He stepped to the cook top and turned the four electric burners on high. Twisting around he punched in ten seconds on the microwave and hit start. He knew the oven was working as he could smell the cobbler, so he twisted back around and placed his hands less than an inch above the burners. All four were beginning to heat, so he flipped them off. He turned off the dishwasher, and as he opened the door, steam rose toward the ceiling indicating it was fine.

"I'm finished with my inspection, Mrs. Addison. There's a few things I need to mention to you. I'll have the final report done early next week, but I want you to be aware of some problems I found." Billy took a deep breath as he prepared to deliver the bad news. He looked at his notes as he spoke. "I noticed several screens were stuck in the windows. It seems all which face the sun during the day have a problem. I'm sorry to say those will need replacing. I also heard a strange noise when the exhaust fans in the bathrooms were first turned on. Those will need to be checked by someone who is more of an expert than me. There's also a leak around the base of the water spout in the tub in the master bath, and I'm pretty sure a plumber will need to check it to fix it."

Billy stopped and looked up to see her reaction. She was unfazed as she looked him squarely in the eyes. "Oh, and one other thing," Billy started again. "Your water heater needs to be double strapped. It's a relatively new California law, and most homes similar to yours in age have to be upgraded. I have a strapping kit in my truck since I anticipated yours might need fixing. I'll be glad to spend the ten minutes or so it will take to do the work if you'd like."

"That would be awfully nice of you, Mr. Riggs. Please. Fix whatever is needed on the water heater. Can you add it to your bill for the inspection, or do I need to pay you separately?"

"I'll just charge you for the kit, and I'll add it to the bill, so you won't have to pay me anything today."

"Well, thank you, Mr. Riggs. Let me know when you're finished. I've got a surprise for you."

Not knowing how to respond to her comment, Billy walked to his truck to get the strapping kit and the few tools required. The job took only slightly longer than ten minutes as no significant problems were encountered, and Billy rang the doorbell in the garage when he was finished.

Mrs. Addison opened the door and unveiled a serving of the cherry cobbler, topped with ice cream, in a small tin pan. "Here, Mr. Riggs. I had a little left over from my mix, so I made some for you. You can come in and eat it if you'd like."

"Thanks, Mrs. Addison. But I do have another appointment this afternoon, and I better get to it or I'll be real late getting finished."

"Wait here then," she said as she handed him the serving and hurried away. She quickly returned with a plastic spoon and a few paper towels. "Here. Use these. You can eat it in your truck on your way."

"Thank you, ma'am. This sure is nice of you. Like I said, you'll get my full report early next week. Your realtor, Mr. Donovan, will be in touch to schedule the necessary repair work. Thanks again."

Billy turned and walked to his truck. He glanced at his watch and saw it was half past three. He wasn't sure he could drive and eat the cobbler at the same time, but he was certainly going to try.

As he took his last bite, Billy threw the tin and plastic spoon on the floor of the passenger side of his truck. He reached for his phone and called Jimmy.

"Billy! Where are you!?" Jimmy shouted without any greeting.

"I'm on my way," Billy blurted as he tried to finish swallowing his last bite.

"What are you eating!?" Jimmy shouted as he could tell Billy was talking with his mouth full. "Did you stop and get a snack!? Is that why you're late!?"

Billy paused as he swallowed the last bit. "No, Jimmy. You'll never believe it. Mrs. Addison was baking a cherry cobbler, and she gave me some."

"Well was it hot, and did it have a big scoop of ice cream?" Jimmy asked sarcastically as if he was talking to a five-year old.

"As a matter of fact, it was and it did. It was really good. And she was a really nice lady."

"Don't get too friendly with the clients, Billy. Just do your job. How much longer is it going to take you to get here?"

"About ten more minutes. Where are you?"

"I'm waiting outside the McVey house, and the buyer's agent is waiting here, too. We expected you around three or three fifteen. Shucks, Billy, it'll be four o'clock when you get here. Mr. McVey won't be too happy about this. He specifically left his office early to meet us here at three, and now we've made him wait for an hour."

"Sorry, Jimmy. I'll be there as soon as I can." Billy hung up and felt his anxiety rising as he prepared for the inspection of the McVey home, knowing a large audience was awaiting him.

FOURTEEN

Billy arrived at the McVey house minutes before four o'clock. The house was on the left side of the road, and Jimmy was standing by his parked car on the right side. Another lady wearing sunglasses was standing outside of a parked car on the left, one house beyond the McVey residence. Billy figured she was the McVey's realtor and couldn't remember if Jimmy told him their realtor was a woman. He turned his truck into the driveway, parked, and took a deep breath in an effort to calm himself.

Billy reached across the seat and grabbed a clipboard from several in the pile. He read the name at the top and realized it was the wrong one. Looking at two more he was still unable to locate the one he needed. When the driver side door opened unexpectedly behind him, he jumped and hit his left elbow on the steering wheel.

"Billy," Jimmy shouted in a whispered tone. "Act like you don't know me real well and shake my hand," he continued softly as he extended his hand toward Billy.

Slowly extending his hand, Billy asked, "What's up, Jimmy?"

Shaking his hand, Jimmy replied, "As we discussed last night, we need to act like we don't know each other real well." Noticing the lady walking toward Billy's truck, Jimmy quickly said, "Listen. Start on the inside instead of the outside, and be sure to take a long time and do a thorough job."

"But I usually start on the outside," Billy pleaded.

"Just do what I say." Jimmy was still whispering.

Releasing Billy's hand, Jimmy took two steps back from the door. Turning to the lady now standing a few feet behind him he said in his normal tone, "Hello, Ms. Rasmussen. This is Mr. Riggs."

"Hello, Mr. Riggs. I'm Jamie Rasmussen," she greeted Billy as she extended her hand. Billy noticed she was a much younger woman, probably not even thirty years old, but quite attractive, particularly in her short skirt.

"Hi, Ms. Rasmussen," Billy returned the greeting as he shook her hand even though he always felt uncomfortable shaking a woman's hand, as he never knew how firm a grip he should use. "I'm sorry to keep you waiting. My last inspection took a little longer than I expected."

"Does your truck always smell like fruit pie?" she asked.

"No," Billy said slowly, being a little confused.

"Well, when I walked up I thought I smelled some kind of berry pie," she explained.

"Oh. Actually, I did just have some cherry cobbler. I guess I must be used to it and can't smell it anymore." Billy was amazed at her keen sense of smell, and it made him worry more about their plan. "Let me grab a few things, and then I can get started."

Billy finally found the clipboard with the paperwork he needed, and he grabbed the other items necessary for inspecting the inside. He walked to the front door where Jimmy, Ms. Rasmussen, and a man and a woman he expected were Mr. and Mrs. McVey were waiting on him. "Mr. and Mrs. McVey, this is Mr. Riggs," Jimmy said.

"Hi, Mr. McVey," Billy said as he offered his hand. "I'm sorry I'm late. I got tied up at my last inspection."

"How long is this going to take?" Mr. McVey asked coldly.

"It depends," Billy replied.

"On what?" Mr. McVey quickly snapped back.

"It probably depends on what he finds," Jimmy interrupted to help his friend combat the obvious aggressiveness. "If things are fine, I'm sure it will take less time than if he finds some problems. Isn't that right, Mr. Riggs?" Jimmy said as he put his hand on Billy's shoulder. Not waiting for an answer, Jimmy added, "Why don't you go ahead and get started? I want to discuss a few things with Ms. Rasmussen while you do your thing. We'll check in with you after a while to see how things are going." Turning to Jamie, Jimmy said, "Why don't we leave them be for a while and talk out here since it is such a nice day?"

Taking his cue, Billy said, "I thought I would start on the inside. Excuse me." He stepped between Mr. and Mrs. McVey, and seeing the kitchen in the back of the house, he walked toward it as the couple followed closely behind.

Still outside the front door, Jimmy's counterpart stated firmly, "Whatever you want to discuss, Mr. Donovan, make it quick. I like to do some of my own checking of a property my clients are buying, and I have another appointment which I need to leave for at no later than five fifteen."

"I understand. This won't take long. I just wanted to reiterate how much I appreciate your willingness, and the willingness of your clients, to work with me and the McVeys to get this deal done. I know we're not done yet, but so far it has been a pleasure working with you. I just wish all of the other agents I have to deal with were as easy to work with as you have been. Thank you."

Being taken off guard by his kind words, she wished her previous tone was not so harsh. "Thank you for the compliment," she responded.

"Well, I was also wondering if you would consider changing companies and coming to work for me. I don't know how long you've been with your present company or if you've thought recently about making a change, but I'd like you to give it some serious consideration."

"Wow. You're just full of surprises. I certainly didn't expect to get a job offer this afternoon."

"I'll tell you," Jimmy started and then paused. "Two of the agents working for me now used to work for other firms. I hired them under similar circumstances, and now they're the best two agents I have." Jimmy knew this wasn't true, but he wanted to drag out this conversation as long as possible to give Billy more time to complete his inspection of the kitchen. "In both cases, they're happier working for me than they were at their former employer, at least that's what they tell me on a regular basis."

"Thanks for the offer, but I'm really happy in my present situation, though I do have to say I'm flattered by the offer. Thanks again for the kind words. Maybe some time in the future." Pausing for a moment to make sure he understood her sincerity, she added softly, "Why don't we go inside and see how they're doing?" She turned and started walking to find the others. Jimmy let her go first but quickly followed not wanting to leave Billy alone without any help.

When Jimmy entered the kitchen he saw Billy opening the dishwasher. Mr. McVey was standing less than five feet away with his arms folded across his chest and a sour look on his face. As steam rose from the open door, Mr. McVey firmly stated, "See, I told you it was fine. What do you think we do around here? Eat with dirty dishes. Of course the water gets hot enough to clean the dishes."

Turning to Mrs. McVey who was seated at the table and clearly dissatisfied by her husband's behavior, Billy said, "Mrs. McVey, I'm not going to take the time to run a full cycle, so I'll just ask you. Are your dishes dry when the dishwasher finishes its cycle?"

"Of course they are!" Mr. McVey quickly interrupted, obviously disturbed by what he was witnessing.

Jimmy was looking directly at Mrs. McVey, and she happened to turn and notice him. Jimmy's expression communicated to her to go ahead and answer Billy's question, so she turned to Billy and said, "There are times, Mr. Riggs, when I have to dry a few things by hand even after the drying cycle is complete."

"But nothing out of the ordinary I would imagine," Jimmy inserted a helpful comment with a tilt of his head, a shrug of his shoulders, and the raising of his spread hands with his palms turned upward as if to indicate it was normal to have to dry a few items when the dishwasher finished.

"It's probably fine," Ms. Rasmussen joined the discussion. "I have to dry a few dishes at my house, too, and my dishwasher is brand new. I'm sure if you've been using it regularly and haven't experienced any problems, it'll be fine."

"Good," Mr. McVey stated firmly, indicating he thought this was a waste of time.

"Shucks," Ms. Rasmussen started. "I can't ever remember a home inspector turning on the dishwasher to make sure the water was hot enough." Turning to Billy she added, "Are you always this thorough, Mr. Riggs?"

"Yes, ma'am," Billy replied as he made a few checkmarks on his top sheet. "I thought everyone was," he added as he turned to one of the pages near the bottom on his clipboard and reviewed the list Jimmy gave him. He crossed off the dishwasher item as well as the oven temperature entry, but added a checkmark by the cooktop, the disposal, and the exhaust fan. The next item was the toilets, so he made his way to the half bath located adjacent to the kitchen.

Mr. McVey began to follow Billy, but Jimmy stepped in his path and held up his hand. "Mr. McVey," Jimmy began in a comforting tone, "I'm sure Mr. Riggs can do his job without us watching his every step. He's done this many times. I do recognize it's quite nerve wracking for you to have someone come into your home and turn every switch and knob to try and find things wrong when you are used to how everything works, but it's required. Mr. Riggs works independently, so he's not here in favor of the buyer or the seller. Part of my job is to help interpret his report, which we will receive early next week, and work with Ms. Rasmussen to determine what needs repairing or replacing and what doesn't. There are a few items I need to discuss with you anyway while I'm here today, so why don't we just sit down here at the table and talk about those things?"

Ms. Rasmussen took the silent hint to leave Jimmy with his clients, so she walked in the same direction as Billy. She stopped in the hallway and saw Billy had the lid of the tank to the toilet removed as he watched the inner workings of the toilet. He flushed it once, and he watched the tank fill properly. He pushed the handle down a second time for a repeat.

"My, Mr. Riggs," she said from the hallway. "You are very thorough. Most people only flush it once, and they don't bother to lift the tank lid to watch."

"Well if it works properly only part of the time, you may not be able to detect a problem if you flush it just once, so I got in the habit long ago of flushing twice to make sure. You'd be surprised the number of times I've seen one work on the first try but not on the second, so you can rest assured if my report says they work, they really do work."

"I believe you," she said with a small laugh. "You've convinced me. I'm still going to check a few things on my own if you don't mind. I like to form my own impression of things for comparing to your report. By the way, when do you expect to have your report completed?"

"I'm not sure. It should be on Monday or Tuesday. Wednesday at the very latest I would expect." Billy knew the report would be done by the end of the day on Saturday, as he and Jimmy already planned on meeting tomorrow afternoon. Their plans were to watch the PAC-10 football game while finalizing the two inspection reports. He didn't commit to a specific day though since he wasn't sure when Jimmy wanted to deliver it to her.

Satisfied his inspection would be adequate and uncover more than she could hope to find in twice the time, she added, "Thank you, Mr. Riggs. I'm going to check a few things in the garage and around the outside of the house before I go. I don't know if Mr. Donovan told you or not, but I've got another appointment this evening, and I need to leave by five fifteen. I don't expect you'll be finished by then, so instead of getting an update when you're finished here, I'll get the details from your report. I'll be looking for it sometime next week then."

"Okay, Ms. Rasmussen. It was a pleasure meeting you."

"My pleasure, too. Do you have a business card, in case I need to get in touch with you?"

"Uh, not with me. I have one in my truck if you'd like to wait for me to get one."

"Oh, don't bother. I'm sure Mr. Donovan has your number. I'll call him if something comes up. I'll let you get back to your inspection. Thanks again."

"You're welcome," Billy said as he watched her walk down the short hallway and through the door to the garage, glad the encounter was over. Convinced the downstairs half bathroom was fine, Billy checked his notes and walked through the kitchen on his way to the downstairs bedroom.

"Everything fine in there, Mr. Riggs?" Mr. McVey interrupted his wife as Billy passed.

"Yes, sir. No problems there, sir," Billy answered as he kept walking.

"Good," Mr. McVey said, as he turned his attention back to his wife and Jimmy. "Now, where were we?"

"I was telling Mr. Donovan our schedule for the packers and movers," Mrs. McVey said as she tried to scold her husband with her tone and expression. "Now as I was saying, Mr. Donovan, I mean Jimmy." She stopped again and glared at her husband. "The packers will be here on Sunday and Monday, the 30th and the 1st, which is only nine days from now. The moving van is supposed to be here on the 2nd, Tuesday. We won't be leaving until Thursday, the 4th, so we'd like everything to get closed then, before we leave."

Jimmy pondered for a moment before he spoke. "So to close on the 4th, we'll probably have to get the paperwork signed next Friday, and that will be difficult. I'll have to lean on the escrow agent pretty hard, but I'll talk to him over the weekend and have an answer by Monday."

"We're bending over backwards to get our stuff in order so we can provide occupancy to the buyers when they requested. For what we're paying you, you better get the escrow agent to perform," Mr. McVey demanded.

Jimmy kept his calm as he explained. "Mr. McVey, we'll get it done. I'll have a much clearer picture on Monday after I've had the weekend to get some things done, and I'll contact you then with an update. The only problem I can foresee is if something comes up from the inspection which requires some time to get it fixed or replaced."

"Isn't there something we can do if something does come up?" Mrs. McVey asked, hopeful other options were available.

"Actually, there is. In some closings we estimate how much money is required to fix items from the home inspection. Then in the closing we take some of the money from your side of the statement and put it into escrow for paying to the different parties who do the repair work. Once everything is fixed and everyone is paid, the money remaining is distributed back to you. We have to be a little conservative with the amount or the buyers and their realtor won't agree to it, but I anticipate Ms. Rasmussen and her clients will be willing to work with us. They showed their ability to compromise to get us this far, so I expect we can work something out."

"Well that will certainly help," Mr. McVey stated, softening his tone slightly.

Seeing they were satisfied for now, Jimmy excused himself to check on the inspection. Mr. McVey began to rise so he could follow, but his wife's scowl made him reconsider, and he sat back down. Jimmy looked at his watch and saw it was shortly after five o'clock. Remembering Ms. Rasmussen would be leaving soon, he changed his course and headed outside to find her.

Jimmy walked out the front door and noticed her car was still parked in front of the neighbor's house, but he didn't see her. He walked around the right side of the house where the garage was located, but didn't find her there either. As he returned to the front, Jamie came walking around the left corner of the house, looking carefully at the details of the home.

"Hello again, Ms. Rasmussen," Jimmy said to her as he walked toward her. "Is there anything you've found we should inform Mr. Riggs about?"

"Nothing. Everything seems fine, although I certainly am not an expert at this. As I mentioned before, Mr. Riggs seems very thorough. I'm sure if there is a problem, he'll find it and put it in his report."

"He does seem to be quite complete, doesn't he?" Jimmy agreed. "And isn't it amazing how well the McVeys have maintained their home?"

"Yes, they have done a fine job. It was one thing which really appealed to my clients about this property. I showed them several other older homes, as they particularly like the architecture from years ago, even though the utilization of the interior space is not as efficient as it is with newer homes. Many homes we looked at were not well kept or were not presented as well as this one. You must have done an excellent job in counseling your clients. Congratulations."

"Thank you. You know my offer from earlier never expires. If you ever want to work with me, please call me."

"Thanks again, Mr. Donovan," she replied, "but I don't expect to change my mind anytime soon." Reaching into her handbag she grabbed her keys and said, "I must be going to make it to my next appointment on time. Let's talk next week when we get the inspection report." She began to walk to her car.

"Will do. If everything is alright, we'll be able to get the paperwork signed next Friday and be closed by the middle of the following week."

"That's what we're counting on," she said over her shoulder.

Jimmy watched her walk to her car and get in. She quickly started the engine and began to drive away. Jimmy waved but she didn't notice as she was looking in her rearview mirror to make sure her hair was still in place. Jimmy was satisfied she was convinced nothing was wrong with the house, so he turned and walked back inside to find Billy.

Jimmy saw the McVeys still seated at the kitchen table. There was no conversation between them, and from the look on their faces Jimmy could only conclude Mrs. McVey told her husband in no uncertain terms to behave. Undaunted, Jimmy said, "I talked with the other agent before she departed for another appointment. She assures me they will be ready to sign the paperwork next Friday so we can close the following week as planned." Getting no response, he continued, "I was looking for Mr. Riggs. Do you know if he is still inside somewhere?"

Mrs. McVey responded. "I think he's in the garage."

"Thanks," Jimmy said as he began to walk down the hallway. "I'll see how he's doin' and how much longer this will take." As he opened the door, he saw Billy and heard the garage door closing.

As Jimmy approached Billy, they watched the door jerk slowly to its closed position. Billy pushed the button again, and the door began to rise. "Any problems with the door?" Jimmy asked.

"Not yet, but I want to run it through three or four cycles to be sure," Billy replied.

"Good," Jimmy said as he winked at Billy. "The other agent has gone, so we don't have to worry about her anymore. She was very satisfied with the condition of the house and your thoroughness. I'm sure she won't question the inspection report she receives. And from the looks of Mr. and Mrs. McVey in the kitchen just now, I expect Mrs. McVey will be a big help in handling him when I give them the bad news of all the things requiring repair. I'm going to go back inside and keep them occupied until you get finished. Be sure to make some noise on the roof so we know you're checking it."

Jimmy walked back to the kitchen and found the McVeys still sitting silently. With some effort Jimmy was able to engage them in a discussion about their plans for buying a house at their new location, which improved the mood significantly. Meanwhile Billy was busy going through his normal inspection checklist as well as the special list Jimmy prepared.

Billy didn't find the garage door to stick on its way down on any of the cycles, but it did jerk as opposed to operating smoothly. He knew it could be fixed with a simple greasing of the springs, which most people didn't do on a regular basis. The circuit panel was satisfactory, although several of the wires contained portions of electrical tape. The water heater was within a few years of the end of its lifetime, and it showed normal wear, but Billy noticed a relatively new valve, so he made a note indicating the water heater was probably recently serviced.

Getting near the end of his inspection, Billy retrieved his ladder and did his check of the gutters and downspouts. He additionally walked on the roof and banged on the top of the chimney, knowing the occupants below would be able to hear him.

"What's he checking now?" Mr. McVey asked in an accusatory tone when he heard the noise. "We already had a roof inspection performed prior to the listing. He doesn't have to inspect something that's already been inspected, does he?" He looked at Jimmy for an answer.

"Actually, Mr. McVey, home inspectors routinely check many things which are checked during a roof inspection, just not in the same manner of detail." He paused briefly before continuing. "However, I was looking back at my notes for this listing earlier today, and we did not have a roof inspection performed previously." Jimmy knew this was a lie, as Billy completed the roof inspection. Jimmy knew the report was in his files, but he never provided a copy to his clients.

Mr. McVey adjusted his sitting position as he stared at his realtor. Jimmy persisted with his sincere tone. "As you know, a roof inspection only has to be done prior to the closing, not before the listing. In most cases I have it done as part of the listing, and I thought I ordered one in this case. But when I checked this morning, I didn't have a report. I checked to see if I paid for one, as normally I would pay for it, and then it would be billed to you as part of the closing settlement. But, I couldn't find anything."

Seeing in Mr. McVey's face some anger about to erupt, Jimmy calmly continued. "So I went ahead and called a roofing company today and scheduled the roof inspection for next Monday. Since I was remiss in taking care of this, I'll pay for the inspection out of my pocket."

"I can't believe this!" Mr. McVey shouted as he got up out of his chair. "I remember you specifically telling us the roof inspection was completed, and everything was fine. Don't you remember, or did I just imagine the whole thing?"

"I'm sorry, Mr. McVey. If I said that, then I misspoke. As I said, I thought I ordered it, but I don't have a report or a bill. Once again, I'm sorry. That's why I figured the least I could do was pay for it when it's completed next Monday."

Mr. McVey was clearly exasperated, but he noticed his wife staring at him with a look of disapproval, so he waited to speak. Mrs. McVey then said, "Honey, I'm sure Mr. Donovan is doing the best he can. He's already made arrangements to get it done on Monday, and he's going to pay for it out of his pocket. What else do you want him to do?"

"I wanted him to get it done when he said he was going to," he snapped at his wife.

The three of them were silent for a few moments as each debated what was appropriate to say. Finally, Mr. McVey said, "Okay. Just get the inspection done on Monday, and thanks for offering to pay for it."

"You're welcome. And once again, I'm sorry for the confusion, and I'm sorry I failed to get it done sooner."

"It's alright," Mr. McVey said, accepting the apology being offered. "Let's just get everything done so we can get moved and get on with our life."

Jimmy didn't smile outwardly, but he knew he scored another victory, so he said, "Why don't we go out and see if Mr. Riggs is almost finished, and then we can all enjoy the rest of our evening." Jimmy turned and walked toward the door as Mr. McVey followed. Mrs. McVey remained at the kitchen table as she stared out the back window.

Billy was tying down his ladder as it appeared he was finished. "Mr. Riggs!" Jimmy shouted across the yard. "How much longer?" Jimmy continued to walk toward Billy as Mr. McVey followed.

"Actually, I'm done," Billy said to both as they approached. "I was just about to come inside and let you know."

Knowing Mr. McVey would prefer a verbal summary now but not wanting to provide it, Jimmy quickly asked another question. "Do you expect you'll have your report completed by Monday or Tuesday of next week? You know we're trying to get closed quickly, so any extra effort to get us the report as soon as possible would be greatly appreciated."

Looking at Mr. McVey and then back at Jimmy, Billy said, "I expect I'll have it done by Wednesday, but I'll see what I can do about getting it done earlier. I have some others to finish up, including the one from earlier today."

"Can't you put this one at the top of your priority list?" Jimmy pleaded. "After all, we waited for over an hour for you to arrive today, and now it's already after six. Could you please try to get it done for us by Monday or Tuesday?"

"You're right. You did have to wait on me, so I promise I'll have it done by first thing Tuesday morning. I'll even drop it by your office to make sure you get it."

"Thank you," Jimmy said. "That will be fine. Thanks again for your help, Mr. Riggs." Jimmy extended his hand.

"My pleasure," Billy replied as he shook Jimmy's hand. Turning to Mr. McVey, he said, "It was a pleasure meeting you, sir. Good luck with your move."

"Thank you, Mr. Riggs," Mr. McVey said as he watched Billy get in his truck.

Jimmy turned to his client and chatted briefly regarding the arrangements for the roof inspection on Monday morning and other details before departing. As he drove back to his office he felt good about the day's events. He was anxious to meet with Billy the next afternoon so the two could prepare the inspection reports and fax them to Mickey. Jimmy also wanted to have a nice dinner with his wife and girls and then turn his attention to tomorrow's college football games, hoping he could pick more winners than losers this week.

FIFTEEN

"How can they let a guy come right up the middle and block a punt without even blocking him!?" Jimmy shouted at the television. "You and I could block better than those guys!" Jimmy and Billy were sitting on Billy's couch this Saturday afternoon watching Ohio State and UCLA while they worked. Ohio State just blocked a UCLA punt and recovered it in the end zone for a touchdown. The extra point was missed, so UCLA still led 7-6 in the second quarter, but Jimmy was upset since his bet was on the twelfth-ranked Bruins and a win by a single point would not cover the spread against the twenty-first ranked Buckeyes.

"You sure let these games bother you a lot, Jimmy," Billy commented as he drank the last ounce of his beer and stood to fetch another. "Would you like another beer?"

"Yeah, sure," Jimmy answered as he shook his head in disgust. His betting day was not off to a good start. North Carolina unexpectedly pounded Florida State in Tallahassee 41-3 earlier in the day, while both Clemson and Notre Dame lost at home to unranked opponents. Once again Charlie's inside information proved wrong as Arkansas lost at Alabama by twenty one points. In addition Jimmy lost his bet on the Thursday night game two days ago.

He did have one winner on the day so far, with Florida winning. Texas and Fresno State were winning easily late in their respective games even though both were playing on the road. The scores from other PAC-10 games in progress were displayed at the bottom of the TV screen, and Jimmy was happy to see Washington State, Stanford, and Arizona leading. If those games remained as they were he would finish close to even if not slightly ahead for the weekend.

Jimmy drank the remaining contents of his beer as Billy returned with two more. They were finished with the Addison home inspection report, having prepared one for the Addisons and another for the buyer. The one for Jimmy's clients indicated multiple window screens required replacing, the exhaust fans in the bathrooms needed to be replaced, the exhaust path from the fans to the roof needed to be checked, and the master tub would have to be checked by a licensed plumber. The report Jimmy would provide to the agent representing the buyers only contained the master tub item, and Jimmy was disappointed he would have to call a plumber and schedule the work, while not being able to garner any profit from this item.

The two also rewrote the roof inspection report Billy prepared for the Addison home a few months ago when Jimmy listed the house. Billy's fears about his former roof report were easily put to rest when Jimmy informed him the report was never provided to the Addisons. Jimmy kept the report to himself and simply informed his clients the roof inspection was done and was fairly normal. In the updated report a few notes were added indicating the exhaust ducts protruding from the roof seemed a little loose, pointing toward a possible minor problem with the exhaust path.

Jimmy's intent was to talk with the Addisons regarding these items on Tuesday. He would tell them he already contacted a licensed repairman to work in conjunction with Valley Roofing to fix whatever was necessary inside the house and on the roof to eliminate whatever the problem really was. A further part of his plan was to tell them the work could not be completed until the week after the closing, but he already contacted the agent representing the buyers and they were agreeable to having money set aside in the closing for taking care of this.

Jimmy and Billy now focused on the McVey house. They reviewed Billy's notes on the list of items Jimmy discovered from Mrs. McVey. The oven temperature, dishwasher drying, floor creaking, water temperature in the shower and sink, and water sprinkler timer were all crossed off.

"Why did you cross off the floor creaking item?" Jimmy asked. "Didn't you hear anything while you walked around upstairs?"

"Sure, I heard a few creaks, but that's normal. I don't think we can recommend they tear down the house and rebuild it to try and fix it. We'd never get away with it. Every house has a few creaks, especially if it's as old as their home."

"Well let's be sure to make a note in the report, even if it doesn't require any work. The more items in the report where something is mentioned which doesn't have to be fixed will help me in my negotiations with Mr. McVey."

"Okay," Billy said as he wrote a note on the list.

"And on the water sprinkler timer item, make another note saying only the manual operation was checked."

Billy made another notation, and the two then turned their attention to all of the items containing checkmarks. The game was for Billy to propose possible problems and solutions with recommend amounts for the repair, while Jimmy judged the validity of each. In some cases they swapped roles.

The heater was an easy item. Billy used an infrared device for measuring the temperature of the incoming and outgoing air, but he never knew a home owner to have the same capability, unless they did home inspections or worked for a company installing and repairing furnaces. The measurements at the McVey house were fine, but a simple change of the numbers would indicate a problem. The proposed fix was to replace the rods, which did routinely wear out more quickly than other components, at a cost of one hundred dollars per rod for all four rods. Jimmy determined the McVeys would not be able to check the heater themselves, so the numbers were changed as needed.

The garage door was deemed to be another easy item since Billy could fix it himself while it was possible to bill the McVeys for the materials and labor to replace the springs and tracks. They agreed to put in the report a recommendation for a garage door company to perform an additional check. Jimmy would attempt to schedule the appointment for after the closing. If the McVeys went along with it, Jimmy would simply have Mickey generate an invoice for payment to a company which happened to be in Billy's name, without any work being done. If Mr. McVey insisted on having it checked before the closing, Jimmy would take care of it by having one of Billy's employees make the service call and provide the necessary lubricant, with a smaller bill still being paid to the same company.

Another item listed as requiring repair was the circuit panel. Billy and Jimmy knew most people were fearful of opening the box and messing with the wires, so they expected Mr. McVey would readily accept a licensed electrician coming to fix a problem if the report stated too much electrical tape was present to be considered safe.

Even though Billy did not find a toilet with any difficulty, they stated two had problems. They additionally agreed to list concerns about the disposal, the kitchen exhaust fan, and two eyes on the cook top. Each item would be a negotiating point for Jimmy in dealing with Mr. McVey, although Jimmy expected Mr. McVey wouldn't be worrying too much about these lower cost items once any discussions regarding the roof began.

Jimmy and Billy decided to indicate the roof as nearing the end of its lifetime and showing unusual wear in some locations. Billy had notes as to where the shingles were slightly discolored or cracked, and having these locations identified by the home inspector would set the stage for a more damaging report from the roof expert.

Once the list of potential problems was exhausted, Billy asked, "So what should we indicate is wrong in the inspection report you are going to give to the buyers?"

"Nothing," Jimmy firmly stated. "Everything works reasonably well, and if something breaks soon after they move in, they'll be covered by the home warranty."

"What about their agent? Do we know if she found anything?"

"You know, the real beauty of this whole deal is Jamie Rasmussen."

"She sure is a good looker," Billy agreed.

"Yeah, but that's not what I meant," Jimmy started to laugh. "She was completely snowed by your thoroughness," Jimmy continued to laugh and talk at the same time. "Particularly the dishwasher drying bit."

"I was pretty convincing, wasn't I?" Billy said as he began to laugh, too.

"And then you went on with your toilet flushing business." Tears were beginning to form in Jimmy's eyes as he was now laughing uncontrollably. He had to pause every few words as he said, "I only wish she could have been in the kitchen when you began banging on the chimney." Billy now had tears running down his face, too, as the two fraternity brothers rolled on their sides and grabbed at their stomachs in their amusement.

Several minutes passed without any more conversation as the two tried to compose themselves. They found it difficult as every time either would try to look at the other and speak, they both would begin to laugh again. Finally, the laughter subsided and they continued drinking beer as they watched the football game.

UCLA shut out Ohio State in the second half, and on the strength of two field goals, won the game 13-6. It was an excellent defensive performance as UCLA overcame four lost fumbles to win and cover the spread. Jimmy won his bet on this game and the Arizona game, and Washington State and Stanford were also winning by wide margins late in the fourth quarter. It would be four wins and no losses for Jimmy in the PAC-10 games today, putting him ahead by one bet with only a single night game between Auburn and Syracuse remaining.

The events of the day left Jimmy in a good mood as he left Billy's house and headed home to take his family out for a nice dinner at his favorite Mexican restaurant. Billy needed to put the reports in their final form, but he would deliver them to Jimmy at ten o'clock the next morning for faxing to Mickey. The remainder of Jimmy's day on Sunday would be spent completing his usual research at several homes which just listed. Billy's agenda for Sunday was to prepare one of his employees to complete a roof inspection of the McVey house scheduled for Monday.

Even though it was nearing the end of September, Monday morning ushered in another beautiful day. Temperatures were expected to reach ninety. It wouldn't be an all-time high, as temperatures rose to more than one hundred in September almost ten years ago, but it was hotter than most days in the middle of summer. At half past nine in the morning, a truck displaying the name Valley Roofing pulled in the driveway of the McVey house.

The employee Billy counseled on Sunday got out of the truck and rang the doorbell. Mrs. McVey greeted him, and he explained he would be completing the roof inspection which was ordered by the realtor. He wouldn't require access to the inside of the home, but he wanted her to know he would be the one making some noise on the roof and around the outside of the house. He expected it would take about an hour, and he planned to leave when he was finished without bothering her again. When she asked how long it would take to receive the report, he told her it would be ready the next day, as he was told it needed to be done promptly. He quickly excused himself to get to the job at hand while not wanting to engage in a long conversation, consistent with Billy's advice.

Untying the ladder from the top of the truck, he leaned it against one of the gutters and gained access to the roof. Having limited experience as he had only been with Billy on two other occasions to inspect a roof, he tried to pay careful attention to the checklist his boss prepared for him. He first drew a top view of the roof. Unhappy with his result, he started with a second blank sheet. After three tries he was finally satisfied it was reasonably accurate. As he checked the condition of the roofing material, his legs were beginning to hurt, and he remembered Billy told him to draft the top view of the roof from the ground so he wouldn't have to stand on the roof in an awkward position for as long.

He continued his inspection, and as he neared the end he stopped to look at his watch. Almost two hours had passed, and he knew he needed to finish quickly and hurry back to the office so Billy wouldn't think he was loafing. In his haste to get to the ladder he stumbled and almost lost his balance. His clipboard flew out of his hands as he tried to stay erect, and out of the corner of his eye he saw it sail over the fence and land in the neighbor's yard. Happy he didn't fall, but disappointed his notes were temporarily lost, he carefully climbed down the ladder and breathed a sigh of relief when his feet finally touched the ground.

He put the ladder back on the top of the truck and walked to the fence to see about his notes. His head was slightly lower than the top of the fence, so he placed his hands on the fence and tried to pull himself up. Getting a splinter in each hand he let go and uttered some profanity. As he tended to his hands he was frightened when a loud bark came from just on the other side of the fence.

"Be quiet, Sheba!" came a woman's voice from the back of the neighboring yard, but the barking continued. "What is it, girl?" the same voice asked.

Finding a small gap in the fence, he said, "Ma'am. Ma'am. Excuse me, ma'am." The dog let out another load bark.

"Hush, Sheba," she said to her dog. "Mr. McVey? Is that you?"

"No, ma'am. It's the roof inspector," he replied.

"Who?"

"The roof inspector. I just finished inspecting the roof, but I dropped my notes over the fence. Could you be kind enough to get them and hand them to me?"

"Oh. I see them. Here, let me get them for you," she said to her unseen guest. "It's okay, baby," she muttered to her dog in a voice people reserve for speaking with pets and babies.

He lost sight of her through the small gap in the fence as she walked to where his notes were, but he could still hear her movements. She returned in a few moments, and handing the clipboard over the fence said, "Here you go." Still curious she asked, "How'd you drop them over here?"

"Well, while I was up there I tripped and almost fell. Luckily I didn't fall off, but I lost control and my stuff fell in your yard."

"Wow. I'm glad I'm only returning your notes over the fence and not you. You should be more careful, or you're not going to last very long in your job." Not waiting for a reply, he heard her walking away and saying in her dog voice, "Come on, Sheba. Let's go inside. That's enough excitement for one day."

"Thank you," he said loudly, although he knew she wasn't listening. He returned to his truck and started the engine. Being anxious from all of this he was cautious before he backed into the street. He put the vehicle in a forward gear and headed down the street. He was startled as he heard something crash around him. He slammed on the brake and looked around him to see what it was. In his side view mirror he saw his ladder laying in the street several feet behind him, and he realized he forgot to fasten it.

Feeling stupid he put the truck in park and returned the ladder to the rack, being certain to strap it this time. As he walked back to the door, he saw the neighbor looking out of her window at him. He also noticed Mrs. McVey staring out of her window, and he hoped Billy didn't find out about this.

Tuesday was another pleasant day, although not nearly as warm as Monday. The cloudless sky was its normal shade of blue, and there was a steady breeze of five to ten miles an hour. Jimmy was driving his Cadillac, and he was in route to the McVey house having finished a successful meeting with the Addisons. They readily agreed to have the screens replaced, the master tub fixed, and the exhaust fans and ducts repaired. Additionally, they were pleased their realtor would be handling all of the arrangements with the necessary repairmen while their only requirement was to pay for the work. The proposed amounts did not seem excessive to them, and some of the money set aside for repairs might even get returned to them. Jimmy was hoping things would go as smoothly with the McVeys, but somehow he knew it would be much more difficult.

Jimmy's plan was to present the home inspection report first with its many items requiring repair or further examination by a more qualified person, and then address the roof inspection report. The first part of his strategy was to utilize Mrs. McVey as an ally since she seemed to be able to control her husband on occasion and provided Jimmy with her concerns regarding the operation of many different items. Second, he would use the original disclosure as a weapon since Jimmy knew Mr. McVey was not totally honest when it was completed and signed. Third, Jimmy would point out some things were not checked, like the timer on the automatic water sprinkler. Last, he would promise to negotiate with the buyers and their agent to not require fixing some items. Then, after hopefully having gained his clients' confidence by showing them his willingness to work in their best interests, he would present the roof inspection report which stated a new roof was recommended.

When Jimmy arrived shortly before eleven o'clock, Mr. McVey greeted him at the door and ushered him to the formal dining room. Not seeing Mrs. McVey, Jimmy asked, "Will your wife be joining us?"

"No. She's not feeling well and decided to take a nap."

"I'm sorry to hear that. I'm sure the stress of your upcoming move is having an affect on her. Hopefully she'll be feeling better when she wakes." Jimmy felt unlucky she chose today to not be feeling well.

"I'm sure she'll be fine," Mr. McVey said in a tone without worry and clearly wanting to get on to the business at hand.

"As I said on the phone earlier, I received the inspection reports for the home and the roof. There's some things we need to cover, and I thought we would go over the home inspection one first." Jimmy reached in his folder for the correct papers and set it on the table at an angle between them.

Mr. McVey was silent as he waited for Jimmy to go through the important points. "There are several items which either need to be repaired or require someone with more expertise to check," Jimmy said as he looked at the man to gauge his reaction. Seeing nothing positive or negative, Jimmy continued. "It seems as though the garage door doesn't operate as smoothly as it should, which causes it to not go down completely on occasion. Is this something you've noticed recently, as there was nothing in the disclosure regarding it?"

"I haven't seen any problem," Mr. McVey responded.

"Hmm," Jimmy started as he debated how to present the information Mrs. McVey gave him about the door being open while they dined in San Francisco. "I thought I remember your wife saying something about it having difficulty from time to time. Maybe she comes and goes more than you and she has more opportunity to witness it not functioning correctly. Is that possible?"

"Maybe. But I come and go quite often, too. Surely I would have seen it since I use it more every week than Mr. Riggs did while he was here."

"Well he checks those things all the time, and he seemed to pay a lot of attention to the details. He certainly would have a better view of the door's operation during his inspection than you or your wife would have if you're operating the door from inside your car as you leave every morning." Jimmy was hoping Mr. McVey would accept his logic as it would otherwise be a long and probably unprofitable day.

"Maybe. But I just can't see how something which works every day for me can be a problem for someone who tries it two or three times."

"Well when was the last time it was serviced, Mr. McVey?"

"That's a good question. I can't remember ever having a serviceman out to look at it."

Sensing he was on the winning track, Jimmy tried to clinch this small victory. "I know I've had mine serviced twice in the last five years or so. In one case the springs, tracks, and ball bearings were replaced because I didn't have everything greased on a regular basis. Now I have the serviceman come once a year whether it needs it or not so I am sure to avoid such a costly repair."

"Okay. We'll have someone look at it."

Glad his client finally agreed with him, Jimmy persisted to gain complete control. "I'll be glad to handle it for you if you'd like. I know you're busy with your job and your move. I'm always amazed at how much work it is for my clients to actually get everything done, so I usually take care of as many if not all of these items as I can, just to make it easier on you."

"Thank you. It would be very kind of you to coordinate it with the serviceman."

Having won the first item, Jimmy went to the next. "There seems to be a concern with the circuit panel. Mr. Riggs noticed a lot of electrical tape on the wires, and he recommends an electrician come and take a look. Have you ever done any work on it yourself, Mr. McVey?"

"No, I haven't. I always leave the electrical work to someone else. When I was little my father almost killed himself doing work on our house, and it made quite an impression on me. That's what's confusing to me, though. I'm surprised it's not acceptable since I've always had an electrician do any electrical work in this house."

"Well I haven't looked at it myself. And I'm like you. I tend to shy away from electrical work. Why don't we have someone else take a look just to make sure?"

Jimmy saw Mr. McVey nod his approval, but knowing he couldn't win three in a row, he went to the floor creaking item. "There's a note in the report stating the upstairs floor creaks in a handful of places when someone walks there." Before Mr. McVey had a chance to jump in, Jimmy put him as ease. "But that's something which doesn't have to be fixed. Mr. Riggs recognizes most if not all two-story houses have a similar characteristic, so it is only included as a note just for information."

Wanting to win another easy one, Jimmy mentioned the toilets next. Mr. McVey didn't argue, so Jimmy figured his client noticed the same problem his wife mentioned.

Feeling more confident, Jimmy next raised the concern about the heater. Mr. McVey was amazed a device could measure the temperature of incoming and outgoing air, but astounded better described his reaction to the estimated four hundred dollars for replacing the rods, whatever they were, plus another one hundred dollars for the labor.

The two men continued to discuss every item of Billy's home inspection report. Mr. McVey acknowledged the disposal was quite old and his wife complained about the noise it made on occasion, and he wasn't bothered by the kitchen exhaust fan being listed as requiring servicing, but he took exception to the report saying the cook top had two eyes which did not heat properly. Jimmy calmed him by informing him the same repairman who would look at the disposal and exhaust fan would be able to examine the cook top, too, so there wouldn't be another charge for an additional service call.

Nearing the end of the home inspection report, Mr. McVey asked, "Instead of having all of these different repairmen come to check each of these items in more detail, can't we just get another home inspection, preferably from someone with less scrutiny?"

Recognizing his experience with real estate transactions was a big advantage, Jimmy simply answered, "No."

"Why not?"

"Well, in this case the other agent knows this inspection was done. She's going to get a copy of this same report. So even if we were to commission another inspection, things would only get worse. If the next inspector found something else, then we'd have to worry about it, too."

Mr. McVey didn't have a reply, so Jimmy continued. "Also, I think we better hope she doesn't spend much time looking back at the original disclosure. I know it's been a few months since we completed it and signed it, so some things could have gone from being completely operational to having problems, but I don't think they'd agree all of these items are in that category. Hopefully, since the closing is so quick and we've bent over backwards to provide them occupancy when they demanded, they either won't notice or we'll be able to negotiate favorably with them."

Mr. McVey shook his head in agreement. Jimmy sensed his client felt fortunate Jimmy was working so hard to help him, so he proceeded to the roof portion of the home inspection report, which he intended to set the stage for the full roof inspection report. "There is one other item of importance here. Mr. Riggs stated some concern for the condition of the roof. He did note some discoloration and cracking in places on the roof. Further, the report says the roof has unusual wear in many locations and is near the end of its lifetime."

"So what does that mean," Mr. McVey quickly switched to his unfriendly tone.

"Nothing by itself, except it supports the really bad news I have to deliver." Jimmy reached in his folder for the roof report Billy prepared the previous night. "Here's the roof inspection report, and it says basically the same thing."

"You've got to be kidding!" Mr. McVey shouted as he stood and was now as upset as Jimmy experienced previously over the phone when the contract was finalized. "The roof should be good for another five to ten years! This report is totally bogus! We're not putting on a new roof! We're just not!" Mr. McVey turned and looked out the front window.

Jimmy heard footsteps on the stairway and turned to see Mrs. McVey coming down the stairs. Recognizing her husband's mood, she turned the opposite way from the men when she reached the bottom of the stairs and walked into a different room. Jimmy expected her to join them, so he didn't even greet her, which he knew was a mistake.

"What options do we have?" Mr. McVey asked as he turned back toward Jimmy. "Can we get another roof inspection? Surely we can get a second opinion on some things around here!"

Jimmy pondered for a brief moment and answered, "Yes, I'm sure we can get another roof inspection. The biggest problem is getting it done in time. It's already Tuesday, and we're supposed to sign the paperwork this Friday in order to close by the 4th."

"Well this is totally unacceptable right now. If we don't get another roof inspection, the buyers will just have to make other arrangements. I don't care what problems it causes. I'm not going to pay several thousand dollars for a new roof when the roof inspector is a buffoon who can't complete his work without falling off the roof, bothering the neighbors, or remembering to tie down his ladder."

This caught Jimmy by surprise. He didn't know what his client was talking about. Billy did not tell him anything about anyone falling off the roof, so he wondered what really happened. In his anxiousness and uncertainty, an idea happened to pop into his head. "How about this, Mr. McVey? I've done some work with another roofing company, Foothill Roofing. Actually, they installed the roof on my house several years ago when I built it. I'll give them a call this afternoon and see if they can get out here and do another inspection soon. I doubt if they can do it today on such short notice, but I'll see what I can do. I think the man who ran the place years ago is still in charge, so maybe I can get him to do me a favor."

"But what are we going to do about this report?" Mr. McVey asked, reminded of Jimmy's answer about a second home inspection report.

"Leave that to me. I'll contact Valley Roofing and the other agent and simply tell them we are not satisfied with the report and want to get a second opinion. I'm a little confused by your comment from a minute ago, though. Did someone fall off the roof?"

Relaxing a little since his agent was agreeing with his proposal for having someone else take a second look at the roof, Mr. McVey said, "Well I wasn't here, but my wife tells me the young man almost fell, and in the process he dropped some things in the neighbor's yard. This is all secondhand from the neighbor, but she is pretty nosy about things. But both ladies saw the ladder fall off the truck when he tried to drive away. He must not have strapped it on after almost falling. I guess I might have been a little shaken, too."

"Wow," Jimmy replied. "Sounds like we have a right to question this report. Thanks for sharing that with me. I'm sure it will help me convince the other agent we need another inspection. I'll also tell Valley Roofing we aren't going to pay them for their work."

"Good," Mr. McVey said very satisfied. "Is there anything else?"

"No. Let me work on getting the other roof folks over. I'll call you and let you know when they can make it, but I expect I'll be lucky to get them here even by tomorrow."

The two men bid each other farewell as Jimmy left the home inspection report with his client while keeping the roof inspection report for himself. As he got in his car and drove to a nearby deli, he wondered what Billy knew about the events from yesterday. He hoped Billy could find another more capable employee to return under the guise of Foothill Roofing the next morning. He dialed Billy's number as he shook his head in dismay.

"Hello," Billy answered on the first ring.

"Billy! It's J.D.! How ya' doin'!?" Jimmy yelled his normal greeting.

"Fine, Jimmy. What's up?"

"Have you checked your insurance to make sure your premiums have been paid?"

"No," Billy replied cautiously, not knowing what his friend was hinting at. "Why?"

"Well, rumor has it one of your boys almost fell off the McVey house yesterday. Did you know that?"

"No, I didn't," Billy said in amazement. "How do you know?"

"And you better check all your ladders to make sure they're tied down properly. I'm told those things have a tendency to fall off when you're driving if they're not." Jimmy would normally be laughing at his own kidding, but this was too serious for laughter.

"I guess I'll have to go back and ask a few more questions," Billy couldn't help but wonder what really happened.

"Yeah. You do that. I'm sure it's quite an amazing story."

"How'd it go with Mr. McVey, Jimmy?"

"Okay on the home inspection part. The roof's another matter. Do you think you can send out someone else tomorrow in a truck with a Foothill Roofing sign on the side?"

"Sure, why?"

"I've agreed to get another roof inspection done, and it's got to be quick. I told Mr. McVey I'd be lucky to get someone here by tomorrow morning, so we'll have this afternoon or tonight to prepare. Can we meet later today? How about three o'clock?"

"Gee, Jimmy. I'm sorry. You remember the roofing project for the production home builder developing the neighborhood I mentioned to you. Well, I'm supposed to meet with them again this afternoon to go through some of the numbers. I should be done by five, maybe a little sooner."

"That's fine. Just meet me at my office as soon as you can. Be sure to call me when you finish with your meeting and are on your way. Talk to you then." Jimmy hung up before he heard Billy say goodbye.

Wednesday morning at half past ten o'clock a truck bearing a sign advertising Foothill Roofing pulled into the McVey driveway. Less than a minute later Jimmy Donovan arrived at the same location from the opposite direction. Jimmy followed the driver from Billy's office to the edge of the neighborhood, where he then took a different route to make it look like a mere coincidence the two arrived at the same time. Jimmy hoped the meeting at Billy's office earlier provided sufficient preparation.

Mr. McVey arranged to be home this morning so he could witness for himself any strange events since he only received a secondhand description of the amazing happenings from the roof inspection two days ago. He greeted the young man from Foothill Roofing coldly, but did have a kind word for Jimmy as he didn't expect his realtor to be present. Jimmy had two pages of notes regarding repairs for the items from the home inspection report, and he reviewed them with Mr. McVey while the two stood in the driveway as today's roof inspector made his way to the top of the house.

Jimmy's notes showed multiple servicemen were called and different dates arranged for them to complete their house calls. The earliest date was October 5th, and the last date was October 10th, all conveniently later than the expected closing on the 4th. When Mr. McVey questioned why it was going to take so long, Jimmy said it was typical. Jimmy went on to say he already contacted Jamie Rasmussen regarding these dates, and although she was disappointed her clients would be troubled by the intrusions, they agreed it was acceptable.

"I also did not discuss the roof with her," Jimmy said to Mr. McVey. "She was so distracted by the other items she must have forgotten about it. And since we didn't want her to see it anyway, it may all work out for the better."

"That would be nice," Mr. McVey replied. "But won't the other roofing company send her their report anyway?"

"I don't think so. She wasn't the one to order it. I was. She doesn't know who I called to do it, so when she gets the report from Foothill Roofing, she'll think it was the only one we did."

"Good."

"By the way, I used the information you provided me about the other inspector and told his boss we wouldn't be paying them for their services since he was clearly incompetent. They didn't like it, but they really don't have much choice. They know it's not worth the time and effort for them to sue us for the hundred and fifty dollars they were going to bill, and there's plenty of other roofing companies for me to work with in the future."

"Thank you," Mr. McVey replied, happy his realtor was looking out for him. Jimmy on the other hand knew most roof inspections only cost seventy-five dollars, so Billy would now be able to charge one hundred and fifty dollars for the one performed by Foothill Roofing, thus covering his costs for both inspections.

As Jimmy and Mr. McVey continued their discussion, they could see the young man on the roof continuing to move about while constantly checking and making notes. The man made his way to the ladder and descended to the ground without incident.

"Let me handle asking him what he thinks," Jimmy said to Mr. McVey as the two watched the young man grab his ladder and carefully strap it to the truck.

"All finished?" Jimmy asked.

"Yes, sir," the young man replied.

"So what do you think about the condition of the roof?" Jimmy continued to lead the conversation.

"I'm sorry to say it's not good. There are a lot of areas with problems which need fixing." The young man was trying to state his words exactly as he just read them on one page of his notes. He and Jimmy also practiced this four times during their earlier meeting.

"But is it a major deal or just a lot of minor things?" Jimmy continued with the script as Mr. McVey listened intently.

"Well each area could be repaired separately, but by the time you add it all up, you'd be better off getting a new roof."

"Do you really think so?" Jimmy asked in a tone hopeful there might have been a mistake, noticing his client lowered his head and was now staring at the pavement.

"I'm sorry I don't have better news, but that's what I'm going to recommend in my report." Opening the truck door he asked, "Are you going to want us to do the repairs?"

"We're not sure. Why do you ask?" Jimmy replied.

"Well, we're pretty busy right now, so it might be a few weeks before we can get to it. You can always have someone else do the work, but if we do it we won't charge you for the inspection."

"We don't know what we'll be doing yet. Just finish your report by tomorrow morning and we'll have an answer for you then. Thanks for stopping by."

"You're welcome, and once again I'm sorry about the bad news," the young man said as he started the engine and departed.

Jimmy turned to Mr. McVey who was surprisingly subdued as opposed to angry. "I guess we'll just have to go ahead and get a new roof."

"Yeah," Jimmy agreed with his client. "I guess so. With two similar reports, I don't think it will change if we were to try a third time. Do you want me to handle scheduling the work with this second company?"

"Yes. I'd appreciate it. It would certainly help me and my wife get everything else associated with the move done."

When Jimmy and Mr. McVey finished their conversation, Jimmy headed back to his office, stopping first at a deli for a sandwich with plenty of roast beef, a thick slice of kielbasa, jalapeno cheese, lettuce, tomato, and a tangy sauce. He knew he was close to the finish line on the Addison and McVey closings, and he wanted to celebrate with a quiet lunch in his office.

As he was about to take the last bite of his lunch, Jimmy's phone rang. Mickey's voice was on the other end.

"What's up, Mick?" Jimmy asked.

"I've run into a little problem, Jimmy. It's with the McVey closing."

SIXTEEN

"What's the problem, Mick?" Jimmy asked anxiously.

"A few things actually," Mickey responded. "First is Foothill Roofing."

"What about it? When we talked yesterday you said it would be fine to use the name Foothill Roofing. What's changed?"

"Well I spoke too soon, before I checked it completely. I was so busy trying to get all the paperwork done for both of these closings, I didn't go back and verify if Foothill Roofing was actually a company. I thought it was, but for some reason I got to thinking about it late last night. So I checked it out this morning, and it turns out Foothill Roofing doesn't really exist."

"Can't we just make it a company?" Jimmy asked, hopeful there was a quick solution.

Mickey breathed a heavy sigh before answering. "Yeah, I can, but it will take a few days for the papers to get signed and filed with the appropriate offices. With the paperwork signing for the closing scheduled for this Friday, it won't get done in time."

"Can't we use the name Foothill Roofing in the paperwork, do the work to make it a company, and generate the invoice for the new roof and have it paid to Foothill Roofing once it is a real company?"

Mickey once again was slow to answer. "We could, but I expect someone would find the discrepancy where the inspection was done on a first date, the company was created on a later date, and then money from an escrow account was sent to the company against an invoice soon after. I just don't feel comfortable leaving that kind of trail."

"So what can we do?" Jimmy asked bluntly after having his suggestions rejected so quickly.

"A couple of things come to mind. Do you think we could swap the names of the two roof inspections? Since we're not going to charge the McVeys for the first roof inspection, why don't we treat it like Foothill Roofing did the one on Monday and Valley Roofing did the one on Wednesday? That way, the name Foothill Roofing will never appear anywhere."

"I don't think it will work, Mick. Turns out the guy Billy sent out on Monday made quite an impression on Mrs. McVey and her nosy neighbor. Mr. McVey was informed pretty well by his wife and possibly the neighbor, so I'm certain he would recognize the name Valley Roofing in the paperwork and want to know why he was being charged by them when I've assured him he won't have to pay them anything due to their incompetence."

"I knew it was risky having someone other than Billy involved," Mickey said with a tone indicating he told Jimmy it wasn't a good idea.

"Well if the guy just didn't almost fall off the roof, things would have been fine. He only thought he was doing a basic roof inspection. Billy did the report, and his employee didn't know a new roof was being recommended." Jimmy stopped his defensiveness as he remembered the mishap with the ladder and realized Mickey was probably right on this one.

"Well Billy needs to be more careful in the future."

"I agree, Mick. But I also know we need Billy's help. We couldn't do all of this without him. He's a key player."

"I know," Mickey agreed as he focused back to the business at hand. "The other thought I had was to use the name Bay Roofing. We've used it in the past, and it's a real company I previously created with Billy as the sole proprietor. It would be fine."

"Other than the fact the truck we used this morning had Foothill Roofing on the side," Jimmy said as he thought about this suggestion.

"Well, if there are questions when the paperwork is signed, you can just say Bay Roofing owns Foothill Roofing, so even though the truck said one thing, the roof inspection report, invoices, and any other correspondence will say Bay Roofing. Can you pull it off, Jimmy?"

Jimmy thought for a few moments before speaking. He stared at the maps on his wall, and saw the names Santa Cruz Mountains, Coyote Valley, and Almaden Valley, all which either were used or were heavily considered for fictitious company names. He wondered how much attention people paid to the name of companies as he considered Mickey's suggestion. Convinced he gained Mr. McVey's trust in their last meeting, Jimmy decided. "Yeah. Let's use Bay Roofing. I'll make it work, Mick."

"Good. Do you want to tell Billy to use Bay Roofing, or would you like me to handle it?"

"I'll take care of it, Mick. Anything else?"

"There is one more problem," Mickey said as his tone indicated this item was worse than the first one.

"What is it?" Jimmy urged his friend, not knowing what to expect now.

"It's Jamie Rasmussen." Mickey replied.

"What about her?"

"She's called me three times this morning."

"Three times! What's she want, and why is she calling you instead of me?"

"It's certainly her right to call me instead of you, Jimmy. What she wants is her copy of the settlement statement for review. She was expecting it today, and I've been trying to put her off without telling her the roof inspection report isn't done yet. Since I thought the roof inspection from Monday was going to be sufficient, I promised her I would have everything by today. Now it's going to be tomorrow, only with a lot of work on my part tonight."

"Let me call her," Jimmy offered. "I'll just tell her you're real busy doing the work for several closings right now, and it has taken an extra day. I'll tell her you are the type to not want to make excuses or you would have told her yourself. I think she'll be alright with it."

"That would be a big help. If you can buy me one more day without me having to call her, I'll be able to manage."

"No problem, Mick," Jimmy said, happy to solve the last problem for now.

"There's more, Jimmy," Mickey continued with his hesitant tone. "She's also demanding to see a copy of the settlement statement for the McVeys in addition to the one for her clients. She seems to really have a lot on the ball. She worries me, Jimmy."

"Don't worry, Mick. Most people's first impression of her is similar. Billy was a little worried when he first met her, too, but we completely fooled her during the home inspection. She thinks

177

everything in the house is fine, so she won't question anything related to her client's settlement statement."

"But what about her request for a copy of the McVeys statement? I know we don't have to legally provide it to her, but if we refuse it will only raise her suspicions."

"Why don't you make three settlement statements, Mick?" Jimmy asked as he wondered if Mickey was thinking clearly. "Instead of making one for the buyers and a second one for the sellers, generate a third one for the sellers which is consistent with the one for the buyers. We'll give the first and third ones to Ms. Rasmussen, and I'll use the second one with the McVeys."

"I don't know, Jimmy. I have the feeling we're pushing our luck on this one."

"I'll tell you what, Mick," Jimmy said realizing he would have to expend more energy working with his friend on this one. "I'll drive down to Monterey this afternoon after I finish meeting with Billy and getting him squared away on the Bay Roofing versus Foothill Roofing thing. He'll be able to complete the reports while I'm on my way, and I'll tell him to fax them to your office. We'll work on all of the statements together to make sure we don't have any holes. We'll work as late as we need to tonight until it's done. I'll even tell my wife I'll be spending the night at your place. She won't like it, but I'll live with it. Then I'll bring the copies back with me early tomorrow morning so I can deliver them personally to Jamie Rasmussen."

"Sounds like a plan," Mickey said as he felt some relief. "Oh, don't forget to call her today."

"Thanks for the reminder. I'll call her after I leave Billy's. Then I'll call you after I finish talking with her to let you know when to expect me. Hopefully I'll make it by six. We can order some sushi from the delivery place with the cute Japanese waitresses."

"I just ate there last night."

"Well I didn't, Mick. You once told me you could eat there every night without getting tired of it. Now's your chance to prove it. See you later."

"Bye, Jimmy."

Jimmy cleaned his desk of the remnants of his lunch and grabbed several folders before heading out the door for an afternoon of work not planned. His meeting with Billy lasted less than twenty minutes, and he realized he was thirty minutes ahead of the afternoon commute. He decided to drive to Monterey via Santa Cruz as he enjoyed the scenery on this route more than the alternative of highway 101. As he headed south from San Jose he dialed Jamie Rasmussen's number as his Audi TT continued its climb toward the summit.

Jamie was not in a particularly good mood, having not received the paperwork from Mickey. When Jimmy explained how busy Mickey was with other closings, she said she understood, but Jimmy could tell she wasn't sincere. She also made a snide comment about Mickey being located in Monterey, further indicating she didn't care much for his choice of escrow agents in this transaction. When Jimmy told her he would be delivering the paperwork personally the next morning, she had an additional sarcastic remark regarding another offer of employment.

When Jimmy hung up at the completion of the call, he wondered where she was born and raised. He knew it wasn't the South, and now he wished it was. He just couldn't stand for such a young and physically attractive woman to be so forceful and outspoken in the business world. Her mother probably dominated the marriage, he expected, providing a completely liberated woman as a role model. If she grew up in the South, he expected she would be a little less pushy and have more respect for older people.

Jimmy's thoughts then turned to his wife, who he needed to call to inform her of his plans for staying with Mickey. Susan was certainly as attractive at the age of forty-five as Jamie Rasmussen was now. Susan was much more polite at Jamie's age than Jamie was presently displaying, but Jimmy recognized Susan changed over time. Maybe it was his influence, he pondered. Maybe it was the influence from other women in her volunteer groups. Probably some of both he concluded as he dialed their home number.

After four rings the recorder answered, but Jimmy decided not to leave a message, not wanting her to receive this from a tape recorder. Instead he dialed her cell phone, hoping she would have her phone turned on and not be talking with one of the girls. When her voice mail answered immediately, Jimmy expected she was indeed involved in a conversation with one or both daughters. He would just have to wait and try again once he was on the other side of Santa Cruz.

Meanwhile, Mickey was busy working on the paperwork for the McVeys while his assistant was working on the Addison closing when the office phone rang. Thinking it might be Jimmy or Jamie Rasmussen yet again, Mickey hollered to his assistant to let him answer it. He was totally caught off guard when his ex-wife's voice was on the other end. It was several months since Mickey last talked with her, and he didn't want to talk with her on this occasion either. Now he was kicking himself for not letting his assistant answer the call.

Mickey mostly listened as his ex-wife made a plea for him to get involved with their children again this school year. His son was a sophomore and an above average athlete. He was presently playing on the sophomore football team, and he was expected to play on the junior varsity basketball team this winter and on the varsity baseball team in the spring. She begged Mickey to come to some of the games to show his support for his son. Mickey saw him play a few years ago when he was in Middle School, but he didn't enjoyed it then and didn't expect it would be different now. It wasn't watching his son he didn't like. He just didn't like reminders of his ex-wife and their failed marriage.

Mickey's daughter was in the seventh grade, and nothing she was doing excited him. Her passion was playing the piano, and she performed several recitals, none of which Mickey witnessed. Now his ex-wife was asking him to attend at least one this year. He politely but firmly refused and then listened as she scolded him at the top of her lungs. When he calmly asked if she was finished, he heard the phone slam in his ear.

Immediately after he hung up Mickey heard the phone ring again. He instinctively picked it up, and as he started to utter his greeting he wished his assistant answered the call. Fortunately it was Jimmy, which made Mickey breathe easier.

"I'm just coming down the mountain a few miles from Santa Cruz, Mick. I should be at your office in about an hour. When I left Billy he was going to finish up the roof reports and fax them to you. I also called Jamie Rasmussen, and everything is fine. I have an appointment to meet her in the morning with all the paperwork. How's your afternoon going?"

"It was fine until a few minutes ago," Mickey replied.

"What happened?"

"My ex-wife called. I can't stand talking with her anymore. How we ever stayed married for as long as we did is still one of the great mysteries of the world."

"What's she want now?" Jimmy asked.

"She's constantly asking me to get more involved with our children. You'd think it was enough for me to send them money every month, but no. No, it's not enough. I have to be the father they want me to be. I guess some mistakes we just keep paying for."

"Well at least you're able to hide some of your income from them or they would be getting even more. Just treat the calls and other forms of harassment as requirements for getting to keep more of your money than you otherwise would."

"I guess. By the way, was Susan real bent out of shape when you told her you'd be spending the night?"

"I haven't been able to reach her yet. She's not home, and her cell phone is busy. I expect she's talking with the girls. They have to recap the school day once it ends. It can't even wait until they get home. Shucks, for me to get more involved in their lives, there would have to be more hours in the day. Between their school activities and the mother-daughter relationship, not much time is left."

"Lucky you," Mickey said solemnly.

"Cheer up, Mick. Finish what you can and I'll see you soon. We'll have a nice dinner, get all of the paperwork done, and tomorrow will be a better day."

"If you say so. See you when you get here, Jimmy."

After the call each had different thoughts. Mickey was depressed. He wondered if another career change was appropriate. Maybe he should follow his ex-wife's advice and get more involved with his kids. Maybe he just needed to quit working with Jimmy on their scams, but he needed the money. He wasn't sure what would help, although he sure wished his golf game would be consistently good.

Jimmy on the other hand felt alive and satisfied. He had a beautiful wife and their marriage was strong, particularly the sexual part of it. He was proud of his girls, even if they were more influenced by their mother. He still enjoyed the real estate business, and he cherished every victory in a swindle, however large or small the financial reward. He liked being with his fraternity brothers, whether it was discussing some new outrageous scheme or simply sharing a beer while watching a game. It was fulfilling for him to help them gain financially, particularly since tough times were falling on them for one reason or another. He did wish his gambling luck would change, as he seemed to have two losing weeks for every winning one.

Having driven well south of Santa Cruz, Jimmy once again tried to reach Susan. She didn't answer her cell phone, so he tried the home number. She answered on the second ring, and her tone indicated this was not going to be an easy conversation.

She just didn't seem to understand why he needed to drive to Monterey to help Mickey finish some real estate paperwork. Couldn't all of this get done over the phone she wondered. Although she knew Mickey was a long-time friend, she also questioned why her husband didn't use someone closer to Palo Alto. The clincher was having to spend the night. She didn't like sleeping alone in their bed and didn't like the thought of her girls not being protected by their father. She warned him in no uncertain terms if this was all a front for him to cheat on her, she would divorce him instantly and he would never see his girls again.

Reassuring his wife this trip was a necessary part of his job which provided the financial support for the entire family, Jimmy bid her farewell. As he continued his drive he felt fortunate he wasn't too fond of Jamie Rasmussen's personality, particularly in light of his wife's most recent threat.

As he approached Monterey Jimmy admired the view. He liked how the houses and other buildings covered the hillside and looked over the bay. He figured if he ever retired he might try to convince Susan to move to Monterey so they could enjoy the northern California weather and the ocean without being surrounded by as many people as there were in Palo Alto. He knew it would be a difficult sell as Susan mentioned on many occasions how nice it would be for their girls to attend college somewhere in the South, and he knew she longed to someday move back closer to home.

Jimmy exited the highway and easily navigated the streets to Mickey's office. Once he parked and got out of his car, he stood and took several deep breaths. A strong wind was blowing in from the ocean, and he sensed the salt and fish in the air. He enjoyed the smell but knew he would grow tired of it if constantly exposed to it. He was glad he worked in real estate as opposed to having developed a love for fishing.

Jimmy's energy was uplifting to Mickey. The two worked for more than two hours before realizing they should consider ordering some dinner. When Mickey grabbed the delivery menu for the sushi place they discussed earlier, Jimmy suggested a few other cuisines as alternatives. Mickey appreciated his friend's willingness to compromise, but he was warm to the idea of having sushi a second night in a row, so two orders of the house specialty were made.

Once the delivery arrived the two stopped working and chatted about their fortunes in life as they ate. They talked about their college days, their marriages, their kids, their careers, and various other topics. Jimmy realized his friend was depressed, but he remembered seeing Mickey much worse at other times, so Jimmy figured Mickey would overcome it as he did on the other occasions.

As they were both almost filled and the food just about gone, the discussion turned to Jamie Rasmussen. Mickey never met her, so his impression of her was less complete than Jimmy's. As Jimmy described her physical appearance, Mickey seemed genuinely interested in meeting her. Knowing this would be a mistake for the business relationship, Jimmy quickly described the faults he noticed. Mickey's interest seemed to be eliminated when Jimmy likened Jamie's personality to Mickey's ex-wife's at a similar age, so they began again working on the settlement statements.

The paperwork was completed long after midnight, and Jimmy realized he would have to get up far sooner than he wanted the next morning. As the two left Mickey's office it was suggested they just stay up all night to avoid the early alarm. They remembered having done this many times while in college, and never did it seem to be such a good idea during the afternoon of the next day. They laughed as they felt good at having learned at least one lesson from their college days.

Jimmy left Mickey's house the next morning shortly after five o'clock. The sky was still dark and the traffic light as he departed Monterey, but he knew both would change as he neared San Jose. He intended not only to beat the heaviest part of the morning commute, he also wanted to meet with Billy prior to his appointment with Jamie

Rasmussen at nine o'clock. He hoped he would make it to San Jose by half past six, allowing plenty of time for some breakfast at a diner followed by the preparation of an additional roof inspection report.

Jimmy and Mickey decided to use the name Bay Roofing for the paperwork the McVeys would see. They were still hoping their explanation of Foothill Roofing being owned by Bay Roofing would suffice. However, they didn't want Jamie Rasmussen or her clients to see any reference to either Bay Roofing or Foothill Roofing, as Jamie or her clients might decide to call on their services at some point in the future. Jimmy and Mickey decided only bad things could come from such a scenario, so they decided to use Valley Roofing for the paperwork Jamie and the buyers would see. Thus Jimmy needed another roofing report from Billy.

As expected traffic steadily increased the further north Jimmy drove. He chose to take highway 101 through Gilroy and Morgan Hill as he didn't like driving over the mountain on route 17 at this time of day. Bad accidents on two previous occasions caused him to be late for important appointments, and he wanted to avoid the possibility. Highway 101 wasn't immune to mishaps and slow traffic, but it was less frequent.

Jimmy arrived in San Jose and found his way to a restaurant which served breakfast twenty-four hours a day. After he ordered a small stack of pancakes with a side of bacon, he called Billy's house, expecting him to either be asleep or just getting up. To his surprise Billy was about to head out the door as a big day was planned, including a meeting with the production builder developing the neighborhood. Jimmy told his friend another roof inspection report was needed by half past eight, and Billy agreed to juggle his schedule to accommodate the request.

Armed with all of the paperwork Mickey and he generated and multiple roof and home inspection reports, Jimmy parked in front of an office park where Jamie Rasmussen's company was located. He much preferred doing this in his office, feeling the comfort of his usual surroundings provided him with a home court advantage, but Jamie said her schedule couldn't accommodate a drive to Palo Alto.

When Jimmy walked in the door, Jamie was waiting at the front desk to greet him. She again was wearing a skirt, and this one was shorter than the one she wore during the home inspection.

Additionally, the top three buttons on her blouse were undone, providing more than a peek at her lovely figure. Jimmy was used to this as most young female real estate agents seemed to dress provocatively in their efforts to get the single men and even the married men to better enjoy the working relationship. It usually did have a positive influence on clients, and probably on other agents as well, but Jimmy knew he needed to not be distracted. Remembering his wife's comments from their phone conversation yesterday was the perfect antidote for him to stay focused on the business at hand.

When they were seated at the end of a large conference table, Jimmy handed Jamie two folders. He explained the first contained a copy of the papers her clients would sign. The two went through the entire set page by page, and Jamie agreed everything looked fine for a first pass. Next they reviewed the contents of the second folder. The numbers and reports were consistent with the first set, so she was pleased things were properly prepared and the signing of the papers would take place as planned the following day.

Jamie indicated she would take another look through the paperwork later in the day, but she didn't expect to find any problems. If by chance there was something, she said she would call both Mickey and Jimmy to figure out how to get it resolved. She reiterated how important it was to sign the papers the next day and complete the closing the following Thursday to allow her clients occupancy at that time.

Jimmy left her office confident things were going to go as he planned. He intended to do some research at a few new listings the previous day, so he drove to his office to make appointments to preview some homes and see what could be accomplished this afternoon. Ever since the meeting with Charlie where Jimmy was advised to find people who pay their monthly mortgage via bill paying as opposed to bank draft, he searched many people's private desks and computers.

He presently had identified four candidates with mortgage payments ranging from fifteen hundred dollars to more than three thousand. The problem was all of these homeowners could possibly sell their houses before his target date of November 1st, so he wanted to grow his list of candidates to a dozen. His hope was at least eight would remain unsold, and with an average of two thousand per mortgage payment, sixteen thousand dollars would be redirected to his friends and him.

Friday morning Jimmy woke without the need of his alarm. His research the previous afternoon was fruitless, except for identifying another coin collector and adding three more duplicated keys to his library. His wife was a little cold toward him during dinner, but after a few glasses of wine she softened, allowing them to enjoy a wonderfully playful evening. He also did not receive a call from Jamie Rasmussen, so it seemed things were going to work as planned. His excitement this morning was in anticipation of getting the paperwork signed by the McVeys and the Addisons, and once he awoke at five o'clock he was unable to go back to sleep.

The Addisons were kind enough to drive from Cupertino to Jimmy's office in Palo Alto to sign their papers. They would be vacating their home the following Monday as their moving company accelerated the schedule by two days from the plan they communicated to Jimmy at the first of this week. Even though they were busy packing many things themselves and not yet finished, they wanted to get out of the house for a few hours and enjoy another drive along the bay before they departed the area for good. They were tremendously thankful their house was almost sold and quite appreciative of Jimmy's efforts, especially his handling of the screens, tub, and exhaust fans. As Jimmy saw on most occasions, his clients asked a few questions on the first three or four pages, and then blindly signed the remainder of the pages he put in front of them.

The McVey signing was scheduled for two o'clock in the afternoon, and Jimmy agreed to meet them at their home in Mountain View. Jamie Rasmussen was meeting with her clients at three o'clock to have them sign their set, and Jimmy planned to meet her at her office at four to collect everything.

When Jimmy arrived at the McVey residence, Mrs. McVey answered the door. She was busy packing books as Jimmy noticed more than thirty small boxes throughout the front room either empty, partially filled, or already taped shut. She escorted Jimmy to the garage where her husband was mostly throwing away items not used in many years. A dusty tire pump was on top of the pile of trash in a can, and not noticing any bicycles, Jimmy figured it was a long time since the pump's last use. Several lawn mower blades covered in rust were also laying against the can. Jimmy concluded this garage was fairly typical of people who lived in the same house for quite some time, and he knew Mr. McVey was experiencing both good and bad memories from his stay here.

When the three sat at the table with the pile of papers, Mr. McVey put his hands on top of the stack and looked across at Jimmy to address him. Jimmy was caught completely by surprise when an apology was being offered by Mr. McVey for his previous behavior. The contentment Jimmy noticed on Mrs. McVey's face indicated she played a major role in convincing her husband it was necessary.

Few questions were asked as the signing progressed. Jimmy highlighted all of the money being reserved for the repairs and new roof without incident. When the roof inspection report was viewed, Mr. McVey didn't ask about the Bay Roofing name and must have forgotten about the Foothill Roofing truck as he only commented he was glad no money was being paid to Valley Roofing.

When finished with the paperwork Jimmy and the McVeys chatted kindly about their moving plans. The packers were still scheduled to arrive Sunday and take two days, with the moving van appearing the day after. A few nights in a local hotel would be followed by a flight to their new destination the afternoon of Thursday the 4th. They wanted the money due them deposited directly into one of their accounts, and they planned on verifying the deposit prior to their departure.

Jimmy indicated he expected everything to happen according to the same schedule, as he personally met with the escrow agent to help matters move in a timely fashion. Jimmy also was picking up the signed papers from the buyers later in the afternoon, and he said he would phone the McVeys once those were in his possession. A quick farewell included a kiss on the cheek from Mrs. McVey, and Jimmy left to make his next appointment with Jamie Rasmussen.

Jimmy had a little extra time as he arrived in the neighborhood of her office at twenty minutes to four. He debated about going ahead a little early, but he didn't particularly want to meet the buyers. He figured preserving his anonymity from them might be helpful if they didn't change the locks and he was to use his key for access to their new home.

Instead, Jimmy parked around the corner at a sandwich shop devoid of customers as the lunch crowd departed long ago and the early evening activity was yet to start. He grabbed the morning sports section and headed inside to take another look at the betting lines for tomorrow's college football games. He ordered a glass of lemonade as a final tribute to the summer which was now gone and sat at a table near the front windows.

After checking the point spreads and reading a few short articles about Cal's poor performance this football season, he checked the time. It was almost four o'clock so he made his way to Jamie's office. He didn't see anyone entering or exiting, so he grabbed his folders and headed for the door.

When he was less than ten steps from the door, it opened and he saw Jamie Rasmussen leading another couple. She again was wearing a short skirt and a revealing top, and she greeted him with big smile. She introduced him to the couple behind her, who were the two buying the McVey house. He shook hands with the husband and said hello to the wife as they thanked him for helping them to get occupancy of the property when they desired. He commented it was all part of the job, and when they departed he was disappointed knowing his identity was no longer a secret with this couple.

Once inside Jamie's office, Jimmy asked if there were any problems or if she or her clients had any questions. There were a few with one being related to the geological survey. The sellers paid for it, but the buyers were unaware of this California requirement, so Jamie took the time to explain a little of the history of earthquakes and resulting legislation. Jamie and Jimmy agreed this seemed ridiculous, but acknowledged it was a law they could work for a lifetime and not change.

Jamie made another comment about her commission being reduced more than Jimmy's, and asked if he would have conceded another quarter of a percent if she demanded. Jimmy's answer was no but he could tell she didn't believe him and would probably try if the occasion presented itself in the future.

The meeting lasted less than fifteen minutes as Jimmy collected everything and said he was in a hurry to get to his next appointment. All he wanted was to get an early start on the Friday commute so he could be home before six. He wanted to make good on his promise to his wife to take her and their girls out for a nice dinner.

The weekend was fairly uneventful other than the baseball regular season coming to a finish. San Francisco was not in the playoffs, but Oakland qualified and was paired against the New York Yankees in the first round. Jimmy was also glad the Cardinals and Braves both made the playoffs in the National League, as he continued to follow both teams since his days growing up in Tennessee.

With the closings of the Addison and McVey properties expected on Wednesday and Thursday, Jimmy decided a celebration was appropriate.   He spent almost two hours on Monday morning searching the internet for tickets to Friday night's game between Oakland and New York, and he finally located four. Instead of taking his wife and girls, who wouldn't want to bear the cold of an early October evening at a ballpark, he invited Mickey, Billy, and Charlie.

Mickey thought it was a great idea, and Charlie agreed to attend even though he didn't care much for either the A's or the Yankees since he was a fan of the National League. Surprisingly, Billy said he would not be able to make it, blaming another meeting with the production builder. This sounded strange to Jimmy since Billy was always eager to spend time with his fraternity brothers, but Jimmy recognized how much Billy was hoping and trying to improve his business.

No strange events occurred as the closings approached for the Addison and McVey transactions. The recording of the deals and disbursement of funds happened without incident on Wednesday for the Addisons and on Thursday for the McVeys. Invoices for repair work were generated on Friday afternoon with dates ranging from the 5th to the 12th of October, and Mickey would easily be able to direct money from the escrow account to various other accounts, all in Billy's name, over the course of the next two weeks.

Although having cheated previous homeowners of money in this fashion, this was the first time a seller was conned out of the entire cost of a new roof. Billy gave a raise to his employee who completed the second roof inspection at the McVey home. Mickey was relieved everything was completed other than disbursing the money in the escrow account for repairs. Jimmy was ecstatic with a grand feeling of accomplishment for himself and his friends, and he was eager to meet with Mickey and Charlie on Friday evening at the game to discuss additional plans.

SEVENTEEN

Jimmy's mood was extremely good on Friday. The events of the week pleased him, and he was looking forward to chatting with Mickey and Charlie while hopeful the A's could win the game. This was the third game of the five-game series, but it was the first one played in Oakland as the series opened in New York on Tuesday. The A's were ahead two games to none having won each of the first two games on the road. Jimmy fully expected Oakland to win this game which would clinch this series and place them in the American League Championship series, most likely against Seattle, and he bet four thousand dollars on his feeling.

The game was scheduled to start fifteen minutes after five o'clock, but Jimmy arrived well over an hour before the first pitch as he wanted to experience the fanfare which accompanies a post-season baseball game. The stadium was decorated for the occasion, as red, white, and blue bunting was draped along the front of the stands in the lower and second decks. Instead of only a few personal signs typical of a regular season game, Jimmy counted thirteen banners draped over the railing in the outfield alone, ranging in size from about two feet on a side to one real large one communicating a loathing for the Yankees because of their large payroll.

The crowd was clearly excited as the pitch of noise was significantly higher than normal, and Jimmy was sure those tuning in to the pre-game television and radio shows would notice a louder buzz in the background. As he looked around it seemed about half of the crowd was already sitting or standing at their assigned seats, but he wondered if traffic was going to deter the remainder from arriving on time.

Jimmy was still drinking his first beer when Mickey approached with his hands full. He was carrying a tray containing nachos, a cheese steak sandwich, and two large beers. "Hey, Mick," Jimmy greeted his friend.

"Hi, Jimmy."

"Man, did you bring enough food and drink?"

"I knew you'd be here early, so I figured I'd save you the trouble of getting another beer. You know in California they don't vend the beer at sporting events like they do in most other parts of the country, so next time it will be your turn." Mickey stretched his arms so Jimmy could grab one of the beers and make it easier for him to sit.

"You can help me eat the nachos, too, if you like," Mickey continued once he was seated, "but the sandwich is mine."

"That's okay. I was going to get some spicy chicken strips in a little bit anyway. Thanks for the beer. Here's to an Oakland victory," Jimmy said as he raised his first cup for a toast.

Mickey raised his beer as well and took a hearty drink. "So I take it you bet on the A's."

"You bet your bottom dollar," Jimmy said with a huge smile. "During the season when these two teams played, the home team won every game. Back in May the A's were struggling, and the Yankees won the three games in New York fairly easily. A week later it seemed like a miracle when Oakland won three games from the Yanks here. They played one more series in August, and the A's were clearly the better team. Now with two big wins at Yankee Stadium, their confidence is sky high. Oakland has the better of the pitching matchup tonight, so I'm looking forward to enjoying an exciting game and an A's victory with this big crowd. I hope you are, too," Jimmy concluded as he failed to contain his excitement.

"I hope they win, too," Mickey responded, "but I'm not as confident as you it'll happen. The Yankees always seem to find a way to win."

"Not tonight my friend. This day belongs to the A's."

The two continued their discussion as they ate and drank. When the nachos were finished and the beers were getting low, Jimmy excused himself to buy another round and purchase the chicken he was craving. While he was gone, Charlie arrived.

"Hi, Mick," Charlie said as he smiled and extended his hand toward Mickey. Charlie had a beer in his left hand and was cradling a hot dog between his left forearm and his body.

"Hey, Charlie," Mickey returned the greeting as the two shook hands. "Jimmy told me you'd be here tonight. Glad you could make it."

"Jimmy told me you were coming, too. Thanks for making the drive up from Monterey. It's good to see ya'."

"Well the drive wasn't too bad until I got north of San Jose. Then things slowed tremendously. I'll bet it was slow for you, too, coming across the bay."

"Very slow, but it could have been worse. I usually come across the San Mateo Bridge, but I happened to catch the traffic update on the radio just as I was leaving Palo Alto. They said there was an accident on that route and to avoid it at all costs, so I used the Dumbarton. It wasn't too bad until I got into Fremont and got on 880. It's a good thing I gave myself plenty of time. I'm sure some folks will have a tough time making it by the first pitch."

"How's your wife, Charlie?"

"She's doing fine, Mick."

"How long you been married now? It's got to be what, seven years or so?"

"Actually, we celebrated our eighth anniversary earlier this year, and we're well on our way to number nine."

"Still no kids, I guess," Mickey said softly as he knew Charlie and his wife were unable to have children of their own.

"Yeah. Same as before. We're still considering adoption, or at least I am, but it's not clear if we'll ever do it. How are your kids? Do you see them much?"

"Not really, and to be honest with you, it doesn't matter to me. The last few times I spent a day with them all they talked about was how depressed their mother was and how I was the cause of all of her problems. She just brainwashes them."

"So I take it she's still not working," Charlie surmised, well aware of the events of Mickey's and his ex-wife's life surrounding their divorce.

"I don't expect her to ever work again," Mickey stated without hope. After pausing for a moment he continued. "You know the story, Charlie. The courts ruled I was to blame for her physical and emotional problems. You'd think from their statement I took a baseball bat to my pregnant wife and beat her until she lost our child,

193

when in reality all I was trying to do was make a career change so I could have a better life, which my family would benefit from as well. Now all I do is send them money every month."

Charlie could see Mickey's irritation rising so he changed the subject by asking, "How's your golf game? Have you played any new courses since we last talked?"

"It's been up and down. I was in Scotland earlier this year, and I really started to play well near the end of the trip. I'll tell you, it's tremendously difficult getting used to the time change. At least it was tough for me. I never admired the pros as much as I have since I made the trip. All those guys who go to the British Open every July and play well after being there just a few days are much tougher than me by a long shot. And I don't know how the ones in Europe who play a mixture of tournaments in the U.S. and in their home country do it. They probably don't know what day it is or when they're supposed to sleep, but they're still able to gain their focus and play good, steady golf."

"Yeah," Charlie agreed. "Jimmy and I were talking a few months ago about traveling and getting adjusted to the time change just here in the U.S. between the east coast and the west coast. It's funny," Charlie let out a small laugh as he started his comment. "Jimmy thought he had it all figured out one night in San Francisco, but then his team lost and it was back to the drawing board."

"He's got a new theory for tonight's game. Something about the pitching matchup and how these teams have played at home this year."

"Let's hope he wins. I remember he bet a pretty tidy sum, and I'm sure he hasn't backed off any."

"He's a big gambler, Charlie," Mickey said as he switched the conversation from the light discussion to a much more serious tone. "We both knew he bet on games as far back as when he was in college. Shucks, he spent a whole summer in Las Vegas during college. But it was only a hobby, then. Unfortunately, it's gotten much worse, especially in the last year or so."

"How bad is it, Mick?"

Taking a deep breath, Mickey decided to answer. "Charlie, I probably shouldn't be telling you this, but you and I go way back to when we were initiated into Sigma Chi during our freshman year, so I know you won't use this information the wrong way." Mickey looked his friend squarely in the eyes before he continued. "One weekend last fall, Jimmy lost over twenty thousand dollars. He bet on something like fifteen different college games, and I think he only won one or two of his bets. Now he may have made it up some other weekend, but I don't think so. And I'm pretty sure he hasn't changed. He told me earlier tonight he bet four grand on tonight's game alone."

Charlie sat stunned. He knew Jimmy was a gambler during his college days and beyond. Charlie remembered during his own freshman year, when Mickey was also a freshman and Jimmy was a sophomore, being mesmerized by Jimmy's descriptions of Las Vegas on many late nights around the fraternity house's lone pool table. Jimmy spent the previous summer there, and all of the fraternity brothers, particularly the new ones like Charlie and Mickey, were constantly wanting to hear this contagious person paint unbelievable pictures of the Vegas strip with his words, from the bright lights which were never turned off and kept people from knowing whether it was daylight or dark, to the long-legged showgirls with huge breasts whose appearances and inviting smiles made your knees feel like jelly.

"Hey, Charlie!" Jimmy yelled at his friend. The sudden sound made Charlie jump, causing some of his beer to spill out of his cup.

Turning and seeing Jimmy, Charlie said, "Hi, J.D. You know, one of these days I'm going to get used to the way you greet people. You'd think I'd be used to it having known you for more than twenty years, but you still scare me every time."

"Here, guys. Grab these two beers and I'll go get us two more," Jimmy said as he held his tray forward for his friends to capture the two cups. "You know, Mick, not only do they not vend beer at this ballpark, they also only let you buy two beers at a time. No wonder the lines at the beer stand are so long."

Charlie and Mickey watched as Jimmy hurried up the stairs to purchase more beer before the game started. "He's amazing, isn't he?" Charlie asked.

"Certainly is," Mickey agreed. "A real piece of work. One of the best salesmen I know. If anyone could sell ice to Eskimos, my money would be on him."

"I thought he was crazy when we were in college, and he's stayed the same since."

Pausing for a moment from their conversation, Charlie and Mickey both knew there were more serious things to discuss, but neither knew how to break the ice. They also knew Jimmy would be back from his latest beer run in less than twenty minutes, so recognizing time was limited, Charlie made the first move.

"Mick, I don't know what you and Jimmy have been doing, or what your business relationship is, but I imagine you two are involved in some fashion. You obviously don't have to tell me anything you don't want to, but I've got to believe it's no coincidence Jimmy has invited the two of us here for a reason."

Mickey waited for a minute to answer. "It would scare you, Charlie, if you knew all we were doing. It would truly shock you." Mickey paused for a moment and took a sip of his beer. "And since I expect you're better off not knowing, I'll simply say we've been working together and leave it at that." Pausing again, Mickey decided to confide further in his friend. "I'll also tell you I know you've agreed to work with us on some things. I don't know all you and Jimmy have discussed, and I'm pretty sure I don't want to know, but I agree it is no coincidence the three of us are here tonight."

"His imagination is phenomenal," Charlie commented regarding Jimmy, avoiding Mickey's comment about agreeing to work with them on some things. "And with his persistence and personality, it's a compelling combination."

"I am constantly amazed at how his mind works. The thing I find most interesting is he really understands people. He has a broad knowledge of a lot of different topics, more than I see in most people, but I'm still most fascinated with how he reads people. Somehow he knows how they think, or how they'll react to something. But surprisingly, in light of the number of people he takes advantage of, he is extremely loyal to a certain group of people."

"Who all is included in his loyalty ring?"

"As far as I can tell, his family and his fraternity brothers, because he thinks of them as family. I guess he subscribes to the old adage of blood being thicker than water."

"Well I suppose it's a good thing I'm on his side as opposed to being on the opposite one."

196

"I agree," Mickey said as he took the final bite of his sandwich and washed it down with another swig of beer.

Jimmy returned with two more beers and an order of spicy chicken accompanied by a honey mustard sauce. As he sat on the aisle with Charlie to his immediate right and Mickey in the next seat, Jimmy raised his cup of beer and said, "Here's to good friends and a good game. May the A's win tonight and may Sigma Chi live forever." Charlie and Mickey joined in the toast as they raised their cups and drank with their fraternity brother.

The first three innings were dominated by the pitchers, and Jimmy provided his explanation, attributing it to two factors. The first was the earlier than normal game time. Indicating the start was dictated by the television schedule, Jimmy said the sun would reflect off the windows in the outfield sky boxes until at least half past six or maybe even seven o'clock, insuring few if any hits for the first four or possibly five innings. Jimmy's second reason was his belief the pitchers had the advantage the first time facing the hitters in the opposing lineup, so he didn't expect any runs until at least the fourth inning. Jimmy's thinking sounded logical to Charlie and Mickey, although each knew Jimmy's insight into the intricacies of baseball and all sports was well beyond their knowledge, which was fine by them.

As the A's were batting in the bottom of the fourth with one man out and no runners on base, Jimmy pulled a paper from his pocket and handed it to Charlie. "Here, Mick. Take a look at this."

Charlie handed the folded page to Mickey as he heard Jimmy say, "You need to look at this as well, Charlie."

As Mickey unfolded the sheet he saw MP111 written in blue ink across the top of a printed page. Charlie also saw the blue letters but didn't know what it meant.

Mickey was the first to ask, "What's this MP111 at the top?"

"Mortgage Payment November one," Jimmy replied with a smile. "I told you we were going to figure out how to do this, and here it is." Jimmy waited for his statement to register while also giving his two friends some time to look at the information.

"The name and address and other personal information at the top are what we should use for our bank accounts. The two banks below the name and address both have branches in Santa Cruz, and using them will avoid conflicts with the accounts of the people at the bottom." Charlie read the names silently and was glad neither was his bank.

"All of the other stuff at the bottom," Jimmy continued but then paused for a moment to provide a dramatic effect, "are people, their addresses, their phone numbers, their banks, their account numbers, their social security numbers, their online user names and passwords, the institution and account number they pay their mortgage to, and their monthly mortgage payment amount to be paid by electronic bill pay on November 1st." Jimmy smiled as he watched his two friends look in astonishment at the completeness of the fourteen records.

"This is amazing, J.D.," Charlie said. "How'd you get this?" Charlie couldn't believe someone could gather all of this data for this many people without the help of someone at each of the respective banking institutions listed.

"I told you before, Charlie," Jimmy replied. "A realtor has access to a phenomenal amount of information about homeowners whose houses are for sale. With enough care and work, it's all there for the taking."

Mickey sat and stared at the piece of paper, and then he closed his eyes as he realized Jimmy expected him to walk into a branch of each of the banks in Santa Cruz and open the accounts. Mickey opened his eyes when he heard Jimmy start talking again.

"What we need to do Mick, at the advice of our friend here, is open two accounts on Monday and generate a lot of electronic banking activity. Mainly do transfers between the accounts while also withdrawing money using an ATM. Just rotate the same five thousand dollars between the accounts in amounts of one to two thousand dollars, and make sure neither of the accounts gets overdrawn. If you do it correctly, they will look like normal accounts with fairly high traffic."

When Jimmy stopped talking Mickey looked at Charlie to judge if what Jimmy said seemed reasonable to a long-time banker. Charlie nodded his approval, so Mickey turned his eyes back to Jimmy.

"Then on the 30th of October, which is a Tuesday, we will change the bill pay directions for any of the fourteen people who have not sold their homes. With some luck, there may be as many as ten or more remaining. My expectation with the way the real estate market is presently moving is for five to eleven to still not be sold.

"Once the transfers of the mortgage amounts are completed on the first day of November, that evening we'll change the bill pay directions back to what they previously were. Then we'll close out both accounts on the morning of the next day. With the accounts being opened for almost four weeks with significant activity on a regular basis, no one will question the sudden closing of either.

"The first time anyone will see a problem is when the mortgage companies send notices to the homeowners informing them their payments were not received. When they check and see the payment went to the wrong account, they'll call the banks in Santa Cruz. The first bank will see the activity and also see the account is closed. The bank trail will lead to the other account, but it will also be closed and will lead back to the first account. Both accounts will point to the name and address of the account holder, but that will only show the way to the poor soul listed at the top, who just moved to Pleasanton from New Jersey three weeks ago and may not even know where Santa Cruz is.

"You'd think people from New Jersey would know better than to not change the locks on a house they just purchased. Maybe we can convince Billy to become a locksmith and make an unsolicited telemarketing call on this guy," Jimmy said as he laughed with a huge grin.

Charlie laughed at the joke, but Mickey only smiled, the gears in his head turning as he contemplated the feasibility of this latest concoction. "I think I'll get us two more beers," Mickey said as he started to get up from his seat.

"Don't bother, Mick," Jimmy spoke as he got up and motioned with his hand for Mickey to sit back down. "Let me go. I need to make a pit stop anyway."

After Jimmy walked up the stairway and was out of sight, Mickey looked at Charlie with raised eyebrows and a blank stare. Taking this as his cue to comment, Charlie said, "I agree with Jimmy it will work. There's no way to completely cover your tracks, so having them point in a circular fashion between two accounts and to a real person and address different from one of us is the only way."

"So what are the three most likely mistakes we can make?" Mickey asked. Then he added, "or I can make?"

"First would be being recognized at one of the two banks when you open or close the accounts, or when you make ATM withdrawals. I know Jimmy has some way of helping provide identification and a disguise. Please don't ask me how I know, 'cause I don't know the details and you're better off not knowing why I know. I'm sure it's similar to some of the secrets you and Jimmy should rightly keep from me.

Seeing Mickey nod in agreement Charlie continued. "Second would be the computer access you use for doing the electronic modification of the bill paying. You should go to a library which provides computers with modems and phone lines. Third is one thing Jimmy said. Generate a lot of activity between the accounts, including transfers in each direction and ATM withdrawals for each, but be sure not to get overdrawn. Transfers between accounts which get overdrawn are a big red flag to a bank."

"I may want to call on you for some additional advice," Mickey said as he remembered Jimmy's comment at dinner long ago saying Charlie would get an equal share for providing counseling.

"I'm sure you'll be fine, Mick, but feel free to give me a call if you want to chat. I should caution you though. If someone was to recognize you and some checking was done, any calls out of the ordinary would raise more questions."

"We've been fraternity brothers since we were in college, Charlie," Mickey said defensively.

"I know, Mick, but we haven't called each other on a regular basis for many years, pretty much since about a year after I got married. Except for when you were going through your divorce, of course, 'cause we talked quite often then for several months."

Recognizing his friend was a little afraid, Charlie tried to reassure him. "Oh, don't worry about how often you call me. As I said, you'll do fine, and the plan is solid."

Jimmy returned to his seat with two beers in hand. "Hey, guys," he started. "Why don't we all make the trip back to Memphis for homecoming this year? It's been two years since I've made the trip, and I thought it would be fun to go. Billy goes back every year, so

I'm sure he'll be going again. When's the last time you went back, Charlie?"

"Let me think," Charlie said as he looked to the sky in a thinking pose. "Seven years I think. I remember going back the first year after I got married. My new bride wasn't too warm to the idea, but I went anyway. Boy, what a mistake. I didn't hear the end of it when I returned, so I agreed with her to only do it every so often. Once I missed the following year, I haven't made it back."

"See," Jimmy started. "You're way overdue to go back then. Why don't you find a time when she's in a really good mood, and tell her you're thinking of going back this year since it has been so long? Surely she'll understand."

"I don't know. It sounds like fun, but I'll have to wait and see. When is it this year anyway?"

"The first weekend in November," Jimmy said. "It's later than normal for some reason, but hopefully it won't be as hot as it has been some years when it was in the first half of October. How about you, Mick?"

"I'm in, Jimmy," Mickey replied. "I usually plan a golf trip around the homecoming weekend with some of my golfing buddies in south Mississippi. The last two years we've actually played in Alabama on the golf courses which are part of the Robert Trent Jones Trail. One of them told me the state of Mississippi was approached first about the idea of a series of courses throughout the state, and for some reason they balked on it. Alabama couldn't jump fast enough or high enough when they were asked. It's probably a good thing, as some of the venues in Alabama have more hills and there are more locations with hardwood trees as opposed to pines. I don't mind a course carved out of pines, 'cause I grew up on those, but it gets a little old after an entire week."

Just as Mickey finished the Yankee batter hit a liner to left. The fielder continued to chase the ball as he neared the warning track. Not expecting the ball to carry the fence, the fielder stood at the base of the wall in astonishment as it barely sailed over the top of the scoreboard used for scores of other games during the regular season.

The crowd was incredibly silent as they tried to understand what they just witnessed. As the A's fans realized the score would now be 1-0 in favor of the visiting Yankees once the runner rounding third crossed home, they began to boo. A large number of fans were cheering however, indicating how many Yankee fans were in attendance.

"I can't believe it!" Jimmy shouted. "The ball cleared the fence!" he shouted in amazement. "I thought it was a routine fly ball! That guy's not a home run hitter! That's ridiculous! How can we let that guy hit a home run!?"

"Easy, Jimmy," Charlie tried to console his friend. "There's still plenty of innings left, and it's only one run. I'm sure the A's will catch up," he added hopeful of a comeback.

The A's did have rallies during the next two at-bats, but neither effort resulted in a score. In one inning an Oakland runner starting from first was thrown out at the plate on a double to right on a magnificent play by an infielder. The runner was slow and didn't slide, but it still took an outstanding defensive play to get him.

The anger Jimmy felt was obvious on his face as the game approached the final two innings with the score still 1-0. His fear was the Yankees star reliever would now be able to pitch the final two innings to preserve the win. Unfortunately, his fear became reality as the Yankees went on to win by the single run.

"Tough loss, Jimmy," Mickey said as the three stood to make their way to the exit.

"Yeah," Jimmy retorted. "The home run was the difference. One pitch. It's like this so many times in the playoffs. A pitch, a hit, or one missed play in the field is the difference between a win and a loss. Same thing tonight."

The three walked through the short tunnel leading to the parking lot with the remainder of the mostly disappointed crowd, as some sparse cheers could be heard coming from those wearing Yankee caps. Jimmy and Mickey were parked in one direction while Charlie was in another. After saying goodbye to their banking advisor, Jimmy and Mickey walked together in silence for several steps. Then Jimmy said, "Mick, I've got another idea I'd like to discuss with you." Mickey didn't answer as he wasn't sure he wanted to hear what his friend had on his mind.

"I've been thinking about another way to cheat a homeowner out of some money during the closing. I got the idea from a closing about three months ago when one of my agents was representing the buyer.

The seller had a lien against their property they knew nothing about. It seemed like a fairly petty thing. I remember the amount was only a few hundred dollars, but the seller was forced to pay it before the closing was complete."

"Anybody can file a lien against a property, Jimmy," Mickey commented. "It happens all the time. That's part of the work I do for the title search, check for any liens against the property. That's part of the basis for title insurance, to protect the buyer from inheriting liens which may not have been found."

"I'm not interested in collecting money from any title insurance, Mick. I just want the seller to pay some money in the closing which is paid to us. What would keep us from filing a lien against someone's property and getting them to simply pay it as part of the closing?"

"The filing's not the problem. Getting them to pay it is where the difficulty would be. I assume you would be the realtor for the seller?"

"Certainly," Jimmy responded, "although I'd like to figure out how we could pull it off when I represent the buyer, too. What would be the ultimate is to pull it off when I don't represent the seller or the buyer."

"You should really go to a doctor and get him to prescribe something for you to contain your imagination and greed, Jimmy," Mickey said jokingly before he continued. "Let me give you my take in the case where you represent the seller. When your client saw such an entry on their settlement statement, they would first ask you a lot of questions and then they would want to track down who filed it against them and why, particularly if they didn't recognize who wanted money from them or if they didn't remember some significant situation where they didn't pay someone for something. And it would have to be something which warranted having someone go to the trouble of filing the lien. Most people just keep asking for someone to pay them. They may threaten legal action, but it usually stops there."

"Well here's my thought, Mick," Jimmy interrupted as he listened carefully in his efforts to learn and understand, but he was getting a little disgusted his friend's tone was one of wanting to dismiss the idea without giving it a fair chance. "I came across a homeowner three weeks ago who belonged to two country clubs. Now most clubs here in California require you to provide them with bank account information on your application, which doesn't authorize the club to withdraw any money, but it certainly informs the applicant up front who is in control.

"If a member doesn't pay their monthly bill at the club for one reason or another, the club usually maintains the balance and charges a significant interest rate. It's kind of like a credit card, but in some cases the rate is tremendously high, as they really try to discourage members from not paying their bills on time. It's all legal since it's part of the bylaws and all members have signed something saying they will abide by all rules, without really knowing everything in the bylaws. Plus, some of the policies and regulations change over time anyway, so most members can't keep up with all of it, particularly if someone belongs to multiple clubs.

"Also, all clubs usually reserve the right to assess their entire membership whenever they want for any amount they want. Sometimes the assessment is counted as being an addition to the initiation fee, so the member gets part of it back when they sell their membership, but that's not universally true. Sometimes the assessment is just a bill which has to be paid either immediately or over time with some finance charge added.

"So what keeps us from starting a company with a name resembling a country club, and filing a lien against a homeowner, supposedly for not paying some previous assessment?"

The two continued their walk toward their cars as Mickey contemplated Jimmy's latest idea. "I'll have to give this some more thought, Jimmy. It actually sounds possible. Maybe I should go back through all of my records and see what liens were paid at different closings to refresh my memory on the specifics of what's been done. I could also check other closings. Let me do some research, and then we can discuss it again."

Satisfied with this proposed action, Jimmy smiled and said, "Good. But don't take too long as the information I have is only valuable until a house sells. After it sells I have to start all over with someone new."

"I think I'm parked this way," Mickey said as he pointed to his left and began to take a few steps in that direction.

"Hang on a minute," Jimmy quickly replied. "I'm just up here, and I've got something for you. It'll only take a minute, and it's something you'll need."

Jimmy increased his pace as he reached in his pocket for his keys. Mickey followed not knowing what to expect. Jimmy pushed the button on his keyless entry to open the trunk. He reached inside and grabbed a grocery sack with the top closed and rolled down about halfway. Mickey could tell the contents were light as Jimmy easily picked up the sack.

As he accepted the sack from his friend, Mickey wasn't sure he should open it in the parking lot. "Go ahead, Mick. Open it," Jimmy said with encouragement.

Unrolling the container Mickey peered inside. He saw three hats sitting on top of some kind of cloth. "What's this?" he asked.

"It's your disguise, Mick. There's three hats and two shirts. They were previously owned by a New Jersey man now living in Pleasanton. I'm sure he won't miss them as I found them near the bottom of a moving box. Just wear them when you go to open the bank accounts on Monday, when you go to the ATM for making withdrawals, and when you close out the accounts after we've captured the mortgage payments. Trust me, it'll work perfectly."

"If you say so, Jimmy. I'll call you next week."

"Okay, Mick. See you later."

"See you," Mickey said as he was already walking toward his car. As he walked and thought about the sheet of paper in his pocket labeled MP111, he had a different idea for his disguise for opening the bank accounts on Monday. It was one he intended on not telling Jimmy or Charlie about.

EIGHTEEN

The sky was clear as morning dawned on the Monterey peninsula on Monday, October 8th. It was fairly brisk, as a cool wind was blowing in from the ocean, but the temperature was expected to rise into the mid to upper seventies by the afternoon. Mickey was at his office much earlier than normal as he was editing a file Jimmy sent to him.

In addition to the hats and shirts in the grocery sack Jimmy gave Mickey on Friday evening, a fake California driver's license was present. Jimmy generated it the same way he always did, but Mickey called on Saturday stating it contained a picture which was somewhat outdated. Jimmy knew the picture was one from three or four years ago, so he agreed to email the computer file to Mickey for editing.

Mickey spent Saturday afternoon talking with his assistant, and dinner in the evening was also included. Another meeting on Sunday culminated with a promise, a handshake, and the taking of a picture with a digital camera. Now on Monday morning Mickey was not swapping the older picture of himself for a more recent one on the driver's license. Instead, he was exchanging his picture with the one of his assistant.

When Mickey's assistant arrived at the office on Monday morning shortly before nine o'clock, Mickey recognized the shirt as one from the grocery sack. When Mickey asked about the hat, he was told it was in the car. Armed with the fake identification, a page full of information about a person now living in Pleasanton who previously resided in New Jersey, and thirty-five hundred dollars in cash, Mickey's assistant left the office for the drive to Santa Cruz.

The instructions were discussed in the meeting yesterday, and they were also written on one side of a small index card. The other side of the card contained the personal information of the man who had no idea his name and identification were being used for this purpose.

The instructions were fairly simplistic. A first account was to be opened with one thousand dollars. Electronic banking was to be included, and this service was expected to be free based upon a radio ad Jimmy heard on his drive home from Oakland on Friday night. Instead of mailing the checks and ATM card to the home address, a request to keep them at the bank for personal pickup was to be made. If the bank personnel asked why this was necessary, a simple explanation of still being in the process of moving and not yet occupying the new house was to be provided. A second account was to be opened at another bank with two thousand dollars and the same services and arrangements for checks and debit card. The last line of the notes on the index card specified the remaining five hundred dollars was an employment bonus.

At quarter of eleven Mickey left his office for a long walk. For the last hour he didn't do any work since he couldn't focus on anything other than his thoughts about how his assistant was doing. Knowing his assistant was probably nearing Santa Cruz or possibly walking into the first bank, Mickey didn't want to answer the phone if it rang. He decided to walk to the wharf and watch tourists shop for souvenirs which he expected would be junk when they arrived home at the end of their vacations.

In one shop Mickey noticed an older couple purchasing a fairly unique wind chime. The top was bright green and had white lines representing the markings on a baseball diamond. Hanging from the top were four small baseball bats of different sizes to provide different tones. In the center on a small string was a baseball, which was positioned to hit the bats somewhere close to their sweet spot. The string continued downward and a catcher's mitt was suspended at the bottom. The glove would easily be moved by the wind, causing the baseball to clang against the bats, thus producing a pleasant melody. If only the chimes could play a recognizable baseball tune Mickey pondered as he admired the distinctive gift. He also wondered if the same company designed a similar version for golf enthusiasts. He walked closer to the display to identify the manufacturing company so he could later contact them or check their web site.

A few stores further along his walk Mickey saw a young couple he expected were on their honeymoon. The new bride had three Christmas ornaments in one hand and was begging her husband to buy another one. He was resisting in a soft tone as he looked around to see if anyone in the store was paying attention to them. Mickey saw the young man simply walk away in his final effort of resistance, but it was to no avail as his bride grabbed the extra one in an angry gesture with a sneer on her face. Mickey wondered how long the marriage would last if so much disagreement over a few dollars was already present.

A restaurant which served clam chowder and chili in bread soup bowls caught Mickey's attention as his stomach began to growl. With a little of the chill from the early morning remaining, he thought a warm bowl of soup matched with a sandwich and fries would be appropriate. When he entered he decided to sit at the bar as opposed to waiting to be seated. Being a local he saw the bay and ocean regularly, so he decided to let the tourists have the more desirable seats at the tables against the windows. Mickey knew the service was quicker from the bar anyway, particularly for drinks, so he found a stool near one end which allowed him a view of the foot traffic passing by the front.

It was well past four o'clock when Mickey finished the walk back to his office. Maybe if he sat at a table instead of the bar he wouldn't have drank well into the afternoon, but he didn't really care now. What was done was done he figured, and he was in a much better mood to accept whatever his assistant reported regarding the events in Santa Cruz.

When he walked into his office his assistant was busy working. The two greeted each other as if nothing special happened, and when Mickey finally asked if everything went fine at the banks, his assistant merely nodded affirmatively and stated, "The account numbers and receipts are on your desk." When asked about getting the checks and ATM cards, the response was simply, "They'll be ready on Wednesday at one bank and Thursday for the other, so I'll get them both on Thursday."

Mickey sat at his desk and wished he could be as carefree as his assistant as he looked at the messages awaiting him. He flipped through the stack and chose to call a friend in Mississippi who phoned earlier with some questions about the golfing trip in November.

Over the next two weeks Mickey completed several electronic transfers of money between the two accounts. His assistant also made regular deposits and withdrawals, usually via an automatic teller but sometimes in person inside the banks. Both carefully tracked the banking activity, making certain neither account was overdrawn.

Mickey's office phone rang on Tuesday, October 23rd, at fifteen minutes after ten o'clock in the morning. His assistant announced it was Jimmy Donovan and transferred the call to Mickey. After a brief greeting Jimmy focused on the business at hand.

"How ya' doin' with our special accounts and activity?" Jimmy asked.

"Things are fine. They've been open for two weeks now, and there's been a transfer, deposit, or withdrawal for at least one of the accounts every day. Neither account has been idle for more than a day, and every transaction has shown up the very next day when I check the activity electronically."

"Good, Mick. I know it's a lot of trouble for you to have to take the time to drive to Santa Cruz to use the ATM, but it'll be worth it."

"It's okay, Jimmy. I enjoy getting out of the office for a drive in my jaguar from time to time," Mickey said in a calm tone, fairly confident Jimmy would not detect he was lying. "And it's certainly better only having to go to Santa Cruz versus what I used to do for law school in San Jose. Plus, this won't last nearly as long."

"Well I wanted to touch base with you regarding our list of candidates. Three are no longer available, and those are numbers two, six, and nine on your sheet. A fourth one will probably go away later this week. I can't tell you for sure if any are definite winners for us, but I'm pretty confident in five. So we're somewhere between five and ten right now."

"When do you expect to have a final list for me, Jimmy?"

"I'll call you again next Monday afternoon after I check on what if anything happens this coming weekend. I won't have a final list then, as I'm sure there will be one or more where an offer is made but not yet accepted. That's the easy part though. The harder part will be trying to determine if an offer is being prepared. I have no way of finding out for sure how many prospective buyers look at a particular property on a given weekend, or any day of the week for that matter, so I don't know what everyone is thinking. Plus, many homes have open houses on Saturday or Sunday, and the results of those are completely random.

"I'll be able to tell you on Monday which ones are definitely out. On Tuesday I'll give you the ones which are definitely in, and you can change the bill pay directions for those. I'll continue to monitor the ones we pick through the end of Thursday to see if anything unusual comes up. Even if there is one where an offer is made and accepted, it shouldn't affect their mortgage having to be paid on the first of the month, so we'll be fine.

"Once we see how this works, we may be able to change our timing a little in the future. I expect we would be safe choosing anyone who didn't get an offer seven or even as many as ten days before the end of the month, but I think it's better to error on the safe side this first time around."

"I agree," Mickey said as he thought Jimmy had now told him this last part on at least three previous occasions. A little tired of hearing it again, Mickey tried to end the call by saying, "Just call me next Monday with an update, and then we'll talk again on Tuesday. Anything else?"

"Yeah. Have you finalized your plans for the homecoming trip?"

"Not yet. I'm still working out the details with the rest of my golf group. It would be so much easier if just three other guys would simply agree to play every day for a certain number of days. But what is happening is two guys want to play these three days, two other guys want to play these two days, and another guy wants to play every other day 'cause he wants to bring his wife and kids along and says he can't play every day. So even though I want to have either four guys or eight guys, I'm not sure how many we'll have. I'm sure we'll get it all worked out, but it definitely takes a lot more work than it should."

"Sounds like you should tell the guy with the wife to forget it," Jimmy said. Not waiting for a reply he added, "I'm glad it's you and not me dealing with it. When are you planning on flying out?"

"Sometime on Friday. What are you doing, and do you know what Billy's or Charlie's plans are?"

"Billy's going out a few days early to visit some of his relatives first. Charlie and I are on the same flight out of San Francisco on Friday morning. Charlie's got some free upgrades to first class for us to use."

"Sounds sweet. Maybe I should take the same flight. Reckon Charlie's got another upgrade for me, too. I love flying first class."

"I know you do, Mick, but we're taking an early flight Friday morning. You can't leave until the afternoon since you've got to close out those two accounts in the morning, or did you forget?"

Knowing his assistant would be tending to the bank business, Mickey forgot Jimmy expected him to be taking an afternoon flight. Now realizing his mistake Mickey said, "Oh, yeah. That's right. Trying to make all of these golf arrangements along with this bank stuff is making it difficult for me to keep up with all of the dates and details. I guess I'll probably just take an afternoon flight from San Jose. Where are you staying?"

"I was thinking about spending the night with my parents there in Germantown, but Charlie knows someone at the Peabody, so we'll be there. He booked two rooms, both with two double beds. You're welcome to stay in one of those rooms, as it's just Charlie, Billy, and me. We were expecting you to join us."

"Sounds good. Thanks for taking care of it. I've been so busy keeping up with other things I completely forgot how difficult it is to get a room in Memphis during homecoming weekend."

"Well, I hope you get all of your golf stuff figured out, but be sure to stay on top of the accounts. I'm sure you'll play much better once we collect the money from those accounts."

"Okay, Jimmy. I'll talk to you next Monday."

The two said their goodbyes and hung up. Jimmy was a little mystified Mickey hadn't booked his flights or hotels yet, but he didn't know how difficult it was to organize a group of golfers, so he turned his attention to a section of the map on his wall he planned on visiting sometime in November.

Mickey on the other hand sat and stared at his phone after the call. He almost made a serious blunder in not remembering what his schedule was versus what Jimmy thought his schedule should be. In thinking about his travel itinerary, Mickey did not want to arrive in Memphis in the evening, and it was his plan to let his assistant close the accounts on the Friday morning while he was on a flight. He now decided it would be better to amend his plans so he grabbed his personal calendar and made a note to drive to Santa Cruz on Friday morning. He explicitly wrote down two shops where he could shop for new golf attire and three restaurant options for lunch to make sure he didn't schedule a flight until the early afternoon. As he finished writing he grabbed the phone and hit the speed dial button for his travel agent. As the phone rang he reached for his list of golf contacts which contained his latest notes about when everyone said they could make it.

The following weekend was busy for Jimmy as he made and kept appointments to preview all eleven houses remaining on his mortgage candidate list. In eight of the eleven cases the homeowners were home when he visited, allowing him to ask a few questions to get a feel for how much traffic each home recently received. The other three were out of town for the weekend, so he chose to make his stop late on Sunday afternoon to gauge the amount of activity by seeing how many business cards of other realtors were left at the respective homes.

One of the three houses had five cards sitting on a sofa table near the front door and three more cards laying on the kitchen table. The house was quite breathtaking on the inside as the carpet looked new, the inside was recently painted, the kitchen contained new appliances, and the presentation was obviously done by a professional decorator based upon the position of the furniture, the setting of the dining room table, the fake greenery everywhere, and the absence of normal clutter usually seen in an occupied home. Jimmy placed a star by the name of this candidate on his list as he expected one or more offers to come from the large number of prospective buyers who obviously visited in the last few days.

On Monday morning Jimmy spent from shortly after nine o'clock until well past noon contacting the agents for all eleven houses. As expected, the house with the significant traffic went pending as the seller was able to choose from two written offers and a third verbal one. The agent for another listing was expecting an offer later in the day based upon the comments she received from a buyer's agent, so Jimmy made a note to call back on Tuesday morning to get another update.

After a well-deserved break for lunch, Jimmy phoned Mickey to provide an update. The list was now reduced to ten, and it was expected to be pared down an additional one. The good news was at least nine of the original fourteen remained, which was more than Jimmy originally anticipated.

Jimmy and Mickey once again discussed their plans for the upcoming weekend in Memphis, and Mickey was now much happier about the final golf arrangements. Three golfers committed to playing six consecutive days while all of the others, including the one who was considering bringing his family, opted to skip this year while promising to get better organized sooner the following year to avoid so much confusion. Mickey's flight was scheduled to arrive in Memphis at 7:52pm, and Jimmy volunteered Charlie, Billy, and he would meet Mickey at the airport before heading to a favorite barbeque place for some ribs and beer.

On Tuesday morning when Jimmy phoned the agent again, he learned an offer was made and accepted, so he crossed off the entry and studied the remaining nine. As he looked at the names and addresses, he tried to picture the color and style of each house. He attempted to remember the faces and clothes of the homeowners he met while he also struggled to recall parts of the conversation with each. He did this as a final mental check to convince himself his research was sufficient, as he determined if he couldn't remember certain things he probably was a little remiss in doing his homework. After engaging in this cerebral exercise for more than forty minutes, he felt satisfied with each of the nine. He saw from the clock it was almost eleven o'clock in the morning, so he picked up his phone and called Mickey.

"Hi, Mick. It's J.D. How ya' doin'?" Jimmy familiarly started.

"Good, Jimmy," Mickey replied. Then he asked, "Anything new from yesterday?"

"Yeah. Number twelve on the list needs to be deleted. As we discussed yesterday, they did get an offer which they accepted. The realtor wouldn't tell me the price, but I expect they took less than they were asking."

"You know they don't have to tell you the price while the sale is pending," Mickey reminded his friend.

"Yeah, I know. But usually one agent will tell another agent as a courtesy. Kind of like a fraternity sharing information within its membership. It just makes it easier for all of us to work together. Oh well, hopefully the agent cut their commission to help close the deal," Jimmy added as he let out a fake laugh.

The two reviewed the list one last time to make sure Mickey deleted the appropriate five and was targeting the right nine. Content the list was correct, the two made plans to talk on Wednesday after Mickey changed the electronic bill pay directions.

In the middle of the afternoon on Tuesday Mickey left his office and headed to the library where for the last few weeks he used the available computers and internet access to complete the electronic transfers of money between the two accounts. As Mickey entered through the back entrance a man seated by the door once again greeted him generically, not knowing his name. Mickey returned the greeting and quickly walked to the computer section.

Seeing all of the terminals occupied Mickey decided to browse in the adjacent legal section until a machine was available. As he mindlessly looked at some of the books on the shelves, he heard a familiar voice one aisle over asking for some help from a librarian. He felt his body go stiff and his mouth go dry as he recognized his ex-wife's voice. Not wanting to have a chance encounter with her, he made his way to the exit as quickly and as quietly as possible. The man at the door once again said something to him, but Mickey wasn't listening in his haste as he forcefully pushed the door open and took the stairs two at a time before turning in the direction he was parked.

When he got in his car and started the ignition, Mickey realized his heart was pounding, his knees were shaking, and his palms were sweaty. He decided to drive to a nearby bar and have a drink. He parked along the street directly in front of the establishment as very few were gathered since it was still early. After ordering a pint of beer and downing more than half with two big drinks, he gazed out the front window. Suddenly he began wondering if he should have parked in a more concealed spot on the chance his wife might drive by when she made her exit from the library. He finished his beer with another big drink and decided to leave his car where it was as he ordered a second pint.

Not knowing it was almost eight o'clock Tuesday evening, Mickey reached in his wallet and handed the bartender a fifty dollar bill and told him to keep the change. The bartender politely indicated the charge for the beers, snacks, and sandwich was slightly more than fifty dollars, so Mickey found another twenty and gave it to the man. Mickey wondered how many beers he consumed and the price of each since many should have been at the lower price of happy hour, but he let it pass and left without questioning the bartender's math.

When Mickey looked at the clock in his car and saw the time, he realized the library closed at seven on Tuesdays. He pounded the steering wheel and cursed himself as he drove. When he pulled into his driveway, he turned off the car and remained inside as he debated his options for completing his computer work.

He first thought about postponing it until the next day, but he knew this was not what Charlie recommended. His next thought was to do it from home, but this was another item Charlie instructed him to avoid. Finally he thought about his assistant.

Mickey gave his assistant five hundred dollars to open the accounts. Their deal was for a second five hundred to be paid for all of the deposits and withdrawals, followed by a third and final payment of five hundred for closing the accounts. From Jimmy's initial estimation Mickey expected eight from the original list of fourteen candidates to remain, but now there were nine. Mickey's share from this ninth mortgage payment would easily cover giving his assistant another five hundred dollars, so he got out of his car and eagerly went inside.

The assistant answered the phone on the first ring, and twenty minutes later Mickey was parking his jaguar in front of his assistant's apartment. Three hours later the ninth and final bill paying direction was changed. Once finished Mickey declined the offer for another beer and headed for home in the dark.

Wednesday and Thursday passed without fanfare as Mickey did little work while he worried about the accounts. He stayed in his office from the time he arrived until it was time to return home, not wanting to venture out for lunch or even a short walk. He had difficulty sleeping both nights, but Thursday was particularly tough as he contemplated all which could go wrong and tried not to think of the potential consequences. Although he cheated many people out of money with a variety of schemes over the years, he concluded he was clearly way out of his comfort zone with this latest mortgage and banking concoction. He swore he would tell Jimmy to find someone else to participate in this specific activity in the future, and the thought comforted him enough to allow a few hours of uninterrupted sleep.

On Friday morning Mickey chose not to go to his office first, but rather to wait until the library opened at nine o'clock and go there instead. The library had few patrons as he made his way to the computer room. He logged onto the internet and typed in the username and password for the first account. After he positioned the mouse over the login button and clicked, a screen unfamiliar to him was displayed. He read the message which stated the account was protected by a special mechanism requiring a change to the password on the first day of each month. Since it was now November 2nd, the account holder would have to visit one of the branches in person to regain electronic access.

Mickey couldn't believe his luck. It must be related to the free electronic banking he thought, so he tried to access the second account. This time he was successful, and he clicked on the appropriate link to view the balance. A broad smile came across his face as he saw a much larger number. He struggled to control his excitement as he wanted to jump up and down and shout. He made a note of the balance and recent transactions and quickly logged off. Hoping the other account was also credited with new deposits from yesterday, he gathered his things and exited the library for the drive to his office.

When Mickey walked in the door to his office, his assistant was dressed in one of the shirts Jimmy provided. Mickey recognized one of the hats on the desk sitting on top of a manila folder. Mickey handed an index card with notes for one of the accounts to his assistant while he explained the problem with the other account.

His assistant now remembered the safety feature, but indicated it would be no problem and told Mickey not to worry since the account was going to be closed in a few hours anyway. The two shook hands as Mickey restated their agreement to have all but the final five hundred dollar fee deposited into his personal account. His assistant wished him good luck on his golfing trip, and the two exited the office and walked to their cars.

The destinations of both were Santa Cruz with Mickey intending to shop for golf clothes while his assistant was going to the banks. Mickey drove well over the speed limit and arrived in Santa Cruz at eleven o'clock. Within thirty minutes he purchased several shirts, a few pairs of pants, and a sweater. With a drive of an hour or more to San Jose ahead of him, he decided to have a quick lunch so he would be certain to catch his flight.

As Mickey drove to San Jose, he wondered if his assistant successfully closed the accounts. He also hoped there were no problems with depositing the funds into his personal account. After arriving at the San Jose airport and parking in the long-term lot adjacent to a shuttle pickup location, he grabbed his golf clubs, suitcase, and shopping bag from earlier and climbed aboard the bus as the driver was kind enough to wait for him. As Mickey road to the terminal he looked at his watch and saw it was a few minutes before one o'clock. Mickey's wait in line for checking his luggage was surprisingly short, leaving him with about an hour until takeoff.

Mickey made his way through security without incident and walked down the corridor toward his gate which was located at the far end of the concourse. Halfway to his gate he found a quiet spot in the corner where a flight just finished boarding, and he used his cell phone to call his office to see if his assistant returned.

After several rings the answering machine began to play the greeting his assistant recorded several months ago. Mickey decided not to leave a message but to try again just before it was time for him to board his flight. He continued his walk toward his gate and then stopped at a newsstand to hopefully find a book which could occupy him. He purchased a paperback from the bestseller rack, and as the young lady behind the counter pulled his change from the cash register he noticed several copies of a new hardcover release by the same author. Mickey stuffed the book and receipt in his shopping bag from earlier in the day and resumed his walk.

When he arrived at the gate Mickey looked at his boarding pass and saw he was seated near the middle of the plane in a center seat. He cursed himself and his golfing friends for not finalizing their plans soon enough to allow him to get a better seating assignment, and he hoped it would be better next year. As the first class passengers were called he thought of Charlie and Billy and expected they already were in Memphis after a pleasant ride in first class. As those with seats in the back rows of the aircraft were allowed to board, he decided to try his office one more time.

Once again his assistant did not answer, and Mickey began to worry if anything went wrong. He debated about whether or not he should delay his departure until he confirmed the money was in his account, but he didn't know what excuse he would use with Jimmy and Charlie who were planning on meeting him at the other end. Deciding to trust his assistant he boarded the plane when his row was announced.

Fortunately for Mickey the book he purchased was one he found to be very consuming. A young mother almost in poverty won the state lottery with the help of a man who rigged the outcome. The man was an expert in chemistry, but Mickey didn't understand all the technical details of how the numbered balls matching her ticket were selected via some special magnetic mechanism. It made for a good plot though, and he enjoyed the style of the author's writing.

Mickey chose not to eat the meal provided during the flight. Instead he only drank a few beers and ate some peanuts since he wanted to be able to fully enjoy the upcoming meal Jimmy promised, and his stomach started growling as the captain announced the final approach into Memphis. Mickey found a good stopping point in his book and looked out the window at the landscape west of Memphis. As he looked at the farms below Mickey's thoughts turned back to his assistant, and he hoped everything was fine.

Once the aircraft stopped and the seat belt signed was turned off, most of the passengers stood to gather their carry-on bags stored in the overhead bins. Mickey continued to sit and looked at his watch. It was almost eight o'clock in Memphis, meaning it was nearing six o'clock in California. He didn't expect his assistant to be at the office, yet he dialed the number anyway.

When he heard the answering machine again, he terminated the call and dialed his assistant's home number as a last resort. He didn't expect an answer since Friday evening was just beginning in Monterey, but he found he was disappointed nonetheless when he hit the end button after the tenth ring. Mickey was out of options since his assistant didn't have a cell phone or a pager, so he grabbed his bag and slowly made his way toward the gate. As he walked he contemplated what he should tell Jimmy and Charlie who would be waiting with Billy at the baggage claim.

NINETEEN

"Hey, Mick!" Mickey heard a voice yelling from somewhere in the baggage claim area. The crowd of people from his flight and another arrival left little room for him or the others to walk.

"Hey, Mick!" he heard again as this time he was able to detect the voice coming from over his left shoulder. As he turned his head he saw Jimmy waving and fighting his way through the mass.

"Hi, Mick. How ya' doin'? How was your flight?" Jimmy asked, his exuberance overflowing.

"Fine, Jimmy. The flight was fine," Mickey responded as he saw Charlie and Billy now approaching.

"Hey, Mick," Charlie greeted his friend as he extended his hand with a smile. "Welcome to Memphis. I hope you enjoyed the flight."

"Hey, Charlie. Thanks. The flight was fine," Mickey said. "This book I bought in San Jose is pretty interesting. I'll have to give it to you when I finish. I think you'll enjoy it."

"Thanks. I always like a good book when I have to fly to the east coast, and I might be making the trip next month."

"Hi, Mickey," Billy offered his welcome.

"Hi, Billy," Mickey replied as he shook hands with Billy. "I heard you came out a few days early to visit some friends and family. How's your sister doing?"

"She's good," Billy answered. "Happily married to a chicken farmer, and they've got four kids."

"Wow. Four kids. I'm sure that's a handful. How old are they?" Mickey asked as he heard a loud buzzer and saw a red light flashing, indicating the luggage from his flight was arriving at the carousel.

"The oldest is fifteen and the youngest is eight," Billy said as he raised his voice to talk over the noise. "Three boys and a girl. The two oldest are boys, and they're now able to help with the raising of the birds, so it's a lot easier for them to manage than when the youngest was just born. He was a surprise, and it was really tough for them both financially and physically for several years. But now things are much better and they are very content, as the youngest is a joy."

"That's good to hear. Where are they living?" Mickey asked as he tried to peek through a gap in the heads in hopes of seeing his bags.

"They're in Boaz, Alabama.

"Boaz? Where's that?"

"It's in northeast Alabama, about halfway between Birmingham and Chattanooga, closer to Birmingham, though. It's a real small place, but she likes that kind of environment."

"Yeah, I remember when she would visit you in college. She was completely overwhelmed with the size of everything and the number of people."

"She certainly wouldn't enjoy living in San Jose. That's for sure," Billy concluded.

"Aren't those your golf clubs, Mick?" Jimmy asked. Not waiting for an answer he fought his way through the large number of people to get to the front.

"We don't have to worry about what Jimmy will do when he retires, Mick," Charlie said as the two watched Jimmy bump and excuse himself through the crowd. "He can always be a sky chief."

"I keep telling him he should consider being my caddie when he retires," Mickey replied.

"I'm sure he takes kindly to that suggestion," Charlie said sarcastically.

"Yeah. About as well as he does to the one about being a bartender or a chef," Mickey said as they both laughed.

"What color is your suitcase, Mickey?" Billy asked.

"It's green. It supposedly matches the color of the greens at Pebble Beach, but either it's faded or the greens have somehow gotten darker," Mickey said as he tried to look carefully at each new suitcase as it dropped onto the carousel.

Mickey, Charlie, and Billy continued their conversation as they watched Jimmy make his way back to where they were standing with Mickey's golf clubs in tow. Seeing his other bag Mickey fought through the crowd and retrieved it. After trying to recall how many bags he checked in San Jose, Mickey also looked at the baggage receipts stapled inside the jacket of his ticket. He concluded he had all of his luggage, so the group exited through the sliding glass door into the darkness of the night.

It was half past eight, and with the recent time change back to standard time from daylight saving time, the sun was down for the day long ago. Mickey noticed it was colder in Memphis than it was in California, and he hoped the temperature would be warmer by Monday for his first round of golf. A large number of cars were moving about, but the flow seemed efficient, unlike the really slow traffic at the San Jose airport every Friday evening.

After getting everything stored in the large trunk of the full-size rental car, Jimmy got in the driver's seat and easily drove through the traffic and exited the airport. Their destination was a barbeque house, where the popular lunch choice was a pork sandwich served with cole slaw on the bun, and the evening specialty was a rack of baby back ribs accompanied by baked beans and corn on the cob. The conversation was light and the mood jovial as each commented about their last visit to Memphis.

The parking lot was full of both cars and people when they arrived at the restaurant. They could see what looked like an even number of people entering and exiting the front door as the early crowd was leaving while the late crowd was just now arriving. The hostess said they would have to wait about thirty minutes to be seated, and suggested they find a spot in the bar in the meantime.

The bar was quite crowded and filled with smoke, reminding all of them of the difference in the smoking laws between California and Tennessee. Jimmy noticed a couple preparing to leave and quickly staked claim to the small round table barely big enough for four. Charlie walked to the bar and gained the bartender's attention by holding up a twenty dollar bill. He ordered four draft beers, and when the bartender brought fourteen dollars in change with the four mugs, Charlie was reminded of the difference in the cost of living between San Francisco and Memphis. He left a tip of two dollars as he grabbed the frosty mugs.

When Charlie set the beers on the table, Jimmy grabbed his and offered a simple toast. "Here's to good friends, cold beer, Sigma Chi, and Memphis State," he said as he hoisted his mug in the air and waited for the others to raise theirs before taking a swig. After taking a big drink Mickey excused himself to find the men's room.

"So who's going to win the game tomorrow, J.D.?" Charlie asked, certain he knew the answer to come.

"Memphis, of course," Jimmy said as he took another swig from his glass. "We're five and two after last week's win, and three and one in the conference. Plus, we've won three games in a row after getting beaten at Louisville the last week in September. A win tomorrow guarantees us a winning season, a winning record in the conference, and makes us eligible for a bowl game. If we keep playing as well as we have the last two games, it could turn out to be a really good year."

"I saw the score of the win against Southern Mississippi a few weeks ago," Charlie commented. "But I remember the game was fairly close, maybe four or five points, and I figured if we couldn't beat them by very much at home we would have a tough time of it on the road."

"Yeah, the first five games of the year were fairly typical of many recent seasons," Jimmy responded. "We played better at home and won, while we played lousy on the road and lost. But something just clicked when we played at Houston. We scored fifty-two points and beat them soundly in Houston. Then we won a real close road game, so the team should be playing with a lot confidence. With three of the last four games at home, it's possible we could win the rest."

"But we do have to play at Tennessee next week," Billy said. "It's been a while since we've beaten them."

"You know something, Billy," Jimmy said as he turned and faced his friend. "I can't stand Tennessee. I don't like anything about them. I don't like their fans. I don't like their field, the way they paint those stupid orange and white squares in the end zone. And I certainly don't like that horrible orange color. If I never see that color again in my lifetime, it would be better." Jimmy grabbed his beer, took a big drink, and slammed the empty mug on the table to help show his disgust.

"I don't like them either, Jimmy," Billy responded, "but they do have a good football team." Seeing Mickey walking to the table, Billy said, "I'm going to make a stop in the men's room before we eat, too."

"Let me get us another round of beers," Charlie said as he turned and walked toward the bar.

When Mickey returned he grabbed his glass and took another drink. Jimmy waited for him to sit his beer down and then asked, "So how did it go today with our special accounts, Mick?"

Wishing this discussion could be postponed or cancelled, but knowing it was inevitable, Mickey quietly answered, "It was okay."

"Just okay," Jimmy said as he sensed something uncomfortable.

"Yeah. It went fine." Mickey was frustrated his cell phone could not pick up a signal in the bathroom, so he still was unable to confirm what happened with the accounts.

"No problems, Mick?" Jimmy prodded. "No questions at either bank about closing the accounts so soon, particularly with the recent deposits? All of the money from all nine mortgages accounted for?"

"Yeah, Jimmy. It was all there," Mickey said not knowing if he was lying or telling the truth. "Everything went smoothly."

Jimmy looked at his friend and shook his head. "I can't believe this, Mick. We pull off one of best scams ever, and you're not more excited than this. My heart's beginning to pound with just the thought of strutting into a bank and getting someone else's money."

"Jimmy," Mickey started with a big sigh. "I've got to be straight with you. This was way beyond my comfort zone. For some reason, this one scared me to death. I know we've done many other things much harder and riskier than this, but I just felt so out of control on this one." Mickey looked at Jimmy with eyes pleading to be excused.

Recognizing the fear in his friend's voice and face, Jimmy backed off. "It's okay, Mick. Once the dust settles from this you'll probably feel differently. Let's just wait and see."

Charlie returned with four new beers as Billy also returned to the table. "This is amazing," Charlie said. "Four beers for six dollars. I can't remember the last time I bought a beer for a buck and a half in California."

"And wait until you taste the rack of ribs waiting on you," Jimmy said. "You'll know you're back in the South again."

The young hostess walked to them and said their table was ready. They grabbed the glasses which were not empty and followed her to a remote corner of the restaurant. It was much quieter there than in the bar, and it was a welcome change. All four ordered the house specialty, and no one was disappointed as only a pile of bones remained when the last bite was swallowed.

When the four arrived at the Peabody Hotel it was nearing midnight, and there was a line of people waiting to get checked in by the three women and one man working behind the registration desk. Having registered earlier they were able to bypass the wait. Jimmy asked, "Anyone want to have another drink before calling it a day?"

No one answered immediately, so finally Charlie said, "No thanks, J.D. The flight wore me out. I'm ready for bed."

"I'm going to pass, too," Billy said. "I was up early this morning at my sister's, so it's pretty late for me."

"How 'bout you, Mick?" Jimmy asked, certain Mickey would accept his offer since Jimmy couldn't remember a time when Mickey rejected a drink.

"Not tonight, Jimmy," Mickey replied. "I'm pretty worn out, too, from all of the day's activities."

Jimmy was stunned, but he knew Mickey expended a lot of energy recently simply worrying about the special accounts. Realizing it was probably better to wait until another more opportune time to talk with Mickey, Jimmy did not persist.

Jimmy and Billy shared a room, and both were fast asleep soon after their heads hit their respective pillows. Mickey and Charlie shared the adjoining room, and as Mickey was crawling into bed, Charlie asked, "How did it go today at the banks, Mick? Any problems?"

Comprehending this was the first time he and Charlie were away from the company of either Jimmy or Billy since his flight arrived, Mickey realized Charlie probably was anxious for the entire evening, not knowing for certain if everything was executed according to plan. Mickey debated whether or not to confide in his long-time friend, but chose not to by saying, "Everything was fine, Charlie." Mickey reached to turn off the light and said, "I'm beat. Let's get some sleep."

Mickey laid still in his bed with his eyes open as he wondered about his assistant. He thought about getting out of bed and calling his assistant, but in the darkness of the room he could hear Charlie breathing, and he knew Charlie was not sleeping. Mickey tried to think back to the book he read during the flight, speculating what fate awaited the young mother in the pages ahead. His mind wouldn't cooperate as his thoughts quickly returned to his assistant and the accounts. At some point in the night his worry went away and he fell into a deep sleep.

Mickey was awakened when he heard a bang on the door of the hotel room. When he opened his eyes he could tell it was morning as there was some light peeking through the crack in the curtains. He next heard the shower running and looked to see Charlie's bed vacant. The clock showed 7:17, and he knew he wasn't very well rested. Another knock on the door was followed by Jimmy's voice calling for Mickey and Charlie to get up, so Mickey got out of the bed and answered the door.

"Good morning, Mick," Jimmy said as the door opened. "You and Charlie can meet Billy and me downstairs when you get ready. Billy's already down there having breakfast. I swear he eats like he's still in college. We'll see you in a little while." Not waiting for Mickey to respond, Jimmy turned and walked toward the elevator.

The shower was still running, and Mickey didn't know how long Charlie would remain, but he walked to the coffee table and turned on his cell phone. He pushed a few buttons to retrieve the home phone number of his assistant and placed the phone next to his ear to wait for an answer as he stood facing the drapes.

The phone continued to ring as Mickey lost track of whether it rang four times or five. Finally he heard someone on the other end pick up the phone and mutter something sounding like a greeting.

"Hello," Mickey said. "It's Mickey. Who's this?"

"Mickey!" he heard his assistant exclaim. "Do you know what time it is? It's five-thirty in the morning. What is it? Is something wrong?"

Mickey realized he completely forgot about the time difference between Memphis and California, but he knew the damage of having woken his assistant was already done. "Sorry. I forgot about the time change. I was calling to find out how things went yesterday." Mickey waited for a response while he held his breath.

"Everything went fine, just like we expected."

Mickey let out a huge sigh of relief. He was so happy, yet he was amazed his assistant seemed so calm. "Well I tried to call you a few times yesterday, but I couldn't reach you at home or at the office."

"It was such a nice afternoon, and the boss was not in the office, so I did what any normal employee would do." Mickey heard a pause and sensed a yawn on the other end. "I played hooky. I spent the afternoon in Santa Cruz, and when I got back to Monterey I decided to continue the celebration. I didn't get home until about two this morning. And like any normal employee I was hoping my boss wouldn't find out. No chance of that now. I wonder how many other employees get a phone call from their boss at five-thirty on a Saturday morning after having been out until two o'clock the night before."

"Only the ones who play hooky on Friday afternoon," Mickey kidded. "Why don't you go back to sleep? I promise I won't bother you next week while I'm golfing, so you can play hooky every afternoon if you like."

"Thanks, but it's still not payment enough for getting called after less than four hours of sleep after such a late night. Now I've got a hangover."

"You'll get over it. I'll see you in a week when I get back."

"Bye, Mickey."

Mickey pushed the end button on his phone and sat it on the coffee table next to his wallet and keys. He smiled broadly at the favorable news. As he turned around he saw Charlie standing near the bathroom door with a towel wrapped around his waist.

"Who was that?" Charlie asked.

Mickey felt his heart miss a beat. He wondered how much of the conversation Charlie heard. "I was just checking in with my office."

"It's awful early on Saturday morning in California to be checking in with your office, Mick."

"I know. I forgot all about the time change. I should've waited until later."

"Everything okay, Mick?" Charlie asked.

"Yeah, it's fine."

"You sure, Mick," Charlie prodded as he could tell Mickey was uneasy.

"Yeah. Let's just leave it for now, Charlie. We can talk about it some other time."

"Okay," Charlie said as he decided not to push on his friend. "Did I hear Jimmy at the door while I was in the shower?"

227

"Of course. Who else would be knocking on our door to make sure we didn't miss anything? He said we should meet Billy and him downstairs when we're ready. I better get in the shower or they might leave without us."

Only Billy ate any breakfast as the others just had coffee or orange juice. Jimmy spent his time in the scoreboard section of the sports section, reviewing the point spreads for the day's games against his mental recall of the bets he placed Thursday night, while also glancing through the real estate section to compare home values. Charlie only glanced at part of the finance section, having read Friday's entire edition of the Wall Street Journal on yesterday's flight. Mickey and Billy chose not to bother with the morning paper as they only watched other guests of the hotel.

As nine o'clock approached they decided to drive to the campus for the annual homecoming lunch provided to the Sigma Chi alumni and their guests by the present members of the chapter. It was a fun time allowing present members of the fraternity and their parents and other family members to converse with the men who preceded them. The common bond was membership in Sigma Chi, and all who pledged and were initiated felt proud of their association.

Several alumni present graduated within the past few years, and many of them were still close friends with those still enrolled. In many cases they recently shared the fraternity house. Most in attendance lived in or around the Memphis area, or at least within driving distance, although there were others like Jimmy, Billy, Mickey, and Charlie who flew from fairly distant places to participate in the homecoming activities.

There were several people Billy and Mickey knew from participating previously in this annual event. There were also a handful of men they remembered from their college days since they were active members at the same time. Jimmy saw many new faces when he arrived, and whoever stood or sat near him soon became his friend as the discussions varied from the upcoming game to people's present employment situation to stories from old.

By the time the meal was served there were close to two hundred and fifty people in attendance. The inside dining room had tables and chairs to accommodate eighty, but most people chose to eat outside in the bright sunshine of the late morning. A stage intended for use by the band performing at the homecoming party later in the evening was already full of musical equipment, and the hope was for the sky to remain clear, as many previous homecomings were dampened significantly by thunderstorms.

Once everyone was almost finished eating the barbequed chicken and boiled crawfish, there was a short program. Several awards were presented, but the highlight was when three random names were drawn from a fishbowl, and those three were required to tell the entire gathering a story from their college days at Memphis State and Sigma Chi. The names of Jimmy, Billy, Mickey, and Charlie were not drawn, but an older man stole the show as he told a hilarious version of a story from his college days he claimed was true.

The old man said people called him Jack, although it wasn't his real name and he couldn't recall how he ever got the nickname in the first place. He said it was typical of the South where so many people were referred to by something other than their real name. In his story he and his girlfriend were caught in a very compromising situation late one night by a policeman, and the old man claimed he accidentally backed into the officer's police car when he intended to drive away. When he said he thought the cop was ramming him, everyone in attendance laughed so hard they had tears in their eyes.

The football game was enjoyed by everyone, but particularly Jimmy as Memphis beat TCU by the score of 37-14, easily covering the spread and allowing Jimmy to win his bet on the game. With the win Memphis now had six wins against two defeats, with four of the wins and only one loss in their conference. With the sixth win, the team was now eligible to play in a bowl game. Another win would almost certainly assure the team of getting a bid to play in a bowl, and if they could win all three of their remaining games, a major bowl was a possibility.

After the game as Jimmy drove his three friends back to the hotel, he suggested they agree to make another trip to wherever Memphis was playing in a bowl game. They agreed it was a good idea and all committed to making the trip. They debated whether any family members should accompany them, but nothing was decided for sure regarding the matter.

Although they were invited to the evening homecoming party at the fraternity house, they decided to leave it to the college kids.

Instead they went in search of their own entertainment in downtown Memphis. At one point during the evening Jimmy and Mickey were separated from Billy and Charlie. Having been concerned from the previous day's conversation, Jimmy took the opportunity to check on his friend's well-being.

"How are you feeling today, Mick?" Jimmy asked. "You seemed pretty upset last night."

"I'm sorry, Jimmy," Mickey replied. "Actually I'm feeling much better today. I was just very anxious about everything, but now things are fine."

"Good." Jimmy waited for a few moments to make certain Mickey was ready to chat about another item. "Then let's talk about the false liens again for a minute. I have a different idea from what we previously discussed. Instead of trying to make it look like someone's country club has made an assessment which they haven't paid, why don't we use a company name resembling some tax collecting agency and make it seem like someone didn't pay some county or state tax they were supposed to."

Mickey thought for a moment. "That's actually a good idea, Jimmy. Much better than the country club version. I expect most people would be afraid of not paying something they think is owed to some government organization."

"My thought exactly. Why don't we decide on a name and you can do the paperwork to create the company?"

"Should we make Billy the sole proprietor?"

"Yeah. I'll tell him what we're up to and he won't mind, as long as we give him a share of what we get."

The two were interrupted as Charlie and Billy rejoined them. The four enjoyed a wonderful evening which included a meal consisting of seafood gumbo, fried catfish fillets, raw and fried oysters, fried shrimp, french fries, cornbread, hush puppies, and plenty of cold beer. As they ate they kidded each other about whose cholesterol would gain the most by the end of the trip. Jimmy didn't expect it would be him as he was planning to have Sunday dinner with his parents, and his mother changed her cooking several years ago to provide a much healthier diet for his father. Charlie also claimed it wouldn't be him as he was flying back to California in the morning, and he didn't plan on eating any more fried food for quite a while. Billy said he had a good chance of winning since he ate bacon and eggs with homemade biscuits and gravy the past few days at his sister's house, along with country fried steak and fried chicken in the evenings. Mickey thought he might be able to win only because he would be staying another week on his golfing trip to Alabama.

They all felt comfortable with the camaraderie they shared. The bond of being fraternity brothers was strengthened from the day's events, as they recognized themselves in many of the students they met earlier. At this most enjoyable time, however, none of them could predict the fate which was awaiting them over the next few weeks.

TWENTY

A few minutes after seven o'clock on Monday morning, Charlie Bates walked into his bank. He was in a good mood and wanted to get an early start to the day, hoping to catch up on anything from Friday he might have missed.

His return flight from Memphis on Sunday was amazingly smooth, and he enjoyed the extra room and amenities of first class. Not wanting to wait until Mickey finished reading the book he recommended, Charlie bought his own copy at the Memphis airport and read a good portion of it during the flight. He did like the plot and the writing style, and he hoped he would be able to dedicate some time to finishing it during the next few days.

Charlie was glad he accepted Jimmy's invitation to attend the homecoming activities, and he hoped to participate again next year. His wife didn't mind since he was only gone for a few days, and she was even receptive to the possibility of Charlie going with the guys to the bowl game at the end of the year, whenever and wherever it might be, and with or without her.

When Charlie unlocked the door to his personal office, he saw a stack of papers about seven inches high on the corner of his desk. This seemed a little much to him since he only missed work on Friday, but he figured he could deal with it. After taking his coat off and hanging it on the hook mounted on the back of the door, he walked to his desk to take a seat.

As he sat his briefcase on the floor beside his desk, he noticed a single sheet of paper placed in the center of his desk. It was a memo from the chairman of the Board of Directors of his bank. He quickly read it without bothering to sit in his chair. The memo stated there would be a special meeting this afternoon at two o'clock which he was required to attend. The memo didn't state the exact purpose of the meeting, but said it would last less than an hour and was an important step in the future of the bank.

Charlie knew some of the active members of the Board of Directors, including the chairman, were rumored to be considering retirement, and he wondered if the meeting would be the forum for them to internally make the announcement. He further wondered if the president of the bank would become the chairman, and he found himself getting quite excited with the possibility of being named president, which is what he was striving to achieve all of these years.

Since no one else was yet to arrive for work this morning, Charlie could not discuss what was being rumored about the meeting with any of his co-workers. Instead he moved the memo to the edge of his desk, sat down in his chair, and grabbed the large pile of papers to begin work.

There were many of the normal things in the stack. Weekly reports were present, and since October ended just last Wednesday, there were some monthly charts and graphs also included. Charlie easily organized the work into categories and worked with a vigor through some of the easier items.

When his assistant arrived shortly before eight o'clock, Charlie stopped working for a few minutes and chatted with her. She wanted to know how he enjoyed his weekend in Memphis, and she shook her head in disgust when he described all of the fried food he consumed. He enlightened her with a shortened version of the story the older man told at the fraternity lunch, and she also laughed to the point of having tears rolling down her face. They briefly discussed the schedule for the day, including the two o'clock meeting, but she didn't have any additional information regarding the agenda of the special meeting. He expected she knew but didn't want to ruin the surprise.

The morning was quiet as Charlie worked diligently. He skipped the usual morning coffee break in his efforts to get caught up on his work, but he found himself quite hungry shortly after eleven o'clock. Not wanting to take too much time for lunch, he asked his assistant what her plans were for lunch. When she said she was having an early lunch with a friend, he asked if she would be kind enough to bring him back a sandwich. She agreed, of course, which allowed him to continue his work uninterrupted.

By one-thirty, Charlie was almost finished with everything waiting for him this morning. A few new things were added, but he expected he could finish them by five o'clock, even if the special meeting lasted as long as an hour and a half. With some regularly scheduled meetings on Tuesday morning to attend, including his weekly staff meeting with his subordinates, he knew getting caught up by the end of the day was necessary. He also wanted to have some time in the evening to get back to the book he was reading, and it seemed like accomplishing all he wanted was likely.

The special meeting was held in the bank's largest conference room. Extra chairs were placed around the perimeter of the room to accommodate the expected crowd. At most special meetings there was food available in the back of the room, but today there was none as the furniture was rearranged to allow for more chairs.

When Charlie walked in at five minutes before two, he saw almost every seat filled. Some people were standing and talking, as he saw a few groups of men chatting, but most were sitting quietly or talking softly with the person seated next to them. Four seats in the front were empty, and Charlie expected one of those was for the chairman, one was for the vice-chairman, and one was for the president, but he couldn't determine who might occupy the fourth.

As he found an empty seat near the back corner, Charlie saw the chairman of the bank walk in from a door near the front of the room. He was talking to a man beside him who Charlie recognized as the vice-chairman. Another vice-president much younger than Charlie was next, followed by the president. Charlie wondered why the young vice-president was walking in with these other three powerful men, and then suddenly the reality of what was happening hit him.

Seeing the entrance of the chairman and his group, everyone remaining standing was quickly seated and became silent. The chairman stood behind the chair reserved for him and thanked everyone for coming while reminding them the meeting would not last long. He then said he always loved this bank and all the employees and customers who made it successful, but he planned on stepping down as chairman. He said he felt he was getting old, planned to play more golf while he was still able, and wanted to give others the opportunity to run the show. He told a few stories from when he first joined the bank. He encouraged everyone to continue their hard work and dedication to the task at hand, while reminding them how important the customers are. He informed everyone his resignation would be effective at the end of the calendar year, and the vice-chairman would take over as chairman when the new year started. He continued by saying the president was to become the vice-chairman, and then he relinquished the floor to the president.

The president stood and first thanked everyone for coming. He said when he took his new post as vice-chairman, he would step down as president. The man who would replace him was the young vice-president seated to his left, and everyone stood and clapped at the announcement.

Charlie couldn't believe it. He was crushed. He worked so hard and every indication was he would be the one chosen to replace the president when the time came. Instead, a man several years younger was selected. Not only was he being passed over now, his career probably wouldn't outlast the man who would now be his boss, meaning he would never become president of this bank.

The young vice-president did address the group, but he kept his comments brief, knowing there were several people like Charlie who weren't very happy right now, while also realizing nothing he could presently say would matter. The vice-chairman who was to become the chairman chose not to talk, so the meeting was adjourned after only thirty minutes.

Charlie left the meeting without talking to anyone. He hurried back to his office and closed the door after entering. He sat at his desk and simply stared at the work on his desk in disbelief. After fifteen minutes he heard a knock on his door and saw his assistant peeking through the window adjacent to the door. Normally she would have walked right in, but he expected she knew what was announced at the meeting.

Charlie waved for her to come in, and she opened the door and walked timidly toward his desk. She said she heard the news and added how sorry she was he was not selected for the promotion. Charlie gazed at her face and realized she also was hurt by the announcement, as she wanted to be the president's assistant as much as he wanted to be president. Charlie dismissed it as just the way it goes and told her everything would be fine. She once again said how sorry she was and turned and walked out of his office.

Charlie didn't do any more work until it was time to leave at five o'clock. As he walked through the bank on his way to the door and heard the normal noise of the building, he thought of how quiet it was upon his early arrival this morning. He reflected on the good mood he possessed hours ago, and how it changed so abruptly. As he drove home he debated about how he would break the news to his wife, but he wasn't sure what he should say.

The weather in Alabama turned warmer early in the week but then became colder again on Friday. By then Mickey was completely frustrated with his golf game. He played acceptably on Monday, and slightly better on Tuesday, although he was on the losing end of most bets both days.

Wednesday his game left him completely as once he hit his drive on the first tee he didn't seem to have any sense for where his ball was going. One drive would go to the left followed by the next one to the right. When he did hit a shot straight, he seemed to choose the wrong club as he hit it over the green twice while coming up short on several other holes.

Thursday was much of the same except his putting was now also causing him problems. He three-putted four times on Thursday on his way to an eighty-seven, his worst round of the year. By Friday morning his losses from the previous four days totaled more than four thousand dollars, and he wondered why he did so much work to arrange this golfing week.

Friday and Saturday were a little better as Mickey broke eighty both days and actually won a few hundred dollars each day. He birdied the last hole on Friday by making a short putt after an excellent approach shot, and he birdied the last two holes on Saturday when he holed a bunker shot on seventeen and a long putt on eighteen. The two good finishes lifted Mickey's spirits somewhat, but he still was discouraged at his poor play and big losses.

While Mickey was finishing with his struggles in Alabama on Saturday, Jimmy was enjoying an afternoon of additional research in the Bay Area. He identified two recently listed homes requiring roof inspections and made a note to call Billy on Monday morning with the information. Jimmy's car radio was tuned to KCBS, the all news station, so he could catch the sports updates at fifteen and forty-five minutes past each hour. When the early games played on the east coast were finished he was slightly ahead on his bets for the day, but as more games in the Midwest and South progressed he found his losses beginning to mount.

The game most interesting to him was being played in Knoxville, as Tennessee was hosting Memphis State. Jimmy bet on Memphis, and although he really wanted them to win, he knew they only needed to stay close enough to keep Tennessee from covering the spread. The amount was triple his standard bet, as he was sure Memphis would play well again after having seen them win easily just a week ago. The game wasn't even close as Memphis lost 49-28, bringing their record to six wins and three losses. With home games against Army and Cincinnati remaining the following two weeks, Jimmy expected at least one win, which would at least help their chances of playing in a bowl game.

Billy's return from the homecoming trip to Memphis was filled with promise as he met once again with the production home builder regarding the neighborhood development. Billy felt confident he was going to win the contract as he modified his proposal multiple times during the last few months in his efforts to show the builder how much he wanted to work with him. Billy even compromised more on the price than he originally intended, but his math still showed a substantial profit for his company over the next two years, which was particularly better than the performance during the previous two.

"Billy! It's J.D.! How ya' doin'!?" Jimmy greeted his friend shortly after eight o'clock in the morning on Monday, November 12th.

"Hi, Jimmy," Billy replied. "Things are fine."

"How can things be fine with Memphis having gotten trounced by Tennessee Saturday? You sure you remember which school you attended?" Jimmy kidded his friend.

"All I said was they had a good football team. It's not going to change just because you dislike them so much."

"Well I can certainly root against them," Jimmy stated firmly, pausing for emphasis. Then he added "And you should, too, dog gone it."

"I don't like them either, and I agree their orange color is pretty annoying."

Not wanting to dwell on the disappointing game from the weekend, Jimmy focused on the purpose of his call. "I've got a few new clients for us. One is in Cupertino, and the other is in San Jose."

Jimmy proceeded to give Billy the names, addresses, and phone numbers for the new contacts. When he told Billy the address for the one in San Jose, Billy said, "That's near where the production builder is going to develop the new neighborhood."

"How's the deal coming? It's sure been dragging on for a long time. Aren't they going to decide sometime soon?"

"I met with them again last week, and they told me they'd make their final decision in a week or two."

"What are your chances of getting it?"

"Pretty good, I think," Billy answered. "I've changed my proposal to accommodate everything they've asked for, and I even compromised on the price some, even though I think I could have won it without any adjustment."

"Well good luck with it, Billy. I hope you get it. Let me know what happens, and we'll celebrate when you win it. Talk to you later."

The celebration never happened, as Billy received the bad news the following day. The production builder's secretary called to inform him, and Billy was really disappointed. He couldn't remember the number of times he met with the builder or the number of changes he made to his proposal, and now it was all wasted effort. Not only did he lose the major part of the work, he did not even get a small portion. What made him feel worse was the builder didn't even have the courtesy to inform him personally. Billy felt depressed, certain the builder used him just to get more favorable terms from whomever he chose.

Mickey returned to Monterey on Sunday, November 11th, his flight arriving in San Jose as the sun was going down. He was seated by the window on the right side of the plane, and as they approached the airport from the south, Mickey was able to see the houses, buildings, and roads which seemed to completely cover the valley. He noticed several houses located closer to the top of the hills than he remembered and wondered when the hillside would be totally covered with homes.

No one met him at the airport, so Mickey walked alone among the crowd of passengers on their way to the baggage claim. Once again his golf clubs and other luggage were delivered successfully to him, and he quickly exited knowing the drive to Monterey was still ahead.

Mickey didn't have to think about his route, as he knew it well from having driven it so many times. Instead, he spent the entire drive contemplating the bank accounts, the money transfers, and his assistant. The split of the profits was one-third each for Jimmy, Charlie, and Mickey. Because he enlisted the help of his assistant for two thousand dollars, Mickey's share was reduced from somewhere around seven thousand to roughly five thousand. Mickey wondered if he should take the chance the next time as opposed to relying on his assistant. Not determining if the two thousand dollars was well spent or not, Mickey wasn't sure what he would do the next time.

On Monday morning Mickey arrived at his office promptly at nine o'clock. His assistant was already present when Mickey walked in. The two greeted each other and then chatted for almost ninety minutes about their activities of the previous week. Mickey recounted his poor golfing performance, the events from the homecoming festivities, and the various meals. In between, his assistant filled him in on the important pieces of business during his absence.

As the conversation was winding down, the bank accounts became the topic of discussion. The assistant was nonchalant in describing what happened, and anyone listening would think it was just a normal bank transaction. Mickey was told all the receipts were in a folder on his desk, so the conversation ended without additional detail.

After the discussion Mickey sat at his desk and reviewed the contents of the folder. On top was a receipt indicating a cash deposit made into Mickey's personal account for the amount he anticipated. There were also receipts confirming the closing of the two accounts which were opened just last month. Additionally there were business cards and brochures from the two banks, making it clear both banks hoped to be of help in the future. Mickey wondered if they were going to have the same helpful attitude once they started receiving calls from the other institutions and customers whose money was transferred to a wrong account.

The next few days were fairly normal at Mickey's office, but then the mail arrived on Thursday. Mickey vaguely recognized the name and address of the law firm on the outside of the envelope, but he didn't have a clue what was inside since he couldn't remember having a business relationship with this particular firm. Mickey started skimming the two-page letter, but after the first paragraph he slowed his pace considerably.

His ex-wife was now being represented by this new law firm. There was a claim she was terminally depressed, stemming from her abortion of their third child years ago. A reference was made to the previous court ruling, that the abortion and her mental state were a direct result of the financial and emotional support she was forced to provide Mickey and their two children while he attended law school. The letter then informed Mickey they intended to ask for alimony payments to not only continue beyond an already extended time period, but for a significant increase in the amount. Further, monthly payments into a college fund for the oldest of the two children were being requested, and a similar request was promised in the future for the other child.

Mickey was shocked. He read the letter a second time in disbelief. He was presently paying alimony and child support, and the alimony continued well beyond the normal two or three years. Now her lawyer was asking for the alimony to continue, with an increase of all things. The payments for the children were supposed to stop when each turned eighteen, and now they wanted him to pay for their college.

Mickey read the letter a third time with real anger. This was ludicrous. She wasn't terminally depressed, only terminally vindictive. Mickey stood and walked around his office contemplating what to do. He looked out the window and saw an old couple walking on the sidewalk across the street. They were moving slowly due to their age, yet they were holding hands, and he wondered if the woman ever angered the man to the point where he simply wanted to strangle her. Surely once or twice in all the years, he thought. Then he turned away from the window in disgust.

Mickey sat at his desk and made several notes on a legal pad. He hoped he could capture enough thoughts to build a legitimate case against his ex-wife. As he scribbled he tried to organize his thoughts into categories. After almost two hours of working on it, he suddenly stopped, laid his pen beside his notes, got up from his chair, and walked out the door on his way to the nearest bar.

Mickey stayed drunk through the weekend. He didn't go to the office or answer his phone, and he didn't care.

One of the calls he missed Saturday evening was from Jimmy. Earlier in the day Memphis hosted Army and won 42-10, improving their record to 5-1 in the conference and 7-3 overall. A bowl game was almost a certainty now, and Jimmy wanted to chat about making a trip to wherever they might play.

Another call Mickey missed on Saturday was from Charlie. Charlie was still stinging from the announcement of almost two weeks ago, not knowing more bad news was soon headed his way.

The following Monday, November 19th, Charlie received a call informing him another of his investments in a startup company was headed for bankruptcy. This was a company which previously was struggling, but a change in strategy coupled with the hiring of three new top-level managers only four months ago provided new hope. It didn't last long though as the company was going to be unable to meet its payroll demands this week, which was particularly bad timing for the employees since Thanksgiving was three days away.

Still steaming over the bank's decision of whom to promote, and now having received the bad news about another poor investment, Charlie was truly angry. He called Jimmy, and they agreed to meet the next day.

TWENTY ONE

"Hey, Charlie," Jimmy greeted his friend as he took a seat opposite Charlie in a booth located in the corner of a small Mexican restaurant famous for their large burritos.

"Hi, J.D. Thanks for coming," Charlie said. Charlie was drinking beer from a longneck bottle. One empty bottle was standing at the edge of the table against the wall, and four more were in a bucket of crushed ice, ready to be consumed. "You want to help me drink this beer?" Charlie asked as he slid the bottle opener laying in front of him toward his friend.

"Of course," Jimmy said as he grabbed the opener with one hand and reached for a cold one with his other.

It was fifteen minutes after six o'clock on Tuesday evening, and only two other customers were seated and eating. They chose one of the eight small tables in the center, and they also had a bucket of beer, although the bucket was empty as they nursed their last two. A young couple was in line to place their order, and they were trying to decipher the menu written on a big sign hanging from the ceiling and angled toward customers below. They spoke in a whisper, not wanting the others to hear their discussion. Three other people were waiting on their order as they stood near a counter where several sauces ranging from mild to extremely hot were available. Jimmy knew the hottest sauce would probably give him heartburn, but he expected he would have enjoyed it when he was younger. Two Mexican men worked behind the counter, as one took the orders and money while the other was busy making burritos.

Jimmy couldn't recall exactly when he last visited this place. Once or twice a month during the spring and summer he would buy a burrito here and take it back to his office for lunch, but he guessed his last visit was probably sometime in September. He couldn't remember ever being here in the evening, but he expected he and

Susan may have bought some burritos and taken them home for a simple dinner with the girls on at least one occasion.

The restaurant was typical of so many other small, family-owned and operated eating establishments located in shopping centers or strip malls. Their main business was servicing the lunch crowd, yet they were open until eight or nine o'clock at night in their efforts to make as much profit as possible for themselves.

Charlie on the other hand had never been here. He frequented two other similar locations closer to where he lived, but he didn't want to go to either of those places for tonight's business.

"You want to get some food before we talk?" Charlie asked.

"Whatever you want to do, Charlie," Jimmy replied. "Either's fine by me."

"Let's just talk while we work on this bucket then."

"Okay," Jimmy agreed as he took another sip of his beer. "What's on your mind?"

Jimmy could tell Charlie was really bothered by something, and he also knew Charlie would tell him what was on his mind if he simply sat back, waited, and listened. Jimmy detected both urgency and anger in Charlie's voice the previous night when he called asking to meet, and Charlie's expression and demeanor so far were consistent with the call.

"Two weeks ago the bank made a big announcement," Charlie started. "The chairman of the board is retiring. The vice-chairman is taking his place. The president is stepping down as president but will become the vice-chairman." Charlie paused for a moment and took a deep breath. "And a young vice president was chosen to replace the president."

Jimmy could hear the hurt in Charlie's voice and see the pain in his face. Jimmy knew his friend was hurt, but he chose not to speak.

After another swig of his beer Charlie continued. "The thing which ticks me off the most is they did it all behind my back. I took off the Friday we flew to Memphis for homecoming, and when I got back to the office on Monday morning there was a memo laying on my desk informing me of a special meeting in the afternoon. When I show up at the meeting, the big dogs are courting this young vice-president, and they don't even hardly acknowledge the others in the room. The meeting lasts thirty minutes, and then we're all sent back to work. It was ridiculous. They could've been a little more personable with those of us who clearly have more experience with the company and in the banking business than the guy they chose. I don't know what repercussions they were expecting, but I anticipate several people are looking for other jobs since it's clear they'll never get promoted, unless we acquire some other bank and bigger jobs become available."

"Any likelihood of that happening?" Jimmy inserted a question.

"Not any time soon, as best as I can tell. You never know now though. They may be considering something and keeping me and some others completely in the dark."

"So what are you going to do? Are you going to look for another job?"

"I'm not sure. I might, but I'm really not prepared to relocate. Not yet at least. I was hoping to find my way back to the South after maybe another ten years, certainly not before I turn fifty but I also didn't want to wait too close to retirement. It's also not clear if I'll ever move back since I've got a big selling job to do on my wife to convince her."

Jimmy waited to see if Charlie was finished before he inserted any comments. When Charlie lifted his beer for another drink, Jimmy said, "Well, Charlie. You're probably better off staying put where you are for a while until you decide what you really want to do."

"Yeah. I agree, but I'm still mad over the whole promotion thing. I just felt like a pawn in their big chess game. Like a loose piece of meat they think they can just throw around. It's amazing the politics associated with a large company. Sometimes I envy you, J.D., since you have your own little business to run without all the hassle."

"Well, Charlie, there's good and bad to having your own business. You should know that from Mickey's and Billy's situation. Billy is constantly struggling to make enough. Do you know he lost the big roofing contract with the production home builder he was hoping for?"

"No. I hadn't heard. I know he was pretty excited about it while we were in Memphis a few weeks ago. He told me he thought it was only a matter of time before they were going to decide, and he thought he was the front runner."

"Yeah. That's what he said. Turns out the builder was just using him to help negotiate a better deal with another roofer he wanted to use all along. Hopefully he'll learn from this experience and either win the next one or at least not waste his time."

"I'm sure Billy's really disappointed," Charlie said as he grabbed his bottle and angled it slightly to see the few ounces remaining in the bottom.

"He sure is," Jimmy said as he raised his bottle and took another drink.

Charlie finished his beer and grabbed two more out of the bucket. Jimmy opened both bottles with the opener and threw the caps in the ice.

"Did you hear about Mickey's ex-wife?" Charlie asked after testing his new beer.

"No. I tried to call Mickey over the weekend, but I couldn't reach him."

"Me, too. I tried to call him Saturday three or four times, but I didn't get an answer either. I tried again on Sunday with no luck, but I finally was able to reach him yesterday, just after I called you. Turns out his ex-wife is at it again. She's hired a new lawyer, and now they're asking for an increase in alimony."

"That's amazing, Charlie. Does Mickey think he'll have to pay it?"

"Not sure. But that's not the worst of it. They're also asking for him to start paying money into a college fund for their oldest, who is fifteen. And they've informed him they'll be asking for the same thing in a couple of years when the other child is a little older."

"Sounds more like a warning or a threat to me," Jimmy said as he shook his head and took another sip.

"I agree."

"So what's he going to do," Jimmy asked.

"So far all he's been doing is drinking," Charlie answered. "Once he gets beyond that, I don't know what he'll do. I think he should fight her on this. He's already paid alimony for longer than anyone I know, and I also can't recall anyone being forced to set up a college fund for their children. Many people do the college fund thing on their own since they truly want to help their kids get an education, but it's not forced upon them."

"I'd like to see him fight, too, but he should get another lawyer to represent him instead of doing it himself."

"My thought exactly. I've always told him to let someone else handle these kinds of things, but he never listens."

"He can be pretty stubborn about some things."

"Yeah," Charlie said as he noticed they were now the only customers. "Hey. Let's go ahead and order a few burritos before they decide they want to close early due to a lack of business."

"Oh, I think they'll stay open as long as we're here drinking beer, but I am getting hungry. Tell me what you want and I'll order for us."

Charlie told his friend what he wanted, and Jimmy walked to the counter to order two of the same. The employee taking the order punched the necessary keys on the cash register as Jimmy stated he wanted both with sour cream but without guacamole. The man asked if they needed any more beers. When Jimmy hesitated, the man said something resembling half price for a bucket, so Jimmy shook his head in acceptance. After he paid the requested amount he returned to the booth with a fresh bucket of beer.

"Do we need all that?" Charlie asked in amazement when Jimmy sat the new bucket on the table.

"Maybe. Maybe not. But it was half price so I figured we should try."

"How'd you swing that?"

"I guess it's the Tuesday night special for two," Jimmy said with a shrug of his shoulders.

The two continued to chat as they waited for their food to finish being prepared. The discussion centered around their recent trip, the outcome of the Memphis football games since seeing them in person, and their hopes for where they could possibly go for the anticipated bowl game.

The burritos were delivered to them along with a paper plate filled with tortilla chips. The chef turned waiter asked what sauce they wanted, and he retrieved a large cup containing one of medium spiciness. Charlie unwrapped the foil from his burrito, laid it on its side, and covered it with some of the sauce as he prepared to eat it with the plastic knife and fork. Jimmy peeled back a few inches of the foil and took a bite while holding it upright in his hands. After a few bites Jimmy spooned some of the sauce where he intended his next bite.

Charlie finished first and munched on the remaining chips while he waited for Jimmy to complete his burrito. As he noticed his friend taking his last bite, Charlie reached for two more beers and opened them. He sat one within Jimmy's reach and took a big swig from his.

"I told you I wasn't sure what I was going to do regarding my job at the bank, but here's one thing I am going to do, J.D.," Charlie said as he cleared some of the mess of the meal from between them. "If we can convince Mickey to handle opening two more bank accounts and doing the electronic banking necessary to redirect payments, I'll provide a long list of our customers who pay their mortgage to some mortgage company or other financial institution using bill pay. And we won't have to worry about them selling their house soon and us having to cross them off our list."

Jimmy sat stunned. He knew Charlie was hurt by the recent events at his bank, but he was utterly amazed at the vindictive tone his friend was using. Thinking quickly Jimmy said, "Wait a minute, Charlie. It's not going to be that easy. When we redirected those payments previously, I was able to gather all the information I needed about a person since I had access to their home, only because it was for sale and I'm a realtor. Even if I have the names, addresses, account numbers, and so on, I don't expect you can provide their username and password for doing electronic banking. At least I thought the names I use for my personal banking weren't readily available to anyone at the bank."

"You're right. They're not readily available. But we do have something called Super Access which we can use."

"Do you always have this type of access, Charlie?" Jimmy asked very intently.

"From time to time. It depends upon the circumstances."

"And who else at the bank has this capability?"

"Only a few people, and it varies. From time to time it's given to someone to allow them access to different people's accounts, usually to solve some kind of problem."

"But how often is it changed, Charlie?"

"I don't know for sure, but I imagine every few days depending upon how many different people learn what it is."

"So what good is this Super Access if we're not guaranteed of being able to use it a day or two before the payments are made?"

"Think about it this way, J.D. If we set up two accounts and have them ready to accept a bunch of redirected mortgage payments, and if it happens I know the Super Access password at the right time of the month, then we'll be able to take advantage of the situation. If I don't know the password, then we just wait until the next month."

"What about the bank statements which get mailed to the account holder for our two special accounts each month? When those get mailed to the person we stole their identity from, they'll call the bank and the accounts won't be any good to us. What's worse, the money we put there for moving between accounts may get withdrawn by the other person."

"I thought about that, J.D. There's two solutions. The first and easiest is we set up the accounts to have the statements mailed electronically. It's more and more common every day for people to do it without having a piece of paper mailed via the post office, so I'm pretty sure it will work. We can easily generate our own screen name on some internet service provider so the statements will come to us. The second way is to close the two accounts and open two more accounts. It requires we get a second identity for the second set of accounts, but I trust you can easily do that."

"It certainly sounds possible. Let me think more about it. If you give it more thought, too, then we can talk again. Maybe this weekend or early next week.

"Okay. It's a deal," Charlie said with a satisfied look on his face.

"There's one other thing, Charlie. You mentioned convincing Mickey to handle the accounts again. I'm not sure it's a good idea. I have a funny feeling, and I'm now also worried about how this whole new issue with his ex-wife is going to weigh on him."

"Who else do you suggest?" Charlie asked.

"Well," Jimmy started and then stopped, not certain he should share this information with Charlie. "Billy's been helping me with some things. You remember those withdrawals we did for a while." Jimmy saw Charlie nod his head affirmatively. "Billy did those. He might be able to pull this off, too, but we'd have to be careful which banks we choose since he's been to a lot of them, and not too long ago. Let's think more on that part of it, too. In the meantime, why don't you call Mickey again and see how he's doin'? I'll do likewise and we can compare notes."

"Sounds good," Charlie said, happy Jimmy was agreeing in principle with only the details to be figured out.

The two finished the last of the beer and left with a lot to think about.

Jimmy and Charlie talked on the phone the following afternoon, and again the day after, which was Thanksgiving. They agreed to meet on Saturday, and they planned on watching a college football game at Billy's, as they wanted to enlist Billy to help them.

One highlight of Saturday for Jimmy was Memphis beating Cincinnati in the season finale by a close score of 36-34. The win was their eighth of the year against just three losses. The conference record was an even better six and one. The final bowl bids would not be announced until another week or so, but it seemed likely Memphis would be playing in the Peach Bowl in Atlanta.

The plan Jimmy and Charlie developed this time was for the two accounts to be opened and operated in two cities in the East Bay. Deciding San Ramon and Danville would suffice, and knowing Billy was the one with the best access to those places, they asked Billy to assist them. Billy was more than happy to help since he was still stinging from the lost roofing contract.

Mickey spent the Thanksgiving weekend golfing in San Diego. Charlie chatted with Mickey a couple of times since the burrito meeting with Jimmy, and his analysis was Mickey was over the initial shock of the news from his ex-wife's lawyer. Jimmy intended to pay a personal visit to his friend in Monterey early the next week to cover the role they planned for Mickey.

The plan was for Billy to open the accounts, handle the regular ATM withdrawals, and ultimately close the accounts. Mickey would do the electronic transfer of funds between the two accounts along with the electronic change of the bill pay instructions for the mortgage payments, provided Charlie could garner the Super Access password a few days before the end of the month.

It was Jimmy's and Charlie's hope for Mickey to have a successful golfing weekend in San Diego, expecting it would help him return to his normal self again. Both Jimmy and Charlie were still worried about Mickey, but they knew Billy would not be able to perform the changing of the electronic transfer instructions, so they decided to rely on Mickey.

The Tuesday after Thanksgiving Jimmy left his office shortly after eating his lunch and drove to Monterey. He arrived at Mickey's office in the middle of the afternoon, and the two chatted there for a few hours. Mickey's golf game was good the previous weekend, and even though his winnings were only a few hundred dollars, he felt redeemed since he played well and was a winner instead of a loser.

As Jimmy and Mickey discussed the next mortgage payment redirection scam, Jimmy said he and Charlie decided the accounts should be somewhere other than Santa Cruz, and Carmel or Monterey also did not seem like good choices. Jimmy mentioned the profit would be split four ways instead of three since Billy was signed up to open and close the accounts, but Mickey didn't care. He was comfortable with what was being asked of him.

To celebrate they decided to drive to the sushi bar where they previously received the delivery when Jimmy drove to Monterey in late September to work on the McVey closing with Mickey. They wanted to experience the atmosphere of the restaurant versus eating in Mickey's office.

When they arrived at the sushi bar, the hostess asked if they preferred to sit at a table or the bar. They opted for the bar where they sat on two of the stools surrounding an area where three Oriental men were preparing orders by slicing fish and packing rice. Random items were placed on little plates which acted as boats and floated along a narrow stream of water running along a track between the preparation area and those seated. It allowed those on the stools to grab what appealed to them as it passed by. The empty plates were collected by a waitress to figure the amount of the check.

Jimmy sat and wondered why other restaurants didn't offer their buffet in a similar fashion. He remembered just a few weeks ago treating his wife and girls to their favorite pizza place and having to walk from his seat to the buffet arrangement numerous times, and many times being disappointed with the available selection.

Jimmy liked this much better since he was a big fan of sushi. Mickey also thoroughly enjoyed all of the selections. The two ate, drank only a few beers, and talked about how care-free their lives were when they were in college. It was amazing to them they felt comfortable so long ago when they only had twenty dollars in their pocket with no idea when or where the next twenty would come. Now twenty dollars barely filled their cars with gas.

After the pleasurable visit with Mickey, Jimmy returned home. He made certain to be home before ten o'clock so Susan would not be mad. He drove fifteen to twenty miles over the speed limit, but his pace was the same as most other cars, as he passed a few cars every so often while also getting passed occasionally. When he pulled into his driveway at quarter till ten, Susan met him at the door with a big hug and a kiss and led him upstairs to their bedroom for another fun evening followed by a satisfying night of sleep.

The same night Billy struggled to sleep. He worried about what awaited tomorrow when he was supposed to drive to San Ramon and Danville and open two accounts using the identity of a man originally from Ohio who recently bought a home in Los Altos.

TWENTY TWO

Although tired from a poor night's sleep, Billy felt alert as he drove from Valley Roofing in San Jose toward Danville on highway 680. It was almost nine o'clock on the final Wednesday morning of November, and once he got to Milpitas he was clearly going opposite of the commute. The cars heading southbound were moving slowly, and Billy judged them to be doing about twenty miles an hour. If this is what it is like at nine, he wondered how slowly cars moved between seven and eight when traffic was even heavier. He expected and hoped it was much lighter on the other side when he returned in a couple of hours.

Billy was driving fifty-five since he was in an unfamiliar car he borrowed from one of his employees earlier. It was an old Buick in need of a paint job, but the engine ran smoothly enough and the inside was much cleaner than his truck. The few drivers going north were passing him easily, but he didn't mind as he tried to enjoy the scenery.

Billy couldn't recall exactly when he last drove this route, but he thought it was probably when he played golf on one of the two courses at Sunol Valley. As he descended the Sunol grade he saw some of the holes on the left of the highway, and he noticed several golf carts and golfers already playing even though it was a brisk morning. Knowing the community of Sunol was less than a hundred people, he wondered where those who were playing lived. Probably different parts of Fremont, he decided, as he didn't expect anyone from Pleasanton, Dublin, or Livermore would want to fight the commute to play golf on an average public golf course.

As he approached Pleasanton he saw a housing development on his right in an open field where a sign advertising red oat hay for sale indicated the land's previous use. He counted five or six two-story homes packed tightly together in the middle of the flat area he guessed was about a hundred acres in total. It looked strange to see the houses built so close with so much open area surrounding them, but he knew in a few years the entire space would be filled with homes. Everyone living there was certainly going to hear the noise of the highway twenty-four hours a day, but he knew people would pay the high prices and live with the sound to have access to the high-tech job market in such a temperate climate.

He glanced to his left and saw heavy equipment moving dirt. He expected this would also be covered with homes soon enough. He wondered who was doing the roofs for these two developments and if he might be able to garner some business for himself. He quickly looked back to the right to see if there was a sign indicating the builder's name, but he already passed it. If he thought about it after finishing his bank business he would take a detour and drive by the model homes.

After exiting the highway and finding his way to the bank in Danville, he parked the car and grabbed an envelope laying beneath a hat in the passenger seat. The envelope contained two thousand dollars in cash, and the personal information matching his fake Ohio driver's license was written in blue ink on the outside. The hat was a light shade of blue and displayed the name of a university in Ohio Billy didn't know. According to Jimmy it was located in the northeast part of the state, but Billy didn't think it mattered. He put the hat on his head and strolled confidently into the bank.

The lady who assisted him said she was recently employed and asked only the necessary questions required to open the account. She seemed nervous about getting the information in the correct spots, and this actually calmed Billy. He thought about how anxious he previously was when he made the first unauthorized withdrawal, but now he felt much more comfortable. When Billy requested to have the checks and bank cards delivered to the bank for him to retrieve in a few days, she checked with one of her co-workers to determine if it was possible. When she said they would be available in about a week, he said not to bother calling him when they were ready as he would return on Thursday or Friday of the following week to pick them up.

At the second bank in San Ramon, Billy was assisted by a young man who looked no more than fifteen years old. Billy expected he was at least eighteen to be working at the bank in this capacity, but he couldn't imagine the boy was old enough to drink legally. Billy noticed the efficiency, and he wondered if the youngster was like Charlie at a similar age.

Billy returned to his car with a handful of literature from the bank, mainly brochures promoting one thing or another. He sat it in the passenger seat on top of a what he was given at the first bank, expecting the special services were similar between the two. He and Mickey would sort through all of it in a few days when they planned to play a round of golf. Billy last played more than three months ago, and he hoped to at least go to a driving range before the weekend so he wouldn't totally embarrass himself. As he drove back to the highway for his return to San Jose and thought of his schedule for the next two days, he remembered the new housing developments on the south side of Pleasanton and decided to see what the business possibilities were.

Meanwhile Jimmy was on the phone with his travel agent planning his trip to the Peach Bowl. It wasn't yet certain Memphis was playing in the New Year's Eve game in Atlanta, but the San Jose Mercury News, the FOX national sports report on television, and the ESPN and NCAA college football web sites indicated it was decided, just not formally announced.

Jimmy and Susan discussed their plans the previous evening, and they agreed to spend Christmas in Palo Alto and then fly to Memphis the day after. They would spend a day with Jimmy's parents in Germantown before driving to Susan's home in Jackson, Tennessee. Although Susan liked going to a few college games on Saturdays in the fall, she wasn't too excited about going to a bowl game, so she told Jimmy to go without her. Jimmy would go to Atlanta on Saturday, December 29th, while Susan and the girls would remain with her parents. He would return on New Year's Day, and then the entire family would fly back to California the day after.

Charlie was also planning on making the trip to Atlanta. His wife didn't want to fly across the country and back just to attend a college football game, so she declined his offer but wanted him to go and have a good time. Not wanting to be away too long Charlie decided to fly to Atlanta on December 29th and return to San Francisco on New Year's Day. Plus, he needed to be at work on Friday, December

28th to make certain he knew the Super Access password to give to Mickey for use on Monday the 31st.

Although wanting to attend the bowl game, Mickey had a few conflicts. Earlier in the year he committed to play in a golf tournament on New Year's Day with a buddy of his in Los Angeles. The tournament included a New Year's Eve party followed by an eight o'clock shotgun start the next morning. The flyer generated to provide information about the tournament emphasized the availability of bloody Mary's and other drinks throughout the golf course to help postpone the inevitable hangovers from the night before, and Mickey taped it on the wall of his office beneath the golf calendar displaying courses from around the world.

The other conflict for Mickey was dealing with the changing of the bill pay instructions for the mortgage payments Charlie provided. The plan was to change the instructions on Monday, December 31st, and Mickey wanted to do it early in the afternoon, which precluded him from being on a flight to Atlanta. Charlie also advised him to do it from somewhere in California as having bill pay instructions changed from a remote location not associated in any way with the account holder raised immediate suspicion. With the need to be in California on New Year's Eve coupled with the golf tournament in Los Angeles, Mickey chose to miss the bowl game, but planned on going to New Orleans with Jimmy at the end of January for the Super Bowl.

Billy also decided not to make the trip to Atlanta. He intended to close the accounts in San Ramon and Danville on Thursday, January 3rd, which would allow him ample time to return from Atlanta and do his business, but he wanted to sit with Mickey while the electronic bill pay instructions were changed. Billy wanted to learn how it was done, but he also wanted to be available to go to either of the banks if necessary in case a problem arose. He, too, was planning on attending the Super Bowl in New Orleans, and if he had to choose one game over the other, he figured going to a Super Bowl versus a college bowl game would be more memorable.

Jimmy and Susan sat in first class while their girls sat in coach on the flight from San Francisco to Memphis. Charlie provided them with two upgrades, and Jimmy was unable to purchase two more first class seats as his travel agent said it was full. Even though Susan didn't like the idea of being separated from her girls during the flight, she did enjoy the extra room and attention.

It was cold and windy in Memphis upon their arrival, as snow flurries were in the air but nothing was sticking on the ground. Jimmy's parents met them at the airport for the short drive to their home in Germantown, and Jimmy's mother said she couldn't remember the last time it snowed on or around Christmas.

After spending a day with his parents, they borrowed his dad's car for the drive to Jackson, Tennessee. The weather on Friday was warmer than when they arrived on Wednesday, and the girls were disappointed there was no more snow in the forecast. They chose to make the drive in the early afternoon, and as he drove, Jimmy thought about Charlie and whether or not he was going to be successful getting the password Mickey would need the following Monday. Jimmy also wondered if the bank would change the password over the weekend as a security measure, but he figured Charlie knew more than he about how the bank operated.

In the middle of the afternoon on Friday, December 28th, Charlie looked through several accounts to find one fitting a specific criteria. He remembered what triggered his need to know the Super Access password previously, and he searched for accounts showing similar characteristics. Once he found two candidates he jotted down the home phone numbers for each and picked up his phone to dial the first.

A lady answered his call, and after a brief introduction Charlie inquired about some of the recent activity for her account, which she shared jointly with her husband. Without any prompting the woman stated she and her husband were in the process of getting a divorce. He moved out several weeks ago, and she didn't know his exact whereabouts, but she expected he was somewhere in the Bay Area. Charlie said there were checks clearing through a bank in Phoenix, and she said it was certainly possible he was there. Charlie gathered a few more details and politely thanked the lady for her time and said he hoped she wasn't bothered by the interruption.

An elderly woman answered Charlie's second call, and she was more guarded with her information. Charlie's good manners finally won her over, and she explained her hesitancy. When she banked at another institution her grandson stole her ATM card and was withdrawing money from her account. She requested the bank refund her money since the withdrawals were clearly not performed by her, and the bank agreed to the refund but said they would prosecute her grandson. She decided she would spare her grandson the legal action and solved the problem herself, with one result being a change in banks.

Armed with a few details Charlie proceeded to make the request for the special password. He explained why he needed it and identified which accounts he was going to inspect. He also asked how long the password would be valid, and the answer was probably through next Monday and until next Wednesday, since Tuesday was New Year's Day and a bank holiday.

Charlie left his office promptly at five o'clock, and on his drive home from work he called Mickey with the password. The two chatted briefly, mainly about their plans for the next several days. Mickey was going to change the bill pay instructions on Monday around noon, and then drive to Los Angeles for the New Year's Eve party followed by the golf tournament. He expected to drive back to Monterey the day after New Year's. Charlie's plans were to fly to Atlanta early the next morning, spend a few days there with Jimmy while also attending the Peach Bowl, and also return to the Bay Area on January 2nd.

After he hung up and continued to drive toward home, Charlie debated if he was doing the right thing. He wanted to get revenge against the bank for the way the whole promotion thing was handled, but he presently was feeling some remorse, particularly for the people whose payments were about to be sent to the wrong account. He knew if he got caught his banking career was over, and he wondered if it was worth throwing away the work of so many years for such a small sum over what many would consider a petty issue. As he thought more about the meeting announcing the retirement of the chairman and the planned changes and promotions, his anger returned. When he pulled into his driveway he was once again determined to get his revenge on the bank.

Charlie sat in coach on his flight to Atlanta the next day, having given his last two upgrades to Jimmy and Susan. It wasn't too bad though as he was able to get assigned a seat on an exit row, providing him with more leg room even if the seats were more narrow than what was in first class. He started a new book by an author his assistant read regularly and recommended—one he hadn't read—and he found the descriptions of the medical examination processes quite interesting. It was amazing to him so much detail could be uncovered regarding someone's death by cutting them open and analyzing what was inside.

Charlie was a few chapters short of finishing the book when his plane touched down at the Atlanta airport. He folded the corner of the page marking his place and grabbed his carry-on luggage for the walk through the terminal to the shuttle. After riding to the main terminal, he made the walk, including riding the escalator, to the baggage claim area where Jimmy was waiting with a big smile.

"How ya' doin', Charlie? How was your flight?" Jimmy greeted him with an extended hand and a big smile.

"I'm fine, thanks. The flight was fine, too. How are you, J.D.? And how was your drive from Tennessee?"

"I'm ready for a Memphis win in the Peach Bowl. Isn't this great! Our alma mater is playing in the Georgia Dome, and we're here to enjoy it. I thought we would drive to the hotel and get checked in, and then we can have a nice dinner."

"Sounds good," Charlie said, happy to be in Jimmy's company again.

During the drive to the Marriott Marquis hotel, Jimmy asked Charlie about the bank password. Charlie's reply was everything was fine, and he told Jimmy about the two ladies he called regarding their accounts. He recounted the details of his call to Mickey while driving home from work, and Jimmy was satisfied things were going as planned.

The two enjoyed a nice steak dinner accompanied by a cabernet from a winery in the southern part of Napa Valley. Charlie was impressed the waiter knew the location of the winery, and the waiter commented he and the other waiters and waitresses were required to attend informal wine classes once a week to learn about all aspects of the business. Charlie advised the man to learn but not to bother investing, based on his persona, painful experience.

The discussion during dinner centered mainly about the upcoming football game, still two days away. Charlie knew how much Jimmy wanted Memphis to win, and he was certain his friend bet significantly on the game. Jimmy could tell Charlie was curious, so without being asked, Jimmy said his bet was fifteen thousand dollars.

Charlie didn't know how to respond to the amount. He remembered Jimmy mentioning he bet a few thousand on the baseball game in August between the Giants and the Mets. Mickey's comments about Jimmy's betting at the Oakland playoff game against the Yankees also stuck with him. He knew Jimmy's bet was in the thousands on the Memphis homecoming game, but well short of ten thousand, although it was a winning bet. Charlie was simply speechless Jimmy was now betting fifteen thousand on a single game.

Jimmy could tell his friend was astonished, so he compared the bet to Charlie's investments in the wineries. It was true the bet was smaller while the timeframe to see if you won or lost was shorter, which to Jimmy seemed much better. It didn't matter if you couldn't control the outcome as he knew you couldn't control everything in the business world either. Although not yet ready to become a gambler on sporting events, Charlie did see some logic in Jimmy's thinking.

Being a little tired from the flight while also wanting to read the last few chapters of his book, Charlie declined Jimmy's offer to go to a nightclub after dinner. They still had all day on Sunday to enjoy Atlanta along with most of the day on Monday since the football game wasn't until eight o'clock Monday night.

The next morning was Sunday, December 30th, and Jimmy and Charlie were eating breakfast in the hotel shortly before nine o'clock. Charlie was not as well rested as he wanted as he was struggling to get adjusted to the three-hour time change, which reminded him of Jimmy's theory about baseball teams on the different coasts. Jimmy was reading the sports section to see if the betting lines for the remaining college bowl games were still the same as when he placed his other bets. He also reviewed the pro football standings since today was the last Sunday of the regular season, and he was preparing himself for who might be facing each other in the first round of the playoffs.

"Well look who's here," Charlie suddenly said.

Jimmy looked up from the newspaper and saw Charlie looking beyond him. Jimmy turned around and saw a man he recognized.

"Hey! Brian Nichols! How ya' doin'!?" Jimmy said loudly, gaining the attention of several of the others seated nearby.

Brian walked up to Jimmy and returned his smile. "Jimmy D. How are you? Somehow this doesn't surprise me you'd be here," Brian said as he shook hands with one of his Sigma Chi fraternity brothers from Memphis State. Turning to Charlie and extending his hand he said, "Hey, Charlie. I certainly didn't expect to see you here this weekend. You a big football fan now?"

"Not nearly like you or Jimmy," Charlie answered as he firmly shook Brian's hand. "Wow. It's definitely been a long time. Here, have a seat." Charlie pulled the empty chair next to him away from the table. "Please join us and we can chat for a while. I'd like to know how you're doin' now."

"Well I'm in a little bit of a hurry. I was supposed to meet a friend in the lobby, but I haven't seen him. I thought he might be getting a bite to eat, but I don't see him here either."

"Please, have a seat," Charlie begged. "Maybe he'll be by in a minute or two."

"Well, we were supposed to go over to the Georgia Dome this morning for some meetings. He may have gone on without me."

"Sounds like a fun place for a meeting," Jimmy said.

"Yeah. Part of the perks of my job, but it's not as glamorous as it seems."

"Why don't you join us for a few minutes and maybe your friend will show after all?" Charlie asked. "Please. Sit down and tell us where you are and what you're doing."

"Okay, but I've got to leave by nine-twenty. You see, Memphis gets to practice for an hour on the field this morning at ten, followed by North Carolina for an hour. I was going to watch the practices and then meet with some folks over lunch."

"You get to watch them practice inside the Georgia Dome?" Jimmy asked in child-like amazement.

"Well, I'm a sports agent now. Actually, I've been one for a long time. Even though I can't legally talk with any of the players as an agent until after their eligibility runs out, the coaches I know will always let me watch them up close. There's a couple of players on Memphis' team I hope to represent in their pro careers, but nothing's for certain. If the players see me at a few practices talking with the coaches, then it gives me a leg up on my competition to become their agent."

"So where are you living, Brian?" Charlie asked.

"I'm in Tampa, now. I started here in Atlanta which you may remember is where I grew up."

"Yeah, I remember," Jimmy said.

"But when a few players I represented years ago were drafted by the Tampa Bay Buccaneers, I decided to move. I thought I was going to save myself some time and trouble with traveling, but I don't think it matters where I am. I guess there's just a lot of traveling no matter what."

"So how are you enjoying, Tampa?" Charlie asked.

"The move's been good for me, particularly with the expansion of the NBA to Orlando and Miami and with the NFL adding a team in Jacksonville. Being in the state of Florida has also allowed me to represent a few players from Miami, although I still haven't been able to crack the nut at Florida or Florida State. The coaches at both those schools are in so tight with agents they've known a long time I can't even get the time of day from them. The Gators and Seminoles always have a lot of good pro prospects, but I've about given up on trying to land one of them.

"It's funny how much time, energy, and effort it takes to get the first college football player from a particular university to sign with you. After the first one, the second one is much, much easier, especially if the first one goes high in the draft and gets a lot of local press. It helps even more if they're drafted by a team close by, 'cause the press coverage is phenomenal in those cases.

"So what are you two up to now?"

"I'm in real estate in northern California. I'm living in Palo Alto and I've got my own agency now. You probably remember I married Susan Graham. Well, we've got two teenage daughters who are just like their mother—very pretty and very capable of spending money."

Brian laughed at Jimmy's comment. "How about you, Charlie?"

"I'm still in the banking business. I'm also living in Palo Alto. I married a lady eight years ago who was born and raised in California, so I'm not sure if I'll ever get back to the South again."

"Any kids, Charlie?" Brian asked.

"No. My wife was in a bad accident, and it's not possible."

"That's too bad," Brian commented.

"How about you, Brian? Did you ever get married and have any kids?" Jimmy asked.

"No," Brian answered. After a brief pause and a sigh he said, "I guess I just spent too much time watching and following sports to develop a meaningful relationship."

"You did follow the Atlanta sports teams pretty closely in college," Charlie said. "Do you still root for them?"

"Yeah. Once a Braves fan, always a Braves fan. It's certainly been a lot more fun the last ten years though. The one nice thing is no matter where I am, I usually can find the Atlanta baseball game on the television."

"I think the Braves were the first team to start televising all of their home games back in the eighties," Jimmy commented. "It's amazing how so many teams would only televise the road games, thinking they would keep people from coming to the ballpark if they showed the home games."

"Yeah, I agree," Brian responded. "Now there are so many more dollars generated from some of the local television contracts, it doesn't matter whether ten thousand fans stay home and watch it instead of going to the game. Listen, I've got to run. It's about a twenty minute walk if I hustle. Good to see you both again."

Brian stood and shook hands again with Charlie and Jimmy. "Are you staying here at the hotel?" Charlie asked.

"Yeah," Brian responded.

"Maybe we'll run into you again before the end of the weekend, then," Jimmy said.

"Maybe so. See you later," Brian said as he quickly departed.

Jimmy and Charlie sat back down as they watched Brian leave. "I wonder who else we'll run into this weekend who we haven't seen in a long time," Jimmy mused.

"Yeah. That was amazing. I can't remember the last time I saw Brian. It must have been right about the time I graduated."

"Wasn't he a year behind you, Charlie, or was it two?" Jimmy asked.

"I think it was only one, but I seem to remember he didn't join the fraternity until he was a sophomore." Charlie stopped and thought more about something which happened over twenty years ago.

"Yeah. I'm pretty sure he was a year behind me, but I only knew him for two years since he didn't join as a freshman."

"Yeah. That sounds familiar. I think I was a senior when he joined, so he and I only overlapped the one year. I guess I didn't realize he was a sophomore."

"Well I think he majored in physical education. I don't recall ever having any classes with him, and I do remember he was involved with the baseball or basketball team as a student-manager or whatever they were called."

"That rings a bell," Jimmy said as he began to remember more from so long ago. "He was always over at the athletic department."

"Certainly makes sense he would become a sports agent, as much as he loved all of it. He seemed to be enjoying it okay."

"You really think so, Charlie. I got the impression he was spending a lot of time, energy, and probably money struggling to get college players to sign with him."

"Oh well. It doesn't matter," Charlie said to let it pass. Trying to change the subject he asked, "What do you want to do today?"

"Why don't we walk over to the Georgia Dome? I would love to watch the teams practice."

"I doubt if we can get in."

"Oh, Charlie," Jimmy said with an exasperated tone. "Why don't we give it the old college try?"

Charlie looked at Jimmy and knew his friend was now determined to find a way inside the Georgia Dome. "Just don't get us thrown in jail. I'd hate to go back to California and tell my wife I missed the football game because you and I were locked up."

"Twenty bucks says we're watching practice an hour from now," Jimmy said as he got up from his chair and started to walk.

"You're on," Charlie said as he stood and laughed and began to chase after his friend after leaving a tip on the table.

Forty-five minutes later Jimmy and Charlie were standing on the sidelines of the football field near the twenty yard line.

"You see the big two and big zero there, Charlie?" Jimmy asked as he pointed to the paint on the turf.

"Yes."

"You know what it stands for?" Jimmy asked another question.

"It's the twenty yard line, Jimmy."

"Monday night it will be the twenty yard line," Jimmy said with a smile. "Right now it represents the twenty bucks you owe me." Jimmy laughed at his joke. Charlie laughed too as he knew better than to underestimate what small things Jimmy could get away with if he wanted.

After doing some sight-seeing in Atlanta and enjoying another wonderful dinner, Jimmy and Charlie decided to stop in the hotel bar for a drink before bed. It was after eleven o'clock, and the bar was three-quarters full. It was a little dark and noisy, as the lights were turned down but the conversation was lively. Jimmy saw a handful of open tables, and he selected the one adjacent to where three women he expected were in their twenties were sitting. A cocktail waitress with long legs accentuated by a short skirt and high heels quickly came to take their order. Jimmy settled for a draft beer, but Charlie opted for cognac.

"I don't know how you drink that stuff, Charlie," Jimmy said. "Last time I tried it I thought I was drinking rocket fuel. How can you stand it?"

"I just like it, J.D. But tell me one thing, how do you know what rocket fuel tastes like?"

"Very funny. Very funny. I'll tell you this, though. Those people who spontaneously combust as they're walking down the street probably drank one of those and then lit a cigarette."

"I'll be careful not to smoke then," Charlie replied as he saw one of the young ladies at the next table light a cigarette, once again being reminded of the difference in the smoking laws between California and most other states.

The waitress returned with their drinks, and as Jimmy paid her for them, Charlie casually waved to someone near the other side of the bar. Jimmy glanced in the same direction and saw a familiar face. It was Brian Nichols, and he was sitting and talking with a large, young, black man. Brian did not return the wave as he was engrossed in a conversation. There were two full beers and two more with only a few ounces remaining on the table between them.

"I wonder who Brian's talking to?" Charlie asked.

"It looks like Bruce Tate, the star running back for Memphis," Jimmy answered. "Brian must be working on him to try and become his agent."

264

"I thought Brian said this morning he couldn't meet and talk with a player until after his eligibility is complete."

"He did, but I'm sure he's like any other agent. I doubt if any pro prospect isn't already locked into an agent long before they finish their last college game. If he plays by the rules and waits, he probably won't be representing anyone of any value."

"Probably so," Charlie said as he saw Brian and his guest stand and shake hands as the young man then turned and walked out of the bar.

Charlie once again waved at Brian, and Brian stared across the bar in their direction. Brian looked down at the beers on his table, and he grabbed the two full ones and walked toward Jimmy and Charlie.

"Hey, Brian," Charlie greeted him as he approached. "Please join us."

"Hi, Charlie. Thanks," Brian said. "Either one of you guys want to finish these last two beers."

"I'll have one and you can have the other," Jimmy offered.

"It's a deal," Brian agreed.

"Wasn't that Bruce Tate you were meeting with?" Jimmy asked.

"Yeah," Brian answered, somewhat surprised Jimmy recognized his departed guest.

"Are you going to be able to sign him and represent him?" Jimmy asked matter-of-factly.

A little startled by the directness of the question, Brian waited a moment and then replied, "I hope so. I think I'm getting close."

"He'd be a good one to land," Jimmy said. "He should go in the first round, don't you agree?"

"No doubt," Brian replied, "but you never know with these young kids. Sometimes the littlest things turn them toward you or against you. Sometimes it's just the way you greeted their mother over the phone when you called them and she answers. Other times it's their girlfriend liking or not liking your hair or your clothes. You never win it based upon your capability as an agent."

"Good luck in trying to sign him," Charlie said with encouragement.

"Thanks."

"So who's going to win tomorrow?" Jimmy inserted another pointed question.

"As much as I would like to see Memphis win," Brian started, "I think North Carolina will win."

"Why do you say that?" Jimmy asked, thinking about his large bet.

"Curfew," Brian answered in a single word. Then he elaborated. "I go to one or two bowl games every year, and I spend several days at each one. It doesn't matter who the best team is, it usually matters who is better rested. The teams who don't impose a curfew on their players and let them stay out to all hours of the morning, they never seem to play well. And it's particularly difficult when the team and coaching staff aren't used to everything associated with the bowl game. There are so many distractions, and it's always a long time since you played your last game.

"If you were to go to the hotel where the North Carolina players are staying, you'd find them all in their rooms right now. They probably aren't sleeping, but they're not out getting drunk, chasing women, or causing trouble. As for Memphis, you saw for yourself. Their star running back is out late, having a few beers with some agent in the bar of a hotel, two miles from where the team is staying. And I guarantee you most of the other players are doing things much worse."

"I don't know, Brian," Jimmy said, thinking of his bet and hoping Brian was wrong about his prediction. "I always figured the biggest factor was the length of time since their last game. Since it's usually four to six weeks between the end of the season and the bowl games, I think the team with the better athletes, better defense, and an offense which relies on the running game more than the passing game has the edge. The better athletes can play better after the long layoff, and defense doesn't rely on the same level of execution as offense. Plus, a team with a better running attack doesn't have to depend on getting their timing back for their passing game."

"I agree with all of those things, Jimmy, and that's one reason I favor a playoff in college similar to the pros or similar to the NCAA basketball tournament. The revenue from a college football playoff would be phenomenal. Although I will say the present bowl system has its advantages for people like me. For the great players not on the really good teams, the other agents, scouts, and I all get to see them play one more game, under conditions quite different from the regular season. Being able to see how they play under these circumstances is a good indicator to me of how well they'll play in the pros. The scouts and other general management of the NFL teams pay attention as well, so there is benefit to the whole bowl setup, even though I'm sure the average fan would rather see a playoff. But getting back to who's going to win, my experience says the discipline a team has is more important."

Jimmy pondered what Brian said while Charlie just shook his head. "You two are amazing. So many theories about who's going to win and why. I'll just wait and see who wins tomorrow night."

"Well I've got to go, guys," Brian said as he stood to leave. Jimmy and Charlie both stood and shook hands with their friend before he departed. The two sat back down, ordered two more drinks, and continued to talk in their efforts to postpone the end of the day.

The next morning was cold and rainy in Atlanta. In Monterey the weather was a chilly fifty degrees with a strong wind. Mickey hoped it would be warmer the following day in Los Angeles for the golf tournament, but he didn't spend much time worrying about it as his eyes and mind were focused on his computer screen.

Billy arrived at Mickey's house around ten-thirty, and the two immediately drove to Mickey's assistant's apartment. Mickey's assistant was away on a long skiing weekend at a resort near Lake Tahoe and unaware of the intrusion.

Mickey plugged in his computer, turned it on, and accessed the bank's website with no problems. The password Charlie provided didn't work on the first try, and Mickey was reading the message in front of him in his efforts to understand the problem as Billy watched silently over his shoulder. Not being able to decipher it, Mickey clicked on the back button and tried the password a second time.

This time he was allowed access. Expecting he simply typed the word incorrectly the first time, he looked back at his notes for the account number of the first person on the list. Mickey entered the number and other information into the appropriate fields while Billy double-checked the data. A few screens later they received confirmation the bill paying instructions were changed.

Mickey clicked on the button for the next account and repeated the procedure. A little over two hours later the last change was finished. Thirty-four accounts in all were modified, and Mickey was glad when he exited without any problems and shut off his computer. He turned to Billy and raised his hand over his head. Billy slapped his friend's hand as they both smiled in celebration.

The two returned to Mickey's town home and continued their celebration with a few beers and some snacks. As he saw the time approach two o'clock, Billy decided to depart for his drive back to San Jose while Mickey grabbed his things, including a cooler full of beer and ice, for his trip to Los Angeles. Mickey wished him luck in closing the accounts as he gave Billy the address and phone number where he could be reached until he returned home later in the week.

On the drive Mickey listened to music by Van Morrison. He was a fan of Van's from long ago, but he enjoyed several of the more recently released albums, too. When he looked at his watch and saw it was after five o'clock, he remembered Jimmy and Charlie were at the Georgia Dome attending the Peach Bowl football game. Mickey hoped Memphis would win, but he really didn't care too much. He was looking forward to the evening party and hoped he could play well early the next morning, certain he would be fighting a hangover along with everyone else.

A few hours later in Atlanta, Jimmy and Charlie watched in disappointment as North Carolina recovered an onside kick attempt by Memphis. The kick followed their only touchdown of the evening, which reduced the deficit to six points, but it was too little and too late. As the Tarheel quarterback kneeled after the next snap, Jimmy endured the chanting of the fans across the field. They were wearing Carolina blue, and Jimmy now hated the color as much as the Tennessee orange. As the game clock descended toward zero, many fans counted aloud in rhythm, and Jimmy wondered when and where this tradition started while wishing it hadn't.

The final score was 16-10 in favor of North Carolina. The Tarheel defense recovered an early fumble by Memphis, setting up the first touchdown. A field goal near the end of the second quarter made it 10-0, and although totally dominant in the first half, North Carolina's lead was not insurmountable.

The play breaking Memphis' spirit was a scramble by the opposing quarterback in the middle of the third quarter which first looked like a sack for the defense. The result was a 62-yard touchdown and a 16-0 lead, and the Memphis players clearly were hanging their heads after the play. A mistake late in the game on a punt by North Carolina provided a glimmer of hope for Memphis when they turned it into a touchdown to make it 16-10, but it wasn't enough.

On the way back to the hotel Jimmy and Charlie walked quietly and quickly. Many dressed in light blue made snide comments to anyone they saw with a hat or jacket supporting Memphis. Jimmy was ready to punch one particular fan who was particularly obnoxious and obviously drunk, but Charlie convinced him to let it go. When they arrived at their destination they wanted to stop in the bar for a beer, but it was so crowded they opted to skip it.

As they rode the elevator to their floor, Jimmy looked through the glass wall at the crowd of people below. He saw two youngsters he guessed were still in high school, and they clearly were big enough to be football players. He wondered if they might someday be playing in a bowl game, and he knew they probably had similar dreams.

The sight of the two boys made him think of Bruce Tate's three fumbles in the game tonight. Although Carolina only recovered one of the three, it gave the Tarheels their early lead and killed any other chance to sustain a drive. Tate's performance clearly hurt his chances of being a first-round draft pick in the NFL, and Jimmy pondered how many dollars this one game might cost Tate in his contract negotiations. Jimmy also wondered how many dollars in commission Brian Nichols would lose if Brian was able to sign the running back.

As Jimmy crawled into bed he remembered Brian's prediction for the game. Brian was confident Carolina would win, and confident or not, the game's outcome matched his forecast. Jimmy knew Charlie's inside information about Arkansas during the season didn't help win any bets, but he wondered how much information Brian possessed via his conversations with players and coaches. Jimmy struggled to get to sleep as he continued to think about Brian, Bruce Tate, the game, and his bet.

The next morning Jimmy drove Charlie to the airport. It was New Year's Day, and although traffic was light this morning, Jimmy knew he would have to push it to make it back to Jackson, Tennessee by mid-afternoon in time to watch some of the bowl games being played. Jimmy needed almost all of the games to go his way to allow him to overcome his huge monetary setback from last night's game. Susan and the girls were still with her parents, and Jimmy hoped they enjoyed New Year's Eve more than he did.

The radio was on as Jimmy drove, but a few hours away from Atlanta he switched it off when an idea popped into his head. He wondered how easy or difficult it would be to convince Brian Nichols to go along with him. Jimmy was certain Brian would welcome the chance to represent more players, but Jimmy wasn't sure how far Brian was willing to bend the rules. Brian did meet with the star running back in a public place, so he clearly played by his own rules on some occasions and took chances. Knowing it was possible Brian might be willing, Jimmy continued to think as he drove on the fairly isolated highway.

The following morning was cold, and snow was in the forecast for the weekend. Jimmy's two girls were disappointed they would miss it, but they were also happy to be going home. More than four days with the old-fashioned habits of their grandparents was difficult for the teenage girls.

On the flight from Memphis Jimmy and Susan were once again in first class while the girls were in coach. Normally preferring the aisle, Jimmy sat next to the window. Instead of reading or talking he simply stared out the window as he continued his thoughts from the previous day's drive. He was convinced his plan had significant merit, and he debated when, where, and how to present it to Brian.

If Susan hadn't said something to Jimmy about how much she and the girls spent during the past week and thinking her credit cards were charged to their limits, he wouldn't have remembered Billy was supposed to close the accounts the next day. Jimmy hoped things would go smoothly, and it reminded him of how far Charlie had come since the time of their meeting in August at the baseball game and later the same evening at the café. Jimmy smiled as he thought of possibly adding Brian to his team.

TWENTY THREE

Thursday, January 3rd, was a cold morning in the Bay Area as Billy drove from San Jose north on highway 680. The analog clock on the dash indicated it was nine-thirty as he fumbled with the controls below the clock. He was in the same car he used when he opened the two accounts five weeks ago, and he couldn't get the heater to turn on. He expected the temperature was in the low thirties, but whatever it was, it was cold enough to cause him to shiver from time to time as he drove. The sky was clear and the sun shone brightly, so Billy hoped things would warm up as the day progressed.

Traffic was extremely light on his side of the highway, and Billy noticed it was light on the other side as well. With the recent slowdown in the economy, many companies forced their employees to take vacation during the holidays both last week and this week, so Billy expected most of the normal commuters were still off and would probably return to work next Monday. He knew many people took advantage of the time off by going skiing at Lake Tahoe, as he remembered seeing a segment on the news last night discussing how crowded the slopes were.

Even though the temperature was near or below the freezing mark, Billy noticed some golfers playing as he passed the two courses at Sunol Valley. He thought they must be crazy, and it reminded him of how poorly he played when he and Mickey golfed last month. Billy hit some balls a few days before the round, but it obviously didn't help much, and he wondered if playing in the cold as these golfers were doing was required to improve his game. If it was, Billy resigned himself to always being a poor golfer, as he certainly had no plans to endure this cold weather by chasing a little white ball around an open field. Knowing Mickey would play golf on days like today, Billy wondered about the outcome of his friend's golf trip to Los Angeles.

As Billy drove further north he descended a small hill about a half-mile south of Pleasanton. He saw the housing developments on both sides of the freeway, and it reminded him he should call the builder again. He talked with the builder two days after his trip here to open the accounts, and he was told there might be some possibilities and to call again after the new year. Billy hoped he could get some of the business, but he felt it was unlikely, as the developer didn't sound too promising during their conversation.

As he continued to drive Billy thought more about his business and the offer his brother-in-law made to him a few months ago. The idea was to sell his roofing company, move to Alabama, buy some land adjacent to his sister's and her husband's chicken farm, and start his own chicken farm. His brother-in-law knew all the key people at a chicken processing plant and said they wanted to contract with some new chicken farms. He offered to assist Billy in whatever way was necessary to get him established.

Billy knew his sister was excited her older brother might possibly agree and take the offer, but Billy wasn't sure it made sense. He just didn't know if he wanted to give up what he worked so many years in California to build. Even though his company wasn't doing as well as he wanted or as it previously did, he wasn't sure he should sell it, as he felt it would be like quitting before being finished.

Billy also enjoyed his many friends here, particularly Jimmy, and he didn't really want to jeopardize that. As he exited from the highway, he decided he would continue considering the offer, but he didn't expect to accept it.

Billy parked in the bank's lot between two fancy cars. On his left was a white Lexus with a tan interior. A red BMW with black on the inside was on the right. He expected the black interior was hotter in the summer than the tan one, and he also imagined the leather for both was cold in the winter, but he would certainly bet their heaters worked, unlike what he was driving. He grabbed the hat from the passenger seat along with a folder of information and a bag for the money and strolled toward the front door.

Very few customers were inside as Billy noticed a teller on the end not helping anyone. She smiled at Billy and asked if she could help him. Billy approached her and said he wanted to close out his account. He handed her the account number and his identification, and she punched some keys on her keyboard as she looked at the screen Billy couldn't see. She stated the balance as she wrote it down on a note pad containing the bank's logo.

"Does this sound correct?" she asked.

Billy checked the number against what was written on a sheet of paper in his folder, and he saw they matched within a few dollars. Knowing the discrepancy was from the interest earned, Billy said, "Yes ma'am."

The lady said she would be a minute as she retrieved this much cash, so Billy watched her walk away and waited patiently for her return. As he stood and waited Billy was careful not to look up toward any of the security cameras. He did turn around when he heard two men talking who entered the bank. Billy looked at the floor and turned in their direction. He first saw both men had dark shoes and blue pants with yellow stripes down the sides. He recognized the pants as part of a uniform, and he couldn't help but look up at their faces. It was two police officers in their full uniforms, including a night stick on one side and a gun on the other.

One of the men looked right at Billy and said, "Good morning, sir."

Billy paused briefly and then returned the greeting. The other officer simply nodded at Billy as the two walked by.

"Here you go," Billy heard behind him as his teller returned with a handful of cash. She proceeded to count out the entire amount. Billy put the money in the bag and thanked her for her assistance. She smiled and wished him a good day. He walked calmly out the door and got in the borrowed car.

Billy drove to the next bank to repeat the procedure. The bank was a little busier, but he only waited in line two or three minutes before being helped. The amount was again within a few dollars of his calculation, and he barely had room in his bag to hold all of the bills. As he walked out the door of the bank toward his car, he didn't notice the coldness in the air due to the satisfaction with his performance.

On the drive back to San Jose Billy called Mickey to inform him everything went smoothly. Mickey was relieved and ecstatic in his congratulatory remarks. Next Billy dialed Jimmy's number. Jimmy's cell phone was busy, so Billy called the number of the real estate office. The receptionist answered and said Jimmy was busy with another call. Billy debated about what message to leave regarding the accounts, but he finally decided nothing was appropriate. He knew he'd be able to tell Jimmy everything when the two met for dinner later to divide the money.

Jimmy missed Billy's call since he was on the phone with Brian Nichols. Brian was impressed Jimmy was able to get his phone number since his home phone was unlisted and he didn't remember telling Jimmy the name of his sports agency. Jimmy decided not to tell Brian he sweet-talked a secretary in the Memphis State athletic department into giving him the necessary information, determining it would be better to let Brian contemplate how he accomplished the feat.

Jimmy was outlining to Brian the first part of his plan. There were two parts, but Jimmy wanted to see how Brian reacted to the initial phase before discussing the second half.

The first piece of the plan was to identify a young college player, preferably a freshman, who was a definite professional prospect while also coming from a very poor family. Jimmy expected the best match would be a player with a single mother and other younger siblings, but he knew an athlete with both parents still married and living together without any other children might be possible.

Jimmy wanted Brian to identify such a candidate. If Brian could convince the athlete to sign a contract agreeing Brian would be his agent during his entire professional career, Jimmy's offer was to provide financial assistance to the player and the player's family during his college career. When Brian asked about the amount of assistance, Jimmy said it could be anywhere from twenty dollars per week to as much as a hundred dollars.

Brian could benefit in two ways. The first was growing his list of clients, as he would have an advantage over his competition by being able to capture athletes much earlier in their career by offering something many college players needed—cash. The second benefit to Brian was he could possibly get a higher percentage than normal for his commission associated with negotiating the professional contract. Jimmy's thought was to lock in the commission percentage when the athlete signs the original contract, when they can be lured by the

274

weekly payments without realizing how many future dollars they are promising.

In return for providing the financial aid Jimmy would receive a portion of the commission paid from the athlete's professional contract to Brian. Jimmy only asked for the extra dollars from the higher commission, so Brian would still get his normal portion.

The plan had two definite weaknesses. The first was the athlete may never make it to the pros, possibly due to injury, but perhaps due to performance. It was a risk Jimmy was comfortable taking, but he knew he was depending upon Brian to identify the right players. Jimmy and Brian agreed Jimmy was taking more of this risk, as Brian wasn't providing any initial funds, and the money Jimmy paid to the athlete would never be recovered if there was no professional contract. Jimmy accepted this without telling Brian how he planned on mitigating this risk. Jimmy intended to share this risk with Charlie, Mickey, and Billy by having them participate in the financial funding, while also sharing in the reward. Jimmy expected Brian may never need to know this detail.

The second problem with the plan was the illegal nature of what he was proposing. It was definitely against all rules for a sports agent to have this kind of relationship with a player, but Jimmy's concern was different. At some point in their professional careers, the athletes would realize they were paying a higher commission percentage than their peers, and it was likely they would try to renegotiate or retaliate.

Brian's comment regarding this issue was he often times had power of attorney for the athletes he represented. The rumor in the newspapers and throughout the sporting world was many players could not read or write, even though they attended and sometimes graduated college. Brian knew it was true, and he and other agents dealt with it by being able to sign everything for their clients. Brian knew the power of attorney could be revoked, but he expected it was yet another obstacle for a disgruntled professional athlete to overcome.

Brian was intrigued by the idea. He knew boosters and others at different universities were handing out money to the star players. He also knew agents were giving gifts, including money, to athletes. He wasn't sure anyone was going so far as to lock in the player by having them sign a contract, but he expected some might already be doing what Jimmy was suggesting.

Brian liked his potential benefits, and Jimmy felt part of this was due to his suspicion Brian was struggling to garner clients. Brian agreed in principle to Jimmy's cut, but he wanted to go through the numbers including inflation, particularly in light of the recent escalation in professional sports contracts and the long duration from first identifying a collegiate freshman athlete to the final contract of an average football or basketball career. The two decided to give it some more time and thought, and they agreed they would meet in New Orleans at the upcoming Super Bowl in a little over three weeks.

Jimmy was satisfied with the outcome of this first discussion. He wasn't sure what to expect since he didn't know Brian real well, having only overlapped with him in the fraternity during college for one year, and having spent much of the year focused on Susan as opposed to the new pledges. Jimmy knew Brian might dismiss the idea immediately, but he expected his hunch regarding Brian's struggles was correct, so it didn't surprise him too much when Brian was willing to listen.

Jimmy sat in his office and stared at the maps on his walls as he considered the second part of his plan. It was dependent upon the first, but it was the part which excited him so much more. The second piece was to offer bonuses beyond the weekly or monthly stipend, based upon performance, to the athletes already signed up with Brian. The twist was the bonuses would not be paid for outstanding performances, but for poor ones in key games, and those games would be ones Jimmy would make significant bets on. Having struggled against the point spread in college football games this past fall, Jimmy knew the players didn't need to throw the game enough to lose, only enough to not cover the spread.

The way Jimmy figured it, he would make enough money on these bets to easily cover the weekly payments to the athletes. Whatever he collected from the higher commission paid to Brian would just be an extra bonus at some future time.

As Jimmy looked at some of the names on the maps, he decided this scheme needed its own unique name. He first thought about calling it Operation Oakland, thinking he could call it Double-O for short, and it would represent the two zeroes he hoped to add to the balance in his gambling account. But then his eyes were drawn to the San Francisco Bay, to the small island north of Fisherman's Wharf, and he decided the name should be Operation Alcatraz.

The following week Jimmy dined with Charlie. The first piece of business was delivering Charlie's portion of the latest mortgage payment redirection scam recently concluded. When Billy and Jimmy dined the previous week in the evening of the day Billy successfully closed the accounts, Billy gave Jimmy three-fourths of the gain while keeping one-fourth for himself. Jimmy delivered Mickey's share to Monterey on Saturday while taking Susan and the girls on a day trip to the Monterey Bay Aquarium and 17-mile drive. It was the first time for the girls to eat at the Pebble Beach Lodge, as Jimmy and Susan usually dined alone on the other special occasions they visited this beautiful place, and Jimmy pitied the poor boys who married these girls since they were learning to like yet another expensive thing.

The second item on Jimmy's agenda was learning what Charlie knew about Brian Nichols. Being one year older than Charlie, Jimmy knew Charlie spent two years at the Sigma Chi fraternity in college with Brian. Jimmy wanted to learn as much as possible about someone he hoped would be an excellent partner.

"I talked with Brian Nichols over the phone last week, Charlie," Jimmy started.

"Something tells me it wasn't just a social call," Charlie replied.

"Certainly not. You remember how I suspected Brian was struggling to get clients. Well, I was right."

"How do you know for sure? Did you just ask?"

Jimmy laughed slightly at Charlie's question. "Of course not, Charlie. I have an idea I've been thinking about. Actually I thought about it a lot during my drive back to Susan's parents after I dropped you off at the airport in Atlanta, and I thought about it the entire flight back here the day after.

"It involves getting Brian to help, so I called him and discussed a mutually beneficial proposal. The main thing he stands to gain is more clients, and since he was willing to listen and discuss it, I'm sure he is struggling as a sports agent.

"The thing I want to know from you, my friend, is whether or not you think he'll play ball with us."

Charlie laughed at first. "That's an interesting choice of words, J.D., 'play ball'. The one thing I remember most about Brian was his constant focus on sports. Being from Atlanta he was a huge Braves fan. Being a big baseball fan he followed all the teams and players. And being a sports fan, he followed everything.

"On the few occasions when I went to the kitchen in the fraternity house late at night to get a snack after studying or something, Brian would almost always be in there eating a sandwich. He'd have the newspaper sprawled out over the entire table as he looked through the box scores of the games, whatever sport was in season. He absolutely loved looking at how many hits, runs scored, and runs batted in certain baseball players had, or how many field goals, rebounds, points, and fouls basketball players had, or who scored the goals and made the assists in hockey games. And if it was a Sunday night in September, he would pour over the batting averages and other statistics of all the players which were published in the Commercial Appeal each Sunday."

"But what did you know about him personally, Charlie?" Jimmy asked.

Charlie had a non-expressive look on his face as he answered. "Not too much really. Brian was involved as a student-manager for the different sports teams. He was a good athlete, but not good enough to play in college. He played on our intramural teams, although I only played on the softball team since I wasn't good enough in flag football or basketball. Since he spent so much time working in the athletic department, I didn't spend as much time with him as I did with the others. Plus I was back and forth to Little Rock so many times trying to help out with the local bank, I missed my share of fraternity activities, too.

"Can we trust him, Charlie?" Jimmy asked directly.

Charlie waited for a few moments to answer. "If he is struggling, I expect he'll work with you. If it helps him with his business, and you said he would get more clients, I expect he'll go for it."

"What about his loyalty to his fraternity brothers?"

"I assume it'd be similar to anyone else. I've got no reason to think otherwise."

Jimmy and Charlie sat silently for a while, each thinking but not speaking.

"Well here's what I have in mind, Charlie," Jimmy said breaking the silence. "I named it Operation Alcatraz."

"Catchy name, J.D." Charlie interrupted his friend. "We should have you help our marketing department at the bank. If we used a name like that, our customers might think they were stealing from the bank instead of the other way around."

Jimmy laughed at Charlie's comment and continued to tell his fraternity brother about the first phase of his plan, once again keeping the second piece to himself for the time being. Charlie listened carefully as he thought of the merits and pitfalls of what he heard. When Jimmy was finished, he asked Charlie what he thought and if he was interested in participating.

"A couple of things come to mind right now, J.D. First, I would like to participate, but my preference is to do it as a silent partner. It will be easier if there is only one contact with Brian, and I trust you can handle it.

"Second, I agree with your concern about a player wanting to renegotiate the commission percentage. The best way I see to structure it is to have the college athlete sign a contract which is forward dated enough so it will seem like a legitimate contract if someone searches through the old records at some point in their professional career. Make sure to get power of attorney for everyone initially, whether they need it or not. Then take as much commission as possible from the first professional contract, so if you have to renegotiate later, you've still collected a huge sum of money and have some room to maneuver.

"As an example, most players get a huge signing bonus, which is cash up front. From what I've heard, and this may or may not be completely true, but I'm sure you can find out from Brian, more and more contracts contain performance incentive bonuses—a player getting an extra fifty or hundred grand for being an all-star, that kind of thing. If you structure the contract correctly, Brian can get a commission on those items, whether or not they are ever earned and paid to the athlete by the team. The player just has to pay a bigger fee, but it comes out of the money he received as his signing bonus. So he pays it and doesn't know any better until someone else clues him in at some future time."

A huge smile came across Jimmy's face as he listened to his friend. He couldn't believe his ears. He wondered if only a banker would think of this wonderful twist to the basic plan, and he was glad his work in recruiting Charlie was reaping such huge rewards. Jimmy also wondered what ideas Brian might have six months or a year or two from now regarding some other scheme he developed.

From the time he finished his dinner with Charlie until the day of the flight with Billy and Mickey to New Orleans for the Super Bowl, Jimmy thought constantly of Operation Alcatraz. A few times while he was driving his excitement was so great he almost ran red lights. Jimmy also thought more about his conversation with Charlie, and it made him wonder about the roles for Billy and Mickey. Jimmy expected Billy would go along with whatever was proposed, but he wasn't sure if Mickey would agree to be a silent partner as well. Jimmy decided to be cautious and wait to explain the first part of his plan to Billy and Mickey until after he worked more of the details with Brian.

Jimmy, Billy, and Mickey arrived at the San Jose airport before dawn on Thursday, January 24th, for their flight to New Orleans. The sky was dark when they arrived and first checked their baggage, and as they waited at the gate prior to boarding they watched it turn through several shades of blue and purple on its way to daybreak. When the older gentleman employed by the airline called for their row to board, they handed him their tickets and proceeded to walk to the plane. The top of the sun was just now peaking through some of the trees in the distance, indicating another beautiful day for the Bay Area. Jimmy knew the sunny day would be welcome since several days during the last two weeks were filled with rain, and he hoped their arrival in New Orleans would be greeted in a similar fashion.

Mickey was seated in an aisle seat and read most of a book during the flight. Sitting across the aisle from Mickey, Jimmy read the USA Today newspaper, particularly the sports section, while he worked through some numbers in his head. Billy was seated next to the window with an empty seat between Jimmy and him. Billy spent some of the flight reviewing several annual reports from previous years for both construction companies and a chicken processing plant in his efforts to learn more about both businesses and do an initial comparison. He and Jimmy conversed about many random topics during the flight, but Jimmy decided to wait until later in the weekend to talk with both Billy and Mickey about Operation Alcatraz.

The trio arrived in New Orleans in the middle of the afternoon, and they were greeted by temperatures in the fifties and a strong wind. Although somewhat disappointed the weather wasn't better, at least it wasn't bitterly cold, and the forecast called for things to improve over the duration of the weekend.

They took a taxi to their hotel and registered without incident. After dropping their things in their respective rooms, they departed on foot for the French Quarter. The wind was in their face for the one-mile walk, but their excitement easily overcame any discomfort. They saw only a few other people during the initial part of their journey, but once arriving at Canal Street the scene changed dramatically.

Finding Bourbon Street they walked slowly toward Jackson Square, allowing themselves time to experience the ambience of this wonderful place. After browsing through a few t-shirt and sweatshirt shops, they stopped at a small bar on a corner. They didn't debate long about what to order as the hand-written sign behind the bartender advertised hurricanes at a special price. The drinks were prepared in tall glasses, but the bartender poured them into plastic cups with lids and straws when they said they wanted them to go. It was still not quite four o'clock in the afternoon on this Thursday, but from the crowd of people already gathered it seemed much later or like a weekend day. Jimmy expected the draw of the Super Bowl was responsible for the large crowd, although he didn't have anything to compare it to.

They stopped at one restaurant for some raw oysters, and after ordering the waiter indicated everything required for making a cocktail sauce was on the table. A red plastic squirt bottle contained ketchup, and a similar clear one contained horseradish. Wedges of lemon were also present along side small paper containers similar in size to what some fast-food hamburger places provided for ketchup for french fries.

Jimmy, Billy, and Mickey each made their own sauce, but all three versions had far too much horseradish when the first oysters were consumed. Each added ketchup to their mix after each bite, but the horseradish was still overpowering. As they ate they noticed their waiter telling another group of women all the ingredients for a sauce were in front of them, and the three men laughed at the wry smile they saw on the waiter's face, expecting the women too would add way too much horseradish into their concoctions.

A few more blocks down the road they stopped at a small café and ordered three bowls of gumbo. Jimmy thought it was adequately spicy, but Billy added a little more Tabasco while Mickey added quite a bit more to kick it up a few notches. It was still windy outside when they finished this course of what was turning into a progressive dinner, but they headed outside amongst the growing crowd nonetheless.

After perusing several more shops and consuming a few more hurricanes, they decided to continue their feast at a restaurant famous for po-boy sandwiches. Jimmy order one with fried shrimp, Billy chose one with roast beef and cheddar cheese, and Mickey opted for one with smoked sausage. Although the sandwiches were quite good, each agreed the atmosphere of the French Quarter probably would accentuate any marginal cuisine.

After a few more drinks and more window shopping, the three noticed it was almost nine o'clock and decided to head back to their hotel. They figured they could make another visit or two before departing on Monday, and they were all a little tired from the early start and the long ride on the plane.

The next morning Jimmy was up early and sitting in the hotel's restaurant reading the morning newspaper when Mickey and Billy entered walking side by side. They easily spotted their friend and took seats on each side of him.

"So what's our plan for today?" Mickey asked.

"I don't care other than I'd really like to eat some warm beignets for breakfast," Billy replied.

"That sounds good," Mickey said.

Looking at Billy while shaking his head sideways, Jimmy said with a smile "Is there ever a time you don't think about food, Billy? You're forty-five years old, and you still eat like you're in high school."

"I do like eating, Jimmy," Billy replied. "Mom always put plenty of food on the table, and Dad didn't like to eat the same thing two nights in a row, so he always encouraged us to eat everything in front of us."

"Well unfortunately, I've already had some breakfast," Jimmy said as the plate on the table had some remnants of scrambled eggs, bacon, and toast. Additionally, there was a glass half full of orange juice close by. "And I've also got a few real estate things I need to take care of this morning. I wanted to do a little research on my own, and if I'm lucky, I think I can get it done by noon. Why don't you two go ahead and hunt down your beignets while I take care of my business? We can meet back here at noon or so and go somewhere for lunch. Then we can figure out what to do this afternoon."

Billy and Mickey looked at each other and decided the suggestion sounded reasonable. "That works for me," Mickey offered.

"Me, too," Billy added.

"We'll see you in the lobby around noon," Mickey said as he and Billy stood in preparation for their departure.

"See you then," Jimmy said. "Have fun while I do the work," he added as they hurriedly made their way toward the exit. As he watched them Jimmy thought about their roles in Operation Alcatraz.

Jimmy knew he didn't have any real estate business this morning, only other dealings. He glanced at his watch and saw it was twenty minutes before his scheduled meeting, and he was glad it was so easy to free himself of Billy and Mickey and have the remaining part of the morning to conduct his business.

TWENTY FOUR

A few minutes after Billy and Mickey left to find their breakfast, Jimmy returned to his hotel room one floor from the top and waited. Fifteen minutes later there was a knock on his door. He opened the door and extended his hand to greet his guest.

"Hey! How ya' doing'?" Jimmy said as he smiled.

"I'm fine, but it's windy outside, just like yesterday."

"Maybe it will die down later," Jimmy responded. "Come on in. Thanks for taking the time and trouble to meet with me here at the hotel."

"No problem. Always a pleasure to see you, Jimmy D."

Brian Nichols entered Jimmy's room and walked toward one of the three chairs surrounding a round table near the window. Jimmy closed the door and followed Brian across the room, sitting in one of the other two chairs. The drapes were open providing a good view of some of downtown New Orleans.

"Nice view, Jimmy."

"Yeah, it is nice, although I'd really like to stay in one of the hotels in the French Quarter on a future trip. Wouldn't it be neat to sit out on one of those second-story balconies and watch all the action on the street below?"

"I'm sure you could only watch for a short while before having to join the fun," Brian said.

Jimmy laughed. "You're right. I agree it would probably take less than ten minutes for me to get tired of watching."

"What's on your mind?" Brian asked, wanting to get to the point of the meeting.

"Well, Brian, the last time we talked I described the first part of my idea to you. I told you I'd be willing to fund an athlete during his college career if you could convince him to sign a contract guaranteeing you would be his agent when he turned pro. I've thought more about it, as I'm sure you have, so we need to cover a few more details regarding that portion."

Jimmy paused while Brian shook his head in agreement and then continued. "But I want to discuss a second part of my idea with you as well." Jimmy proceeded to describe how he wanted the college athletes under contract to help control the outcome of some games so he could win significant bets on those games.

As Jimmy talked, Brian listened with fascination. As Jimmy finished he asked, "So what do you think of Operation Alcatraz, Brian?"

The idea was indeed phenomenal. Brian knew there were many rumors of athletes working with different underworld and disreputable organizations to fix different sporting events, and he expected many if not most of them were true. He also knew athletes were receiving monetary payments from boosters and agents, and imagined some of the athletes were somehow locked into working with the agent providing the funds. He didn't expect anyone was marrying the two ideas, and he was somewhat surprised it was a realtor who put the two together. Brian suspected Jimmy's only motivation was a history of continuously losing more bets than he won.

"I have to admit I'm quite amazed. I guess being to close to the business like I am I can't see the forest for the trees, so maybe being far enough removed from it allows you to see things I'm unable to." Brian paused as he noticed the satisfaction on Jimmy's face.

"It's certainly an interesting proposition, Jimmy," Brian continued. "I'll have to give it some thought. When did you hope to get this whole thing rolling, by next fall's college football season?"

"Actually, if you want to proceed, I was hoping we could do something during the present college basketball season. As I'm sure you know, Memphis has a good basketball team this year, and I would expect we could identify a few key games near the end of the season or in the conference tournament or NCAA tournament where they would be favored and we could take advantage of the point spread."

Brian couldn't believe the man seated across from him wanted to move so quickly. "Wow. I'm not sure it's possible to do it so fast. It's already the end of January, and the regular season only lasts five more weeks. Then there's the conference tournament the week after, followed by the postseason. I can't imagine being able to convince someone between eighteen and twenty-two years old, who is a pro prospect and can have enough control over the outcome of a basketball game, to work with us in something clearly as illegal as what you're suggesting, especially in only a few weeks."

"Well, I've been doing some research, Brian," Jimmy said in a soft voice to provide a calming effect. "I've looked through all of the box scores for this year's games, and I've researched the backgrounds of a few players. You probably pay more attention to it than I do, so I expect you already know who we should target. It's clear to me Dante Lewis fits any criteria we would set."

Jimmy paused for a moment to let his suggestion sink in. Seeing the defensive expression on Brian's face subside, Jimmy continued. "Dante is the second best player on the team, and he's playing much better recently than he did early in the year. Being a junior this year, if he continues the same kind of progress during his senior season next year, he should put himself in a position to be drafted in the first round.

"Now as more of a defender and rebounder as opposed to a scorer, he has the most control over how many points the other team scores. If he throws in a couple of bad passes or other mistakes on the offensive end, I expect he can easily impact the game by anywhere from five to fifteen points, certainly enough to cause Memphis to not cover the point spread in a game where they are favored.

"Plus his family is dirt poor. His mother works two jobs in her efforts to support four kids. His father died several years ago, and who is going to marry a forty-five year old woman with four kids and provide financial support for them? I'm sure no one will."

Brian was amazed Jimmy knew all this about Dante. Brian additionally knew Dante did not yet have an agent. Brian was aware of these things since he followed Dante's entire collegiate career and even talked with Dante just two weeks ago. Brian was shocked Jimmy suggested Dante, since Brian first thought of Dante when Jimmy called him over three weeks with the first part of the plan.

"I agree Dante is a prime candidate. I'm just not sure we could convince him so quickly. For someone like Dante who is showing significant improvement in their basketball skills at this point in the college career to agree to play so badly in a game is a tall order."

"I agree, Brian. But if we propose it to him along with guaranteeing payments throughout all of next year to him and his mother, I expect he'll be willing."

"You may be right, Jimmy. Let me do some work next week. I was planning on being in Memphis anyway, so I'll make an appointment with him to feel him out regarding the idea."

"Good," Jimmy said with a smile.

The two continued their discussion of the details of both parts of Operation Alcatraz. Brian wanted to split the extra commission differently than Jimmy first proposed, and Jimmy thought Brian's proposal was acceptable. As the details of the plan were concluding Jimmy realized it was ten minutes before noon. Knowing Billy and Mickey would soon return, Jimmy decided to let the conversation end without subtly inquiring more about Brian's present financial situation. Jimmy expected his initial suspicions about Brian struggling were additionally confirmed based on Brian's proposal for splitting the commission, so he didn't delve further. The two made arrangements to talk the following Friday after Brian's trip to Memphis and conversation with Dante was complete.

After Brian's departure from the hotel room, Jimmy stood at the window and looked down toward the street. It was difficult to see the sidewalk on the side of the street closest to the hotel due to how high up he was, but he could easily see the walkway on the opposite side. He didn't observe Brian walking anywhere outside, but he did see Billy and Mickey returning. They were a few blocks away, so he quickly left his room to catch the elevator so he could meet them in the lobby.

One block from the hotel Mickey thought he saw someone he recognized exiting the hotel, but he couldn't recall the man's name, and he didn't get a good enough look at the man's face since the man turned and walked away from them after looking in their direction briefly. Billy also saw a glimpse of a familiar face, but he didn't think twice about it since he already saw many people in New Orleans during this weekend who looked similar at a glance to people he either met or knew at some point in his life. Neither bothered to mention it to the other as they continued their walk to the hotel's entrance.

Brian on the other hand recognized both Billy and Mickey when he left the hotel. He planned on walking in their direction, but when he saw them he quickly changed his mind and headed in the opposite direction. When Brian reached the corner, he waited along with several other pedestrians to cross the street, making sure he was concealed by a taller man to his left. When the street light changed and the lighted red hand changed to a white person in a walking position, Brian proceeded across the street along with the others. The others continued but Brian turned and walked back toward the hotel on the opposite side of the street.

When he was directly across from the hotel entrance, Brian turned away from the hotel and faced the window in the front of a store. In the reflection of the window he could watch who entered and exited the hotel. After about five minutes he saw Jimmy, Billy, and Mickey exit and walk to the east, expecting they were in search of some lunch. A few minutes later Brian turned and walked down the street toward the west.

The following day was Saturday, and the crowd of people descending on New Orleans for the Super Bowl was continuing to grow. It was amazing to Jimmy, Mickey, and Billy so many people would come to a city for a football game when they didn't have a ticket and couldn't afford the price being requested by the cheapest of scalpers, but they expected many were present for the fanfare and party, particularly in New Orleans.

The three spent Saturday morning at the Riverwalk since they planned on going to the French Quarter again in the evening. It was well after one o'clock in the afternoon when they decided to dine at a small café offering Cajun cuisine. Most of the tables were full of people, but the room didn't seem overly loud. Mickey ate the jambalaya while Jimmy enjoyed the crawfish etouffee. Billy started with a bowl of gumbo and also had a plate of red beans and rice with two sausage links, yet he was the first to finish.

The conversation was light during the meal as the three discussed the crowd of people and the upcoming game between St. Louis and New England. St. Louis was favored by more than ten points, yet the sentiment of most people in the city was St. Louis would win by substantially more. Jimmy hoped so, too, as one of his bets for ten thousand dollars was for St. Louis to cover the spread. His other bet of ten thousand was simply for St. Louis to win, but the odds were two-to-one against him, meaning he was risking ten thousand for the chance to win five. The three also recounted much of the wild activity they witnessed the previous night in the French Quarter.

Once all three finished their respective lunches, the restaurant was only about half full of people. Deciding this was as good a place as any to discuss Operation Alcatraz with his friends, Jimmy said, "I've been working on a new idea for about a month. I thought each of you might want to participate, so let me explain." Knowing Jimmy masterminded the previous schemes and well aware of the success rate, Mickey and Billy listened intently for the next fifteen minutes as their trusted friend explained the first part of Operation Alcatraz.

"So how much money do we need, and when can we expect some money in return?" Mickey asked.

"Here's my thought for one candidate I've identified," Jimmy started, thinking about Dante Lewis. "He's presently a junior, and the draft after his senior season is about a year and a half away. If we give the athlete a hundred dollars a week, and also give his mother a hundred each week, it's a little short of a thousand every month. For a year and a half, it works out to around fifteen thousand. If the three of us go in equally, the cost is about five thousand per man.

"Now most players can sign their initial contract within four to eight weeks after the draft, and they get paid their signing bonus immediately, so our payback will be less than two years away. Now the biggest unknown in all of this is the size of the contract and the payback. Looking at the last few year's contracts and signing bonuses, and figuring what it will be for our player, I expect he'll sign for about five million per year for three years, along with a signing bonus of at least one million. We hope to capture one percent of the total value of the contract, which is a cool one hundred and sixty thousand dollars. Dividing by three gives each of us around fifty thousand dollars on an investment of five thousand. It's got to be the easiest way to multiply by ten in less than two years in the world." Jimmy smiled as he finished his numerical analysis, noticing a broad smile on Billy's face but a somewhat perplexed look on Mickey's.

"But how do we know he'll get drafted and sign such a contract? And how do we know we'll get one percent of the total value of the contract paid to us from the signing bonus?" Mickey asked.

"Well that's the risk, Mick," Jimmy explained. "There are no guarantees in this. If the player gets hurt and never makes it to the pros, our money is down the drain, plain and simple." Jimmy refrained from explaining the second part of the plan, which would provide return on the investment by winning bets on fixed games, effectively funding the athlete for free, as he didn't want to give them too much to think about in this initial presentation.

Instead he offered a different mitigation against the risk. "If we fund more than one player, say four or five, then we'll be almost assured of hitting it on one or two. Even if our hit rate is one out of five, we'll still double our money, and I expect our hit rate will be much closer to eighty percent instead of twenty percent."

Billy was mentally going through some numbers of his own. When Jimmy and he cheat just one homeowner out of several hundred dollars for roof work not performed, enough money is captured to pay his portion of the funding for a month. He and Jimmy routinely cheated far more than one homeowner per month, so Billy thought funding four or five athletes at a time could easily be done. It all sounded good to him, so Billy didn't ask any questions other than when they start. He was so excited he completely forgot his thoughts from earlier this morning in the shower about what to do regarding the chicken farm with his sister and brother-in-law.

Mickey on the other hand was more skeptical. He wanted to know more about how the athletes would be identified and recruited. Jimmy didn't offer the complete solution, only telling Mickey to trust him, as always. The answer was sufficient for now, but Mickey expected there was more to this latest scheme and wondered what Jimmy might or might not be hiding from him.

Some of the activity in the French Quarter Saturday evening was certainly a sight to behold. The streets between Canal Street and Jackson Square were absolutely filled with people, and it reminded Jimmy, Billy, and Mickey of the last time they were in a crowded bar, only this was outside where there should be ample room. No one wanting a drink was without one for long, as many bars provided what was similar to the drive-thru at fast food restaurants, only this was a walk-thru.

There were glimpses of nudity quite often, both male and female, but on four different occasions the three witnessed groups of women ranging in size from three to almost ten walking completely topless down the middle of the street. Jimmy knew Mardi Gras every year was advertised as a promiscuous party, but he made a mental note to never allow his girls to visit New Orleans on any occasion while they were living at home. Billy just laughed at the lack of self-control he was witnessing, while Mickey wondered if any of the women might know anything about golf.

Early the next morning was fairly quiet as Jimmy read the local newspaper hunting for the results of the Memphis basketball game. Predictably the entire front page of the paper contained numerous articles about the Super Bowl, scheduled to start much later in the day. The sports section was also full of every piece of information imaginable concerning the history of the Super Bowl, particularly the ones played in New Orleans, and the details of the teams participating in this year's extravaganza. Finally, Jimmy found the college basketball scores among the small print on page eighteen of the sports section, but he couldn't find a box score or a news brief giving any details of how Memphis won. He was interested in seeing if Dante Lewis played well, and from the relatively low score and wide margin of victory, Jimmy expected Dante did have a good game, but there was no confirmation.

The crowd around the Louisiana Superdome stretched in every direction for several blocks, as scalpers and people hunting tickets searched for each other among the outside pregame activity. Even though he already had tickets for the game, Jimmy still asked every scalper he passed how much they wanted for their tickets. The prices varied, sometimes based upon the location of the seats, but most often due to the individual scalper Jimmy surmised.

Jimmy also entertained himself by asking every scalper where the seats were located. While reading the morning paper earlier Jimmy tore out the seating diagram, and he would pull it out of his coat pocket just after each scalper stated where the seats were for the tickets being offered. He did find it interesting every scalper said the seats were either lower or closer to midfield than they really were, but he knew the buyers had no possible recourse.

When Jimmy, Billy, and Mickey entered the Superdome and found their way to their seats, they were surprised so many seats were empty, even though it was less than an hour before game time. It seemed only half of the seats were occupied, and the number of people they saw walking through the concourse certainly would not fill the remaining chairs. Jimmy expected the price of tickets from scalpers outside would be dropping the closer it got to kickoff, and he wondered if any of the final seats would actually be sold for face value or less. The cat and mouse game the scalpers and buyers played intrigued him, and Jimmy wondered if maybe he shouldn't participate in the future.

The game started fairly slowly, disappointing the large number of St. Louis fans who made the trip from one city on the Mississippi River to another, as they were used to their team scoring quickly and often. At the end of the first quarter St. Louis held a slim three-point lead.

Jimmy watched in dismay as turnovers by the Rams in the second quarter allowed New England to score two touchdowns to take a 14-3 halftime lead. Now he was worried about losing not only his bet requiring St. Louis to cover the spread of more than ten points, but also about losing his bet against the odds for the Rams to win the game outright.

Another field goal by the Patriots in the third period extended the lead to 17-3. It was looking grim until St. Louis rallied in the final quarter. A first touchdown closed the gap to 17-10, and then another score with less than two minutes remaining in the game tied it. The bet against the point spread was clearly lost, but a win in overtime would salvage Jimmy's other bet.

St. Louis kicked the ball to New England after the tying touchdown, and the crowd's mood was patient, as evidenced by its quietness, as most everyone expected the Patriots to kneel on every snap and let the game go into overtime. When New England began throwing passes deep in their end of the field, it was quite a surprise, but a few first downs later made a winning field goal before the end of regulation a definite possibility.

With a few seconds remaining on the clock, the Patriots lined up for a 48-yard field goal. The snap was solid, the kick was high and straight, and the ball sailed squarely through the uprights as time expired. New England won the game 20-17, and all the players celebrated by piling unto one another near where the ball was kicked. The players for the Rams simply walked off the field with their heads down or stood and stared at the goal posts in disbelief. It was hard for them to imagine losing after being such a decided favorite.

Jimmy stared in disbelief, too. Twenty thousand dollars lost on the game. A bad end to a horrible football season for him. He thought back to his anticipation and excitement in early September when he won eleven bets against seven losing bets the first weekend of the college season. At the time he was eight thousand dollars ahead, but he quickly got behind the very next weekend and was never able to catch up. Now in his efforts to get even for the entire year, he dug a deeper hole, and his determination to make Operation Alcatraz a success became greater.

The mood at the hotel was somewhat somber as it seemed more guests were fans of St. Louis than New England. Occasionally a group would show outward joy based on the outcome of the game, but it wasn't sustained for too long. Jimmy, Mickey, and Billy chose to dine at the hotel's fine restaurant and skip another evening at the French Quarter as they prepared for their flight back to California the next day.

Billy was in a deep sleep at six o'clock when the phone next to his bed rang. On the first ring he thought it was something in a dream. On the second ring he opened his eyes but couldn't remember where he was. On the third ring he saw the red light on the top of the phone blink, and he realized it was a phone ringing which awakened him. After one more ring he answered it, although his voice wasn't working quite right for the first try of the day.

"Billy!" he heard the woman sob into the phone, and he recognized his sister's voice.

"What is it, sis?" he alertly said, knowing something was seriously wrong for her to be calling him at this hour in New Orleans at his hotel.

She proceeded to tell him about the horrific accident her husband suffered on their chicken farm just an hour ago. She didn't know how it happened, or what exactly happened, but he crawled through the back door of the farm house with blood all over his face and clothes. She immediately called 911, and fortunately the medical team arrived within ten minutes.

Her husband was now in a coma, mostly due to the large amount of blood he lost, and they weren't sure if he would make it or not. She was at the hospital, and she wasn't sure what to do. Billy told her to stay where she was and he would rent a car and drive to Boaz as quickly as he could possibly get there.

The events for Billy left Jimmy and Mickey with glum feelings as they boarded their airplane for their early afternoon flight to California. The two were seated across the aisle from each other, but there was little discussion.

Jimmy oscillated between two basic thoughts. The first was about his good friend Billy and what might happen if his sister's husband died from the accident. Jimmy remembered the hurt Billy endured when his parents died the spring of their senior year in college. Jimmy knew Billy badly wanted to graduate from college to show so many others he was more capable than they thought, but Billy's spirit was crushed beyond immediate repair at the time, so Jimmy agreed it was better for Billy to start anew with the purchasing agent job in California.

Jimmy's other thought was about Operation Alcatraz. Being constantly beaten by the point spread this past football season weighed heavily on his desire to have some control over the outcome of future games. He knew his plan would work as long as Brian recruited a few good but desperate athletes. Being able to follow the careers of athletes so much easier with the information available on the internet comforted Jimmy, as he expected he could do much of the research on the players, similar to what he did in investigating Dante Lewis.

Mickey read off and on during the trip while also doing some thinking of his own. He knew there was more to Operation Alcatraz than Jimmy told him, and he wondered when his friend planned to inform him of the rest, if ever. Mickey also speculated there was probably more to some of the other schemes he was unaware of, and he now felt uncomfortable with this unknown exposure. His sense was something was wrong, but he couldn't put his finger on why he felt so uneasy.

As Jimmy and Mickey made the long journey, Charlie was busy meeting with the new president of his bank. It was about three and a half weeks since the change in management took effect, and he was meeting with his new boss for the third straight Monday. Charlie couldn't remember when he met with his previous boss on three consecutive weeks, but the new president was a firm believer in a weekly staff meeting and weekly one-on-one meetings with his direct reports.

Charlie was impressed by many things he witnessed. His new superior had wonderful ideas, exciting plans, and a likeable demeanor, but more than anything else he was a good listener. Charlie already saw how the man worked to get the best ideas from a group of people and further develop those ideas, without being a bully about wanting things to be done his way. It was refreshing for Charlie, and he realized this man was better suited for being the president than he was. Charlie expected he would be able to learn significantly from his new boss, and his hopes of advancing in the company at some point in the future were renewed. The thing he didn't know how to deal with was his behavior as part of his relationship with his college fraternity brothers.

TWENTY FIVE

Federal agent Brandon Williams' cell phone rang shortly before ten o'clock on Tuesday morning, January 29th. He wasn't expecting a call as the only case presently assigned to him was at a slow stage. Plus it was a day off for him, so his superior or someone else from the office wouldn't be calling him unless it was an emergency.

The phone rang a second time. Brandon couldn't place the phone number being displayed as part of the caller identification function of his phone. He knew he'd seen the number before, but he just couldn't remember when. This was strange for him since one of his amazing characteristics was his ability to retain and recall an immense data base in his personal memory, from people's birthdays and anniversaries to specific dates and days when seemingly insignificant events happened.

Brandon let the phone ring a third time as he continued to try to mentally match the phone number to someone's name or location. He was simply drawing a blank, but he knew he was supposed to recognize this number.

Finally on the fourth ring he answered with a simple, "Hello." His training as a federal agent was clear about how to handle unknown calls. The first part was to usually answer if at all possible. The second part was to say as little as possible until certain the caller's identity was confirmed. He remembered the instructor during his first week of training many years ago stating things were not always clear or precise in this business, and vague terms and phrases like 'usually', 'if at all possible', and 'as little as possible' were common but necessary. Brandon thought it strange at the time for such a serious business to openly require vagueness, but after several years he now understood how to interpret imprecise things.

"Is this Uncle Bart?" the caller replied, using Brandon's code name.

The voice sounded familiar, but Brandon knew there were many ways to dub someone else's voice onto a phone line, so he continued to be cautious. Remembering from his training and experience not to give an unidentified caller the benefit of knowing they reached whom they intended, Brandon used a tone one would use if a wrong number was dialed and responded, "Who is this?"

"It's Red Man," was the answer.

Hearing the caller's code name from an investigation a few years ago allowed Brandon to immediately recognize the voice, and he instantly recalled the location of the area code which puzzled him only moments ago. Brandon was still cautious however, as early in his career he loosened his guard during a call too soon, allowing the criminals to gain an advantage and escape.

"Code four," Brandon said into the phone.

"Two plus two," the caller replied.

"Code four," Brandon repeated.

"Two times two," the caller replied.

"Hi, Red Man," Brandon greeted his intruder, feeling confident the caller was indeed whom he claimed.

"Hi, Uncle Bart," the caller returned the greeting. Not knowing quite how to get to the purpose of the call, Red Man started by saying, "It's been a few years since we last talked. I hope things are going okay."

"Things are fine," Brandon replied. "What's on your mind?"

Brandon's comforting tone allowed the caller to continue. "I need your help. I'm involved in something, and I want to get out." The caller paused awaiting a response.

"Just stop doing it then," Brandon stated the most obvious course of action.

"It's not that simple. It's not enough for me to get out. I want the others to pay."

"Pay," Brandon repeated the last word. "Pay in what way?"

"I just want them to get caught and suffer the consequences for their actions."

"Sounds like there's a lot more to this than you're telling me, Red Man. Do you mind starting closer to the beginning and filling in some of the details?" Once again Brandon's soothing tone helped provide some calm, so the caller started again with much less distress than the first attempt.

After listening and taking notes for quite some time while only asking a few questions, Brandon had a much clearer picture of what was happening, at least from the caller's perspective. He wanted to ask an important question, but he opted first to make a statement. "I agree it's all illegal. I'm not sure it should fall on the radar screen of my agency, but I'm willing to take the initial look into it since I've presently got a little extra time and the agency and I are grateful to you for your help a few years ago."

Then Brandon got to the heart of the matter by asking, "So why are you so intent on these other men getting caught?"

The caller paused and took a deep breath before answering. "It's the fraternity. It's Sigma Chi, and all it stands for. The pain and humiliation of the initiation is horrible. It's no fun being initiated, or even conducting the initiation. Since I don't know how to stop it, I'd like to see society make them pay for any other wrongdoing."

Brandon understood the motive as he'd seen many similar personal vendettas over the years, but this one surprised him since he knew the caller attended college more than twenty years ago, and he expected time could've healed this wound. He was certainly intrigued by the conversation, which in itself was reason to further investigate, but he was also concerned about the future of college athletics, knowing one man's idea was most likely being contemplated by many others.

"Let's do this, Red Man. Let me do some of my own checking on your fraternity brothers. You keep doing what you're doing, and we'll chat again in a week or so. I'll call you after I've done a little more research."

"Thanks, Uncle Bart."

"You're welcome, Red Man."

After the call Brandon looked at the names from his notes. He didn't recognize any of them, so he wasn't sure what profiles his agency had. He dialed the number of his office and passed along the names, giving instructions for whatever information was available to be on his desk and ready for review the first thing tomorrow morning. He expected more calls to other federal and local agencies and organizations would be necessary, but he wasn't prepared for what he was going to uncover or how he would respond.

Later in the week on Thursday Brian Nichols was sitting with Dante Lewis in a corner of the cafeteria on the campus of Memphis State University. The two were finishing their lunch which was nothing spectacular, although Dante ate three times as much as Brian. Brian was proposing a business deal to Dante, and the explanation was quite simple. If Dante agreed now to let Brian be his agent when he was eligible for the NBA draft more than a year from now, Brian would provide monthly payments to Dante and his mother.

Once finished with lunch the two began walking across the campus toward the library. It was a mild day for the end of January with the temperature in the mid fifties, but both wore coats—Brian because he was used to the warmer weather of Florida, and Dante because he didn't want to jeopardize his health. At six feet and ten inches tall, Dante towered over the much shorter Brian. Dante was also very recognizable by most other students, and as Brian and Dante walked, many other students, both male and female, said hello to Dante and offered their congratulations for his excellent play and the big win of the previous night.

Brian told Dante the offer twice during lunch, but Dante wanted to hear it a third time, so Brian reiterated the exact same deal. The proposal was attractive for several reasons. Dante agreed he didn't expect to be a high choice in this year's draft, so he wanted to return for his senior season to hone his skills. But it hurt him to see his mother suffer from her financial state, and even a small signing bonus as a lower draft choice would go a long way to paying for many needed things. Brian's offer would help make ends meet for the extra year, so Dante saw it as an easy choice.

After going through the same proposal for a third time, Brian and Dante continued their walk, passed the library and down another campus street. Dante verbally agreed to the offer, but with one change. Instead of paying an equal amount to him and his mother, he wanted the total divided differently, so his mother would get three-fourths. Nothing else seemed to matter too much to Dante, and Brian saw the sincerity in the young man's face. When he talked with Jimmy in New Orleans, Brian knew Jimmy was right about being able to recruit good athletes based on their family situation, and now he had proof.

Brian and Dante continued to walk as they talked about life in professional basketball. Dante asked about contract negotiations, and he was eager to listen as Brian spoke from experience. Dante was keen for the time when his opportunity would come, and he was comfortable Brian would provide him with sage advice throughout his career.

The two made their way back to where Brian's car was parked, and it was a tight fit for Dante in the front seat of the Cutlass Ciera Brian rented at the airport. Brian reached for his briefcase in the back seat and pulled out an envelope containing some papers. Dante signed a contract with a date more than a year in advance allowing Brian to be his agent for the duration of his professional basketball career. Dante additionally signed a power-of-attorney, granting Brian complete authority to act on his behalf, including signing any contract or endorsing any check.

Once the papers were signed Brian placed the papers in the envelope and returned them to his briefcase. He grabbed a second envelope and handed it to Dante. "Congratulations, Dante," Brian said. "Here's your first payment and your mother's first payment. In the future I'll send hers directly to her. I'll give your payment to you personally when I visit the campus. It won't always be the same day every month since I don't always know exactly when I'll be here, but your mother will always get hers on time."

Dante opened the small envelope with his huge fingers and peered inside. There was one twenty dollar bill after another. "Thanks," he muttered with amazement.

"Can I give you a lift to where you're going?" Brian offered.

Dante continued to stare at the money and then realized Brian asked him a question. "Oh. No, thanks. I need to stop in the library anyway for something before I head to practice later this afternoon, and it's not far."

"Okay. Talk to you soon."

Dante thanked Brian again as he struggled to extract himself from the small car. Brian returned the thanks and watched Dante in his rear view mirror. Once Dante turned a corner and was out of sight, Brian started the engine and headed for the airport to catch a flight to Atlanta to meet with another client.

Brian spent the night with his parents, and the next morning his mother fed him a hearty breakfast of fruit, bacon, eggs, toast, and coffee. His appointment with his client wasn't until noon, so he spent a few hours talking with his mother as they walked around the yard. There were no leaves on the trees, and the bermuda grass was dormant, but Brian knew she liked to visit while walking outdoors no matter what time of year it was.

As they walked Brian constantly looked at his watch. His mother noticed and was now annoyed by it. "Do you have to be somewhere real soon, son?" she finally asked. "I thought your appointment wasn't until noon, and it's only a thirty minute drive."

"Yes, ma'am. But I need to call someone on the west coast this morning, and they are three hours behind us. I was trying to figure out when the best time to call would be, 'cause I didn't want to call them at home."

"I don't know why you wouldn't want to call them at home," she said with despair. "You get calls at all hours of the day at your house."

"I know, Mom," Brian said as he nodded in agreement, thinking about all the calls he regularly receives while sleeping. "I think I'll wait until it's seven o'clock there, and then I'll call."

"Suit yourself," she said as she continued through the yard.

Shortly after seven o'clock in the morning the phone in Jimmy Donovan's office rang. No one was in the office, so Brian didn't bother to leave a message with the answering service. Instead he dialed Jimmy's cell phone number. Jimmy's voice mail answered, and this time Brian left a brief message stating the date, time, his name, and his intention of calling Jimmy's home number next.

When the phone rang at the Donovan residence, Susan answered on the first ring, expecting it to be a lady from a volunteer group with whom she was riding to a function early this morning. She was completely surprised when a man's voice asked for Jimmy. Susan told the caller Jimmy was on his way to work, and she asked him if he had the number. Brian said he knew the number and would try to reach him there. When the call ended, Susan didn't think twice about it, since she was preoccupied with her plans for the day. It should've seemed strange since it was the second call she received in the last two days from different men wanting Jimmy. Brian on the other end was miffed Jimmy was not home, not at his office, and not answering his cell phone. Brian decided to wait and try Jimmy's office after twenty more minutes or so.

When the phone at Donovan Realty rang around seven thirty, Jimmy answered on the second ring. "Donovan Realty. Can I help you?"

"Is this Jimmy?" Brian asked.

"Hey, Brian! How ya' doin'!?" Jimmy shouted into the phone after recognizing Brian's voice.

"I'm fine. How are you?"

"Good. Real good. What's up?" Jimmy asked, eager to hear an update from Brian since the last time they talked was one week ago in New Orleans.

"I met with our man in Memphis yesterday," Brian answered.

"That's great, Brian. How'd it go?" Jimmy couldn't control his excitement, and it was beginning to rub off on Brian, too.

"Actually, it went real well. Dante signed the contract and the power-of-attorney. I gave him the first month's payments for him and his mother, and he couldn't be happier. It was just like you said. A little bit of money to someone in need can go a long way."

"Beautiful!" Jimmy exclaimed as he looked at the map on his wall and immediately found Alcatraz Island. A broad smile came across his face. "When can we discuss the second phase of the plan? I saw results of the big win two nights ago, and I've been looking at the remaining schedule. I've got a few ideas on what might work, but we'll have to move quickly."

The two continued their conversation, and Brian was staggered at the amount of research Jimmy completed in less than a week. He wondered when Jimmy took time to sleep or run his real estate business.

Meanwhile Brandon Williams was looking over several reports specially prepared for him. He was always surprised by two things on new cases. The first was the amount of research which was done in a short period of time by different intelligence organizations. The second was the activity present in the lives of everyday people.

Brandon came across amateurs and professionals alike, but the behavior described in the pages in front of him were impressive. Brandon knew the commissioner of insurance in the state of California would be quite surprised at the creativity included in several real estate transactions. He knew several bankers who would be more than mystified at some recent activities. He also wondered what might be included in the same reports in a few more years regarding college and professional athletes if he let fate run its course.

Brandon reached for his phone to place a call to his supervisor. As he grabbed the phone, something caught his attention, causing him to hesitate to dial. He looked at the ring on his finger from his alma mater. The stone was a brilliant shade of red, which he and other fellow alumni always liked. Surrounding the stone was the name of the institution, a small school near the east coast. On one side the year in which he graduated was displayed. On the other side were two Greek letters, indicating the fraternity of his choice, Sigma Chi.

Brandon debated what he should do.

TWENTY SIX

Billy Wicks sat in the recliner in his sister's house in Boaz, Alabama and watched her sleep on the couch. It was a few minutes after nine o'clock in the morning on Monday, February 4th, as Billy looked at the clock on the wall. He knew his sister was exhausted, having been up most of the last several nights at her husband's bedside. Billy knew there would be many more sleepless nights over the next several weeks and months, and he expected she might sleep on the couch often to avoid a lonely bed.

Billy hoped the children were doing okay with their grandparents, although he didn't know much about them, first meeting them at his sister's wedding long ago and being reunited with them several days ago. His sister said they were nice people, similar in many ways to Billy's and his sister's parents. His three nephews and one niece were always disappointed they only knew one set of grandparents, but now their disappointment would be much greater without their father.

Billy continued to watch his sister sleep and he wondered what she might be dreaming. Maybe she dreamed of the past, when she first married or when her children were born. Maybe she dreamed of the future, when she might remarry or see her children graduate from college. Billy didn't know how she would afford for her children to go to college, but he knew in dreams anything was possible. He hoped hers were pleasant right now, but he doubted it.

Billy thought about what help he should provide both now and over a longer period of time. He expected the oldest son who was fifteen, bright, and hard-working could complete most of the work required on the chicken farm, particularly with the help of the next oldest, who would soon be fourteen but was already taller and bigger than his older brother. Billy knew the boys needed some guidance and outright assistance in dealing and negotiating with those who purchased the birds, so it made him think about offering to stay and help. How long would be necessary he didn't know, but he expected a few months would certainly not be sufficient.

Billy decided to call his office to let them know he would remain in Alabama indefinitely, but he didn't want the conversation to wake his sister. He realized it was only seven o'clock in California, so a call now would be fruitless anyway.

Billy saw his sister roll over slightly. Then she opened her eyes and looked directly at him and smiled. Billy hoped pleasant dreams were the reason for the smile, but it didn't last long as she quickly began to cry.

Billy knew her husband dominated her thoughts. The man died in the early hours of the morning, shortly after regaining consciousness from a week-long coma. The brief moment of hope when he opened his eyes was quickly taken away as shortly after he closed his eyes and stopped breathing. Only Billy and his sister were in the hospital room at the time, and the night staff came running when they heard her scream, but all efforts of revival failed.

An hour later Billy drove his sister home without a word being spoken. Around four thirty in the morning they talked briefly, but the conversation was almost incoherent from her exhaustion. Both just sat and stared at the walls in disbelief. Finally around seven she dozed off while Billy remained awake.

Seeing his sister cry pained Billy's heart. It used to be fun when they were growing up to make her cry, but Billy outgrew it and now was sorry for the times he treated her badly. As he watched his sister he bit his lip to fight back his own tears. Finally he walked over to the couch and sat beside her prone body. He rubbed her back softly, just as he knew his mother did long ago, as she continued to cry.

When her tears dried Billy excused himself to make a call. On the second ring a woman answered, "Hello."

"Hey, Susan. It's Billy. Billy Wicks."

"Hi, Billy," Susan Donovan greeted him. "Where are you? Are you still in Alabama or are you back in California now?"

"I'm still here with my sister."

"I hope everything's alright, Billy," Susan said, knowing only what Jimmy told her about some farming accident upon his return from New Orleans.

"Actually, it's not." Billy took a deep breath to calm himself before continuing. "My sister's husband died earlier this morning."

"That's awful, Billy. I'm so sorry for you and her." Susan paused, not knowing what to say to ease the pain she knew was present. "Here, let me get Jimmy. He's about ready to leave for work, but let me run and catch him before he goes. Hang on, Billy."

Billy heard her lay down the receiver. He waited almost a full minute before he heard Jimmy's voice.

"Hey, Billy," Jimmy said much slower and softer than he normally spoke. "Susan told me the bad news. I'm really sorry. I'm sure your sister is just crushed. I wish I knew how to make the pain go away, but I don't."

"Thanks, Jimmy. It is tough."

"Is there anything I can do for you on this end? I assume you're going to stay there for a while to help out."

"Boy. I don't know right now. I'm sure there's something, but let me first call my office later this morning. I'll call you later today or tomorrow and we can talk some more."

"Okay." Jimmy paused but didn't say his farewell yet as he knew his friend was really hurting. "Billy, we're really sorry. I'm sure it's particularly difficult for you and your little sis, as I'm certain it reminds both of you of your parents. But just hang in there. If you need anything from me, just say the word."

Both Jimmy and Billy were silent for a few moments as they contemplated what to say. Finally Billy said, "Thanks. Bye, Jimmy."

Hearing the cracking in his friend's voice, Jimmy said, "Take care, Billy. Talk to you later."

Jimmy hung up the phone and turned around to see his wife standing near the wall with tears in her eyes. He walked over and hugged her for a long time as she cried softly. When she stopped weeping she kissed him on the cheek and walked out of the room without saying a word.

Jimmy looked at his watch and saw it was after eight o'clock. He picked up the phone and dialed Charlie's number at the bank.

After hearing Charlie's greeting Jimmy said, "Hey, Charlie. It's Jimmy. I just finished talking with Billy." Jimmy paused for a moment as he sat on the edge of the bed and then continued. "Bad news. His sister's husband died earlier this morning."

Charlie was shocked. "That's terrible, J.D. From your earlier description of the accident, I didn't realize it was so serious. I bet Billy and his sister are just crushed."

"Yeah. He sounded pretty sad on the phone."

"I'm sure the children don't know how to react either. Any idea what they're going to do?"

"I don't know, Charlie. Billy said he was going to stay for a while, but he doesn't know how long it might be. I get the feeling he's going to stay for quite some time. I also think he's seriously contemplating giving up his business and moving back permanently." Jimmy almost told Charlie about the flight to New Orleans where he saw Billy reading the annual reports of construction companies and a chicken processing plant, but he decided to keep the information to himself.

"You really think Billy would pick up and move back after having been here this long? It's not like he'd be going back to a better life."

"I agree, Charlie, but you never know. It was a big surprise to many when he picked up and moved to California years ago after the accident involving his parents. Maybe this latest tragedy will cause him to make another major change."

"Maybe so," Charlie said slowly. Then he asked, "Is there anything I can do to help? Do you think a call would help? Shucks, I don't even have the phone number. Do you happen to have it, J.D.?"

"Yeah. It's right here somewhere," Jimmy said as he searched through the drawer of the night stand by the bed to find some hand-written numbers in a small address book. Once Jimmy found the number he gave it to Charlie.

After receiving the number Charlie asked, "We're still on for our meeting on Wednesday evening, right?"

"Yeah. All you'll need is the money for your portion of the investment. I'll see you then, Charlie."

The two said goodbye and hung up on their respective ends.

Charlie sat at his desk and looked at the work in front of him. He glanced at his schedule for the day and took notice of the meeting with his boss later in the morning. Feeling sorry for Billy, Charlie wondered what he could do to help ease the pain he knew Billy and his sister were feeling.

Jimmy sat on the edge of his bed and stared at the wall. It was full of pictures of Jimmy, Susan, and the girls in various frames. He pondered how Susan might manage if he wasn't around to pay for their lifestyle. He expected she would probably sell the house and move back near her folks and let them help support her, and he hoped she would choose an honest realtor if required.

Jimmy dialed another number on the phone and waited for an answer. When he heard a greeting from the other end he said, "Hey, Mick. It's Jimmy. How ya' doin'?"

"It's okay. What's up?" Mickey replied.

"Billy called just a little while ago. His brother-in-law died earlier this morning."

"Wow," Mickey responded. "That's sad. How's he doin'?"

"It sounded pretty tough. He'll be staying with his sister for a while, of course."

"Any idea how long, Jimmy?" Mickey asked.

"Don't know. It could be just a few weeks, or it may be for several months. I'm sure he's not thinking completely clearly right now."

"Yeah, probably not," Mickey said in agreement. Changing the subject Mickey said, "I'm probably going to be in San Jose later this week on business. You want to get together for dinner?"

"Sure," Jimmy replied, a little stunned Mickey moved so quickly from the tragic news of Billy's family to an entirely new issue. "Which day were you thinking of being here?"

"Thursday or Friday, but most likely Thursday."

Thinking about his schedule and his commitment to take Susan and the girls out for dinner on Friday, Jimmy said, "Thursday would be much better for me. Can you make it work?"

"I think so," Mickey said, knowing he had no business in San Jose but wanting an excuse to meet with Jimmy to talk in more detail about Operation Alcatraz. "I'll give you a call tomorrow when I have a better handle on my schedule." Pausing for a moment while debating whether to mention it or not, Mickey finally blurted, "I was hoping we could talk about Operation Alcatraz."

"What do you want to know, Mick?" Jimmy asked, as his mind began to work twice as fast as he sensed something strange.

"I'm just interested in knowing more of the specifics."

"Like what?"

"Well," Mickey started slowly, wishing he'd waited until later in the week as opposed to starting this conversation over the phone. Nonetheless he recklessly said, "I'm interested in how the athletes are picked. I'd like to have a better understanding of the entire financial picture. I'm also interested in who's participating. Is Billy still in?"

Jimmy couldn't believe what he was hearing. How could Mickey be concerned about Billy's involvement in Operation Alcatraz while being in the midst of a family tragedy. "I'll tell you what, Mick. Let's deal with all those questions on Thursday if you make it to San Jose. Give me a call tomorrow or Wednesday to confirm your schedule, and we'll go from there."

"Okay, Jimmy. I'll talk to you tomorrow."

"Bye, Mick," Jimmy said as he heard Mickey say goodbye and hang up the phone.

Once Jimmy put his receiver in its place he shook his head in amazement. He still couldn't believe Mickey's insensitivity to Billy's situation, but it was clear Mickey was uncomfortable and outright anxious about Operation Alcatraz, and possibly other things. Jimmy thought for several minutes while he remained seated on the edge of his bed, and he concluded to push forward with his plan.

During the week Jimmy continued to research the performances and backgrounds of several college football and basketball players on many teams throughout the South. He found many players who were previously top high school prospects who decided to pursue their dreams of playing professionally by attending a Southeastern conference school to further develop their skills. Many came from poor and broken homes and would clearly welcome some financial assistance. The discouraging thing was the number of players who didn't develop adequately during their collegiate careers for one reason or another. Several sustained injuries which they never recovered from, but many simply didn't improve as much as needed to become a top pro prospect. This data made Jimmy realize there was still a large amount of luck in making the long-term part of Operation Alcatraz successful, and he became completely committed to making the short-term part of fixing games and winning bets on those games work.

Jimmy's Wednesday meeting with Charlie was fairly uneventful. Charlie reiterated his desire to be a silent partner in Operation Alcatraz when he handed Jimmy an envelope with enough money for his portion of funding the first athlete for a year. Charlie only said to let him know when a second athlete was signed and to tell him his amount to pay. There was some discussion of Billy's situation along with a few comments about the positive change in Charlie's working environment due to his new boss. Expecting Charlie's desire for revenge against his bank would be short-lived all along, Jimmy made a mental note to not pursue any more bank scams for several months requiring any assistance or even advice from Charlie.

Mickey made the special trip from Monterey on Thursday, and he met with Jimmy over dinner in a restaurant in Sunnyvale on a cozy street lined with older two-story and three-story buildings on both sides. Several trees were growing through grates in the sidewalk, and Jimmy speculated how difficult it would be to cut them down when their size became problematic.

The front of their destination contained full-length windows across the entire width. The bar to the right of the entrance was crowded with many younger adults sharing a drink after work to unwind from the jobs they performed during the day. Very few people were seated in the dining area to the left, but Jimmy asked if it was possible to be seated upstairs in a secondary dining area. The hostess was happy to accommodate the request and led the two up the stairs to a table in the front where they could watch the pedestrian traffic below. Only one other couple was present upstairs, and the waitress assisting them smiled at Jimmy and Mickey as they were seated, happy her many trips up and down the stairs would now be twice as fruitful.

Jimmy chose a reuben sandwich and fries, accompanied by a domestic beer. Mickey decided to try the catch of the day, which was a grilled mahi mahi with mashed potatoes and mixed vegetables. Mickey ordered a glass of wine with his meal, but he additionally asked for one of the dark beers brewed on the premises for starters.

Jimmy noticed the discussion seemed forced and segmented throughout the evening. Mickey was clearly bothered by not having as much knowledge of, input to, or control over Operation Alcatraz.

Jimmy remained silent about other participants besides the two of them and Billy, not even telling his friend Charlie was involved.

Jimmy stated he was working to expand the activities, but he provided no other details, citing he was still only in the initial stages and needed to do a lot more research before telling Mickey or Billy his plan. Jimmy said he didn't want to get Mickey's hopes up if he later uncovered a stumbling block and was forced to scrap the entire idea, but Mickey was clearly not satisfied as he felt he was only receiving bread crumbs instead of the main course. It was definitely different from their previous dealings, and both were more cautious and less trusting than before. Jimmy couldn't help but think back to Mickey's insensitive comments from the Monday morning conversation about Billy's situation while Mickey didn't understand why his friend was being so protective of so much information.

Neither opted for dessert, and as they left the eating place they walked quietly along the street. There was a Mexican restaurant with very few patrons across the street, and a small bar displaying a green neon sign above the door was receiving three more customers as two men and a woman, all in blue jeans, entered as Jimmy and Mickey approached. A Chinese restaurant with outstanding food was a few doors further down the lane, and Jimmy tried to remember the last time he and Susan ate there.

The evening air was cool since it was still the early part of February, so both Jimmy and Mickey walked fairly quickly. When they reached the end of the street, Mickey indicated he was parked in the corner of the lot for customers of the small shopping mall located just ahead, so the two said farewell. Mickey crossed the street to find his vehicle while Jimmy made a turn to continue his journey to his car, which was parked in a public lot a few blocks further.

As Jimmy drove home he pondered if Mickey felt slighted by not being the main partner anymore. When it was only real estate transactions, Mickey and Jimmy were the two key players, while Billy was used as needed. Jimmy remembered Mickey's response when Charlie was recruited. Mickey was excited and surprised Charlie agreed to participate, but Mickey also was not happy Charlie would receive the same share of the profits. Charlie was a major player in the second round of mortgage payment redirections, while Billy also played a vital role. With so much focus and energy on

Operation Alcatraz, Jimmy expected Mickey was feeling less important. Jimmy didn't know what was wrong or how to fix it, but he wanted his latest idea to come to fruition, so he continued to concentrate his efforts on it.

On Friday evening after having dinner with Susan and the girls, Jimmy monitored the final minutes of the Memphis basketball game at Alabama-Birmingham from the ESPN internet website. Memphis was 10-0 in the conference after starting the year with ten wins and four losses in their pre-conference games. While only seeing an update to the score every ninety seconds, Jimmy could tell Memphis played horribly, as they were soundly beaten by eighteen points while scoring a season-low forty-six. Next up was a tough road game against North Carolina-Charlotte, but Jimmy actually hoped for another loss, as a few losses now was key to fixing a game later without raising suspicion.

The following week on Tuesday Jimmy and Brian once again discussed Dante Lewis and the Memphis basketball program. Tomorrow night was the game in Charlotte, and only four other games remained in the regular season. A home contest against Houston on Saturday, a game at South Florida next week, a home game against DePaul a week from Saturday, and the regular season finale at Cincinnati were left. Beyond the regular season was the conference tournament, and a post-season bid to the NCAA tournament was expected to cap the good season.

There was some speculation on the part of some sports writers as to what Memphis needed to do in their remaining games to assure themselves of a bid to the NCAA tournament. The argument of the writers centered around the four losses in the pre-conference schedule to Iowa, Alabama, Ole Miss, and Arkansas, which were all losses to teams in major conferences. Memphis did have wins against Tennessee and Temple, but these experts weren't certain those were enough. Jimmy on the other hand felt if Memphis simply won their half of the conference's two divisions, they would be rewarded with a bid. Brian tended to agree, but he also pointed out the weakness of the schedule would not help.

Jimmy expected Memphis would be favored in their games against Houston, South Florida, and DePaul, while highly-ranked Cincinnati would be favored in the last regular season matchup.

Memphis was almost guaranteed of one of the top four seeds in the conference tournament, meaning they would not play the first day while being favored in their game on the second day against a team surviving the first round.

Brian agreed with Jimmy's logic, but Brian wasn't convinced he could persuade Dante quickly enough to impact one of the last four games. Brian was planning on flying to Charlotte to watch the game and meet again with Dante, and Brian was also going to Memphis for the weekend game against Houston. Living in Orlando made the road game against South Florida the following week easy for Brian to make. The plan was for Brian to talk with Dante before and after each game to adequately influence him to agree to participate in the second half of Operation Alcatraz, hopefully in the first game of the conference tournament.

On Wednesday afternoon at four o'clock Jimmy sat in his office and navigated the ESPN website to display an updated score for the Memphis game in Charlotte. Jimmy was happy for the time difference between the east coast and the west coast, as it permitted him to monitor the entire game while also allowing him to make it home for dinner well before seven o'clock.

Memphis played better at Charlotte than in the previous game against UAB, but the result was still a loss by a final score of 75-63. Memphis was now 20-6 for the season and 10-2 in the conference with two games remaining. As he drove home and thought about tonight's outcome and Operation Alcatraz, Jimmy smiled.

TWENTY SEVEN

Saturday, February 16th, was a rather warm winter day in the Bay Area. The temperature was in the upper sixties, and there was barely a hint of a breeze. It almost felt like summer to Jimmy, and he was tempted to drive his Audi TT with the top down. Jimmy was leaving an older gentleman's home after visiting with the man who desperately wanted to sell his house and move back to the hills of Tennessee.

It was the conclusion of a full day of researching new listings for Jimmy, and it was shortly after four o'clock in the afternoon. He hurried home to allow ample time to clean up before taking Susan out for dinner. The girls were with friends and were going to a movie among other things, so Jimmy and his wife were taking advantage of being without any parenting responsibilities, other than the normal worrying.

After dinner Jimmy and Susan walked slowly for the few blocks from the restaurant to where they were parked. The temperature was still very mild, and they noticed several other people walking along the sidewalk as well. The conversation was about Billy, as Susan confided in her husband regarding her thoughts of the last two weeks. Susan felt badly for Billy and even more so for his younger sister, who was now with four children and no husband. Susan knew Billy was providing assistance, but she expected the hole remaining was beyond anything she could imagine. Susan was glad Jimmy didn't work on a farm around dangerous equipment where an accident on any day could make it his last and leave her alone with their girls. It was clear Susan required and valued the emotional and financial security her husband provided.

When Jimmy and Susan returned home their girls were still away and were not expected for a few more hours. They sat in their living room and shared wine from a single glass. One side had some lipstick around the rim while the other was the one Jimmy used. They could've just as easily used two glasses, but Jimmy knew his wife liked it better this way. Susan felt it was a little promiscuous to drink wine from the same glass with a man, and it was part of the foreplay on this evening. Jimmy thought a few times about the unknown outcome to the Memphis basketball game against Houston, but he figured he could wait and check it early the next morning while devoting himself to his lovely wife this night.

On Sunday morning when Jimmy checked the score of the game on the internet, he was surprised Memphis lost by three points. The game was played in Memphis, and it was the second meeting of the year between the two teams. The first game was contested in Houston the weekend of the Super Bowl, as Jimmy now remembered the difficulty he encountered trying to hunt down the result in the New Orleans newspaper on the morning of the Super Bowl. Memphis won easily 84-66 in the January matchup, so Jimmy expected an even easier win in the return game at home.

Jimmy further checked the box score of the game to see how Dante played. It was a solid performance as indicated by the many rebounds, good shooting percentage from both the field and the free throw line, and only a few fouls. A couple of other players fouled out and scored well below their respective averages, so Jimmy expected Dante did all he could.

It was now three losses in a row for Memphis, and it worried Jimmy a little, as he needed Memphis to be a solid favorite in the first game of the conference tournament if his plan was to succeed. He hoped they could get back on the winning track in their next game against South Florida on Wednesday, and if so, Jimmy expected everything would fall into place nicely.

On Monday morning Brandon Williams poured over some reports, records, and documents in his efforts to organize different events. Brandon was trying to confirm what several pages seemed to be telling him regarding a homeowner named McVey. As best as Brandon could tell from what he saw, Mr. McVey paid for a new roof, with a company named Bay Roofing, whoever they were, completing the work. From another set of papers it wasn't clear the buyers of the home or their realtor, Jamie Rasmussen, knew anything about the roof. Brandon thought about calling Ms. Rasmussen to determine what she may or may not know, but he opted not to since he feared she may also be part of this scheme. In other real estate closings several different realtors were involved, and Brandon wanted more research done before possibly tipping off anyone who didn't need to know where he was poking his nose.

Another folder laying on Brandon's desk contained the banking activity and other relevant information of a man who moved from New Jersey to California a few months ago. What was so strange or even ridiculous was the man lived in Pleasanton, which was in the East Bay. He opened two accounts in Santa Cruz, which was well over an hour drive away, and made transactions every other day, if not every day, either electronically or somehow in person. The man's phone bills for the period of time in question showed no calls to the bank or an internet service provider. The man also did not purchase any direct internet access for his home, which meant he was either doing a lot of banking from whatever capability was available at his employer or something else was the case. It certainly didn't surprise Brandon when several mortgage payments from seemingly random people were deposited into his accounts on the first of November, followed by a quick subsequent closing of the accounts. The item most intriguing to Brandon was how the random group of people had two things in common—trying to sell their homes and obviously not protecting their personal banking information.

There was another folder on Brandon's desk telling a similar story. This time the accounts were at branches of banks in San Ramon and Danville, while the holder of the accounts lived in Los Altos after moving from somewhere in Ohio. The main difference this time was the people with redirected mortgage payments were not such a random list of homeowners trying to sell their houses. Instead, they all banked at the same institution.

In viewing different phone records Brandon expected other activities worthy of further review would be uncovered, but he decided not to spend any of his energy on it, since others were continuing to dig their way through the mess. Brandon wanted to focus his efforts on stopping the next scam, which required the help of someone outside of his office. Brandon dialed the phone number and listened as it rang four times before finally being answered.

"Hello," was the simple greeting Brandon heard in his ear.

"Hi, Red Man. It's Uncle Bart," Brandon greeted him.

"Hi, Uncle Bart. What can I do for you?" Red Man replied.

"We need to make a trip to Memphis. We need to meet with school officials and Dante Lewis. Since the Memphis basketball team plays in Florida this Wednesday night and then goes back home for a game on Saturday, I thought I would set something up for Friday morning. Can you make it in on Thursday night so we can meet for a few hours prior to the meetings on Friday?"

Red Man thought for a minute about his schedule before answering. "Yeah. I can make it. Where should I stay? And when and where do you want me to meet you?"

"Just pick your own place to stay, and don't worry about where I'm staying. If you randomly pick a place, I expect it will be different from where I'm staying, which is preferred. Call my cell phone and leave me a message with the name and address of your hotel sometime before noon on Thursday. As for meeting with me, I'll call your hotel room sometime between seven and nine on Thursday night and we'll make arrangements then." Brandon paused for a moment and then asked, "Any more questions, Red Man?"

"Do I need to bring anything with me?"

"No, I don't think so. Unless there's some details you know which you think may be important which you can't remember."

"Okay, Uncle Bart. I'll see you in Memphis Thursday. I'll be sure to leave you a message with the name and address of the hotel."

"Thanks, Red Man. See you then."

After completing the call Brandon looked at the ring on his finger. He twisted it a little to fully display the two Greek letters on one side. One was a sigma and the other was a chi. He thought for a few minutes about his fraternity brothers from his college days. He couldn't remember having a conversation with a single one in the last five years, and he wondered if it was normal to lose track of those who were such an important part of his life years ago.

Brandon also thought back to his initiation activities and ceremony. He remembered several items from the week-long event, but mostly he recalled being tired due to having been allowed such little sleep for so many consecutive days. The ceremony at the end of the week was more of a celebration of the commitment several young men were making to the others present and all of the others who preceded them.

Brandon couldn't remember being asked or forced to do anything tremendously embarrassing, certainly nothing which would stick with him or anyone else for so long and demand such revenge, as was the case with Red Man. It was something he wanted to do some of his own research on before his meeting with Red Man on Thursday night. His flight to Memphis in the morning would allow him to conduct several meetings with present members of the Sigma Chi chapter in Memphis and others associated with the university and the Greek system for many years. As Brandon gazed at his ring he knew being a fraternity brother from a different chapter many years ago would be advantageous in his efforts to learn more about the past from those active in the Memphis chapter of Sigma Chi.

Two days later on Wednesday, Jimmy Donovan ate a deli sandwich with roast beef, a slice of kielbasa, slices of pepperoni, pepper jack cheese, lettuce, tomato, and some spicy barbeque sauce. A large bag of sour cream and onion potato chips complemented his sandwich, and Jimmy chose not to read the nutrition information on the back of the bag since he knew the amount of calories, and particularly the amount of calories from fat, would take away from his ability to enjoy this noon feast.

Jimmy stared at the maps on his office walls and wondered what decoration he should add to Alcatraz Island to properly adorn it. He decided he would add a colored push pin around the border of the island and stick a matching one in a blank corner of the paper for every game fixed as part of Operation Alcatraz. In the blank corner next to the second pin he could write the date and score of the game. He debated about adding the amount of the winnings to each entry as well, but he decided it might be more sensible not to.

Jimmy opened the right-hand drawer of his desk and removed a clear plastic box containing close to one hundred push pins of varying colors. He first grabbed two blue ones, thinking the first set should match the school colors, but then he debated about possibly using a color which matched the colors of the opponent. As he set the two blue ones on his desk and started to grab two red ones, he realized he didn't yet know who Memphis was playing in their first game of the conference tournament in a few weeks.

Jimmy then began to laugh out loud as he realized how ridiculously stupid so many people would think he was in spending so much thought about this color matching. Once he calmed down he simply grabbed two pins of each color until he accumulated close to ten sets. He pushed those pins into the blank corner of the map and shook his head as he smiled.

Jimmy returned to his chair and finished the last few bites of his sandwich and chips. Once he cleared his desk of the crumbs and wrappers from his meal, he picked up the phone and dialed Brian's number. Brian answered on the first ring.

"Hey, Brian! How ya' doin'?" Jimmy shouted into his phone.

"Jimmy D. How are ya?" Brian returned the jovial greeting.

"I'm fine. Just finished my lunch and thought we should talk about our star player. How'd your meeting go with him this morning?"

"It was fine. The team flew down from Memphis last night, and Dante and I were able to sneak in a quick meeting this morning before the morning shoot around."

From the positive sound in Brian's voice, Jimmy was hardly able to control his own enthusiasm. "Good, Brian. Real good," Jimmy said. Wanting to get to the issue at hand as quickly as possible, Jimmy asked, "Is he receptive to working with us on the second half of Operation Alcatraz?"

"I think so, but with the team having lost three in a row, it's gonna take a few wins before he'll agree to it. I think our plan of waiting until the first game of the conference tournament is the right thing to do, provided they win tonight and also win at least one of the last two games."

"I agree," Jimmy said as he was now sitting on the edge of his chair as close to his phone as was possible without sitting on his desk.

"I'm going to meet with him again after the game tonight, and we can talk again tomorrow. I'll meet with him again in Memphis before and after the Saturday game against DePaul, and hopefully we'll be able to finalize the deal sometime next week before the last game against Cincy."

"Sounds great, Brian," Jimmy said as he realized he was talking loudly as a result of his excitement. Calming himself slightly, Jimmy added, "I'll talk to you tomorrow."

"Let's do it first thing tomorrow morning your time. I'll call you at your office."

"Okay. Cheer for a win tonight, Brian."

"You, too, Jimmy D."

After the call Jimmy sat back in his chair for a few seconds. He was so thrilled he couldn't control himself, so he stood up and pumped his fists in the air with the same vigor most often times displayed by fans at a live sporting event. Jimmy was so happy he decided to take the afternoon off and go riding in his sports car. He didn't have an agenda or a destination. He just wanted to feel the wind in his hair since he felt so alive and satisfied.

Later in the afternoon Jimmy returned to his office. It was about half past four o'clock, and he wanted to watch the progress of the Memphis game against South Florida on the internet. Two hours and twenty minutes later Jimmy headed for home with a huge smile on his face since Memphis won the game 71-59. He couldn't wait to talk with Brian again the next morning.

Friday morning in Memphis was overcast, although it wasn't expected to rain until the afternoon, and even then it was only a thirty percent chance according to the local television station's weather man. As Brandon Williams drove from his hotel he looked at the sky and wondered if the rain would hold off for several more hours or not.

Brandon also was trying to put different pieces of information into some semblance of order. Three days earlier upon his arrival in Memphis, Brandon met separately with four Sigma Chi fraternity members of the local chapter. Two were very guarded with their information while a third was open and honest but not particularly helpful. The fourth was a second-generation member of Sigma Chi, and this young man provided significant insight into his view of the differences between the present hazing rituals versus those from more than thirty years ago when his father was in college. Brandon wondered if the boy's father exaggerated or not, and he also wondered if things changed dramatically in the immediate five to ten years after the boy's father's experiences.

On Wednesday morning Brandon met with the university president and was quite unimpressed. The man was clearly a figurehead without a clue about anything of importance. Brandon marveled at how the man was hired with obviously no ability to answer questions precisely or avoid stumbling over his own words.

Wednesday's lunch was much more helpful as Brandon enjoyed for more than two hours the company of the Sigma Chi house mother. The lady was a Memphis State alumnus from the class of '58 and worked as a teller at a bank for almost twenty-five years before retiring. Getting bored a few years after quitting at the bank she somehow found her way to becoming a house mother. Her seventeen years of service were the second longest of all the present house mothers at the different fraternities, and she said she and the others met once a week for lunch and bridge while only gossiping about the college boys for one hour. Brandon wasn't so sure the gossiping lasted only an hour as he expected it continued between every hand of the card game. The woman stated she believed some discussion with others in her same role helped her and the others keep their sanity since they were all astounded at some of the rude and promiscuous behavior they witnessed on a daily basis.

The lady wasn't privy to the initiation rituals or ceremonies, but she did notice significant changes in most boys as a result. Many times the changes were for the better, and she likened it to when someone becomes a Christian, commits their life to another person through marriage, or has their first child. There were occasions however when the effect was the opposite.

She remembered one boy in particular who developed alcohol poisoning and spent almost two days in the hospital at the brink of death. The boy recovered fully and continued to participate in all fraternity activities other than the drinking, but he was a loner and didn't seem to enjoy the experience. She never understood why he didn't quit the fraternity.

Another boy threatened to kill three others and even pointed a loaded gun at one of the three before stopping. The boy dropped out of school a few weeks later and ended up transferring to another school the following semester.

The house mother rarely met any of the boys' parents anymore. She did during her first few years, but the expectations of a few of the mothers regarding her responsibilities led to some late night phone calls. Deciding she didn't need to endure the wrath of a worrying mother who wasn't able to instill sufficient discipline in a child, she simply chose to avoid the parents.

Two Wednesday afternoon meetings with university professors who were Sigma Chi fraternity brothers were also helpful to Brandon, but the most intriguing meeting of the day was with a fairly young woman who was now the university's Greek advisor. The woman was involved in a sorority during her college days, and she benefited significantly from the friendships and activities. She was shocked at the ugly comments she heard from her sorority sisters regarding new pledges though, and she learned what people said to her face versus what they said behind her back was often times the exact opposite. She was nearing the end of her third year in her present role, and her own independent research indicated many dangerous and inappropriate rituals from years ago were still present in some of the smaller fraternities. Also being a psychology major she certainly expected someone subjected to a particularly cruel event during their initiation could hold a grudge for many years with the intent of getting their revenge much later in life. She agreed it was also quite possible for the same person to befriend those being targeted.

Brandon met with other members of the Sigma Chi fraternity on Thursday, including two of the boys with whom he met on Tuesday. One of the boys who previously was very guarded with his information was this time quite open. The other boy was the open, honest, and unhelpful one from Tuesday, and much of his story was different the second time around. Brandon doubted he was hearing the truth, and he expected he wouldn't get any more useful dialogue from any of the fraternity brothers if he was to conduct subsequent interviews, since he fully expected the entire house of boys was now aware of his activities.

As Brandon drove on the overcast morning and pondered all he heard during the last three days, he most believed the woman who was the Greek advisor and the boy whose father was also a Sigma Chi member. Brandon was now convinced Red Man was acting in accordance with the woman's suggestion of suppressing his hatred and being a friend while secretly wanting and working to get his revenge.

As Brandon turned into the driveway of the hotel he noticed a few drops of rain on the windshield. He parked in front of the hotel and left his car running while he hurried inside. He saw who he was looking for sitting in a chair near the registration desk reading the local morning newspaper. The two shook hands without saying a word and walked outside to the car. Having driven a few blocks from the hotel, Brandon said, "Good morning, Red Man. Ready for a big day?"

"Absolutely, Uncle Bart," Red Man replied.

"Do you have any questions from our meeting last night?"

"None."

"Good. As I said last night, we're meeting first with the athletic director, then with the head coach, and then with both of them. Then we'll meet with Dante before having a final meeting with all three. If all goes well, we'll be done by noon, and we can be back home for the weekend."

Brandon and Red Man conducted their meetings during the course of the morning without any problems. The athletic director questioned Brandon about not wanting to inform the president of the university, but it was agreed to follow Brandon's plan. The plan was for Dante to continue his relationship with Brian Nichols and anyone else involved. Dante would agree to throw the first game of the conference tournament in a few weeks while accepting whatever bribe money was paid in advance. Dante would play his best and let the game have its natural outcome while Brandon would take care of the rest.

When the final meeting between Brandon, Red Man, Dante, the athletic director, and the head coach concluded, Brandon asked to have a few minutes alone with Dante.

"Big Dog," Brandon started, using the code name assigned to Dante. "I know you're in a tough spot. I expect you're quite confused by all of this, along with being worried about your mother's financial situation. I can't give you or her any money for your efforts in helping us, and I also can't give you any front page accolades since my office will do all we can to keep this as quiet as possible.

"But I can tell you how much I appreciate what you're doing, and I know you'll feel your own reward later in life for having done the right thing. You may never realize how the next few weeks could've ruined college and professional sports as you and I know them.

"I truly believe and hope your basketball skills will provide you with a comfortable life, although the next twelve to fifteen months will be tough, as I expect you'll wish on many occasions you never heard the code names Uncle Bart, Red Man, or Big Dog.

"I just want to tell you thanks. Good luck in the next few games, and do your best to focus on getting prepared to play well in those games. Thanks again for your help."

Dante didn't say anything as the two shook hands and Brandon left the room. Dante only thought about his mother and how it hurt his heart to see her struggle with so little money. And now her financial state, which he promised would be slightly better during his senior season as witnessed by the first two monthly payments recently received, was headed back to where it started.

Saturday's game against DePaul was the final home game of the year. The seniors were honored in a pregame ceremony, and the appreciation the fans showed the senior players and their families encouraged Dante. He now wanted very desperately to make it through his senior season so he and his mother could participate in this same ceremony the following year.

Dante played his best game of the year, as once the opening tip was tossed in the air he focused entirely on the task at hand and played tirelessly. The result was a lopsided win with a final score of 88-61. In the locker room after the game Dante and the other underclassmen were happy the seniors were able to win their last home game.

Memphis now had a record of 22-7 on the season with a 12-3 mark in the conference. First place in their division of the conference was clinched, and a win in the season finale eight days away against league-leading Cincinnati would give both teams a 13-3 conference record.

Dante and his teammates played hard but lost a close game, 80-75, at Cincinnati on Sunday, March 3rd. With Cincinnati securing the league's best record with the win, the Bearcats hosted the conference tournament, requiring Memphis to make a return trip in only a few days. The seedings for the tournament were now set, as Memphis was the third seed of twelve teams. The first day had four games scheduled between the bottom eight teams, and the winners of those four games were matched against the top four seeds in the four games of the second day. Memphis would most likely be playing Houston for the third time this season on the second day of the tournament, since Houston was favored to win their first-round game.

It was a few minutes before five o'clock in the morning in California on Monday, March 4th, and Jimmy continued to study all the scores and statistics for all the teams playing in the tournament in Cincinnati. He was in his office at home, and he wondered how early was too early to call his bookie to get the initial betting line for Memphis' game on Thursday, even though the opponent wouldn't be known until the end of a game on Wednesday.

Jimmy also hunted through multiple web sites to secure a phone number in Cincinnati where he hoped he would be able to purchase tickets for a suite at the arena where the tournament was to be played. With the time difference of three hours between Palo Alto and Cincinnati, Jimmy wanted to call promptly at eight o'clock in the morning Cincinnati time to have the best chance to buy the limited seats.

Jimmy was glad when a young lady named Daphne answered his call, as he knew his chances for success at sweet-talking this woman were greater than with any man. This situation was no different, as less than ten minutes later Jimmy finished giving his credit card information to her and received his confirmation number in return to allow retrieval of the tickets.

Immediately after hanging up from the phone call for the tickets, Jimmy dialed Brain's cell phone number. Jimmy expected Brian was still in Cincinnati since Brian watched the Memphis loss in Cincinnati, and Jimmy didn't know when he planned to return to Orlando. Brain answered on the first ring and the two made arrangements to have a conference call with Dante later in the day. Brian was flying to Memphis around noon, and he was going to meet with Dante at two o'clock.

At two-thirty Brian and Dante were sitting in a hotel room around a speaker phone. Brian was introducing his partner named Jimmy from Palo Alto as part of the call. After the introductions and other small talk about Dante's career, his professional basketball aspirations, and his mother, Brian handed Dante an envelope containing more fifty dollar bills than Dante had ever seen. There were forty bills in all, for a total of two thousand dollars. It was the initial payment for fixing the upcoming game on Thursday, and a second and final payment of eight thousand would be made after the game.

After the conference call Jimmy called his bookie and indicated he would be placing a bet for eighty thousand dollars on the Memphis game on Thursday. His bookie was suspicious since Jimmy's normal bets were only for two thousand and his special bets were typically for ten to twenty thousand, but he knew Jimmy was hoping and trying to make up for his huge losses during the past several months.

Two days later Jimmy flew to Cincinnati with a stop in Memphis. He arrived in the late afternoon and drove his rental car to the hotel to get checked in. Jimmy knew he was on his own for dinner tonight as the others arranged to arrive tomorrow morning. Jimmy's breakfast many hours ago comprised muffins, fruit, scrambled eggs, and ham. His two girls were kind enough to make breakfast for their father, and the youngest handled the eggs while her older sister struggled with the muffins. The muffins lacked something and the consistency of the eggs was not right, and Jimmy knew his two girls would have to learn cooking from someone other than their mother. He did appreciate their effort and show of love for him though, and he remembered hugging them both very tightly prior to his early departure.

Jimmy skipped the meal on the plane since he didn't want to spoil his plans for dinner. One recommendation Daphne made to him when he ordered the basketball tickets was to eat at the Montgomery Inn overlooking the Ohio River. Brian recommended it as well while also informing him to bring a hearty appetite, so Jimmy was eager to enjoy the feast.

On this Wednesday Jimmy was one of the early customers, so the hostess seated him by the windows at a table for two. His table was located halfway down a long curving line of windows, and many others were being seated as he ordered the king-size rack of pork ribs accompanied by a loaded baked potato and a cold beer.

By the time his order arrived the entire place was full and the noise level was much louder than when he was seated. The ribs were wonderful as Jimmy struggled through the last few ribs. When the plate contained only the bones, he counted fourteen in all, and he couldn't remember when he last ate such a huge rack of ribs.

Eight tables behind Jimmy was another man who also enjoyed a king-size rack of ribs, a loaded baked potato, and two cold beers. Brandon Williams also couldn't remember when he last ate such a huge rack of ribs. Brandon left a reasonable tip since the service was quite efficient, but he expected the man he was watching left a much larger tip in anticipation of an improving financial situation.

TWENTY EIGHT

When Jimmy opened the curtains in his hotel room in Cincinnati on Thursday, March 7th, the sky was beginning to brighten to his left, and far to his right which was toward the west it was still dark. Jimmy looked at the lights of the street lamps and cars below and then fixated his stare on the lights of the bridges crossing the Ohio River into Kentucky. He wasn't sure what the temperature was outside, but it looked inviting. He debated about taking a walk down toward the river and maybe even across one of the bridges since his first guest wasn't scheduled to arrive for a few hours, but he opted instead to order room service for breakfast and spend time reading the local morning newspaper.

Jimmy briefly scanned the front page of the paper and then found his way to the classified ads. He was curious to see the prices of some of the houses, knowing it would be far less than what he was used to in northern California. He noticed many houses for rent, and the amounts stunned him slightly as he saw several which were well over one thousand dollars per month with one asking for an even two thousand. Jimmy knew in the Bay Area the average monthly rent was about one-half of one percent of the total value of the home, providing a six percent return per year. With taxes and maintenance subtracting from that, it was only a good investment if the property appreciated nicely, which is what most investors in the housing market in California expected.

Here in Cincinnati on the other hand, the return per year seemed to be somewhere between eight and ten percent per year, which was much more attractive from a cash flow perspective. Jimmy wondered if maybe he shouldn't buy homes in several different cities around the country and rent them, while hopefully being able to arrange to use the property while vacationing a few days or even a week at some point during each year. It might be a good way to invest the extra dollars he was expecting to make through Operation Alcatraz.

There was a knock on the door followed by a muffled voice from the hallway, and Jimmy expected his breakfast was being delivered. He peeked through the eyehole in the door and saw a young man dressed in a bellhop uniform and holding a tray covered with a silver dome. The man smiled in a quirky fashion, and Jimmy marveled at how happy someone could really be performing this job. Surely the smile would wear off after another hour or two on the job, Jimmy thought. He must be new on the job and the fun hasn't yet worn off, Jimmy further decided.

Jimmy opened the door and let the young man enter. Jimmy quickly picked up the newspaper from the table by the window allowing the tray to be placed on top. The bellhop handed Jimmy the bill and indicated where he could add the tip amount and also where to place the room number to assign it to the room bill. Jimmy smiled at the man's means of demanding a tip, realizing it probably wasn't his first week on the job after all.

The breakfast was hot, and Jimmy enjoyed it more than the one his daughters prepared the day before. He wasn't sure how hungry he would be after consuming the large serving of ribs last evening, but he remembered he did only eat two meals yesterday with his dinner being much earlier than normal. When he finished eating he placed the tray in the hallway and returned to his seat in front of the window to finish reading the paper.

Outside his window Jimmy noticed the sky was much brighter than when he looked out thirty minutes ago. The sky was clear but didn't have the same color as the early morning sky in northern California, and he liked what he was used to a little better. Realizing there may be fog in Palo Alto this morning, Jimmy wondered how many foggy mornings the commuters endure here, knowing it was less than the number where he lived. He figured all things evened out in some fashion and then turned his attention back to the newspaper.

This time he found the sports section. There was a picture on the front page of a basketball player dunking over a defender. The caption below the photo indicated it was from one of the first round games played yesterday of the conference tournament being held in Cincinnati. The player dunking the ball was scoring two of his twenty-eight points for a winning team from one of yesterday's four games, and his team opposed the host team from Cincinnati later this evening.

As Jimmy scanned the headlines of the stories on the front page of the sports section, he saw a lengthy article for each of the four games contested the previous day. It was wonderful not having to navigate through multiple links on the internet from his home or office computer to read about the games interesting him. It was also nice reading from a newspaper instead of on the small screen on his computer's monitor. Maybe he would spend some of his winnings on upgrading his computers, including getting larger monitors, although he knew the largest available could not replace the look and feel of a newspaper.

Jimmy looked through the box scores of all four games in some detail, but he spent a significant amount of time reviewing the one from Houston's win over East Carolina. With Houston winning, Memphis played them at one o'clock this afternoon. Jimmy was interested in how Houston's big men performed, as he hoped they did well since his expectation was for them to have good games today at Dante's expense.

Other college basketball conference tournaments were being played around the country, and Jimmy checked the results from those, too. Near the end of the sports section was a scoreboard page with scores, standings, and statistics from professional sports to high school sports to yesterday's racing results from Churchill Downs. The betting lines for many college basketball games being played today were also contained on this page, and Jimmy checked the point spread for Memphis' game today. It was the same as he expected, and he looked out the window as he debated about calling his bookie and increasing his bet. Realizing it was still quite early in the Pacific time zone, he decided to let the impulse pass. Fifty thousand dollars of his own money along with thirty thousand for the remainder of the partnership was probably enough for the first time.

When Jimmy finished reading the morning newspaper he sat and looked out the window of his hotel room. He thought about all of the ways he cheated people out of money for so long with only the help of Billy and Mickey. When Charlie began participating the ante increased. Now with Brian helping there was another significant bump in the pot. Jimmy contemplated what other fraternity brothers could be tremendously helpful, and he made a mental note to look at his college yearbook and fraternity pictorial when he returned to California and possibly contact some of the others to see what some of them were doing. Maybe he could uncover a few gold mines if he looked long and hard enough.

As Jimmy was thinking he heard a knock on his door. He glanced at his watch and saw it was half past eight and thought it was too early for anyone he was expecting. When he looked through the peek hole he saw Brian waiting in the hallway. Jimmy quickly opened the door and said, "How ya' doin', Brian? Come on in."

"Hey, Jimmy," Brian greeted his fraternity brother. The two shook hands as Brian entered the hotel room.

"I wasn't expecting you this early, Brian. You must've gotten an early start from Indianapolis."

"Yeah, I did. But traffic was light leaving Indy this morning, and it's not much more than a hundred miles or so. A hundred and twenty-five max." Brian and Jimmy took seats at the table in front of the window.

"So what took you to Indy?"

"I was there for one of those workouts pro football teams hold on occasion. They refer to them as a college combine. What it amounts to is a lot of standing around for two minutes worth of work. The college players who are pro prospects show up basically to run a few forty-yard dashes so the pro scouts can time them. The receivers additionally run a few pass patterns and catch a few balls, but it always seems like a big waste of time to me."

"So why do you go, then?" Jimmy asked.

"It's a necessary part of my job. Bruce Tate was one of the invited players for this one. I had to be there to make sure all the other agents know he's mine. It's amazing how the other agents act like vultures, just waiting to steal a star player right out from under you."

"Has Tate signed with you, yet?"

"Not yet. His mother is still a little bit of a problem. Bruce says he's ready, but she's very hesitant about everything, and Bruce just won't go forward without his mother's consent."

"Sounds like you needed to be courting her instead of watching him stand around and run a few races."

"Probably so," Brian said as he chose not say he was already sending money to Bruce Tate's mother in his efforts to represent her son.

"Moving on to the real business at hand," Jimmy started, "is everything in order for today's game?"

"Absolutely," Brian replied. "I met with Dante last night and covered the final details. He's a little distraught 'cause he's heard the rumors of Memphis needing to win the game to get a bid to the NCAA tournament. I used the data you gathered from web sites showing all of the different rankings and predictions by those who follow college basketball closely and other so-called or self-proclaimed experts. And it clearly indicated Memphis was a lock for the tournament versus being on the bubble, but he's hearing every day in practice from the coaching staff how important it is for them to win a game or two in this tournament to be sure. Plus the team really wants to make it to the final game and get another shot at beating Cincinnati after the loss Sunday, so he's having some difficulty with the prospect of failing his teammates."

"So are we okay, or do we need to sweeten the pot?"

"I think we're fine. He was really happy with the two thousand dollars I gave him, and the other eight thousand will go a long way to easing any pain or disappointment he'll experience.

"Good," Jimmy said as he got out of his chair and walked over to the closet. He grabbed his briefcase and laid it on the bed. Adjusting the security lock combination he quickly gained access and retrieved a large, dark-colored envelope. Jimmy walked over to Brian and handed it to him.

"Here's the other eight thousand dollars for Dante. I hope this is the first of many payments like this I get to make."

"Me, too, Jimmy D. Me, too," Brian said as he returned Jimmy's smile.

The two continued to talk about other prospects as Jimmy's research during the last week and a half uncovered three high school seniors already committed to Southeastern conference schools he thought were excellent candidates to participate in Operation

Alcatraz. After close to an hour of discussing future probabilities, the two decided to discuss future activities after the day's events.

As Brian was standing in preparation for departing, Jimmy said, "One more thing, Brian." Jimmy reached back into his briefcase on the bed and grabbed another plain envelope, this one much smaller than the first. Jimmy snatched one of the tickets and handed it to Brian.

"What's this?" Brian asked.

"It's a ticket to today's game, in one of the suites," Jimmy said as he smiled widely.

"How'd you swing this?" Brian asked.

"Oh, it wasn't very hard. I'll see you at the game."

"Thanks. Actually, I've already got a seat on the second row behind one of the goals, but I'll be sure to stop in on you sometime during the game, maybe during the second half. Thanks again, Jimmy."

"You're welcome, Brian. Thank you, too."

The two shook hands and Brian departed the hotel room. He made his way to the elevator and pushed the down button. He looked at the three sets of elevator doors and moved in front of the middle one, guessing it would be the one to arrive first. When the green down arrow blinked as he heard a soft bell, he smiled at his correct guess. No one was inside the elevator so he quickly entered and pushed the button for the lobby and waited for the door to close. As the elevator door was closing he heard another soft bell indicating the arrival of one of the other two elevators to this floor. His door closed too quickly for him to notice Billy Wicks exiting from the other elevator.

Billy walked to Jimmy's room and lightly rapped his knuckles against the door. When Jimmy heard the knock he glanced at his watch. Jimmy looked through the peek hole, and when he saw his good friend he quickly opened the door.

"Hey, Billy," Jimmy said as Billy came into full view.

"Hi, Jimmy," Billy replied as he stepped toward Jimmy.

Instead of shaking hands the two embraced. After a few seconds Billy began to cry. Jimmy knew his long-time friend was still wounded from the events of the past five weeks, and a few tears began to run down Jimmy's cheeks as well. Jimmy loved Billy, and it pained him to see his friend hurting. The two continued to hug each other amidst their tears until a small lady dressed in a maid's uniform appeared with her service cart for cleaning the rooms on this floor. The interruption prompted Jimmy to softly say, "Come on in, Billy."

Billy walked to the window and gazed out while remaining standing. Jimmy stayed by the door and looked at Billy and his reflection in the window against the backdrop of the city and river. Jimmy sensed he knew what was on his friend's mind, but he waited silently until Billy started the conversation.

"Jimmy," Billy said as he turned around. "Thanks for all of the help you've provided over the last several weeks with my business in California. I really appreciate it. I know there's some capable people there, but having someone represent me makes me feel more comfortable they are doing what they're supposed to."

Billy paused for a minute so Jimmy inserted, "You're welcome, Billy. However long you need me to keep on helping, you know I'll do it." Jimmy then walked over and sat on the edge of the bed as Billy continued to stand by the window.

Billy looked down at the floor and kicked at the carpet as he stalled to say what he needed. Jimmy provided encouragement by saying, "You can tell me, Billy. Whatever you decide I'll support one hundred percent. You know that."

Billy looked up at Jimmy and felt the comfort of their friendship, and he knew Jimmy was his closest, most trusted, and best friend. "I've decided to sell my roofing business and move back to Alabama to help my sister. She's really confused about everything right now, and I expect it will stay that way for quite some time. She certainly needs my help, and somehow I feel the change will do me some good, too."

Jimmy expected this based upon their conversations over the past several weeks, and the look in Billy's eyes this morning also confirmed his feeling. "That's fine, Billy. It's the right call. I'm sure she desperately needs your help and emotional support. From some of Susan's and my conversations, I know she would really need the help of an older brother or two."

Jimmy paused for a few moments as Billy also did not say anything. Jimmy then asked, "Do you have any timeframe in mind?"

"Not really. I haven't given it enough thought yet."

"Well, take whatever time you need. I'll be glad to continue to help as best as I can from California."

"Thanks, Jimmy. I really appreciate it." Billy turned and looked out the window, as in the reflection Jimmy could see his friend's lower lip quivering as he fought back more tears. Jimmy knew Billy felt stuck between a rock and a hard place having to decide between staying in California and moving back to the South. He knew this decision would change their friendship, as he was already missing the Monday morning calls to Billy with a list of new clients.

Jimmy excused himself to go to the bathroom, and when he returned Billy was still standing and staring out the window. Jimmy could see a more normal expression on his friend's face from the reflection, so he asked, "So how was the drive up from Boaz this morning? You must've gotten a real early start to make it here by ten o'clock. What is it, four or five hundred miles?"

Billy turned around answered, "About four seventy-five. And yeah, I started early, about three o'clock. I made good time as I drove about eighty most of the way. I figured any patrolman out that early deserves to catch me for speeding."

"There was probably less traffic than in California."

"It's amazing, Jimmy. At four in the morning in the Bay Area the morning commute is already starting. You go through a city like Nashville at four or five in the morning and everyone is still sleeping. The hills are also different compared to what we're used to in California. I didn't see much of them this morning since it was still dark, but here the hills are covered with more trees, and there aren't the long flat valleys with the hills in the distance. Both are pretty. They're just different."

"Well, I'm glad you made it. I knew it was a long drive, but sometimes it provides a nice opportunity to do some heavy thinking and figure some things out," Jimmy said as his statement reminded him it was his long drive from Atlanta to Jackson, Tennessee on New Year's Day when he first thought of Operation Alcatraz.

"It does give you some time to think and reflect," Billy agreed. Then he quickly reached in his pocket and pulled out a wad of bills. "Here's my share of the bet," Billy said as he handed the money to Jimmy.

"Gee. I almost forgot," Jimmy said as he reached to accept it. Then he stopped and opened his palms in Billy's direction. "Just keep it, Billy. I'll just send you the winnings when I collect them. Instead of you giving me your share and then me having to turn around and give it right back to you along with the extra, it just doesn't make any sense."

"You sure, Jimmy."

"Yeah."

"That's awful nice of you, Jimmy. You do all the work, risk all the money, and I get some of the profit. Doesn't seem right."

"It's okay. I insist. We'll figure it all out at some point anyway.," Jimmy said with a shrug of his shoulders and a wave of his hand.

Jimmy then reached in his briefcase and grabbed one of the tickets from the small envelope. "Here," he said as he handed it to Billy. "You'll need this for the game today. It's in one of the suites. I've got a few other things to tend to before the game, so I'll have to meet you there."

"Thanks, Jimmy," Billy said as he accepted the gift. "And thanks again for all your help."

"You're welcome. See you at the game."

The two men shook hands and Billy left the room. When Jimmy shut the door he leaned his forehead against it and stared at the floor for a few moments. He knew he would miss his good friend.

Jimmy made a few more calls from his hotel room before leaving for the arena. He finished his last call at twenty minutes after eleven and decided a few hot dogs at the game would suffice for lunch. Jimmy walked briskly as it was colder than he expected, and he was glad he opted earlier to eat breakfast versus taking the morning walk he contemplated. Not many people were present as the host team wasn't scheduled to play in either of the two games of the afternoon session. The line at the will call window was short, allowing Jimmy to spend only a few minutes before making his way inside.

Jimmy was the first to arrive at the suite and as he stood in the emptiness he gazed at the court. He noticed several men and women dressed from the very casual to some in suits scattered across different areas of the floor. Television lights were shining on some of the groups as reporters and announcers taped their pre-game comments. A small crowd was gathering since few fans from Houston made the long trip according to what Jimmy read in the morning paper about yesterday's game. Jimmy noticed the largest gathering of spectators was in several adjacent sections across the floor to his right, and he was happy to see many of them dressed in blue in support of Memphis. Neither of the teams were on the floor, and Jimmy expected they probably did some shooting earlier in the morning and would return for their warmup about thirty minutes before the opening tip.

Jimmy picked up the service phone and placed an order. Within fifteen minutes a small buffet including snacks and hot dogs was assembled. The older lady delivering the food was very efficient but not very talkative, and Jimmy debated if the young lady in San Francisco who delivered the food order for him and Charlie at the Giants baseball game last August would someday become like this woman. Jimmy hoped not, and he only laughed to himself at his own speculation since he knew he would never know the result.

Jimmy sat and continued to watch the crowd grow as he ate one of the hot dogs. The arena seemed about one-third to one-half full when the Houston team took the court. There was little applause but the players didn't seem to mind as they formed two lines for shooting layups. Within two minutes the group of fans from Memphis began to stand and cheer, and Jimmy knew the Memphis team was taking the floor. The view of the entry from the locker room to his left was obstructed, but soon enough he saw the Memphis players run onto the floor. There was more energy in the arena now, and Jimmy felt his excitement growing as well.

Ten minutes later the door to the suite in the back opened. Jimmy heard a lady's voice telling someone to enjoy the game, and when he turned around he saw Mickey walking in as a woman in an usher's jacket held the door.

"Mickey! How ya' doin', Mick!?" Jimmy shouted as he jumped up and ran the few feet to the door.

"Fine, thanks!" Mickey shouted in return as the two men shook hands with their right hands and hugged each other around the neck with their left hands.

"So, you finally made it," Jimmy said.

"Yeah. Like I said on the phone earlier, it was just an absolute mess in the Chicago airport this morning. When I arrived on the red-eye from San Jose I could tell something was up, 'cause they took a long time to taxi and park the plane, and it was obvious we were not getting off at a normal gate. They never did tell us the whole story, but I'm sure there was some breach of security somewhere. No planes were taking off for a long time, only a few landing. I should've just rented a car and drove the three hundred miles or so, but by the time I'd waited a few hours for them to sort things out, I wouldn't have made it in time for the game. Luckily, they started allowing some of the shorter flights to depart, so mine was one of the first to go."

"I'm sure there were a lot of unhappy people at O'Hare," Jimmy commented.

"Boy. I'll say. You can only imagine how many people were there. I can't remember ever being in a place where there were so many people."

"But at least you made it by the opening tip. Here, grab something to eat. The hot dogs are actually quite good."

"Thanks," Mickey said as he walked to the small buffet. "Oh," Mickey said as he stopped and turned around while he reached in his pocket and retrieved a small envelope. "Here's my portion of next year's financing for our man and my share of the wager," he said as he handed it to Jimmy.

"Thanks, Mick," Jimmy replied. "I'll be returning this and more when we get back to California and I collect our winnings."

"Sounds good," Mickey said as he turned his attention back to the food. "This looks good. The omelet in the coffee shop in the airport was tasty, but it's gone now. Thanks for setting this whole thing up. This is really nice."

Before Jimmy was able to reply the back door opened again as the same usher held the door for another man.

"Hey, Billy," Jimmy greeted his friend with a firm handshake. "I was wondering when you were going to make it."

"Hey," Billy replied. "I decided to spend a little time walking around downtown after I left your hotel room. This is a neat city."

"Hi, Billy," Mickey said while he added some chili and cheese to his hot dog and bun. "Come over here and get some food."

"Hi, Mickey," Billy said as he walked the few feet across the suite.

Mickey stopped fixing his plate and set it down on the counter. He offered his hand to Billy, but as the two faced each other they embraced. "Good to see you again, Billy," Mickey said.

"You, too," Billy said as a tear fell down his face.

"I hope everything's working out for your sister."

"Thanks," was all Billy could muster to say.

Another roar from the crowd interrupted them so they turned their attention toward the floor. The Memphis team was running off the floor back to the locker room for some last minute instructions from the coach, and the crowd was cheering for their team once again. As the Houston team followed a minute later to their quarters, the cheers turned to boos. Jimmy smiled at the excitement and enthusiasm being displayed as he enjoyed this part of sporting events sometimes more than the games themselves.

After the national anthem was played the teams returned to the floor and the game started. There was a lot of fast-paced action early in the game, but neither team was able to find their shooting touch. Finally toward the end of the first half both teams began scoring more easily. The game was close as the horn sounded bring the half to an end, and Jimmy smiled since it looked like Memphis would not cover the spread as he expected, providing Operation Alcatraz with a winning first bet.

The second half started similarly to the first one, with both teams struggling to score. With a little more than fifteen minutes left in the game the back door to the suite opened. Jimmy, Billy, and Mickey all turned around and saw Charlie Bates walking in while the same usher held the door for him.

"Hey! Charlie! How ya' doin'!?" Jimmy shouted. "So you did decide to come, and you made it despite the trouble at O'Hare."

"Hi, J.D. Yeah, like I said on the phone this morning, I just couldn't stand the thought of you and the others enjoying this game without me. But boy, was it ever a mess in Chicago at the airport this morning."

"Hi, Charlie," Mickey greeted his friend. "I was stuck in O'Hare this morning, too. When were you there?"

"I got in early this morning on the red-eye from San Francisco."

"Wow. Me, too. I came in from San Jose. I'm surprised we didn't run into each other."

"Well our plane parked way out of the way, as I'm sure yours did, too. When I heard all departures were on hold, I decided to rent a car and just drive the rest of the way."

"As long as we waited, you might've been able to beat me driving," Mickey suggested.

"Well, it took quite a long time to rent a car," Charlie said. "None of the agencies in the airport were open at that hour of the morning, so I took a cab to another rental place outside the airport. I waited there until they opened at eight, and the two folks trying to help everyone were a little overwhelmed and weren't very efficient. I finally got on the road about nine, and this is as fast as I could make it."

"Well at least you made it before the game ended," Jimmy said.

Turning his attention to Billy, Charlie offered his hand and said, "Hi, Billy."

"Hi, Charlie," Billy replied.

"It's good to see you," Charlie continued. "I'm sure things are tough right now, but I also know you'll do fine. Give my love to your little sis when you get back."

"I will, Charlie. Thanks. She always liked you, you know."

"Tell her we all really like her, too. I still remember how awed she was by the buildings of the campus whenever she would come for a visit. She's a sweet girl. The world would be a better place if there were more people like her in it. It's unfortunate about the bad circumstances surrounding her right now."

A large roar from the crowd once again interrupted the conversation as the four men looked to the court. Several players were standing around on one end of the floor as the referees separated Dante Lewis from one of the Houston players. The replay on the television in the suite showed Dante leaping and dunking the basketball over an opponent who was jumping in his efforts to stop the goal. When the two landed on the floor the defender shoved Dante and was called for a technical foul. The dunk and subsequent free throw put Memphis ahead by two points as the game neared the mid-point of the second half.

"Looks like a good game," Charlie said.

"Yeah," Mickey replied. "It's been pretty close the whole way."

"There's still some food left if you haven't eaten Charlie," Jimmy said. "I'm sure Billy will eat what's left soon, so you better get some while you still can."

"Oh no," Billy said. "I'm done. I've already eaten four hot dogs, two with chili and cheese and the other two with grilled onions and peppers. With all the other snacks, I probably won't have to eat again, for at least."

"For about two hours," Jimmy butted in with a laugh. The others laughed as well at the joke. Billy knew Jimmy was right, and he joined in the laughter, too. Charlie fixed himself a plate of food and the four men continued to watch the game.

With a little over one minute remaining Memphis still trailed by four. Dante's dunk which put Memphis ahead was the last lead for Memphis, as it was followed by two consecutive three-pointers by Houston. Since then the two teams mostly traded baskets, and now the Memphis fans were anxious as they realized their team was running out of time to win the game. The door to suite opened again and Brian Nichols entered.

Turning around first Jimmy said, "Hey, Brian. Glad you could make it."

"Hi, Jimmy," Brian said as he looked at the group.

"Hi, Brian," Charlie said as he walked over an extended his hand to Brian. "Good to see you again."

"Good to see you, too, Charlie," Brian said as he shook hands with Charlie.

Mickey and Jimmy glanced at each other without saying a word, although it was clear Mickey wasn't sure why Brian was present.

Turning to Billy, Brian said, "Hi, Billy."

"Hi, Brian," Billy returned the greeting as the two shook hands.

When Brian turned to Mickey there was an awkward silence. Finally, Brian said, "Hi, Mickey."

"Brian," Mickey said with a nod of the head. The two didn't shake hands, and it was clear to everyone there was some tension between the two.

"Hey! Let's watch the end of the game, guys," Jimmy said to break the silence. "Let's see if Memphis can come back and win this thing," he hoped as he turned his attention to the game.

The group watched as each team scored a few more baskets before the final seconds ticked off the clock. The final score was 80-74 in favor of Houston, and Jimmy and the others were a little disappointed Memphis lost. They were all happy knowing their bet was won, which was the most important thing. Jimmy smiled broadly as he looked to the scoreboard high above the center of the court at the final score.

As Jimmy gazed at the numbers the door to the suite opened. He and the others turned and watched three men with guns in their hands.

"Hey! What's going on!?" Jimmy shouted.

Brandon Williams entered next, and he was followed by his boss.

"Good afternoon, gentlemen," Brandon firmly started. "I'm Brandon Williams. I'm a federal agent. Please give me a few minutes and I'll make everything clear to everyone."

"Boss," Brandon continued as he first looked to his boss on his left, "Let me first introduce you to Mr. Jimmy Donovan." Brandon pointed at Jimmy before saying more. "Mr. Donovan grew up in Germantown, Tennessee and now resides in Palo Alto, California. He's a realtor, the owner of Donovan Realty, and a member of the Sigma Chi fraternity. Most importantly, he's the group's leader."

Jimmy started to say something but was cut off by Brandon. "Mr. Donovan. I suggest you remain silent.

"You're a very imaginative man, Mr. Donovan. It's rare for one man to be involved in so many different illegal activities. You must lay awake at night thinking of new ways to cheat people. Unfortunately, you're a very addicted gambler, too.

"Operation Alcatraz. It does have a nice ring to it. It was also a very clever idea, both parts actually. Clever, but illegal of course. There are a lot of under-the-table payments to college athletes these days, but this was far beyond anything I've seen so far.

"It's also unfortunate you're not always as smart as you think you are, though, as your trail is not very well disguised. We have numerous documents from real estate closings where you blatantly cheated buyers, sellers, or both out of significant sums of money.

"We have search warrants to search your office building and your home, and I expect those searches are presently in progress. Your computers will be confiscated and searched for evidence. I'm not sure what else we'll uncover, but I'm sure it won't be helpful to you.

My expectation is it will only get worse for you as we learn more. With what we know right now, you're under arrest, Mr. Donovan."

Jimmy didn't say a word as he looked at Brandon and then at the men holding guns. He realized he was going to pay dearly for his actions.

"Boss," Brandon once again turned to his boss and then looked at Billy. "Let me now introduce you to Mr. Billy Wicks. Mr. Wicks grew up outside of Tupelo, Mississippi and now resides in San Jose, California. He is in the construction business and owns and operates Valley Roofing. He is also a member of the Sigma Chi fraternity, where he unfortunately developed a friendship with Mr. Donovan.

"Mr. Wicks, you're not a very savvy investor in the market. If only you'd not lost so much money playing options and other things you may not understand, you might could've avoided all of this. I get the sense you're a decent person who just associated with the wrong person or people. I get that feeling based upon our recent surveillance of you in Alabama assisting your sister, who recently lost her husband. I expect you're a very submissive individual, being heavily influenced by others.

"Nonetheless, not only do we have documents showing how you cheated people out of money for roof work which was not performed, we also have videotapes of you making unauthorized withdrawals at banks for accounts owned by others. Further, we have videotapes of you opening and closing accounts in San Ramon and Danville for illegal purposes.

"We also have search warrants to search your office and home. I also expect those searches are being conducted as we speak. You're also under arrest, Mr. Wicks."

Billy had tears in his eyes as he only looked at the floor and wondered how his sister would manage without him. Jimmy looked at Billy and felt a deep sympathy for his good friend.

"Boss," Brandon said as he now turned to Mickey. "Let me introduce you to Mr. Mickey Ross. Mr. Ross grew up in Vicksburg, Mississippi and now resides in Monterey, California. He first was an engineer, but is now a lawyer and an escrow agent. His main company is Ross and Associates, although there are several others he uses to hide income from the government and his ex-wife. He is also a member of the Sigma Chi fraternity.

343

"You're a very selfish man, Mr. Ross. You don't care about your children, and you don't care much about others you represent. You're addicted to golf, expensive hotels, fine wine, and fancy meals. If you cared half as much about your children and others as you do about your golf game and yourself, you'd be a much better person.

"Many of the documents implicating Mr. Donovan also incriminate you, Mr. Ross. We additionally have a signed affidavit from your assistant regarding the two of you and your involvement in opening and closing accounts in Santa Cruz for illegal purposes. We have tapes from the banks which substantiate the activity. We also have search warrants to search your office and residence, and those searches are probably happening right now. You're under arrest, Mr. Ross."

Mickey looked at Jimmy in disbelief. Jimmy returned the look and simply shrugged his shoulders.

"Boss," Brandon now turned to Charlie. "Let me introduce you to Mr. Charlie Bates. Mr. Bates grew up in Little Rock, Arkansas and now resides in Palo Alto, California. From his childhood he wanted to be a banker, and now he is a vice-president. He also is a member of the Sigma Chi fraternity.

"Mr. Bates, you've been a poor investor. Your investments in wineries and technology startup companies have caused you to lose all you've made and more. You were on the path to financial security, but you threw it away. Fatefully, you decided to make it up by getting involved in illegal activities. There is a bit of hope for you, however, as your boss is a very nice and generous man. I expect he may be willing to give you another chance at some point in the future, but when it may be, no one knows. You're under arrest, too, Mr. Bates."

Charlie looked at Jimmy, and Jimmy returned the silent glance.

"Boss," Brandon continued as he turned to Brian. "Let me introduce you to Mr. Brian Nichols. Brian grew up in Atlanta and now resides in Tampa, Florida. He is a sports agent, and his company is Nichols Sports. He is also a member of the Sigma Chi fraternity.

"Brian, however, is not a big fan of Sigma Chi or the fraternity system. The initiation ceremony and hazing rituals he endured as a sophomore in college were, well, inappropriate is the best way to describe them here. We'll cover it in more detail at some later time."

Jimmy, Billy, Mickey, and Charlie all looked at Brian in amazement. They all knew they went through the same embarrassment when they were initiated, but unlike Brian, it strengthened their bond to their fraternity brothers.

"Boss, you may remember I worked with Brian a few years ago in a contract fraud case involving another sports agent." Brandon's boss nodded his head affirmatively as Brandon paused. "Since Brandon is a lifetime fan of all the Atlanta sports teams, but particularly of the Atlanta Braves baseball team, we assigned him the code name Red Man."

Looking at Brian, Brandon said, "Thanks for your help, Red Man. College athletics will be much safer as a result of your recent efforts."

Brandon extended his hand toward Brian. As he did, Jimmy noticed the ring on Brandon's finger with the two Greek letters inscribed on the side, and he wondered why Brian and Brandon didn't share the same love and commitment to the fraternity and its members as he did.

ABOUT THE AUTHOR

After a successful engineering career in the computer industry, Chris "CJ" Jones left the demanding yet rewarding life of running a high-tech business for the unknown and perceived fun of writing novels.

A renowned storyteller at his long-time employer, CJ held firm to his demonstrated creativity and determination for success, trading physics, formulas, simulations, and spreadsheets for a word processor with a spelling checker, hoping to entertain readers.

Having lived in multiple places in the Midwest, South, and Western U.S., CJ and his wife once again reside in the South, where he is writing his next suspense story of white-collar crime, while also working on his golf game and climbing other branches of his leisure tree.

Look for his next novel, *The Foursome*, coming soon.

Printed in the United States
22467LVS00004B/27

9 781410 716385